up all hours

*Scorching tales of sex
around the clock*

**Edited by Gerry Kroll
and Fred Goss**

**alyson
books**

LOS ANGELES   NEW YORK

© 1997 by Liberation Publications Inc.
All rights reserved.

Manufactured in the United States of America.
Printed on acid-free paper.

This trade paperback original is published by Alyson Publications Inc.,
P.O. Box 4371, Los Angeles, California 90078-4371.
Distribution in the United Kingdom by Turnaround Publisher Services Ltd.,
Unit 3, Olympia Trading Estate, Coburg Road, Wood Green,
London N22 6TZ, England.

First edition: August 1997

01 00 99 98 97   10 9 8 7 6 5 4 3 2 1

ISBN 155583-402-7

Library of Congress Cataloging-in-Publication Data
    Up all night : scorching tales of sex around the clock / edited by
Gerry Kroll and Fred Goss. — 1st ed.
    ISBN 1-55583-402-7
    1. Gay men—Sexual behavior—Fiction. 2. Erotic stories, American—
Men authors. I. Kroll, Gerry. II. Goss, Fred. III. Advocate men.
PS648.H57U58   1997
813'.01083538'086642—dc21   97-18781 CIP

Cover photograph by Johnathan Black.
Cover design by Christopher Harrity.

Contents

MORNING

AFTERNOON

NIGHT

MORNING

Coffee Talk
by R. J. March

Glenn dialed Pete's number.

"Ugh...hello?" the gravelly voice on the other line said. It was late.

"It's me," Glenn said. He could hear his friend breathing into the telephone. "You awake?"

"No," Pete said.

"You alone?"

"Mmm," Pete rasped. "Think so."

Glenn leaned back on the sofa and looked at his ceiling. He felt better already, just hearing Pete's voice. *Bad sign,* he thought, running a hand absentmindedly across his chest, his fingertips brushing his nipples through his T-shirt. His dick stirred. *Shit,* he thought. *Another bad sign.*

"Uhmmm," Pete said slowly. "Does my clock really say 3:15? Can that be the correct time, Glenn?"

Glenn looked at his watch. "Uh, yeah, that's right."

"So what the fuck do you want?"

Good question, Glenn thought. *What the fuck do I want?* He had wanted Corinne, but now that she had dumped him, he was glad to be rid of her. "You've forced me to do this," she had told him earlier that night. "I mean, I want to love you, but you don't seem to want to be loved. Not by me, anyway."

Glenn looked up at the ceiling again; it flickered blue from the television. He imagined Pete up on one elbow, eyes closed, twisted up in a sheet. He stretched himself out on the couch, spreading his bare legs here and there, his free hand creeping down to the waistband of his boxers, Pete's breath in his ear. He told him about Corinne.

"Sucks, man," Pete said. "Tell me about it over breakfast. Your treat. Good-bye."

"See you," Glenn said, hanging up and digging his hands into his shorts. He closed his eyes and could see Pete again, half covered, spreading himself across the bed. He had by now memorized every detail of his buddy's body; he had seen enough of it at the gym and the beach and around their apartments, half dressed, undressed, soaking wet, covered in oil, pumped up, half hard. He'd even seen Pete's dick completely hard, the morning after they'd shared a bed and Pete woke up in a hurry, his big cock up-and-at-'em and poking out through the slot of his boxers.

Glenn pushed his shorts down to his knees and gripped his stiff dick in one hand, his balls in the other. He pulled and squeezed, letting his imagination take over. He could see Pete, his longish dark hair swaying as he hopped into the bathroom with his prong bobbing up and down; he could see Pete coming in out of the ocean in shorts that went nearly transparent in the surf, his black pubes shining through the wet white fabric; Pete stepping up to the urinal next to Glenn's and unloading his prick to take a long piss; Pete too drunk to drive home, stripping down to his shorts, getting ready for bed in Glenn's living room.

Glenn spit in his hand and stroked it over his cock. He used not to allow himself to think of his friend when he jacked off. That's what Corinne was for. But she hadn't worked — at least not the way he had hoped. The only way he could fuck her was by thinking of Pete's tight, hot (he imagined) butt hole. Her mouth was Pete's. Her hands, though, were what he had the most trouble with.

They were soft and dainty, and he simply could not pretend they were Pete's big, clumsy, hairy-knuckled, callused, dirty-nailed paws. He discovered that he did not want anything to do with delicacy in bed; he wanted heavy hands, rough hands. Pete's hands.

His toes curled, his feet arched, and he tensed every muscle in his legs. He had quickly worked himself up to popping. He pictured himself with Pete, imagined Pete's hand on his cock instead of his own, and he tightened his grip, slamming his fist into his wiry nest of pubes, pumping the shaft and bothering the sensitive head. His ball sac stiffened, and he let out a little holler as he spewed out another load with Pete's name on it. "Oh, sweet," he said over and over again, squeezing out every thick white drop.

Pete was sitting in their booth, the one they sat in almost every Saturday. Patti the waitress raised her eyebrows when she saw Glenn walk in. "What's this?" she said, bringing him a cup of coffee. "Emergency summit meeting? Not used to seeing you guys in the middle of the week. Now I'm going to keep thinking tomorrow's Sunday."

"Breakfast," Pete said.

Glenn reached for a menu.

"Honey," Patti said. "Nothing's changed in there."

"Oh," Glenn said. "Right."

"The usual?" she said.

"The usual," the two men said together.

"You look like shit," Pete said once Patti had gone.

"Thanks," Glenn said.

"Didn't you sleep?"

"Couldn't," Glenn said, stirring sugar into his coffee. He did what he could to avoid looking at Pete: studying the empty sugar pack, patting his jacket pocket for his truck keys, pretending to give some chick the once-over. He breathed hard, almost sighing, and put his hands on his lap. He glanced at Pete, who was staring at him.

"What?" Glenn said.

"Man, are you okay?"

"Fine, why?"

"You seem wrecked or something," Pete said. "I didn't think you cared too much one way or the other about her."

"What gave you that idea?"

The door opened behind Glenn's back, and Pete looked over his friend's shoulder. Glenn turned around to look too. A big guy walked in wearing tight jeans and a flannel shirt. His sleeves were rolled up, showing off powerful-looking forearms.

"Hey, good-lookin'," Patti called from behind the counter, causing the man to grin and go red.

"You know him?" Pete said.

"No," Glenn answered.

Pete seemed to be staring at Glenn, *into* him. *Don't look too close*, Glenn thought. *You might not like what you see.*

They ate their breakfast in silence, Glenn listening and sometimes turning to watch Patti flirt with her man at the counter. His flannel-shirted back was wide and solid, tapering narrowly at the waist and disappearing into well-worn jeans. His brown, slightly curly hair was buzzed to the bone around his head and left a little long on the top. There was something about this man's exposed scalp that seemed to cause a little trouble in Glenn's sweats. He felt his prick nosing around, wanting attention. He fussed with the paper napkin over his lap, fingering his hardening shaft secretly.

Pete put his feet up on the bench beside Glenn, startling him. He looked up red-faced, feeling guilty. Pete pushed his plate to the side, pulled a toothpick out of his shirt pocket, and twirled it around in his mouth. "So you don't want to talk about it. That's cool," he said.

"See ya, Chuckie," Patti called out, and Pete and Glenn both watched the big man walk out the door. Patti came over to clear their plates.

"That your boyfriend?" Pete said.

"Why, I thought you were," Patti said, putting a hand on Pete's arm.

"No," Pete said, winking at Glenn. "I'm Glenn's man, and don't you forget it."

Patti smiled conspiratorially. "You know," she said softly, "I had a feeling. Now, my brother's gay, and we have the best relationship — he is such a riot."

"Hey," Pete said, looking around. "It was a joke. I was joking."

Patti gave Glenn a look and pursed her lips. "Pulling my leg again?" she said. "Never know with you guys. Never know anything anymore." She glanced at the door, the OPEN/CLOSED sign still swinging back and forth. She slipped the check onto the table. "More coffee?"

They walked out to their cars. "That was fucking weird," Pete said, pulling his hair away from his face. He had a wide jaw, a less-than-perfect nose — a little crooked from a bad wrestling move in high school — and brown eyes that resembled polished mahogany. He was wearing a T-shirt, and his nipples were hard in the chill morning air. He hugged himself, and his biceps, big to begin with, seemed to triple in size. He rocked in his sneakers from his heels to his toes. "What are you going to do?" he wanted to know.

Glenn exhaled loudly, shaking his head. He didn't care that he was dumped. He was actually glad Corinne had done his dirty work, but it was this other thing that was getting him down, that he did not know how to deal with. He felt like he was going insane, out of control. "It's my dick," he wanted to say. "I'm having trouble with my dick. And you."

"Hey, I don't mean the big picture, man," Pete said. "I just want to know what you're doing today. Like, do you have any plans or anything? I was thinking of going to the shore to hang."

"I can do that," Glenn said. He dug his hands into his jacket pockets.

"Follow me to my house. I'll get a sweatshirt and some money. Take your truck?" Pete said.

"Sure," Glenn said, trying hard not to stare at the ever-present bulge in Pete's jeans.

It wasn't a long drive, but Pete fell asleep right away. He managed to spread himself across the seat of Glenn's pick-up, strapped in at Glenn's insistence, the black webbing untucking Pete's T-shirt and baring his stomach, lined with dark hair. He was solid there, ribbed with muscle. The waistband of his jeans showed a dark, thin passage with room enough to slip a hand down, which Pete did often, scratching now and then or just touching. Suddenly he went hard, his dick growing straight up along his hairy stomach, up and out of the jeans, its pointed head resting over the dip of his belly button.

"Fuck," Glenn whispered, gripping the wheel with both hands. "Fuck, fuck, fuck, and fuck again." Pete's knee touched Glenn's thigh and stayed there. Glenn pushed hard on his own prick, grinding it, causing pleasure and pain. Pete snored, slack-mouthed and drooling. Glenn pushed on the accelerator, picking up speed. He glanced at his friend, his friend's dick. *Touch it,* he thought. *Go ahead and touch it!*

Pete sat up suddenly, blinking in the glare of daylight. He pushed his dick back into his pants. "Pull up over here," he said. Glenn looked at him. "Got to piss," Pete said, looking out through the windshield.

Pete got out and went into the brush. Glenn watched him disappear. Glenn thought it was odd, since Pete was never bashful about pissing. He had even taken a leak into a beer bottle one night when he and Glenn were driving home from a concert in a downpour.

Now Glenn waited for him to return. Five minutes passed. He beeped the horn. Nothing. He peered into the brush but could see no sign of his friend. He got himself out of the truck and yelled. "Come on, asshole!" he hollered. "Pete?"

He stepped into the bushes, into the woods. *Some joke,* he thought, but at the same time he began to get a little scared. *What if something's happened? Is there a deep ravine here somewhere that Pete could have fallen into?* He called Pete's name again. Nothing.

He walked deeper into the brush, looking for something that indicated Pete had been through here. The sky was a dull gray, and the woods were bleak. He stood still and listened, hearing his own breathing and heartbeat.

"Pete?"

"Over here," Glenn heard, turning around to find Pete leaning against a tree.

"What the fuck, man?" Glenn said, pissed off and ready to cuff that bastard for fucking with him like that. He got up to Pete, breathing hard, fists clenched. He stared at Pete's eyes. Pete stared back. It was cold enough for their breath to form foggy clouds between them.

"What's going on?" Glenn said, not comfortable with Pete's smile.

"Is anything going on?" Pete said.

"What are you talking about?"

Pete blew out a puff of air. "Can't stop thinking about what Patti said. About you and me."

Glenn looked at him for a moment. "You said it first," he said, almost mumbling.

"I know."

Pete touched the front of his jeans. He fingered his fly. Glenn could only watch, could not keep himself from watching as Pete undid the buttons of his jeans one at a time. The jeans opened to reveal a V of skin trailing down to his dark-colored pubes and the pale flesh of his soft, fat, meaty cock.

"I think it's time one of us had some balls and both of us faced facts," he said quietly.

Glenn stared at the nestling prick, the head hidden, the shaft smooth and pink, thick. *Facts,* he thought.

Pete put his hands under Glenn's jacket. Both men seemed to sigh. Pete's hands gripped Glenn's pecs, and he thumbed his nipples through his shirt. He looked up at the sky as Pete's hands slid down his torso, touching the top of Glenn's sweats. He slipped his hands down inside, and his cool fingers scooped up Glenn's cock and balls, warm and loose.

Pete stepped close, pushing Glenn's sweats down, baring his ass and the rest of him. He pressed himself against Glenn, arms going around, hands grabbing ass cheeks. Glenn did not know what to do with his hands, had no idea where to put them. He tried Pete's shoulders, and Pete went down on his knees.

Glenn felt wet heat, a soft lap of tongue. Pete made a noise, taking all of Glenn's cock into his mouth, but Glenn wasn't quite hard, despite Pete's hungry mouth pulling and sucking, fingers digging into the crack of his ass, pressing gently on the soft spot. He touched Pete's hair for the first time, gathering it up in his fingers.

"Turn around," Pete said, and Glenn turned. "Bend over now," he heard his friend say.

He did as he was told, hands on his knees, and Pete got his face up in the crack, lapping up the hairy knot, slipping his tongue in, out, in again, deeper this time, pushing into the tight ring of his sphincter. Glenn's prick hardened into a curved obelisk, an aching wooden arc that seemed to burn into the crisp air.

"I want you, man," Pete said, pulling his tongue out.

"I want you too," Glenn whispered, his eyes shut. The lips of his hole pouted. Pete poked into it with his finger. He reached between Glenn's legs and grabbed his steely dick, jacking it, smearing the sticky tip. He pushed his nose into Glenn's crack again, making his prick hop.

Pete got to his feet and pressed himself against Glenn, pressed his big hard cock against the split of the man's ass cheeks. "Can I?" he whispered into Glenn's ear.

"You can try," he answered.

It wasn't as easy as it looked in the few movies Glenn had seen. And he wasn't prepared for the sheer size of it, the length and width, its fat hardness. Or for the slip of lips on his neck, the roughness of Pete's stubbled chin, the hard grip of fingers on his hips. Or Pete's hot whisper: "It's fucking incredible, man. You wouldn't believe."

Then the hurt gave way to something else that felt almost good and then very good. He felt the long slide of Pete's cock, the bang of its pointed head on his insides, catching on a spot that made his dick twitch. He grabbed his own pecker and caressed the fat shaft, slicking himself up with some precome.

"Give it to me!" he said loudly, his voice echoing through the woods. "Give me that big cock, Pete. Give it to me now!"

Pete let out a wail, slamming himself up into Glenn's ass, making the man wince and dribble a gooey string of precome. "That's it, buddy," Pete said. "Take the load, buddy. Take my fucking load." He came deep inside Glenn's feverish ass, hitting that spot again and again, making Glenn's cock shoot a heavy white spurt across the forest floor.

They turned around and went home, making the drive in silence, neither of them knowing what to say. Glenn wondered what was supposed to happen next. He knew how he felt about Pete, knew that he loved him. He wanted desperately to say to Pete, "I've been in love with you for so fucking long." Instead he stared at the road, gripping the wheel, aware of his asshole and its wonderful new usefulness. He glanced over at Pete, who was looking out his window. "What are you doing for dinner?" he asked him.

Pete cleared his throat. Looked at his fingernails. "Actually," he said, "I have a date tonight."

Girl or guy? Glenn thought.

"Some chick from work," Pete said, as if Glenn had spoken aloud.

Glenn turned the radio on and cracked his window a bit. Pete folded his hands over his crotch. *I think things are going to be very different from here on in,* Glenn thought, biting the inside of his lip.

Things were different. Pete seemed to disappear with excuses of having no spare time, of being too busy. Glenn left messages on his answering machine — terse recorded

notes with long silent gaps. He felt as though he had lost
something; he wasn't sure what, though.

He lay awake at night, unable to sleep, touching himself
everywhere Pete had touched him. He pushed his fingers
up inside himself, pushed anything cocklike up there: a
beer bottle, a brush handle, a cucumber. He finally broke
down and went to a shop that sold dildos and bought one
that seemed Pete-sized. He felt lost and alone, a little
crazy. He even contemplated calling Corinne just to have
some company but realized the mistake that would be.

He went to the diner alone Saturday morning. Patti
brought the coffeepot and poured him a cup and was
about to pour one for Pete.

"I'm alone," he said, feeling pathetic. Patti looked at
him and put the coffeepot down on the table. She sat on
the bench across from him.

"Are you okay?" she said.

"I guess so." He stirred his coffee, staring into it as if
there were answers there. He stirred and stirred. Nothing.
He looked up at her. She looked concerned, safe. "Tell me
about your brother," he said finally, feeling some heavi-
ness leave him.

Patti spoke to him quietly, discreetly, for nearly two
hours, pausing to serve breakfasts and work the cash reg-
ister. He was pushing his own uneaten eggs around with
the corner of some toast when the door opened. He looked
up, hoping to see Pete. It was Patti's friend, the guy who
looked like a big lumberjack. Glenn looked back down at
his messy plate.

When he looked up again, he saw that Patti was bringing the man over to him. He smiled and held out a huge
hand. Glenn took it. "Glenn. Chuckie," Patti said. "Sit
down, and I'll bring by some coffee, honey. Clean up that
plate, Glenn."

Chuck sat down across from Glenn. "She's a trip," he
said, thumbing at Patti, who was hugging an old lady at
the counter. "Name's Chuck. I think I saw you here earlier this week."

Glenn nodded. "Saw you too."

Patti came up with her coffeepot. "Do you have anything in common yet?" she wanted to know. Both men went red-faced. "There you go," she said. "You both blush." They looked at each other across the table, starting to laugh. "And you both like to laugh. So what are your plans tonight, Glenn? Chuckie?"

Chuck looked at Glenn. "Are you doing anything?" he asked.

"I don't know," Glenn answered.

"Give him your phone number," Patti said, handing Chuck one of her guest checks.

"I can handle it from here," Chuck said, "if you'll let me borrow your pen."

Glenn put Chuck's phone number on his dresser and left it there for a week. He looked at it from time to time, even picked it up and carried it to the phone, but he couldn't bring himself to make the call. He was waiting for Pete. Pete, who was just confused, Glenn was hoping. Pete, who was going to realize that he was in love with Glenn, that Glenn was the perfect match for him.

He picked up the receiver and tried calling his best friend. Pete answered on the first ring.

"Man, I thought you were dead or something. Why haven't you returned my calls?" Glenn said, smiling into the phone.

"Glenn," Pete said. He sounded surprised. There was an awkward silence.

"I'm coming over," Glenn blurted out suddenly. "Can I come over? I'll pick up some beer, a movie, some Chinese food. Have you eaten yet?"

"Glenn," Pete said. "I'm sort of engaged."

"Engaged? For the evening?"

"Engaged," Pete said, "like, almost married, man."

Glenn felt the air all around him go cold. He stared at the mirror, feeling like the floor was about to fall away beneath him.

"W-w-well…that's, uh…that's great," Glenn stammered. "Congratulations, bud. That's really, uh…great. Look I gotta go. There's someone at my door, I think. See you."

He hung up the phone. He reached for the piece of paper on the dresser — Chuck's number.

He had a couple of beers while waiting for Chuck to come over. He checked himself in the mirror; he was himself again and nervous as hell. He paced the living room, wondering if he should change his shirt. He thought about having another beer, and then the doorbell rang.

Chuck filled the doorway. He was holding a bunch of flowers clumsily. "Patti's idea," he said, blushing.

They did not go out that night, not like they had planned. They sat at opposite ends of the couch. Chuck leaned back and spread his legs, holding his beer bottle at his crotch and talking about his job as a contractor. Glenn looked into the open V of the man's shirt where a thin patch of red-brown hair lay. The urge to undo the rest of the buttons was strong, and Glenn put down his beer to free up his hands. It was fast, maybe too fast, and maybe he had had one too many. But he was not drunk, just impetuous, randy, and a little reckless. He thought he had caught Chuck glancing at his crotch once or twice, but he wasn't sure.

Both men shifted in their seats. Glenn put out a hand on the empty middle cushion of the couch, the no-man's land there. There was some music playing, but Glenn couldn't remember putting anything on the stereo. He looked at Chuck, and Chuck looked back at him, putting a hand close to Glenn's.

And then they were kissing.

Glenn put his hands on the front of Chuck's shirt, fingering the buttons there, sucking up the man's mouth. Chuck made a soft noise, opening his eyes, pulling Glenn onto him, his big hands all over Glenn's butt, gripping the denim-covered cheeks, slipping into the split of his thighs. He broke the kiss.

"Is this kind of fast?" Chuck asked, lips wet with spit.

"I guess," Glenn answered. He was wondering what he was going to do with the uncomfortable boner he had trapped in his jeans. He also wondered how Chuck would deal with his own erection. Glenn could feel it under him, a big, straight club that had wedged itself between them. He pressed himself against it, and Chuck let out a groan.

"Not fast enough," Chuck said, flipping Glenn over onto the floor. He opened all of Glenn's clothes, pulled at his shirt, tugged off his jeans. He stripped Glenn down to his socks and shorts. He stopped to look over what he had uncovered. Glenn's dick hopped against the front of his boxers.

Chuck pointed at Glenn's nipples, putting his fingers on them, fiddling with them, swirling around them. He kissed the hollow of Glenn's throat, licking down to the center of his chest, down and down, wetting the hairs that trailed up and out of his shorts. He licked over the waistband, over the head and shaft, sucking on the balls through the thin boxers, pushing his nose between Glenn's legs, sniffing around the pinched-up hole. He snaked a tongue around the crotch of the boxers and swiped at Glenn's tightened snatch.

Chuck looked up from what he was doing, looking a little frustrated. "May I?" he said, out of breath. He gripped the crotch of the shorts and tore them easily, like ripping paper.

"Oh, shit," Glenn breathed, feeling his cock go stony. "Please take off your clothes."

Chuck stood and slowly unbuttoned his shirt, revealing his massive hair-covered pecs and their wide nipples. He smoothed his hand over his stomach, dipping into his jeans, coming up with a few short copper-colored hairs between his fingers. He unbuttoned his pants and pushed them down. Glenn was staring up a mile of big muscled legs into the dark crack of Chuck's ass.

"Suck my cock?" Chuck asked, hands on his hips. Glenn climbed up those legs, getting his mouth close to

Chuck's pale-skinned dick. It hung thick and heavy, almost stiff — not long but a mouthful nonetheless. Glenn choked himself on it right away, eager to get it all into his mouth. He tongued the head and played with the soft ball sac, sucking up the weighty dangle of smooth skin. He heard Chuck groan and felt his prick thicken, letting it ride into his throat. Chuck grabbed his ears, bucking his hips and fucking Glenn's mouth, stretching out his lips.

He got himself off the man's fat cock and looked up at him. The big club swayed by his face, dripping with spit. "Put it in me," he said.

Chuck got down between Glenn's legs and lifted them, putting Glenn's feet on his chest. He spit down into his hand and slicked up his dick, pushing it against Glenn's hole. *That's a lot of cock,* Glenn thought as Chuck pushed it in — not quite gently — and Glenn squinted against the pain. He pushed against Chuck with his feet.

"Sorry, man," Chuck said, taking it easy, fucking Glenn with a smooth long stroke that felt better than anything Glenn had ever experienced. Chuck grabbed Glenn's ankles and spread his legs wide. He tipped Glenn's ass up, staring hard into his eyes. "You're feeling very good," Chuck said. He put his face close to Glenn's and kissed him. Glenn hugged the man's waist with his legs, getting and keeping all of Chuck's thick dong inside his ass.

"Oh, boy," Chuck said, rolling his eyes. He began to chug and pump into Glenn, turning Glenn's ass to mush, fucking it with abandon. He held on to Glenn's hips and pounded into him, grunting through gritted teeth. Glenn grabbed Chuck's tits, pulling on them.

"That's it," Chuck said. He pulled Glenn onto his fat prick and bounced him up and down on it, unloading into the slippery hole while Glenn's spew gushed between them in thick spurts, covering them both with gluey clots.

Glenn kissed Chuck good-bye at the door. "That was a very strange first date," Chuck said. "Can't wait to see what the next one's like. Will there be a next one?"

"Probably," Glenn said.

The phone started ringing. "I'll see you," Chuck said. "I'll call you tomorrow."

Glenn ran to the phone. "Hello?"

"Hey." It was Pete. "I was just wondering…" he said, hesitating.

"Yeah?" Glenn said, looking at himself in the mirror.

"You alone?" Pete said.

"I am," Glenn answered.

"Me too," Pete said.

"Where's the fiancée?"

"Don't know."

"Don't care?" Glenn said.

"Don't care," Pete answered. "I was wondering…"

"So I heard."

"Well?"

"Come on over," Glenn said, smiling at himself, thinking that his crazy first date just got crazier.

Dawn Run
by Grant Foster

For those of you out there doing the old 8-to-5 grind five days a week, fifty-two weeks a year, it won't come as much of a surprise to hear that a lot of guys are up and out before the sun has even had a chance to rise. What may surprise you, though, is just how many of those dudes who walk shoulder to shoulder with you in their three-piece suits and other business uniforms every day are riding high long before the sun gets its act together. Lots of dudes are horny at that hour of the day. I mean really horny.

I was a night prowler for years, staking all my hopes on meeting up with a hot guy when midnight had turned its back on us, then going somewhere and getting it on till the wee hours. Then I got my schedule all messed up, so I didn't have any free time for my daily run unless I wanted to get up early and do it before my job got its hooks in me for the day. What I found out was that not only could I get up in the mornings — but I could also get off.

I tend to concentrate my efforts on early risers like myself, steering clear of dudes just coming off their night shifts and those who've been up all night carousing. The former tend to be too tired, and the latter group is usually too out of it to be of much interest to me. Nope, as far as I'm concerned, I'll put my money on another early riser any old day. They're fresh and alert — and they're likely to be harboring fond memories of the morning hard-on they woke up with not long before they hit the streets.

The key to my success is persistence. These early-rising dudes are generally out with a purpose beyond getting laid. This isn't to say they don't want to get laid, just that it might not be at the absolute top of their list of things to do in the morning. But rest assured: Getting laid is definitely somewhere on most dudes' list. I just do my best to goose it up to the number one position.

I got up yesterday morning about a half hour before the sun. It was going to be a hot day, the weatherman said, and I believed him. Hot weather makes me horny, and when I woke up, my dick was pumped up so hard that it hurt. I hauled it into the bathroom and drained it, but it refused to back off on me even a little bit. I took a cold shower just so I could get it to soften up enough to get it in my jockstrap, slipped into a new pair of sky-blue nylon shorts, laced up my best running shoes, and headed for the door.

I stopped at the mirror in the entry hall long enough to check out the package. No doubt about it, I was looking good enough to fuck. I hadn't shaved, and dark stubble shadowed my cheeks and jaw. I smiled at my reflection, flashing white teeth and crinkling the skin around my green eyes. People often commented on my peepers. I got my mother's Italian coloring but my father's Irish eyes. The swarthy skin and dark curly hair really set the eyes off and made people notice.

They noticed the body as well — I worked hard to make sure of it. I'd been blessed with a good natural build and had spent years refining it till it was as close to perfect as I could make it. I flexed and admired the result. My biceps swelled until veins popped out on the full curve of muscle and snaked down over my thick forearms to my wrists. My pecs had been molded into a chiseled shelf of muscle that cut back sharply into my rib cage, my prominent, sensitive tits perched right on the edge of the drop-off. My belly was distinctly ridged, and my waist was fat-free. Years of daily running had sculpted my thighs and calves to eye-popping proportions and hadn't done my ass any harm either. My forearms and legs were hairy, but my torso was smooth as a baby's butt. I flexed again, looked, then left, knowing that if I stayed to admire the view any longer, I'd end up taking myself in hand and ruining my edge. I didn't want that to happen.

At 6 o'clock there were already quite a few guys in the grassy area where the runners did their stretches. I looked around for a guy I'd had my eye on for over a month, found him, and sauntered in his direction. He was alone this morning, which was good, because when he was with his buddy, he wasn't nearly as friendly as when he was solo. The redhead must've been someone he worked with, because they were always talking business when I came up beside them on the track. The redhead was humpy, but I was pretty sure he wasn't interested, so I had been concentrating on the tall blond dude with the great legs.

I came to a halt beside him and slowly bent down to touch my toes. He was kneeling on the grass, one leg stretched out in front, pressing his forehead to his kneecap. When he straightened his back, I glanced at his sleek hairless thigh and was treated to the sight of his nicely pumped rectus femoris, quadriceps femoris, the vastus medialis — you name it. Hey, I've been reading up on my anatomy. Might as well know what you're looking at, I figure. In layman's terms, the dude had a hell of a hot thigh, the type a man could hump with his hard-on or get off on while it was wrapped around his waist in a clinch.

"Morning, Ben," I said, sitting beside him and extending my legs, flexing a few muscles of my own. "Feels like it's gonna be a hot one."

"Tony, good to see you," he said in reply. "Ready to make these other guys eat some dust?" He grinned at me and stretched his other leg out in front of him. His shoulder touched mine briefly, sending little static sparks down my arm.

"You bet, Ben. I'm primed this morning." We stretched in companionable silence for a few more minutes, and then Ben rose to his feet.

"Ready, Tony?"

"Ready." I rose up from the ground, onto my toes, hands high above my head, getting in one final stretch. Ben moved off onto the track, and I followed him. We loped at a leisurely pace for the first few minutes, getting the blood pumping. Then Ben looked across at me and winked. "Move on out," I drawled, winking back at him and kicking into high gear. Ben paced me, and together we started eating up the distance.

We caught each other's rhythm and flew around the track shoulder to shoulder. By the third circuit even our breathing was synchronized. I glanced over at Ben from time to time, watching the rise and fall of his tightly muscled chest, the way his shoulder muscles rippled and flexed as his arms pistoned back and forth to propel him forward — and, of course, at all those sexy muscles in his legs. It was definitely inspirational.

Our eyes met on a couple of occasions, and it was pretty obvious that Ben was checking me out as well. As we passed group after group of other runners, it became clear that we were competing as a team, not against each other. Ben and I were pretty well-matched for size and endurance, but neither of us put on a burst of speed to leave the other in the dust. Instead, we ran in tandem, concentrating our efforts on besting the other guys on the track. It made a sort of bond between us. It was cool.

Ten turns around the track added up to five miles. As we started around the final turn, Ben looked at me and arched his thick, pale eyebrows. "Sprint?" he asked.

"Sprint!" I agreed, taking off like a racehorse with the barn in his sights. Our legs churned, and gravel flew as we broke into a high-kicking, all-out pace for the final lap.

Man, it was exhilarating! Sweat streamed off us as we pounded our feet against the track, flying by everyone else on the field. The sensations coursing through my body were damn near as intense as really good sex.

"Good job," Ben gasped, throwing his arm across my shoulders as we slowed to a fast walk. We stepped off the track onto the playing field in the center, giving ourselves a chance to cool down and work the adrenaline out of our muscles. Five minutes later we were breathing normally; within ten minutes sweat was drying on our skin, and we were ready to think about facing the workday.

"Got time for some juice and maybe a bagel before you hit the showers?" he asked me. "I just live on the other side of the park." I looked over at Ben and nodded agreement. Hell, I'd been planning to ask him the same question. It was nice when a man got the jump on me. Flattering too.

We loped across the park, crossed the street, and walked halfway down the block to an old brick apartment building that had recently been renovated. It was a great place, and I remembered checking it out a few months back, but it was out of my price range. I figured Ben must have a hell of a job to be able to afford it.

We took the stairs to the fifth floor. I followed Ben into the kitchen and, in a single gulp, drained the glass of grapefruit juice he handed me. I set the glass on the counter and stood looking at Ben. God, he was hot! I really got off on the acrid scent of his sweat and the way his taut muscles bunched and shifted under his skin as he moved around the kitchen.

Suddenly I realized that we were just standing there face-to-face, looking but not talking. I couldn't think of anything to say, and I hadn't quite screwed up my courage to the point of making a move. Then Ben did it for me. His hand rose from his side and came to rest against my chest. His long fingers splayed over the curve of my left pec, the ball of his thumb grazing my swollen nipple.

"Nice," he muttered, rubbing the point of my tit gently, shooting wake-up signals down to my cock and balls.

"Yeah," I replied, my hands settling on his narrow waist, just above the waistband of his sweat-soaked shorts. I wriggled my fingers inside the sodden fabric and pulled, shucking shorts and jock down onto his hard thighs. I pressed my thumbs in toward the center of his belly, then down to his groin. My fingers tangled in the soft, damp curls of his bush, then made contact with his cock. Ben growled sexily and set to work baring my own equipment. My shorts slipped over my hips and down my legs to my ankles.

I knelt on the kitchen floor and pressed my face tight against his belly, sniffing his musk. Then I ducked down a little lower and took his soft, sweaty prick into my mouth. I pressed it between my tongue and the roof of my mouth. Ben's fingers dug into my shoulder muscles as his piece came to life, growing longer, thicker, and harder by the second until his fat knob was crowding my tonsils. I backed off just a little and started working on him, sucking the tender tip, swirling my tongue around the flared rim of the crown. Ben sighed softly, and all those delectable muscles in his thighs popped out in sharp relief under his honey-colored skin.

I mashed my own aching stiffer against the solid mass of his right calf and began humping, my hips matching the stroking rhythm of my mouth. I was so involved in blowing the man that I didn't hear the creak of the door or the footfall on the floor. The first hint I had that we were not alone came when a pair of hands — hands that definitely weren't Ben's — cupped my ass and raised me from my crouching position.

"What the hell?" I exclaimed. Ben's dick popped out of my mouth, and I spun around to face the burly redhead who was Ben's sometime running partner. "Oh, shit," I muttered as the scenario became clear. This big galoot had to be Ben's lover. He was going to beat me senseless and then toss me out into the street. Swell.

"G'morning, Dave," Ben said, totally unconcerned by the impending mayhem. "Tony and I just had ourselves a hell of a run."

"I'll bet," Dave rumbled. Up close — my face was no more than six inches from his barrel chest — the man was huge. He had massively thick biceps, and his hands were damn near the size of hams. I'd also watched him on the track, and I knew that his thickly muscled legs could carry him very fast.

"I wasn't looking for trouble when I came over here," I began, my voice quavering slightly. "I didn't know that you two guys were, uh, you know, together."

"What?" Ben looked puzzled. "Oh, hell, Tony," he said. "Dave and I aren't lovers. We've been known to play around together, but we're just good friends."

"Oh." I breathed a deep sigh of relief, and my fear began to subside, leaving horniness in the forefront again. "I see."

"You guys want to play all alone, or could I maybe horn in?" Dave asked, his pale blue eyes taking in my assets, which appeared to be getting rave reviews from his cock. It was beginning to distend the front of his boxers, giving the impression that it could hold up a good-size tent when fully extended. I glanced at Ben, and he shrugged his shoulders.

"I play well in groups," I quipped, rubbing my knuckles against the solid wall of Dave's ridged belly. He grinned raunchily and shed his shorts. His prick was huge: thick, veiny, and uncut, the skin hanging a good inch beyond the fat knob it was draped over. I grabbed both men by the balls and sank back down to my knees. They scooted closer together, standing hip to hip, their dicks both angling toward my mouth.

I smacked my lips and licked Ben from balls to snout. Then I turned my attention to Dave and touched my tongue to the crinkled skin that hung off the end of his prick. His big piece rose high, then crashed down heavily against the bridge of my nose. I grabbed his thick stalk to hold him steady and worked my tongue up inside the hot, tight sleeve of his dick skin. I licked a little dribble of piss off the tip, then began tonguing his knob, watching his balls climb the cords till they were fighting for seating space on the broad back of his meat.

I fisted Ben's cock as well and went back and forth, licking and sucking both men till they started getting juicy. I was getting some much-wanted attention from them too. They were both bending over, rubbing my back and belly, massaging my horny muscles vigorously. Ben had a firm grip on my cock, working it with his fist. Dave was concentrating on my ass, his big hands planted on my muscular cheeks, his fingers sliding deeper and deeper into my crack. He punched a thick finger up my chute, and I swallowed his cock all the way to the balls, putting down over ten inches of fully pumped tube in the process.

"Come on over here, guy," Dave grunted, pulling me to my feet and leading me over to a counter that separated the kitchen from the dining area. Ben pushed aside piles of papers and books, and Dave tossed a big pillow on the tiled surface, picking me up and plunking me down on the middle of it. Dave grabbed my ankles at about the same time Ben pulled back on my shoulders, and I stretched out on my back, fully armed hard-ons pointing at me both fore and aft.

I opened wide for Ben, and he fed me his stiffer, simultaneously clamping his hands down on my chest and mauling my tits. Dave was taking care of my plumbing, chowing down on my cock while he got my ass stretched for what I hoped was going to turn into a long, deep, satisfying poking.

I wasn't disappointed. A couple of minutes — and about three fingers — into it, Dave was rummaging through a kitchen drawer with his free hand. I heard the sound of foil ripping, then felt a cool circle of rolled latex plop down on my belly. I grabbed it, skinned Dave's big cock knob, and bagged all ten-plus inches of him, all without missing a single lick on Ben's flexing prick.

"Ready?" Dave asked, jabbing at my asshole with his dick. I grunted unintelligibly, and he shoved his cock up my ass. At the same moment Ben leaned down and locked his full lips around the shaft of my throbbing prick. All the bases were covered now, and the only thing I had to do was lie there like a man and enjoy it.

Dave grabbed my ankles and spread my legs wide, stretching the well-pumped muscles. The position also tensed the entrance to my ass, assuring Dave a nice, tight ride. I reached down and secured his fat balls, rolling them against my palm, triggering some strong flexing action in his dick that damn near lifted me off the counter more than once.

The kitchen was completely silent except for the sweet music of sex — sucking and slobbering and the squishing sounds of a man's prick pumping a well-lubed asshole. Ben was starting to leak, coating my tongue with his pungent dick honey. The sticky drizzle drooling out of Ben's mouth and coating my balls clued me in that I was doing the same. I grabbed the blond's hard ass and crammed his dick deep, then massaged it with the muscles of my throat till he started to twitch and moan.

I kept him capped for as long as I dared, then let my head drop down over the edge of the counter. Ben slipped forward and began humping the little valley between the hard mounds of my pecs. From my vantage point I saw his balls snap up and his asshole clench, then felt his hot jism shooting down my torso to my belly.

That did me. I smacked his ass in warning and fisted my dick when he spit it out, pumping madly. Dave kept on reaming my ass, and Ben continued to hump my chest. I exploded in a scorching torrent of jizz that spattered Ben and me with long ropy strings of creamy white. About that same instant, Dave roared, jerked his cock out of me, skinned off the latex, and blasted the two of us with his own scalding load. When I finally hauled myself off the counter, I looked like I'd been attacked by a mad chef with a pastry bag full of white icing.

I wiped myself down, sorted my shorts and jock out of the pile of clothes on the kitchen floor, and jogged back home to shower and suit up for work. I have a feeling that Ben and Dave and I will meet up in the future for more early-morning frolics. Even if I don't connect with them again, though, there are plenty of other hot men on the hoof — bright-eyed, randy, and ready to romp long before the old sun clears the tops of the trees here in the park. I know for damned sure that I'll be out there, all limbered up, pumped, and ready for anything.

Beer Nuts
by Phil Cole

I know I didn't see him, and I don't think I heard him. I may have felt his breath on the back of my neck. Whichever sense was alert, it kept me from jumping out of my skin when a low voice about two inches from my left ear said, "Hey, nice."

I assumed that what the person behind the voice thought was nice was a very intricate piece of eighteenth-century wood carving I was engrossed in repairing. Instead of jumping out of my skin, I turned my head slowly and stared into a pair of intense green eyes that crinkled at the corners. As I focused, I gradually became aware of an incredibly handsome face mere inches from mine, smiling down at me.

To cover my confusion and to put some distance between us, I got up, stumbling over the stool in the process, and grabbed his shoulder to keep from falling. He grabbed my arm and held me upright. For an instant we must have looked like dancing partners about to waltz across the room. This strange image, or something like it, must have occurred to him at the same time. We both laughed and reluctantly separated.

We introduced ourselves (I didn't quite catch his name), and he held out an inlaid mahogany box that looked as if it had been thrown a long distance or dropped from a great height. It was dented and scuffed in several places — badly in need of refinishing. He offered no explanation except to ask if by any stretch it could be returned to normal. As I looked down to take it from him, I almost dropped it. Instead of paying attention to the box, my eyes locked on his navel and the beginnings of a trail of blond hair where his tank top didn't quite meet his jeans. I followed the trail down to its inevitable terminus: a huge bulge in the front of his jeans. Christ! Where had this guy been all my life?

I somehow had the presence of mind to get him to write his name and number on a claim check, tear off his half (mangling it in the process), and say I'd be in touch when the box was ready.

After he left (I watched his butt and even its afterimage as he sauntered out) I sank down onto my stool at the workbench, realizing I was trembling only when I inadvertently tore a gash in the carving with the chisel. It was the damnedest feeling. I'd definitely had my share of gay adventures and had certainly been the aggressor often enough. Maybe it was all that beauty in one fell swoop — he startled me with it.

I figured him to be in his early twenties. His hair was dark blond, and he had to be about six feet tall because I am and we'd been at each other's eye level when we were doing our little dance act together. He obviously spent time keeping his body in shape — but not excessively so. His muscles seemed finely toned without being the bulging, steroid-augmented, heavily veined monstrosities so prevalent among the bodybuilding set. I remembered his shoulder; it had flexed and stiffened when I'd grabbed it. I'd stood there, eyes blank, caressing it until I felt my dick stir in my pants.

But what was his name? I racked my brain but couldn't seem to remember it. I had just about given up trying when my eyes fell on the claim check he'd filled out. How stupid could I be? Why didn't I think of that earlier? I must have really fallen for this guy. There it was: Thiers Larsen, 555-4117.

I must admit that for the next few days, Thiers Larsen, his shimmering image filling my head, fueled quite a few jack-off fantasies. I began to spend too much time looking out the window in case he walked past and not enough time on my work. Every time someone came into the shop, I looked up quickly, hoping to see him materialize in the doorway. Every time I went out, I scanned the horizon, my radar on alert for a sighting.

I decided I was going to have to get to work on that box if I wanted to see him again. Seeing him again was, of course, only a small part of what my raunchy little mind had planned.

Thiers had left the box off midweek. The following Sunday, about 6 a.m., I was driving down to the village when my vigilance finally paid off — or perhaps the gods finally took pity on me. Thiers (it had to be — I'd know that butt anywhere) was jogging along on my side of the road about half a mile from my shop. I drove past him, my mind deep in thought, planning tactics and strategies at lightning speed.

I don't like to work on Sundays, but the paperwork piles up during the week, and I usually need a couple of hours to get at it when the chance of interruption is practically nil. The earlier I'm out of there, though, with a full, free day ahead of me, the better. I parked the van and got out, resisting the urge to glance in Thiers's direction to check his progress. I unlocked the shop door and went in, leaving it ajar. If necessary, I was ready to dash out into the street in hot pursuit, but I was hoping the partially open door would lure him in, saving me from making a spectacle of myself.

I heard someone enter the shop and close the door. I made a pretense of being busy at the workbench, looking up in mock surprise when Thiers was halfway across the room. He must have been running for quite a while. Not only was that magnificent bare torso dripping with sweat, but his (very short) white shorts — with a slit on each side exposing several more inches of upper thigh — were completely soaked through. And he obviously wasn't wearing a jockstrap.

"Hey," I said. "Saw you jogging back there. You always run on August mornings with the temperature already in the eighties?"

"To tell you the truth," he replied, "I've got one hell of a hangover, and I figured maybe I could sweat it out."

"I guess that's no nuttier than my method," I said, laughing. "Hair of the dog. Fucks with my head a little, but at least I feel better than before I have it."

"I know what you mean. The promise of a cold beer at the end of this run is what's kept me going this far. I'm going to crack one as soon as I get home."

What a coincidence! I happened to have six ice-cold Budweisers in the shop's small refrigerator. Was I on a roll or what?

I shrugged. "Have one here," I said. "I just stocked up yesterday. I don't have a hangover, but that's no reason I can't join you." I smiled weakly. Beer at 6 in the morning? Even I'm not *that* alcoholic. Nevertheless, I managed to convince myself that this was a special occasion.

"Sure," he said. "Lead on."

I nodded toward the back of the shop, and he followed me there. The fridge is in my little office, a room partitioned off from the rest of the shop by a thick folding screen.

I got the beers, handed him one, and sat down at my desk. He sat in the visitor's chair at its side and put his bare arm down on the desk — where, of course, it would leave a sweat mark. I couldn't have cared less. In fact, it occurred to me whimsically that I might put a little railing around the area as a sort of shrine to Thiers.

We began to talk. I said something about this being such a small town, I was surprised I hadn't seen him around before. He told me he'd landed a coaching job at the local high school and had come to town early to find a place to live and get settled in before the start of the school year. He was staying at one of the seasonal rental cabins down by the lake. He asked me how long I'd had my shop, and I told him some of my history.

We traded banalities like this for about half an hour, both of us looking for some sort of opening. When I said something about liking woodworking so much that it was probably what I'd spend the rest of my life doing, he found one. It was a little weak, but who was grading? This was not an exercise in high-level diplomacy.

"Hope that leaves time for other good things," he said, looking hard into my eyes and leaving no doubt in my mind what he thought the other good things were.

"Like, for instance," he said, "have you ever tasted beer and sweat mixed together?"

As he said this he lifted his arm off the desktop and tipped the bottle, letting the brew splash against his skin. The frothy liquid flattened the blond hairs on his forearm, and he raised it and started licking. He stuck his tongue out to lap, making slurpy noises. The he withdrew it and stuck just the tip out, darting it around over his skin. All the while he looked directly into my eyes.

My cock began to twitch and stiffen, arranging itself just the wrong way in my pants. It was pleasantly painful, but I didn't know how much more I could take.

Finally he said, "Want to try it?" and poured more beer so that it dripped down and around his arm onto the desk.

I didn't say anything. I just leaned forward, rearranged my cock on the sly, and began to lick the beer and the sweat. I was still licking and breathing pretty heavily long after I'd got it all.

"Good, huh?" he smiled. It was a rhetorical question.

"Let me have some more," I panted.

"Where do you want it this time?"

In answer I rubbed my hand across his pecs, stopping at his nipples to pinch them lightly, feeling them harden under my fingers. I'm a nut for nipples, and his were perfect. They stuck out about half an inch, and you could really get your fingers around them. He wasn't especially hairy, but the hair he had was in all the right places: little swirls of blond around his nipples, silky blond in a line from his pecs to his navel, coarser where it disappeared into his shorts.

As I continued to rub his chest, he flexed his pecs, and I could feel the muscles knot. He tipped the bottle and let the beer pour down on him. It cascaded over his nipples and pooled in his navel. I got down on my hands and knees in front of him, taking his flexed biceps in my hands and caressing them. I licked away at his pecs and nibbled on his tits, running my tongue languidly around his bulletlike paps.

Tilting his head back, he moaned. "Bite them," he whispered. I bit into one, then the other. He arched into me, threw his head back, and gasped, "Oh, shit, yeah!"

I looked down and noticed a huge tent forming in his running shorts. I rubbed my stomach against it, eliciting more moans from Thiers. I licked up his pecs in long strokes now, stopping each time at one nipple or the other to bite and chew. He was writhing in pleasure, and when I loosened my grasp on his biceps, his arms shot up reflexively, and he put his hands behind his head.

I took this as a not-so-subtle hint, so I moved to a sweat-soaked armpit and began lapping at the silky blond hairs there. In this position my body was pressed against his, and while I licked I kept running my hands up and down his sides and rubbing my throbbing dick against his. I moved down to lick his pecs again, then his navel, and finally down the damp hairline to the waistband of his shorts.

By his reactions I could tell that Thiers was enjoying this thoroughly, especially now that I was getting closer and closer to his cock. I moved my fingers around the hem of his shorts, hiking them up his thighs past the tan line, exposing ivory flesh and little hints of blond hair. He took the beer bottle from the desk and poured some over his upper thighs. Then he poured the rest of the bottle on his shorts over his bulging cock and balls. He winced a little as the cold beer made contact through the cloth, but he didn't lose his hard-on, which was now clearly outlined, lying flat against his stomach, the back of it ridged, his balls separate orbs on either side.

I stroked his calves as I leaned forward to lick the beer and sweat from his thighs, my tongue moving nimbly around the taut, almost hairless flesh. When I reached the white skin above the tan line, I started to make little forays under the fabric of his shorts. When I touched his ball sac, Thiers let out a long sigh. I could tell he was getting impatient, but I was determined to do this my way.

I licked and kneaded, watching that cock strain at his shorts. I sucked at the moisture in the cloth all around it. Each time he sensed I was almost on it, he tensed. Then I'd move a little farther away. By the time I started running my tongue up his shaft, his whole body was writhing in ecstasy. When I got to the head, I stretched and manipulated the cloth with my teeth until I had his covered cock in my mouth. "Jesus, Jesus, Jesus," Thiers moaned, making little thrusts with his pelvis.

"Stand up," I ordered, leaning back from him and unzipping my shorts. By the time he was on his feet, I had them down to where I could deal with my own rock-hard cock. I reached up to his waistband and yanked his shorts down around his ankles. Eight inches of cock flailed out at me, the perfectly shaped head glistening with precome. I had the head in my mouth in an instant, sucking at it and working my tongue around it. After a couple of minutes of this, he pushed me off, took it in his hand, and slapped my face with it, back and forth, stopping to tease my mouth and then slapping some more. On one pass I managed to capture it and take it all the way up the shaft, burying my nose in sweaty blond hair.

This was almost too much for Thiers. He yelled out and grabbed the back of my head. I quickly got both hands on his ass, cupping those firm, round cheeks with my trembling hands. I let my fingers run down his crack, teasing his puckering hole mercilessly. I couldn't get enough of that ass.

Thiers seemed to be getting over his surprise at my deep throat and started ever so slowly — and somewhat tentatively at first — to fuck my mouth. I took one hand off his ass to stroke my own cock, which was now well-lubed with precome.

"Finger-fuck me!" he gasped. "Finger-fuck me! I want to come with your whole finger up my ass!"

I gently eased my forefinger into his tight hole, pushing it in knuckle by knuckle until I could jam it in no farther. The rhythm of his fucking picked up speed. He grunted audibly as I moved my finger faster and faster in and out of his butt. I felt his cock pulse wildly, the head getting bigger and harder. Suddenly a torrent of come exploded in my mouth, spurting uncontrollably down my throat. Thiers's body, now jerking spasmodically, lunged over and over into my face. I stopped stroking my own cock, fearing I would come before I got a chance to work on his magnificent ass.

As his spasms diminished and his breathing became more regular, he loosened the grip he had on my head and eased his still-hard, still-throbbing cock out of my mouth. When he took hold of my shoulders and raised me up, I forced his mouth open with my tongue and fed him his own come. I held myself to him and squeezed his ass cheeks.

I wanted that ass as much as I'd ever wanted anything, but I hesitated to ask the question. Once I come I can no more take a cock up my butt than a fly. Nevertheless, I kept kissing and caressing him, thinking I might get him hot again. I soon found out I needn't have bothered — though it was certainly no bother, I must say.

"Your finger really felt good up there," he whispered, kissing me tenderly on the neck. "But your cock would feel much better."

Wasting no words of thanksgiving, I whirled him around so that he was facing the desk, pushed papers off every which way to clear it, and bent him over. He steadied himself and spread his legs apart as I rubbed my cock up and down his crack. Then I stood back to see it better. He flexed it while I watched. His undulating tan line was very pronounced, and the flexing seemed to emphasize the invitation, to beg for my cock. I moved up to ease it in, and I was so hot that I begged my rod not to shoot before I could get it in all the way. I managed eight or ten deep thrusts, bashing my thighs into his cheeks, my hands pulling his hips back roughly toward mine. Unable to hold it in anymore, I came over and over, my pelvis slamming into him with brute force.

When the spasms finally ended, I lay down on his body, panting. Thiers turned his head and, almost out of breath himself, said, "Wow, man! Fuckin' wild. That was hot!"

As soon as I could breathe, I asked, "Where'd you come up with that beer-and-sweat routine?"

"Liked that, huh? I first tried that last year on a swimming-coach buddy of mine. I'd been hot to get into his pants for months. I thought he might be straight and didn't dare do anything in case he raised hell with the athletic director. Then I saw a picture in a magazine of a hunk with no shirt on. He had a beer bottle, tilted up, and was sucking on it. Some of the beer was running out of his mouth and down his chest. It really turned me on! I wanted to lick it off for him. Next time we were having a few, it hit me. I tried the same line on him, and he picked up on it even quicker than you did." He laughed, shaking his head. "Turned out he'd been as hot for me as I'd been for him. Months wasted, but we tried to make up for it."

"You know," I said, grinning, "I have to admit, though, beer and sweat really taste awful together."

He shrugged. "Well," he said, "next time we'll have to try something imported."

Struttin'
by David Wesley

I've always been a sucker for a guy who struts, who moves with confidence and an animal awareness of the space he inhabits. He knows he belongs wherever he wants to belong.

I find that very, very sexy. And it's something that I can't do myself. My approach is more cerebral, more considered. But, boy, I really love that intuitive approach to life.

That's why Rusty, the new gofer at *The Chronicle,* was so striking. Right away he was striding around the newsroom like he owned the goddamned place. He'd pick up some copy or deliver some coffee and smile his shit-eating grin and tell you in one quick glance that he wasn't going to be at the bottom rung for long, that he'd soon be doing whatever he wanted to do and with whomever he wanted to do it. He smiled that same hunky grin at everyone — star reporters, editors, the old ladies at the copy desk, and the gnarled old cleaning man who'd been emptying wastebaskets since there was movable type. And Rusty told everyone who'd listen that he had the tools to make it in the business too. He could take photos and develop his own pictures and was handy at a typewriter.

Most of the staff didn't listen and didn't care. But I did because I could see that big basket bob as Rusty walked around the office doing chores. I saw more whenever I could conveniently sidle up to him in the men's room and grab a quick peek at his pecker. That's when I knew he had the tool to make it. He had a gorgeous cock even when he pissed. He held it as if it were his best friend, and maybe it was. It was a good six inches soft. Cut. Heavily veined. A tasty-looking mushroom head. And it seemed to have as much swagger and sureness as its master. Unless, of course, it was the master.

I was lucky to be busy because I started having big-time fantasies about Rusty and his tool. Driving around town, I'd think about him, about how nice it would be to have him sitting next to me massaging my crotch as we drove the city streets. More than once I found myself kneading my dick and thinking it was Rusty's hot mouth that was on it. In the shower I'd soap myself up and close my eyes, and I'd swear it was Rusty pinching my nipples, squeezing my big soapy balls, or exploring my squeaky-clean ass with some very talented fingers. Then I'd imagine Rusty pulling out his fingers and inserting that tool. I felt like his dick and I were on a first-name basis. Yet I hadn't said more than a few words to its owner.

My beat was murder and mayhem. I covered the city cops, big fires, and disasters of all kinds. It was not my preferred assignment. But I was big and beefy, and the local gendarmes and firemen took to me as if I were one of their own. When my eyes swept up and down their bodies, they thought I was just admiring their courage and heart, not their biceps and buns.

It was already late on a Friday, and I was headed home with major plans to hit the bars and forget about Rusty when my scanner started chirping. An explosion had set off a big fire at the chemical plant southwest of town. I hauled ass and dialed the city desk from my cellular phone to order a photographer to the scene. Angry red flames shot hundreds of feet into the night sky. It looked like the end of the world. There was no loss of life, the fire captain said, because it was Friday night and only a skeleton crew was working. They all got out after the first blast.

I called in the basics, assuring the night editor that I'd stay on the scene as long as there was a story. "And when's the shutterbug getting here?" I asked.

"Should be there, Delaney," I was told.

"No sign of anybody here. Who'd you send?"

"There was no one in the pool," the editor replied, "so I sent out that new kid."

I couldn't recall a new kid. Then it clicked. "Rusty?"

"Yeah, Rusty. He assured me he could handle it."

"Shit!" I muttered softly under my breath.

"What? I think your signal's breaking up."

"Shit!" I said distinctly and hung up. I trotted back to the perimeter, where a cordon of fire trucks faced the worst of the fire. Just then I saw someone slip past the barricades and head in toward the flames. I recognized the broad shoulders tapering to a trim waist. And, God, I couldn't forget that sweet, firm ass! It was Rusty.

He was loaded down with equipment but was still moving like a cat, shooting pictures and scurrying. He was taking pictures of the fire, scrambling up and down platforms, acting like a reckless asshole. No one seemed to notice him but me. I moved down the fire line, yelling and waving my arms, trying to get his attention over the fiery spectacle all around.

Just as he turned my way, a tank blew. The explosion propelled Rusty twenty yards through the air toward me. Clouds of black oily smoke smothered him. He lay motionless on the ground.

I scrambled to him. The heat was terrific. I thought my face was melting. Rusty was still when I got to him. I was afraid to move him, but I knew we'd both fry if we stayed where we were. With my adrenaline flowing I picked him up and carried him away from the smoke and flames.

Once we were at a safe distance, I gently laid him down. I couldn't find a pulse. With the roar of the fire and the popping of detonations all around, it was impossible to tell if he was still breathing. I put an ear to his chest and to his mouth but heard and felt nothing.

Afraid time was running out, I cradled his head, put my lips to his, and started mouth-to-mouth resuscitation. There was no response. I saw firemen running toward us. They could do CPR. I tried to pump in a few last breaths. Suddenly Rusty heaved and sputtered and started breathing on his own. His eyes opened. He was dazed but slowly realized what had happened. He stared into my eyes.

Finally he said, "You look like hell." He took a finger and wiped away some oily soot from my face.

"You, my friend, look like a survivor," I said. He smiled at that. "But," I continued, "you acted like a real jerk."

The firemen took over. They couldn't find any broken bones but took Rusty to a waiting ambulance so the ER at City Hospital could check him out. "Wait!" he shouted. He motioned to me as he took the battered Nikon from around his neck. "Get these developed. And don't forget my credits."

He smirked his usual smart-ass smile and was gone. Soon the fire was under control, although it took another couple of days to burn out. I raced back to the newsroom and handed in the pictures, then went home to bed very tired. And very alone.

The next morning I picked the paper up off my doorstep and saw my story and three great shots of the fire by Rusty. A few minutes later my phone rang.

"Thanks. You saved my life." It was Rusty, sounding cheerful yet reserved.

"How ya doin', kid?" I asked.

"Okay. They kept me in the hospital overnight for observation."

"When are you getting out?"

"In about an hour," he said shyly, not at all like he'd ever sounded before.

"What about your car?" I knew it was still down at the smoldering hulk of the chemical plant.

"Someone will take me down later today or tomorrow."

"I'll be glad to help out," I said. I thought I was just offering — without any ulterior motive. "Why don't I pick you up at the hospital?"

After a lengthy pause Rusty agreed. He was subdued on the ride to his place. He didn't even seem interested when I showed him the front page. He sat way over on his side of my pickup and looked straight ahead. The experience had him scared shitless.

His apartment was homey and spotless. I was surprised.

"Get in bed. I'll make you some tea." He started to protest, but I cut him short. "I'll find it. Climb under the covers and take it easy."

"Okay," he mumbled.

After I banged through cabinets looking for tea or coffee or anything, I went to the bedroom.

"I tried to explain," he said. "I usually don't drink anything but water or juice. And I'm all out of fruit."

"That's what you think."

"What?" he asked, startled.

"Just thinking aloud."

I told him to relax and that I'd run out for some tea, honey, and rum.

"Please don't," he said. "I'm fine. Really."

Just then I saw that he was shivering violently. I put a hand to his forehead. He was burning up. Then I saw he was still wearing his clothes under the covers.

"Scared?" I asked gently.

He nodded in a shy, boyish way.

I started to massage his shoulders. "It's okay to be scared. Fire like that's a nasty animal. Wild and untamed and very dangerous. You're lucky to be alive."

"I know," he said, shuddering worse as I kneaded the knot at the back of his neck.

"We may need to take you back to the hospital. Get you some therapy," I told him. He was shaking violently.

"Please, stop," he said. Rusty was almost sobbing. "Please don't touch me."

"Sorry," I said. "I didn't mean to offend you." His eyes were still cast down. "After last night I thought we couldn't get any closer," I joked.

"You bastard," he said softly, not in anger but with an edge of despair. "You damn bastard."

I was really confused now. "Rusty, I don't...I don't understand..."

He turned and looked at me. His eyes filled with tears. I wanted to take him in my arms and kiss the tears away. "You gave me the kiss of life," he said slowly, "and I woke up and put my hand up to your face. And then I remembered. We're two men." He turned his face away from mine again. "When I knew your lips had been on mine, it was like a dream come true," he continued. "I went out to that fire hoping to show you I was as much of a newshound as you, as much of a man, as much of a—"

"Lover?"

"Yes," he gasped and began to sob convulsively. I wiped the tears away. "And now I'm afraid to be near you because you *know* what I am and how I feel and you'll find me repulsive."

"Guess again," I told him as I cradled his head and brought my lips to his. Our kiss was sweet and tender. His lips were swollen and blistered from the heat of the fire. They parted slightly, and my tongue probed his mouth, delicately at first and then more insistently. His eyes closed, and he kissed me deeper and with more passion.

We came up for air. "I've been wanting that for a long time," he said.

"So have I."

"You never talked to me."

"Because I was always thinking about you."

"I followed you into the john to get close to you."

"But acted as cool as could be."

"We were at work, for Christ's sake."

"We're not now," I said as I pulled back the covers and slid alongside him. There was no need to hurry, and I still wasn't sure of his condition.

I kissed his forehead to cool it as I slowly unbuttoned his shirt, first the front and then the cuffs. I kissed his eyes, his cheeks, his throat. We pulled the shirt off together, and my lips and tongue continued their trail downward, moving up and down and from side to side. I nibbled at his armpits, and I licked a trail across his chest, lingering at each hard nipple for a small feast of pleasure.

The heat from Rusty's fever was moving south. I unbuckled his belt and popped the button on his jeans. My tongue bathed the valley where his navel made a dent in his firm, rippled stomach.

"Oh, God!" Rusty moaned as I reached inside the waistband of his Calvin Kleins and tugged them down with his jeans. He let me do all the work, and I was pleased. I was still gentle. I inspected the dark, purple bruises along his legs, much worse than the scrapes on his arms. I saw a rough, raw abrasion on his otherwise perfect creamy ass cheeks. And I understood why he was called Rusty. His pubic hair was a shiny copper, brighter and rustier than the hair on his head, which must have darkened to a burnished bronze as he grew up.

My journey continued. My mouth played along his legs all the way down to his toes. I took a minute to kiss the soles of his feet before sucking on his toes singly and in combination until he closed his eyes and tensed up at this sensation. I knew no one before had ever lavished that much attention on his feet.

I rolled my tongue up his legs to face the monster. By now his cock was engorged with blood and jutting straight up more than ten inches. It was long and fat, but it was perfectly shaped and proportioned. The dark veins pulsed. The corona was a deep red tending to purple. For a moment I just studied it in mute awe, exploring its classic perfection.

Rusty lifted his head, saw my wonder, and then smiled quietly.

I began by rubbing his erection along the outside of my cheek, feeling its velvety texture before tasting its thrilling hardness. My lips kissed the tip. Rusty moaned. My tongue swathed the mushroom head, swirling across the surface, probing the slit. The first honeyed drops of precome trickled out, and I savored their sweetness. I was still taking my time. My tongue licked every vein, every contour on his fabulous prick. This was an experience to enjoy.

I was very excited. My mouth was dripping saliva. Finally I opened wide and sucked in the top of his cock. His dick made love to my lips. "That's it, baby," Rusty sighed. "Take what you want. Take it all, baby."

I opened wider, and his mighty shaft pushed in. Rusty was rotating his hips now. He was doing a horizontal strut. The kid wanted to fuck my face, and I was eager to swallow all of his thick and juicy hard-on. It pushed past my teeth and inched down my throat. Each time he made his thrust, I bobbed my head, and his love tube slipped farther into me.

Rusty sighed deeply as my jaws relaxed and I swallowed the whole damn thing. "Shit, that feels good!" he said, his hands running through my hair, gently guiding me as I turned up the suction. "You like sucking that big cock, Delaney?" he asked. I groaned in the affirmative. "Enjoy yourself, man, 'cause I love that head work on my prick."

He was relaxed, soothed. I knew that few people — man or woman — had taken his giant dong down to the root before. After what he'd been through, he had a right to enjoy first and shoot later. We rocked and rolled in an easy, deep union.

But I wanted to give him more. I switched my attention to his big, hairy balls, swinging heavy and low in a sac still sharply scented with hospital soap. My tongue washed his nuts, then I sucked first one and then the other into my mouth. They were huge and delicious, and I rolled them around while Rusty closed his eyes and arched his body in pleasure.

He was getting more excited. I let his balls slip from my hot mouth and slid my tongue down the rough ridge to his waiting asshole. I licked greedily at the circle of his pucker. The rosebud closed tighter, and I stabbed at it with my tongue in short, hot taps. Then I let my tongue linger and rotate, nudging it in deeper and deeper. Gradually his sphincter relaxed, and the pucker opened in greeting. I nibbled more insistently at the hole. It opened wider for my tongue and lips.

"Eat that asshole, stud," he urged. "Fuck me with that mouth, Delaney. Let me know you're there, man." I strained to push my tongue in, to suck and slurp until he begged me to stop. But Rusty wouldn't beg.

Instead he took charge. "Get out of those clothes," he ordered. "You don't deserve all the fun." He helped me shed my clothing, wildly tossing each piece to a different corner of the room. He pushed me up so that I was hovering over him and he was staring up at my own slab of meat. It's not the titan his is, but it's not that bad. Hard, I'm just shy of eight inches, uncut but always clean, and rooted deep so I always point straight up.

His mouth stretched and pulled me in all at once right down to my dark pubes. He was like a madman on a crazy mission. He sucked and slurped on my hard rod. One hand worked my nuts like crazy, and the other hand played with my love hole. He came up for air. "Suck me, Delaney. I'm not going to fucking break." He was breathless and frenzied.

I plunged up and down his dick, becoming a maniac too. I caressed his balls, rolling them in my fingers until I felt them draw into his wrinkled ball sac and knew he was close to blowing. Quickly I licked a couple of fingers and shoved them up his ass. He winced but said nothing. Now we were both close. I felt my heart beating in my head. I tried holding back. I wanted us to come together.

He mumbled something. "Shoot, cocksucker," I heard. "Shoot that hot come down my throat." Next his words came loud and clipped; he roared like a rogue elephant. "Suck that big dick," he bellowed. "Take that load. You're gonna get my come, man. Here it...here it...here it comes!" His prick was hard as a brick. My tongue could feel the come run up his juice tube until it blasted out his cock. Each shot was bigger and more intense than the last. I kept swallowing his load until his body shook and he tried to pull away.

Just then I started gushing. My own orgasm came in wave after wave, my load pouring out as if I were still a teenage kid with a bucket of come churning in my balls. Rusty was still rock-hard when I shuddered to a stop and he let me out of his mouth. I still held him in mine. I slurped him clean and polished his knob. I didn't want to let his beauty go.

But I wanted a kiss. I rotated back around and stretched out alongside him. "Thanks," he said, gently nuzzling his head under my chin. "That was like a dream come true."

"You're the dream," I said. I leaned over and gently touched his lips. They were raw and red. The fire blisters had popped, and he hadn't given a damn.

I pulled him into me, his back to my front. I held him like a baby, but I kept my fist around his cock. It was still hard and throbbing when we drifted off to sleep.

When I awoke, though, I felt Rusty's hand around my hard-on. He was jerking my dick, and I was swollen and anxious to go again. His front was at my back now, and I could feel his prick probing at my ass. It wasn't yet like he wanted in or anything. It was just that he was ready for action, and we were locked in this position.

I figured he had a good idea. After all, with his bruises I didn't want to toss his legs in the air and pump my way into him. It might strain those tender spots on his beautiful legs and his inviting round bottom, which looked too sore to bang.

My mouth worked his cock up into a lather. Then I spit in my hand and worked it into my butt hole as a lubricant. I positioned myself over his waiting rod and eased back until the red-hot crown kissed the pucker of my chute. Rusty had a big smile on his face. I let my weight down, and his long, fat dick head pushed up inside. My ass is nearly virgin. It takes a special man to pack it. I knew

Rusty was the right man. The pain was sharp and exquisite. Once his crown slid past the opening, things went great. The pain yielded to pleasure as I felt his monster slap my prostate.

"Oh, yeah, baby," I said. "That's where I want it. Give me that dick, Rusty. Fuck my ass!" I rode up and down, slowly at first and then gathering speed. Rusty lay back. He was still smiling, but his eyes were closed, and his mouth was open in a kind of ecstasy.

I picked up speed. Rusty used his hands on my nipples, working them like an expert. I longed for his tongue, but I was so deeply impaled on his hard dick that I couldn't lean over for a kiss. I reached back and played with his balls. They felt warm and good. He sighed as I squeezed them. I squeezed some more.

My own cock was bouncing up and down on Rusty's chest, sliding around in our sweat so that I was close to coming without manipulation. I twisted around and contracted my butt muscles.

"Man, you've got a tight ass," Rusty moaned. "I love that ass, man."

"It's your ass, Rusty," I told him. "Fuck it, baby. Make it your plaything. Make it obey."

He slapped it once, twice, three times. It stung, and the sting was good. "I'm gonna shoot, man," he warned. "I'm gonna come!"

"I want that hot jizz. Fuck me, Rusty. Shoot it up my ass. Make me feel your fiery love juice!" I was bouncing furiously. His dick was pounding my prostate. "Give me that cock juice." I was going to explode any second. Then I felt him erupt in a steady hot stream up my ass. It was as if he were pissing fire into my guts. I was flooded with a warmth that put me over the edge. My rod started shooting. My dick shot and bounced. Come rained over Rusty's stomach and chest. He was covered in puddles of come.

We kissed. We cleaned up. I stayed the rest of the weekend, attending to Rusty's every need. We made love again and again.

In a few weeks Rusty's wounds healed. By then I had convinced our editors of his courage (but had failed to tell them of his foolhardiness). He got a regular job as a photographer, and we were teamed as a special-disaster unit.

We worked together a lot after that. Nobody thought it unusual that we were always together. We drew no notice when our heads were locked in conversation or when one finished sentences the other had started.

Our lives were entwined. Our lives were forever changed. All because of the kiss of life. Or was it the kiss of a lifetime?

Rise & Shine
by Ram Emerson

"Man, I sure hope I get one of those regional slots this time around." My buddy Matt Simms edged past several of our colleagues and sat down next to me. The auditorium was filling up, and the bigwigs were already milling around on the stage. Today was the day all the merit promotions were to be announced in front of the entire home-office staff. Matt and I had both been working our asses off and were hoping for a new job and a healthy raise as a reward for all those working weekends and long hours of unpaid overtime.

I was a little nervous because my boss and I didn't get along all that well. He was a conservative family man, and he didn't approve of the fact that I was single. He kept on bugging me about getting settled down and starting a family so that I could really be a participating member in Agri-Pure Chemical Industries. I personally couldn't see what being married had to do with increasing the yield of wheat and soybean crops, but that was J.L.'s viewpoint, and that was that.

My stomach knotted when J.L. stepped up to the podium and began to announce the names of the chosen. The two jobs I had rested my hopes on went to Matt and another colleague, leaving me with a sinking feeling that my career was dead-ending before my very eyes. Then J.L. dropped the bomb on me.

"It is now my pleasure to announce my appointment to the regional directorship of the Agri-Pure Demonstration Farms located in Conyer's Point, Nebraska. Paul Gunther, come on up here so I can shake your hand."

"Way to go, guy." Matt was pumping my hand as I rose shakily to my feet. The walk up to the front of the auditorium was like a nightmare — all my coworkers smiling and applauding as I marched off to my doom. Nebraska! Christ, I got nervous if I stayed in a city park too long. I liked concrete and skyscrapers and crowded urban streets. I also liked having twelve gay bars within walking distance of my apartment — a luxury I suspected did not exist in Conyer's Point.

"This'll be good for you, Paul," J.L. said as he shook my hand. "You'll have fewer distractions there. Maybe meet a nice country girl, settle down, and start a family. This is an important move, son. Make the most of it." I walked back to my seat in a daze. Nebraska. Jesus Christ!

I was on a plane the very next morning. J.L. wasn't the type of man who messed around once he'd made a decision. I didn't even have time to revisit my favorite watering holes for a farewell beer — or a farewell fuck — before I was winging my way to the middle of nowhere. I picked up a rental car at the airport in Lincoln and drove out into a landscape that stretched as flat as a pancake for as far as the eye could see.

I was so dazed by the sameness of my surroundings that I almost drove right through Conyer's Point. I spotted the name on a tractor-repair shop on the far side of town, pulled into the parking lot, and asked for directions to the Agri-Pure farms. The man I spoke to eyed my expensive suit and briefcase suspiciously, then traced the route on my map with an oil-stained finger. I thanked him and drove away, my heart heavy as I approached the new center of my personal universe.

The farm was impressive — a vast fenced acreage of soybeans, wheat, corn, and rye that stretched off to the horizon on both sides of the two-lane blacktop. I turned in at the main gate and parked in front of a two-story farmhouse set in the middle of a perfectly manicured lawn. A young man with blond hair and the word CORN-FED practically stamped on his forehead stepped out onto the front porch and waved.

"Mr. Gunther?" I acknowledged him with a curt nod. "Welcome to Conyer's Point. I'm Jim Sebring. I sort of keep the office going around here. Guess you could say I'm your secretary, executive assistant, and man Friday." When I opened the trunk of the car, he dashed around me, lifted out my two heavy suitcases as if they were feather pillows, and made his way back to the house.

I followed Jim through a front hall decorated with county-fair ribbons, needlework pillows, and framed photographs of smiling young men who all looked like Jim's near relations. He preceded me up the stairs, demonstrating how a man with a really hot ass can make even a cheap pair of khakis look good. He stopped on the landing and looked back over his shoulder, catching me in the act of cruising his perky bubble butt. His cheeks flushed scarlet, and he smiled engagingly. I was going to have to watch myself around this guy.

He set my suitcases down on a trunk at the foot of a four-poster bed and would have unpacked them if I hadn't literally taken him by the arm and pushed him back out into the hallway. The arm I grabbed was thick and solid — and not, I suspected, from being pumped up at a gym.

I shut the door and took off my suit, wondering vaguely what I was going to do for a gym way out here. I had worked too long and hard on my physique to give it all up, but I suspected no one around Conyer's Point would notice whether I had washboard abs or a potbelly. I rubbed my stomach reflexively, then began to unpack.

I awoke with a start and sat up in bed, my heart pounding violently. Someone was being murdered. There had been a horrible, anguished scream. Then I heard it again, just outside my room. I crept to the window and peeked outside, fearful of what I might see. Everything was pitch-dark, except for a narrow band of crimson to the east. I could see or hear nothing. Then, just as I was pulling my head back in, the scream pierced my ears again, and I cracked my skull on the raised sash of the window. I cursed and yelped with pain.

At that same instant a rooster — a big one judging by the wind his flapping wings whipped up — flew off the back-porch roof just below me. I rubbed the knot on my head and swore to make that damned bird a real homicide victim if I ever got the chance.

I burrowed back into bed, determined to sleep till a more reasonable hour, but the Fates were against me. I'd had no idea how early farm animals got up in the morning or how noisy they could be about it. Within minutes there was such a cacophony of clucking, squawking, oinking, and mooing that I gave up and crawled out of bed, resigned to watching the sun rise.

I went downstairs and made coffee, then stepped out onto a screened porch that was almost buried in a riot of morning glory. As I sipped the hot caffeine and looked across the yard to the barns, something caught my eye. I moved closer to the screen and made out the silhouette of a man leaning back against the side of the barn. At first I couldn't see much, but as the sky behind him brightened, I began to see plenty.

The sun's early rays glinted off a powerful shoulder and a massively sculpted chest. I followed the light down over a curve of biceps to a thick forearm spiked with hairs that gleamed like copper wires, then to a big hand. The hand was gripping what at first appeared to be a small log, but which on closer inspection turned out to be a big cock — long, thick, and hooded. The biceps bulged, the forearm twitched, and the hand moved down, peeling back dick skin to bare a fat knob that caught the first rays of the light like a beacon.

I've never had much time for early morning hard-ons myself. I usually get relief before I go to bed — either with company or alone — and consider morning stiffers merely the result of a full bladder. This dude, however, was treating his like a gift, his whole big body responding favorably as he jerked himself off in the warm July dawn.

As the sun rose higher in the sky, I was able to make out more and more details. Details such as the veins that bulged in his cock shaft and the lube that drizzled out of him, making little slime trails across his knuckles as he pumped himself from come hole to balls and back again. The light was bathing his nuts now — two fat, furry globes nestled snugly between thick, hairy thighs. They slowly drew up into a tight knot and hugged the base of his prick as the man got closer to tripping his trigger.

I felt a little ache of pleasure in my groin as my own prick rubbed against my gut. Something about the country air and the sight of the guy outside the barn had obviously gotten me going. I set down my cup and took the matter up with both hands, encircling my cock and catching the rhythm of the solitary flogger I was spying on.

Man, it felt good — so good that I began tingling all over and the hairs on my chest rose up in little spikes as my juices got to flowing. The mystery man had a big lead, but I worked to catch up, quickly bringing myself up to the same level of genital tension that he had taken ten minutes to reach. Then I paced myself, teasing my juice tube and thumping my nuts with thumb and forefinger, primed to shoot the moment he started to blow.

The guy pushed away from the barn wall and thrust his hips forward, his knuckles a blur as he kicked into overdrive. His muscles flexed, his thick prong arched like a bow, his knob bulged, and he threw back his head in a soundless howl as a long white streamer shot out from prick. It rose high in the air, glittering in the sunshine, then splattered across the broad expanse of his chest.

I felt it like a fist in the gut, grunting as my own ball juice gushed up over my belly. The guy by the barn was still pumping, blowing a respectable second shot, then letting fly with a spectacular eruption that cleared his head and hit the wall of the barn. The big guy continued to ooze as he sank down onto his haunches, his big chest heaving with his exertions.

"G'morning, Mr. Gunther." I jumped at the sound of Jim Sebring's cheerful voice. "Beautiful day, isn't it?" I stuffed my sticky, swollen prick into my underwear and grunted, hoping Jim would go away so I could get upstairs and put on some clothes without displaying the twitching lump of my recently discharged hard-on to his innocent country eyes.

"You ready to settle into the routine around here?" he said. I glanced over my shoulder, and my eyes widened in surprise. Jim was wearing bib overalls and heavy work boots; he had a straw hat pushed back on his blond hair and a red bandanna around his tanned neck. His fat pink nipples peeked over the top of the overalls' bib, perched on the rise of a delectable set of pecs. His sinewy arms hung at his sides, muscles swollen even in repose. He looked as if he'd just stepped out of a photo spread in an upscale men's magazine.

"Going to a costume party?" I quipped.

"Oh, no, Mr. Gunther. We all work in the fields for half a day around here — 6:30 till 10."

"Is that a.m.?"

"Pardon?" He looked at me curiously, then blushed. "You're just kidding me, aren't you?" He flashed me a smile so sweet, it was all I could do not to jump him on the spot. I took the overalls he handed me and put them on, feeling more than a little foolish. "Not bad, Mr. Gunther," Jim enthused, his eyes raking my furry chest. "You're pretty solid for a desk jockey."

"Thanks, Jim," I replied. "And why don't you call me Paul? I'm not much for formalities." He nodded and smiled again. The guy was dangerous. "So now what?"

"I'll take you out to meet some of the guys…Paul." He held open the screen door, and we stepped out into the hot Nebraska sunshine.

I'd read up on my employees during the lengthy flight to Lincoln. All of them were professionals with degrees in subjects ranging from agriculture to chemistry. As Jim introduced me around, I couldn't help feeling like a total fraud. These men all looked comfortable in their surroundings, while I felt like a damned fool in my hayseed getup. However, they all seemed to accept me at face value, and soon I was being given a crash course in the daily workings of a farm.

The only friction I felt came from Tom Braden, who turned out to be the hunk I'd been watching jerk himself off at sunrise. He seemed to take an instant dislike to me, and I soon figured out why. Young Jim had latched on to me with a vengeance, and it was abundantly clear that Tom resented it. Every time he looked at Jim, he practically pawed at the turf like a rutting bull — not that I could blame him. For his part, Jim acted like Tom wasn't even there — not easy given the man's size and physical presence — and fawned over me till my cock was in danger of exploding from the pressure.

Every time Jim ignored him, Tom's bad mood seemed to intensify. I was very aware of this because much of his hostility was directed at me. Whenever I looked his way, Tom glowered and flexed menacingly. I enjoyed the flexing part, but the man's attitude made me a bit nervous. And Jim's actions did nothing but add fuel to the fire. At one point he damn near had me in a headlock as he showed me how to change the spark plugs on a tractor. The smooth skin of his chest was like silk against my arm and shoulder. By the time the plugs had been changed, I was so worked up that the left leg of my overalls was getting soggy. I made a mental note to steer clear of both of them till they'd worked out whatever it was that needed to be worked out between them.

That resolve crumbled at about 6 the next morning. When the rooster woke me up, the first thing I saw was Jim slipping into my bedroom with a cup of hot coffee in his hand. It didn't take a degree in agribusiness to figure out what was on his mind. He was gloriously naked, his thick, hard cock pointing jauntily at the ceiling. I sat up groggily and attempted to cover myself, but the sheet had wrapped around my calves with a vengeance. I tried to cover my own stiffer with my hands, but I didn't have enough hands to manage the job successfully.

"Morning, Paul," Jim chirped, walking over to my bed as if he had a divine right to be in my room — and naked yet. "I brought you a cup of coffee."

"Yeah. Thanks, Jim. Maybe you'd better—" I never got around to telling him what he'd better do because he set the cup on the nightstand beside the bed and climbed in on top of me. He straddled my hips, planted his hands firmly on my pecs, and began rubbing his hot dick against the fur on my belly. I thought briefly about tossing him onto the floor, but it's tough to generate a lot of willpower at that hour of the morning, so I ended up splaying my hands out on his hard ass instead.

"You are so fuckin' sexy," he purred, batting his cornflower-blue eyes at me as he began pinching my tits. "I just want you to shove your big hard dick up my ass and fuck me bowlegged." The guy knew what he wanted, and since his desires coincided so perfectly with my own needs, I threw caution to the winds. I flipped him around on top of me and plugged my tongue deep into his tight, musky man hole.

Jim bucked and squirmed, pushing his ass crack back tight against my mouth. I felt his breath hot against my cock, then his lips encircled the shaft, and I drove deep into his tight throat. He sucked noisily and enthusiastically, quickly slicking my prick and drizzling hot spit on my tingling balls while I rubbed my hands along his tightly muscled back and pistoned my tongue in and out of his silky chute.

"Put it in me!" Jim panted, rolling off me and sprawling on the bed beside me. He tucked my pillows under his hips and spread his legs wide. I knelt behind him, pumped a thick glob of lube on his hole, and smeared it around with my knob. "Put it in me all at once," he directed, looking over his shoulder, his eyes fixed on my flexing hard-on. I took aim and fell on top of him, spiking him up to the balls in one quick thrust.

Jim squealed and bucked but didn't complain about the volume of cock punched up into him. He reached back and began rubbing my flanks as I began to hump, blissed-out by the heat of his clutching ass channel as it caressed my aching dick. I lifted my hips till the flange on my crown caught on his ass ring, then dropped down hard. My balls slapping against his hot little butt felt so good, I repeated the process several times in quick succession. Jim groaned softly and began balling up the sheets in his fists.

I was getting deep into the fuck when the door to my bedroom banged open and a big hand clamped down on my neck like a vise. "What the fuck are you doing, shagging my guy?" a familiar voice thundered. I would have answered, but the hand pulled me back, arching my back like a bow and cutting off my air supply. His action.also jammed my dick deep into Jim, but the pain in my neck effectively canceled out that pleasure. This was bad.

"Go away, Tom," Jim gasped, looking over his shoulder, his face flushed, beads of sweat popping out on his forehead. "I don't belong to you."

"That's not what you said last week."

"That was then. Go away."

"And leave you here with this city dude's cock packed up your ass? No way." Tom pulled me back farther, and my vision began to fade as I clawed ineffectually at the air.

"If you hurt Paul, you'll never stick your cock in me again, front or back," Jim said. "How'd you like that, Tom Braden?" I, for one, sincerely hoped he wouldn't like that at all, but if he didn't decide soon, the issue would be moot. Everything was fading to black — fast.

"Aw, Jim."

"I mean it, Tom." Tom released his hold on me, and I fell on top of Jim like a ton of bricks, gasping for air. Jim twitched his tight little asshole, doing his best to make sure that my hard-on didn't give up the ghost on him.

"If you're so all-fired horny," Jim went on, "why don't you plug Paul's butt. He's got a great ass — all hard and fuzzy. I bet he wouldn't mind." Before I got a chance to express my opinion one way or the other, Tom's overalls hit the floor and he was clambering up on top of me. I felt something big and hot and hard rubbing my left ass cheek, then I got stuffed. Tom gripped my shoulders, and the race was on.

I hadn't been sandwiched between two hot ones in a long time, and I was loving every minute of it. Tom was riding fast and furiously, grunting and bucking as he tore into my ass. I had a feeling he was taking out his hostility on me by fucking me rough, but it suited me just fine. Poor Jim was trapped on the bottom, and Tom's thrusts were causing a chain reaction that threatened to pound the guy through the mattress. He was wadding the sheets in earnest now, and the veins on his arms were bulging like ropes, but his hole was still grabbing lustily at my hard-on, so I figured he'd live.

We were just pulling into the home stretch when the phone beside the bed rang. I was ready to ignore it, but Jim raised his head and made the effort to speak. "New York, I bet" he groaned. "Nobody else calls at this time of day. Might be important."

"Swell," I groused. Tom braced one leg on the floor and managed to pull the receiver off the cradle without dislodging his rigid prong from my backside. "Hello," I barked. "Gunther here."

"Hey, buddy. Rise and shine."

"Matt!" Jim bucked, and Tom poked, shooting a bolt of pleasure through my frame that damn near blew the top of my head off. "Unh! Uh...how are you, buddy?"

"Doing fine. You sound wide awake."

"Been up for hours." Jim's asshole shuddered, reminding me of just how "up" I really was. Tom started banging my prostate like a pile driver, and Jim was pounding his fists against the mattress. We were rapidly approaching critical mass.

"I had a question about the Forbes account, but J.L. just stuck his head in the door and gave me a summons," Matt was saying. "I'll catch you later. I won't call so early next time."

"No problem," I gasped as my prick began to vibrate like a juicy tuning fork. "I have a feeling I'll be up about this time every morning." I hung up just as a major eruption of jism was unleashed. I felt heat gushing up my ass and over my knuckles as my own load flooded Jim's hot butt. As we all ground to a slow, sweaty stop, it occurred to me that this country living might not be so bad after all.

Putting Out Fires
by Bob Vickery

Fire makes my dick hard. Something about flames roaring and shooting up into the sky, timbers crackling, buildings caving in under an explosion of sparks and smoke — I can't begin to tell you how much a scene like that makes me want to squirt a load. If there had been just one little extra twist in my psyche, I could have been a raging pyromaniac, torching buildings and jerking off in some dark alley across the street as I watched the flames. Instead, I'm a decent, law-abiding guy who would never jeopardize anybody's life or property. It's just not in me. So my fascination has found another outlet: I'm a fireman.

I'm awakened from my sleep by the loud clanging of the alarms, and I'm out of bed. This is a three-alarmer, a biggie, and I'm raring to go. I'm still a Johnnie, a new guy. I've been on the force for a little less than a year, and I'm about to lose my three-alarm cherry tonight. I sit in the tiller seat, tugging on the rear steering wheel as the engine speeds down the city streets with sirens wailing, and all I can think is, *This sure as hell beats Disneyland.*

Even a mile away I can see a glow in the night sky ahead of us, and a little later a huge mushroom cloud, as

if someone had just nuked the neighborhood. A few minutes later we come to a screeching halt and leap out of the
fire engine. I take in the scene while running flat out. The
upper stories of an apartment building are in flames, and
thick black smoke is billowing out from the roof. All the
top-floor windows are ablaze with red light; it's as if the
tenants were all up and throwing a party. The flames roar
so loud, the sound just rolls over me like waves, and I can
feel the heat pounding down on me like a concussion. Hot
damn, is this a kick in the ass or what! I'm so horny, I
could hump the first thing on two legs that comes my way.

We look for an empty hydrant to connect to — not an
easy task since there are already two other engines ahead
of us, each hooked up, with their firemen holding on to
their hoses and spraying the building with water. The
searchlight units are in full operation, and the whole scene
looks like a Hollywood set. My partner, Tom, and I put on
our breathing apparatuses, grab our equipment, and run
into the building.

We race up the stairs, shoving past a stream of bewil-
dered tenants clutching blankets and screaming like the
damned as they flee toward the lobby. On the sixth floor
the smoke pours down the corridor. According to our pre-
arranged plan, Tom goes one way and I go the other,
breaking down doors with our fire axes and making sure
all the apartment units have been evacuated. I swing my
ax against the doors like Thor the friggin' thunder god;
each time I hear the wood splinter, my dick gets just a little harder.

I do this for three separate units with nothing to show
for it — they've all been vacated. That leaves one more
unit at the end of the corridor. Smoke is pouring down
from cracks in the ceiling tiles, so I guess the fire must be
directly overhead now. If I were playing this by the book,
I'd get my ass out of there pronto; in a couple of minutes
the whole damned ceiling is going to come down. But I go
ahead and smash the door down in three swings and dive
into the apartment.

It's like diving into black ink. I'm going by feel alone here. Carpet under my feet, a sofa — I must be in the living room. Linoleum — this must be the kitchen. I find another door, push into the next room, stumble, and fall.

It takes a few seconds before I realize I've tripped over a body. It's sprawled on the floor, bedsheets still tangled around the legs. At the same moment I hear a muffled crash as the ceiling collapses in the outside corridor. There's no going back now.

The adrenaline is racing through me. I heave the body over my shoulders, stumble across the room until I find the windows, and smash them open with my ax. With the rush of air, the fire flares up, illuminating everything. I get a glimpse of a dangling arm and the naked torso of the body slung around my neck, but I can't see the face. There's a fire escape outside, and I clamber onto it. I lumber down as best I can, the flames giving me one final goose before I'm below the range of fire. It's only when I'm in the courtyard itself that I feel safe. I ease the body down, rip my mask off, and by the light of the overhead flames check out just who the hell I've been carrying.

It's a man, buck naked, either unconscious or dead, I can't tell. He lies sprawled on his back, motionless, and I quickly realize that he's not breathing. I check his carotid artery for a pulse and finally find one, though it's weak and fluttering. I drop to my knees, lift his chin up, cover his mouth with mine, and blow hard. His chest rises and falls once. I keep on breathing into his mouth, timing myself, twelve breaths per minute. I take half a second to look around. I'm in some inner courtyard, completely alone with this guy. Everyone else must be in front, fighting the fire. *Where the fuck are the paramedics?* I wonder. I can still hear the flames crackling loudly up above, and sparks swirl all around me. I put my ear to his mouth to see if the guy's breathing on his own. He's not. I continue the resuscitation.

It takes about ten minutes before he finally starts breathing raggedly. He coughs, and it's the most beautiful

sound I've ever heard. I feel a thrill of excitement. *I did it!*
I think. *I brought the motherfucker back to life!* I feel like
God. The man lies there gasping and wheezing, and for
the first time, I take the opportunity to really look at him.
I'm startled to see how young he is, barely out of his teens.
His body is smooth and firm, and as I stare at him in the
ruddy light of the fire, all I can think of is how beautiful
he looks.

His breathing is still shallow and erratic. I plant my
mouth over his again and continue to breathe life into
him. My left hand lies lightly on his chest, above his nipple. Without thinking, I take the nipple between my
thumb and forefinger and squeeze, while my tongue slips
into his mouth. His body stirs, and he bends his left leg up.
My hand crosses his chest and tenderly pinches the other
nipple. He groans. I look down the length of his body and
see that his cock is rock-hard. "Hallelujah!" I laugh. "He
has risen!" I bend over and French-kiss him for all I'm
worth as my hand slips down and encircles his fat, soot-
stained cock.

His tongue pushes into my mouth now. "Oh, yeah,
Susan," he murmurs. I pull back. His eyes flutter open,
and he stares with dilated pupils into the night sky.
"Susan?" he murmurs again, his voice stronger. I quickly
let go of his cock. He turns his head toward me. His eyes
focus with difficulty, and I can see the jolt of shock pass
over his face as he takes me in. "Wha—?" he exclaims,
trying to get up.

"Easy," I say, gently pushing him back onto the pavement. "Lie still. I just pulled you out of the fire." With any
luck he'll think that everything that just happened was a
near-death hallucination. I look up and see Tom in the
courtyard entrance, staring at us. God only knows how
long he's been there or how much he's seen.

"Where are the paramedics?" I holler. "This guy needs
medical attention — now!"

Tom turns his head to the darkness behind him. "Over
here!" he shouts. I hear a trample of feet, and a team of

paramedics bursts into the courtyard. It takes them less than a second to appraise the situation, and it's only a matter of moments before they're carting the man off on a stretcher, an oxygen mask over his mouth.

"Good work, Nick!" one of them calls over to me as they exit the courtyard. "It looks like he's going to make it!"

I follow them out to the ambulance. There's a camera crew from a local news station filming us as we approach. As I pass Tom, I nod and grin. He looks back at me but says nothing. His eyes are quizzical. *Just how much did he see?* I wonder.

The first thing I do back at the station house is strip and jump in the shower. Mike and Lenny, two other guys on my team, are already in there, soaped up and scrubbing the soot off. Mike's good-natured Irish face breaks into a grin as I walk in.

"Hey, it's the local hero!" he cries out. "The kid's first three-alarm fire, and he hogs all the glory!"

Lenny slaps a soapy hand against my back and laughs. "You're quite the star, Nick, saving that guy's life. How do you feel?"

I give an aw-shucks smile and grunt politely. But the adrenaline is still pumping fast within me. I keep remembering the heat of the flames, the explosion of sparks, my game of dueling tongues with that hot naked guy in the courtyard. *I'm feeling hornier than a motherfucker, Lenny,* I think. I look at Mike's tight, smooth body and his beefy Irish cock crowned by a flaming red pubic bush, and it's all I can do to keep from dropping to my knees and swallowing it down to the last inch. Lenny turns his back to me as he soaps down his chest. I sneak a glimpse of his perfect nut-brown ass and wonder what it would feel like to plow it home. I feel my dick beginning to stiffen, and I have to close my eyes and think of baseball statistics to keep it soft.

Tom walks in, and my dick springs back to life immediately. I have to turn my back on all of them and mentally recite "The Wreck of the Hesperus" to get my meat to behave itself again. I've always had a hard-on for Tom. He's so straight-arrow: His dark blond hair is always cut short and per the regulations, his mustache is clipped neatly, and his uniform is always starched and pressed. He is so damned earnest. And yet he's the sweetest guy in the world — true-blue and serious, rock-solid and utterly dependable. Maybe he makes my gonads churn so much because he's so completely the opposite of me. And, of course, because he's fucking gorgeous, with a solid, muscular body; a face off a recruiting poster; and a fat, meaty dick that's now swinging between his thighs like one of the bells of Notre Dame.

Lenny turns off his shower and walks out. Mike does the same. Now it's just me and Tom alone in the fire station's shower room at 3 o'clock in the morning. All of a sudden the atmosphere has gotten very heavy in here. I sneak a glance at Tom and catch him looking at me. He quickly looks away.

I clear my throat. "Some fire, huh?" I say cheerfully.

Tom shrugs and mumbles something. There's another awkward moment. I'm not exactly enjoying the situation, but all this drama is kind of funny; it's like a scene from a bad movie. Played naked. At least Tom's embarrassment gives me the chance to sneak a few lingering looks at his thick, uncut tool. My gaze quickly shifts up to his face as he turns and confronts me, a troubled look in his beautiful slate-gray eyes.

"Nick, I got to clear this up," he says, his voice ragged. "Just what the hell were you doing to that guy in the courtyard?"

I give Tom my best poker face. "I believe it's called mouth-to-mouth resuscitation, Tom," I say calmly.

"Yeah, right!" Tom snarls. Now, this surprises me. I have never seen Tom snarl. I didn't even know he could snarl.

"Is something upsetting you, Tom?" I ask in the same calm tone. Even though I like Tom, I can't help baiting him a little.

"Christ, you must take me for a fucking idiot!" Tom explodes. "I saw what you were doing with that guy! You were practically humping him! What a fucking-asshole unprofessional thing to do!" All this from a guy whom before tonight I've never heard say anything worse than "damn" or "shit." Tom's face is beet-red now, and a vein in his forehead is throbbing. He's pacing back and forth under the shower. "I ought to fuckin' turn you in," he says, his lips curling up into a sneer. "Mr. Hero. Mr. Big Shot. What a joke!"

Old Tom's got a major hair up his ass about something, I think to myself. I'm finding all this righteous indignation a little hard to believe, though. I'm not a sadistic guy by nature, but I feel an overwhelming curiosity to push this and see what happens. I stand there looking at Tom with my arms crossed against my chest and let my dick get hard. I give him my nastiest grin. "What's the matter, Tom?" I leer. "You feeling a little jealous you weren't in on the action?"

That does the trick, all right. "You son of a bitch!" Tom growls. He crosses the shower room in three steps, fists cocked, and swings at me. I duck but don't hit back, even though he's left his right flank exposed for a clear shot. This just enrages Tom more. He throws a body tackle on me, arms wrapped around my waist, and we both go down on the tile floor. We roll around, the water hissing on us from the shower nozzles above. I swing over on top of him, and for an instant I look down into Tom's eyes. Instead of the rage I expected, I see fear. And beneath that, something else. Excitement.

Tom pushes me off and wraps his arms around me in a tight bear hug. I'm a strong guy, but I can't break free, and I feel the air being squeezed out of me. Tom's face is no more than an inch away from mine. I quit struggling. "Come on, fight, you bastard!" Tom snarls. I laugh wheezingly. Tom looks startled, and I quickly take the opportunity to raise my head and plant a big, wet kiss full on his lips. His mouth falls open in surprise, and I push my tongue in deep. Tom tries to pull away, but this time I'm the one who holds on tight. I grind my pelvis against Tom's and hump his hard belly. The blood sings in my ears. It's the burning building all over again — the fire and smoke, the rain of sparks, the excitement.

Tom fights hard and then suddenly stops. It takes a second for me to realize that he's kissing back. His tongue shoves deep into my mouth, and his hands are suddenly all over me, sliding along my torso and kneading the flesh. They move down, cup my ass cheeks, and squeeze; I feel his stiff dick thrust urgently against my abdomen.

Tom is just full of surprises tonight, but I'm quick to shift gears. We roll around on the tile floor, our mouths fused together, humping away at each other like a couple of dogs in heat. I reach down and start stroking Tom's thick dick; the way it fills my palm promises some hot times ahead. I lift his arm and bury my face in his pit. I feel Tom's tongue burrow deep into my ear.

Tom straddles my torso and pins my arms down. He looks down at me, panting, the water plastering his hair against his skull. Without taking his eyes off my face, he reaches up behind him and turns the shower off. There's a crazed look in his eyes that probably should make me a little nervous. It doesn't, though. Something in Tom is trying to get out, and I'm willing to push the situation for all it's worth. He grinds his pelvis against mine, and our cocks slap together. I wrap my hand around both of them and stroke them, cock flesh squirming against cock flesh. Tom grins and bends down, and we kiss long and hard, sucking on each other's tongues as we both fuck my fist.

Tom pulls away and sits up straight again. I take the opportunity to really drink him in. My eyes travel down from his handsome face to the smooth, muscular torso dusted lightly with dark blond hair. His nipples are pink and wide; I reach up and brush my thumbs against them before tweaking them hard. Tom groans. I take in his abs, beautifully chiseled into a sharply defined six-pack, an appendix scar highlighting their perfection. Beneath his dark pubic bush, his dick juts out impressively, red and engorged with blood. It's the first time I've seen Tom's dick hard, and I savor the moment. I trace the veins that run up the meaty shaft and see how the knob of his cock head flares out from the uncut foreskin. His ball sac hangs high and tight, the two plump nuts swelling up inside, begging to be licked.

It's a request I can't refuse. "Slide down," I growl, and Tom is only too happy to comply. He squirms up my torso until his knees pin my shoulders, and he drops his balls into my mouth. I give them a good, thorough washing, rolling them around gently with my tongue, sucking on the sac. Tom slaps my face with his meat, rubbing it over my cheeks, my eyes, my nose. I look up, and our eyes meet. Tom grins. "Yeah, Nick," he moans. "Suck on those nuts. Get all the soot off."

A few seconds later I release his balls. My tongue travels down the dark, hairy path to his asshole. Tom shifts his body again and sits squarely on my face. I feel his fleshy ass cheeks pressing down on me, burying my nose and mouth, and my tongue probes the crack until it finds his juicy hole. I shove my tongue up against his sphincter and give his ass a really good working-over. Judging by the way Tom is squirming on my face, I can tell he's having a grand old time.

Tom lifts his leg and swings his body around. He buries his face in my crotch and starts a feeding frenzy — eating my ass, sucking on my balls, and sliding his tongue up and down my dick shaft. There's a pause, and then I feel him take my meat in his mouth and swallow it down to the base with exquisite leisureliness. I give a loud groan that trails off into a deep sigh. *For a beginner,* I think, *Tom is doing a damn good job. He's a natural.* I start pumping my hips, plowing Tom's mouth with long, quick strokes. Tom's dick thrusts above me invitingly, and I raise my head and swallow it. We both work each other's mouths, fucking each other's faces enthusiastically, greedily feeding off each other's dick meat.

I work Tom's cock like the pro that I am. I take it all in, filling my mouth with it, letting my tongue squirm over the swollen shaft. Sucking hard, I slide my lips back up the thick meat, twisting my head from side to side for maximum effect. When my lips reach Tom's cock head, I roll my tongue around it and then work my lips down the shaft again slowly and teasingly, with loud sucking noises. I'm a real pig when it comes to dick; I just can't get enough of the cock of a handsome man. I feel Tom's body squirm appreciatively, and it isn't long before he starts groaning loud enough to bounce echoes off the tile ceiling of the shower room. I just hope the guys in the fire-station dorm are sleeping soundly tonight.

Tom reaches up to the soap dispenser and squirts a couple of dollops into the palm of his hand. He pries apart my ass cheeks, and his finger works my hole, slipping in up to the third joint. Sweet Jesus, does that ever feel good! He finger-fucks me with short, vicious jabs that keep me gasping for more. "I would really like to shove my cock up your ass, Nick," he says earnestly, like he's asking me to go out to the movies with him.

"Hold that thought, Tom," I say, and with a grin I scramble to my feet and run out into the locker room. There's a box of condoms, I know, sitting on the floor of my locker. I fumble impatiently with the combination on my lock; for some reason I'm all thumbs. Banging the door open clumsily, I grab one of the rubbers, and in my haste I almost forget to shut the locker when I'm through. I rush back to the shower and toss the condom to Tom. "I take it you know how to use this," I say breathlessly.

Tom grins. "Oh, yeah. Up to now only to keep the ladies from getting pregnant. But I can adapt to the situation." He rolls the condom down his dick shaft, pushes me onto my back, and hoists my legs over his shoulders. I feel his dick head poke a couple of times against my hole, and then slowly, with excruciating patience, he works his cock inside me. I close my eyes and savor the sensation of being filled. When I open them again, his face is right above me, his lips pulled back into something between a snarl and a grin, his eyes fierce. Tom starts pumping his hips hard, punishing my ass with quick, savage strokes, daring me to take it.

Okay, Tom, I think. *You want to scrap? Let's scrap.* I wrap my legs tightly around his torso and pivot him onto his back. Tom's face registers surprise. I clamp my ass muscles tight and meet him stroke for stroke, riding his cock like a cowboy on a bucking bronco. Tom gasps with the sudden pleasure. We roll around on the shower floor, wrestling and squirming against each other, hips pumping, bodies joined by Tom's thick, hard meat up my ass. Tom wraps a soapy hand around my dick and slides it up and down. I reach down and twist his nipples. We're in a fierce competition to see who can weaken the other the most with pleasure. We both give as good as we get.

Tom's lips are open, and his eyes are getting glassy. Groans trickle out of his mouth, each time getting a little longer and a little louder. I loosen and tighten my sphincter rhythmically as I ride him, quickening my pace and holding on to his muscular torso to steady myself. Tom shows no mercy as he pounds my ass, which is just the way I like it. I reach behind me and fill my hand with his balls. They're pulled up tight now, ready to give up their load of creamy jizz. I give them a good squeeze as I slide down Tom's shaft.

That does the trick. I feel the spasms move through Tom's body with an almost seismic force, and he cries out loudly. I quickly cover his mouth with mine and kiss him fiercely; this is the only thing that keeps him from waking the whole damn crew up and bringing them into the shower room on a run. Tom's load gushes from his piss slit and slams into the condom up my ass; I can feel each squirt distinctly. His hand slides slickly up and down my dick. In only a matter of seconds, I feel my own body shuddering. I close my eyes and think of burning buildings as I squirt my load, spattering Tom's face and torso with hot, thick spunk. I collapse on him, and after a while I kiss him again, licking my come off his face. We lie together on the shower floor for a long time, holding each other. Eventually we sneak back to our bunks in the dorm.

The next morning the whole team gathers around the TV and turns on the news to see the coverage of the previous day's fire. There's a shot of the paramedics wheeling the guy I saved into the ambulance. The newscaster even mentions me by name.

Lenny laughs. "You won't have any problems getting laid after today, Nickie."

"You think so?" I ask, grinning. I glance at Tom and raise my eyebrows. To my amazement he blushes, but he manages to give a small grin back at me. I turn back to the TV and see another shot of the building up in flames. I sigh. I can feel my dick getting hard all over again.

The Angel, the Devil, and Phillip Bond
by Grant Foster

"Good morning, Mr. Bond." Laurie Heckert. Blond hair. Big tits. Bimbo. You could hear her giggling all the way down the hall to her homeroom. Mr. Bond acknowledged her but didn't watch as she minced away, ass swinging back and forth like a fucking pendulum.

"Hey, Mr. Bond." Bond nodded. He made no other moves, but I could tell he was watching as Dave Taggert swaggered on his way to his locker. Dave wasn't so bad — for a jock. He always wore a stupid expression — like maybe he'd just been beaned by a stray football — but he had a nice ass and pretty impressive biceps. Still, I figured Mr. Bond had better taste than that.

Of course he had better taste than that. Mr. Bond — Phillip Bond, to be precise about it — was a dude. Actually, he was more than that. He was a fox. He was a hard-on. A wet dream. He was the man who ran my fantasy life, in any case. At the age of eighteen, maybe I couldn't claim to be an expert, but I knew what I liked, and he was definitely righteous. Totally cool.

The Angel, the Devil, and Phillip Bond

He was a teacher, but I didn't hold that against him. He actually managed to make math interesting, although maybe I just concentrated harder in his class than in other classes. This was his first assignment out of college, but it wasn't like he was some rank beginner. Not Mr. Bond. He was in charge, in control, in touch. He knew his stuff and could talk it so you didn't think he was speaking a foreign language or something.

I wasn't attracted to him because he could do fractions, of course. The draw was a bit more basic than that. He was about six foot two, weighed 180, and had dark brown hair, brown eyes, and a face like a model in one of those high-class magazines. He wore steel-rimmed glasses, but on him they looked way cool. No way anybody'd call him "four eyes."

Now, to tell the truth, I couldn't tell you what he looked like naked because I'd never seen him that way. The bod was hidden under a layer of baggy clothes, but he carried himself like a man who had lots of self-confidence. There was no hiding the wide shoulders or the narrow waist. For those of us who took the time to watch him walk, there was no hiding the tight, rounded butt under the slacks either. Believe me, I watched. Mr. Bond had big square hands with long, thick fingers. There were short bristly hairs growing across the sinewy backs and on the knuckles. Like total outrage.

"Hey, Eric."

I looked up. It was my friend Tony. How a guy named Antonio Boniface Ventura could end up looking like Tony was beyond me. He was a genuine Italian — his old man ran a pizza joint, for Christ's sake — but he looked like some blond rosy-cheeked cherub. Well, he actually looked like some cherub who'd had a bicycle pump stuck up his butt and been pumped full of air. Only it wasn't air, it was all muscle. Big bulging muscle in all the right places, with perfect, hairless skin stretched over it. Tony could've been a wet dream too, only I don't go for guys my own age. I like them older — older like Mr. Phillip Bond.

"Hey, Tony," I said. "How's it going?"

"Not so good. I didn't get my math assignment done."

"Jesus, Tony. How do you expect to graduate, man?" I grabbed him by the neck and squeezed playfully.

He batted his baby blues at me sheepishly. "I'm sorry, Eric. I got busy."

"Yeah, I know. Busy down in the basement with those weights. You oughta give it a rest. You're gonna bust right out of your skin."

"Got my arms pumped to twenty inches last night," Tony bragged, making a muscle.

I squeezed the knot, just like I always did. Hell, you gotta keep a guy's spirits up. "Fucking marshmallow, Tony," I teased. His face fell. "Jesus, man, I was only kidding. You're a stone wall." His beautiful smile returned. "I'll help you with the math at lunch."

"You're a pal, Eric." Tony draped an arm over my shoulder, and we headed off to homeroom.

"Good morning, gentlemen. You'd better put some power behind it, or you'll be late." Mr. Bond's face was stern, but I could've sworn I saw a twinkle in his eye. Everybody who looked at Tony got a twinkle, so it wasn't such a big surprise.

"Thanks, Mr. Bond," I said, feeling my heart beat just a little faster. When we walked past I got a little whiff of him. It wasn't cologne or anything. Just him. You know. I copped a glance when we slipped into homeroom just under the bell. Mr. Bond was still standing there, looking our way. Probably staring at Tony's ass. Figured.

The alarm went off at 6:30. I rolled over in bed, slapped the clock silly, and stuck my head back under the pillow. Then I remembered and jumped out of bed as if I'd been goosed. It was Saturday, and I had a date. Well, actually it wasn't a date, and Tony was going along with me, but I was as excited as hell. I had overheard Mr. Bond telling one of the other teachers that he was going to be building a fence today, so I had volunteered Tony and myself to

The Angel, the Devil, and Phillip Bond

help. Mr. Bond had seemed a little startled at first, but when he figured I was serious, he had agreed to the scheme. Tony didn't know a hammer from a nail, but I'd taken shop class. Besides, I had other plans for Tony.

I had it all figured out. I was pretty sure Mr. Bond was into guys. It was just this gut feeling, but I was willing to go with it and see what happened. I was hoping he'd get all revved up and maybe jump Tony's bones and I could sort of watch. When you laid it out like that, it sounded kind of like a sicko thing to do, but — hey — I was desperate. I really had this thing about seeing Mr. Bond naked and watching him have sex. I hadn't quite figured out how I was going to make it all happen, but I wasn't about to turn back now.

I went to the can and took a piss, then went back to my bedroom to get ready for the day. I stopped in front of the big mirror on my closet and checked myself out.

I sure as hell didn't look like anybody's idea of an angel. When I was a kid, I was really homely — big nose, floppy ears, huge eyes, and a jutting chin. Now that I was grown, I was no beauty, but at least I'd grown into my features, although my ears still stuck out a little bit. I kept my black hair cropped really short, and when I didn't shave — like this morning — I had a dark shadow that made me look a little sinister. My thick black eyebrows, arched up to little points near the center, added to the impression. Some people said it made me look intense; others told me I looked like the devil himself. At least people didn't mistake me for somebody else when they saw me in the halls at school.

I struck a pose and checked my physique. As a kid I'd been called wiry. To me that translated as skinny, and I'd hated it. Since becoming a freshman, I'd been working out a lot — hanging around Tony helped with that — and although I wasn't bulky, at least I wasn't skinny anymore. My torso was still lean, but I had managed to pump up my pecs full and tight, and my arms were filling out to the point that when I flexed, people noticed. Since I'd never had any fat on my body, the washboard gut had been easy for me, much to Tony's disgust. The legs had been a tougher challenge, but I had finally put a little bulk on my thighs and knots of muscle in my calves. No more bird legs, thank you very much.

"Hey there, pervert!"

"Jesus!" I yelped, jumping about a foot off the floor. "Give me a fucking heart attack, why don't you?" Tony had climbed up the trellis at the end of the porch and was peering through the window of my bedroom. "I was just getting dressed."

"Liar," Tony said, shaking his head and climbing over the sill. "Christ, Eric, I don't know how you keep from passing out."

I looked down. My dick was levitating, jutting out parallel to the floor. Must've been all that flexing and posing I'd just been doing.

"Can't help it," I said, making no effort to hide my boner from Tony. He'd seen it before.

"Gonna let me touch it?"

"You gotta ask?" Tony loved to play with my dick. How can a guy say no to a buddy?

"Too much," Tony muttered, wriggling out of his tight shorts and the skimpy tank top that wasn't doing much to hide his eye-popping muscles. "Door locked?"

"They never get up before 9 on Saturday," I assured him, clapping my hands on his thick shoulders as he knelt in front of me. "It's all yours, buddy." I fisted my meat and smacked it against the solid wall of his chest.

"So fucking big," Tony muttered, his baby blues clouding over with lust. He grabbed my erect member and pressed it into the deep valley between his massive pecs, stroking it with both hands. My cock is pretty impressive, if I do say so myself. It's the one part of my anatomy where I didn't have to fight for bulk. Eleven inches long and as thick as my wrist, my dick sometimes scares even me. Tony didn't look too scared right now, however; he was stroking the broad back, following the big veins from my bush out to my come hole. When he peeled the skin back and rubbed my knob against the hard points of his pink tits, I groaned happily.

"Want me to suck it?" Tony asked, looking up as he licked his full, pouty lips.

"Uh…I don't think so, dude," I replied, shaking my head. "Last time it took me two weeks to heal up. You got too many teeth."

"It's like trying to jam a log into your mouth," Tony said defensively.

"I could stick it somewhere else," I chuckled, leering down at him.

"Not in this lifetime," Tony said, squeezing my cock hard. "You'd split me wide open, man. Nobody could sit on that post and live to tell about it."

"Wanna do the usual then?"

Tony nodded and leaned back, bracing his hands on the floor behind him. I straddled him, bent my knees, and began humping his glorious torso.

"Your balls, man. Your balls."

I hunkered down a little more, and my fat balls dragged along the silky wall of his belly. Tony groaned in ecstasy. My cock pumped back and forth, sandwiched between his bulging pecs, and I groaned in ecstasy myself.

"Eric, what the hell is this? Eric!"

I was about five minutes into it, my mind floating off on a big cloud of testosterone. I opened my eyes and grinned down at Tony. He'd been rubbing my legs and belly, ruffling the hairs up against the grain, making them stand on end. His fingers were currently tangled in the silky moss on my chest. He thumped my left tit, and I blushed.

"Oh, that," I said. "I did it last week." I'd had my nipple pierced on a whim — two tiny gold studs screwed on to a little pin that went right through the fleshy point of my tit. Tony twisted it a little, and my cock rose up high, the knob bulging.

"Cool, man. Like you really needed to do something to draw attention to your tits."

My nipples were bigger than quarters and dark brown,

the points jutting out a good half inch from the rise of my pecs. They were sensitive as hell, and the little stud made it worse. Tony tweaked my tit again, and I damn near came on the spot.

"Come on, man," I said. "We gotta get a move on."

I hunkered back down and thrust my hips forward, banging my rod against Tony's chin. He leaned up into me and wrapped one arm around my waist, the other slipping down to his groin. He jerked his dick a few times, and I felt a hot shot on the back of my calf. His whole body twitched under me, sending all the right sensations through my horny frame.

"Tell me," he begged, both hands on my thighs, eyes glued to the end of my dick. "Tell me in time."

"Now!" I grunted, my balls drawing up tight between my legs. Tony loved to eat my spunk, and he got pissed if he missed any, so I tried to warn him a couple of strokes before the payoff. He clenched my cock in a grip of iron, the hot pucker of his mouth pressed against the spout. Tony started trembling and moaning, making more noise than I was. I slid along the slippery trail one last time, then clapped my hands behind Tony's head and let her rip. I felt the jism boiling up along the fat tube running along the underside of my dick, the tingling in my stalk becoming unbearable, and I popped a thick gusher into my buddy's waiting mouth.

Tony gulped greedily, his throat muscles working as he chowed down on the hot, sticky contents of my big balls. When the pumping stopped he started milking the stalk, smacking his lips, digging around with his tongue in the slit to scoop out the last traces of my load. "I'm dry already," I gasped, pushing his head back and trying to disengage my tool from his big fists. "You're gonna pull it out by the roots one of these days."

"Seems well-anchored to me," Tony chuckled, standing up and stretching mightily. "I love those protein supplements!" He licked his lips and flopped down on my bed.

"Hey, get a move on," I said, wiping the back of my leg

The Angel, the Devil, and Phillip Bond

with a crusty towel from under the bed. "We've got a fence to build."

"Man, I just can't deal with this!" I whined. We were standing on Mr. Bond's front porch, having just rung the bell, and were waiting for him to answer.

"Looks terrific," Tony assured me, a wicked twinkle in his eyes. Well, it had seemed like a good idea at the time, but then I'd just shot about a quart of jizz down my good buddy's throat. He'd rummaged around in my chest of drawers and pulled out this pair of gray workout shorts that laced up the front like a football uniform. Only there wasn't any room for padding. Hell, there wasn't even enough room for me. I tugged at the pouch in the crotch, but it didn't help. I tried pulling down on the black tank top Tony had talked me into, but it missed meeting up with the waistband of the shorts by a good three inches.

"I look like I've been shoplifting at a fruit stand."

Tony had said to wear no jock, and I could clearly see the outline of my cock and balls straining against the flimsy fabric.

"This is—" I shut up when the door swung open.

"Come on in, guys," Mr. Bond said, motioning us inside. He glanced at me briefly, then turned to Tony — naturally. Tony started babbling about something, and I followed them through the house and out to the backyard.

Mr. Bond was wearing shorts — there is a God — and a baggy old T-shirt. His butt, high and round and tight, flexed against the worn fabric as he walked. He also had these totally gorgeous runner's legs — long, with dense, pale brown fuzz. I felt my temperature start to rise.

Mr. Bond offered us orange juice and rolls, then we got down to work. He had everything all figured out, so it was just a matter of hauling lumber and nailing up boards. By lunchtime we were half done, and by 6 that evening we had finished building and cleaned up the mess.

Mr. Bond was so pleased with our work that he fired up the barbecue grill and insisted that we stay for dinner.

Things were not going so well as far as my little scheme

was concerned. For one thing, I wasn't sure how to bring it off — I couldn't just lock the two of them in the basement or the garage and watch through the window till something happened. Tony wasn't being much help either. Oh, he was looking hot, his muscles twitching and bulging as he hauled posts and fence boards around, but Mr. Bond wasn't exactly picking up on him. Not so as I could tell, anyway. Every time I'd go to pick up a load of boards, they'd be talking when I came back around the corner, but I never got the feeling they were plotting to sneak off and screw each other.

I, on the other hand, was about ready to hump a gopher hole. After lunch Mr. Bond took off his shirt, and I about lost it. Funny, he wasn't real built or even all that defined really — he was just perfect. He had a nice chest, smooth and sleek and tanned, and a flat belly — no fat, no deep-cut abdominal ridges, no hair. His forearms were furry like his legs, but there wasn't anything to impede the view of his lean torso. As he worked, sweat trickled down the hollow of his spine, and it was all I could do not to run over and lick it off.

"Oh, hell! I gotta go. My old man'll kill me." Tony had just stuffed the last bite of steak in his mouth when he suddenly jumped up and made his announcement. Tony lives in constant fear of his old man — who is about five foot seven and weighs maybe ninety-five pounds. Go figure.

"What? What is this?" My plans were not only fading, they were running away.

"I...I told my dad I'd help out at the restaurant tonight. I forgot all about it." Tony sucked up his soda, shook hands with Mr. Bond, and ran off into the warm summer evening. My plans had run aground thanks to Tony and his old man's goddamned pizza parlor. Life's a bitch.

"Well," I said reluctantly, "guess I'd better be going."

"No hurry, Eric," Mr. Bond replied. "Besides, I hate to do dishes alone." I took some more salad and listened to Mr. Bond talk about his plans for a deck. When I was finished we cleared the table and carried the dishes inside. I made it a point to walk a couple of paces behind him, my eyes glued to his butt. His shorts had sort of bunched up into his crack while he was sitting, and the globes of his ass looked like full, ripe melons. Oh, man!

"Shit!" Mr. Bond had flipped on the light above the sink. It flickered and popped. "Damn cheap bulbs," he groused. He rummaged in a closet and found a bulb, then turned to me. "I'll need your help, Eric. This fixture is about to fall apart. I'll hold it here on the sides and you can pop out the glass and replace the bulb."

"Got it," I said. He leaned against the sink and reached up. When his long fingers pressed against the rim of the fixture, I could see that the whole thing moved around in the ceiling. I grabbed the bulb off the counter and quickly noticed that there was only one way to get to the socket. I was going to have to lean up against Mr. Bond and reach over him. I bit my lip and stepped forward.

By the time I was able to unlatch the hinged square of glass in the fixture, the lump in my crotch was firmly wedged between Mr. Bond's succulent cheeks. My body was pressed against his back, and my chin was up against his shoulder. I reached for the light, straining upward.

"Jesus!" I moaned, popping the clip on the fixture.

"Hot?" Mr. Bond asked.

"I'm fine," I muttered.

Either I was going totally nuts, or Mr. Bond's ass cheeks were beginning to flex, squeezing tantalizingly at the knot in my shorts. I began unscrewing the burned-out bulb, and the flexing got more intense. Needless to say, my prick started to respond, lengthening and thickening as the blood pumped down into it. The head of it slipped out of the pouch and began to push down along the inside of my left thigh. I tried to think of something that wasn't sexy, but with sex standing right in front of me, it was impossible. My shaft cleared the leg hole of the shorts and thrust down along my thigh. My hairs tickled the underside of the thick tube, and other hairs tickled the broad back of the shaft.

"Ah!" Mr. Bond made this soft, little sound. I had a feeling all of a sudden that he wasn't groaning about the fact that I'd just screwed in the new lightbulb. I popped the glass back up, taking my time about making sure the clip was properly in place. I didn't want to move — and I was afraid of what might happen when I did. I finally dropped my arms to my sides, knowing that no amount of time was going to relieve the pressure on my cock.

Mr. Bond lowered his arms as well, but he made no other move. Neither did I. My cock remained trapped between our two thighs, getting harder and harder by the second. I felt the muscles in his leg flex, pressing hard against my dick. My mouth was dry, and I thought my heart was going to explode. I happened to glance up and see Mr. Bond's reflection in the darkened window above the sink. His eyes were shut, and he was biting his lower lip. There was a small muscle pulsing in his jaw, and a vein stood out on his temple, fluttering rapidly. Hell, he was as bad off as I was!

And he was waiting for me to make the first move. Of course. I was the student, and he was the teacher. Even though I was legal, he was afraid to put the moves on me for fear of getting in trouble. He hadn't pushed me away, and he hadn't spun around and popped me one. Could the guy actually want me? Me instead of Tony? Incredible. In*fucking*credible!

I don't know how, but I finally got up the nerve to slip my arms around him. Man, he felt good! He was warm, his skin smooth and soft against my palms. I rubbed one hand up his chest, the other down his belly. The one going down bumped into something soft and sticky. I explored, touching the arrow-shaped tip of his stiffer, which was jutting up over the waistband of his shorts. He let out a soft moan, almost like a sob.

"Hey, dude," I murmured, tracing the ridge of his dick down lower, pressing the fabric tight against it, "it's cool. Way cool."

I kissed his neck. His right hand slipped back and

touched my thigh. I moved my leg, and his fingers wrapped tightly around the stalk of my hard-on. As he worked his way down to the hooded knob on the end, his moans got louder. When he slipped a fingertip into my foreskin, my moans got pretty loud too.

I couldn't believe that Mr. Bond — Mr. Cool, man of my fantasies — was touching my dick. If I couldn't believe that, what he did next really put my senses to the test. He wriggled around in my grasp, knelt down, and started kissing the shaft of my dick. His lips were real soft, putting the pressure on all the right places. I damn near collapsed when he hooked his lips over the end of my piece and I felt his tongue for the first time. He burrowed into my skin and zeroed in on my piss hole, a gesture that curled my toes back toward my heels.

All the while, he was tugging at one of the legs of my shorts, pulling it up till my balls spilled out and sagged heavily against my thigh. My cock cranked up, and Mr. Bond came right along with it, keeping the knob firmly gripped with his hot lips. He fisted it and pulled forward, sucking the skin out over the tip till it hung down in loose folds. He looked up at me, licked his lips, winked, then got the skin between his teeth and started shaking his head back and forth, like a puppy does when you try to take its chew toy away.

While I was still taking that in, he all of a sudden took a deep breath and started going down on me. I watched in amazement as his head came closer and he swallowed my whole dick right up to the bush. When his forehead was against my belly and he started licking my balls, I knew the definition of bliss. I knew Mr. Bond had teeth, but they weren't raking my meat. All I felt was heat and pressure and the rhythmic flexing of the muscles in his throat.

When he finally came up for air, he gasped, "You are one *big* boy!" Then he tongued my knob for a while, licking every surface till it gleamed, and swallowed me again. He kept it up, his head bobbing back and forth, his hands exploring my body, setting my nerves on fire.

I was thinking life couldn't get any better, and then Mr. Bond said the magic words: "Fuck me!" His voice was hoarse, authoritative. I nodded, too stunned by the prospect to speak, and Mr. Bond clambered to his feet. He grabbed my dick and led me into the bedroom, stripping out of his shorts on the way. I watched his pale, bare, hairless ass flex as we walked down the long hallway. Once we were in the room, he got naked, and so did I. I stood at the foot of the bed looking at him, my cock waving uncontrollably in the air in front of me, spitting clear goo.

I'd never fucked a guy before — or a girl, for that matter. I wanted to, but I wasn't quite sure how to go about it. I sure as hell wanted to do it right. I guess Mr. Bond knew what was up, because he came over to me and started rubbing up against me like a cat in heat.

"How do you want me?" he asked softly. "On my back or belly?"

"Uh…back," I said, hoping I'd made the right choice. I figured that way I could see his face and play with his cock. It must have been okay with him because he kissed me and fell back onto the bed with me on top of him.

I was humping his belly and getting off on kissing him when he pushed me back. I sat up between his thighs, and he hooked his hands behind his knees and pulled his legs up and apart. I stared down at his ass in fascination. His asshole looked like this pouty little mouth, full pink lips all puckered up tight.

"You want it?" he teased, his asshole fluttering. I didn't say anything, but my dick rose up and slapped me in the gut. Mr. Bond chuckled, and his hole fluttered again. I fisted my prick and leaned forward. The first contact was damn near enough to do me in. I could feel his heat shooting up along the shaft of my dick, lighting a fire in my gut. He took a deep breath and looked at me intently.

"Now!" he growled, baring his teeth. I pushed, the tight little pucker gave way, and I was in the hottest, tightest, smoothest place I'd ever been. Mr. Bond's eyelids fluttered, and little beads of sweat appeared on his forehead, but

The Angel, the Devil, and Phillip Bond

since he didn't tell me to stop, I just kept burrowing till my bush was mashed tight in his crack.

Putting my dick up inside a man's body was the hottest thing I'd ever done. My hips were against his smooth ass, his bare feet were pressed against my chest, and I could feel every move he made, even his breathing. I pressed my hands against his belly, but he grabbed my wrists and pulled me forward. He hooked his legs over my shoulders and started kissing me. My hips snapped into action, and I started to fuck.

Man, it was intense! There was the constant pressure of his body, but there was nothing to stop me from pulling my dick out, then shoving it back in as far as it could go. Mr. Bond was loving it, his stiffer poking my belly, his tongue damn near plugging my throat. He was pulling the hairs on my chest, making my balls tingle as if all that hair had roots that grew down into them. Then he found the stud in my nipple. He tweaked it, and I slammed into him so hard that my balls smacked against his ass.

"Yeah," he growled, his voice a low animal rumble. I slowly withdrew, made him wait a second, then barreled back into him. He made this little gurgling sound and twisted my tit again.

I quickly got the feeling that I'd found the rhythm of the fuck. I battered him again and again, trying to remember to go slow, waiting to spear him till he whimpered for it. That lasted about five minutes, and then I sort of lost control. I rolled him farther back onto his shoulders, braced my hands, and dug in with my toes. Then I started working the fuck my way — frantic, hard, and fast. The pressure built, and the sensations rushing through me got to be just too much to bear.

Then all my attention focused on the end of my dick. The tingling started, getting stronger and more insistent. I finally stopped humping and stayed real still, letting the feeling build, grow, and spread until I totally lost control. I howled out loud and began bouncing, shooting jism right up Mr. Bond's hot and steamy ass.

I wedged my hand between our bellies and latched onto his piece. It flexed strongly against my palm, and then I felt the hot flow pouring over my knuckles. I hadn't even jacked him; I just touched him once, and — *bam!* — he came. That was power. I humped him a few more times, then collapsed on top of him like I'd had a heart attack or something.

"Hot fuck, you sexy devil!" Mr. Bond had whispered those words in my ear. I raised my head and looked at him in amazement.

"I don't fucking believe this," I panted, talking to the mattress more than to him.

"What don't you believe, Eric? That I could think you're the sexiest thing on two legs? That feeling your big cock pumping way up my ass damn near blew my brains out? That I'm still so horny, my balls hurt? What don't you believe?"

"I...I just figured you thought Tony—"

"Tony? Not my type." Mr. Bond shook his head, and his long hairy legs somehow got wrapped around my waist, pinning me. Not that I wanted to move or anything. "Those pumped-up little pretty-boy cherubs are a dime a dozen. Sexy devils, on the other hand, are harder to find." His asshole clenched down tight, and my cock surged. "Real devils with dicks like yours are harder still. Much harder."

"Gee, thanks, Mr. Bond."

"Shut up, Eric," Mr. Bond growled good-naturedly, grabbing the stud in my tit and twisting it hard. "Shut up and fuck the hell out of me."

A F T E R N O O N

Psych
by Lew Dwight

Bad night, bad day. A rabid student first thing in the morning, and what next? Exhausting enough just trying to keep up the pedagogical exterior let alone when the grass is finally turning green after half a year of bitter New England winter and you'd rather be outside shedding your clothes. You must conduct yourself in front of these boys as though you have a grip on things, when actually you lost it long ago; you've still got to come across like you know what you're doing, so wing it. Maintain the authoritative facade, try to focus on the material, and keep your eyes — which have lives of their own — from crawling like a couple of spiders up hairy shins and into inviting leg openings to examine microscopically the black wiry hairs that creep along the tight seams of Jockey shorts.

You can't go home and nap until you've met with the last of your students — conferences, what a strain, when enacting the authority role reaches its most pathetic and awful pitch. Communicating with just one student, face-to-face, eye to eye, is most difficult: No prepared lecture, no script, you have to make it up as you go. You talk convincingly of papers and exams and attendance, meanwhile hallucinating that Joey V., the baseball player with the thighs (who can hardly write a sentence), is dripping sweat into your mouth as he groans toward climax. How lucid these dreams are, the unconscious giving you shocking glimpses vivid as experience. For example, this Joey V. — six-two, 180 pounds, blond hair (even the eyebrows), legs thickly haired from the bare ankles to the exposed thighs —

"What was that?" Putting aside his paper.

"I said I have to miss a few classes next week. We've got games scheduled."

"You'll have to make up the work somehow."

"Can't I do anything for extra credit?" Knees creeping open a few millimeters.

"Stand up and press your groin against my face."

He stands up, looks down at you, places his hands on the top of your head, buffets the musky bump in his sweaty cotton-knit shorts against your nose and mouth — your hands moving up the backs of those hairy thighs and up under his shorts to the curve of his muscular butt —

Back to the sweep of the minute hand on the wall clock: Joey sitting there looking at you blankly as livestock, waiting for a response. He's only the second one to come in this morning — already you're off-balance, the first appointment having been a doozy — and six more to go.

— pulling out of your mouth at the last moment, the erection points up and shoots a load up under your glasses —

"Just get your work in as soon as you can. Anything that comes in late will be docked half a grade. There's also an attendance policy, you know. I have to be fair to everybody."

He gets up, walks toward the door. "Fucking fag. I ought to piss all over that ugly tie of yours, you fag." You look at the clock: two minutes till your next appointment.

"See you Monday, Mr.—"

"Good-bye, Joseph."

Will you make it through the day? The heat in this damn office could make an iguana sweat. You lay aside the (piss-stained) tie, unbutton the top button of your shirt collar — ah. These private colleges with their dress codes. Even on days like this — your day off, which you've reserved for meeting with students individually to go over their paper drafts — you're required to wear "attire appropriate to an academic setting," faculty offices being considered academic settings. But these boys obviously don't care about dress codes. Out your window, on the quad, students lounge in exposed skin — patent leather black, book margin white, every shade in between. They come partially exposed to your office, where the heat doesn't shut off, yet you're supposed to keep your button-down shirt on. Oh, open another button, for Christ's sake. They're not going to be scandalized by the sight of the professor's T-shirt.

There's a whole list of them to go through this morning, one by sweaty one, mostly French last names, some with the last names of presidents, an Italian name here and there. This next kid will be easy — Ethan: smart; hands in work on time; paradoxically a "special" student, one with a disability, to whom you've agreed to grant extra time for exams. Has cognitive impairments — dyslexia, attention deficit, a stammer, etc. — but requires only a little more time and does much better than the rest on exams. That's why you don't let these jocks like Joey off the hook — they have all their faculties and yet can't seem to get their act together, whereas this Ethan, who has stumbling block after stumbling block to deal with, hands in impeccable papers and receives A's on his exams. You'll simply sing the praises of this Ethan, make a few suggestions for his rewrite, send him on his way — if all goes well.

"Hello, Ethan. Have a seat."

There's something both neat and unkempt about this Ethan: hair well-combed above startlingly black eyebrows and yet just a tad too glossy, as if he hadn't washed it the night before — or maybe he gels it, who knows; always a little unshaven, although he barely has a whisker on his chin. And those eyes! The way a cat's eyes get when it's about to pounce on something — as if permanently dilated to take in more than others can. And why the baggy pants, that hip-hop-gone-mainstream look, which reveals nothing about the boy underneath? Belt cinched so tight at the waist that the pants bunch up like sackcloth; therefore, you can formulate nothing about Ethan's tough little body. All you have to go on is his silence in class; he sits at the back of the room absorbing simply everything, taking in what you say and writing it down — slowly, to be sure — in a scratchy, tiny, cramped hand that you can barely read but you know is flawlessly written. He won't speak up in class because of his impediment, a stammer and a lisp, the words seeming to come at him sideways and jamming in his mouth — he feels embarrassed about stalling the class. Even when you tell him privately that he shouldn't be afraid to speak up, he says it's best if he just listens and hopes you won't dock him for lack of participation.

"I kuh-can take thtuff in buh-better than I kuh-can get it out. I'd ruh-rather abth-abth—"

"You'd rather absorb what's being said?"

"Yeah."

During lectures there will come a sort of spark to Ethan's eyes — a half smile edged with irony and mischief — when he picks up on some finer point that the others miss. And yet sometimes that mischievous look comes over him at unexpected moments, and you think, *Now, what did I just say that he finds so amusing?*

"Ethan, you're doing excellent work this semester. I'm really impressed by your writing skills and your grasp of the subject. You're doing much better than almost everyone else in class."

"Thuh-thuh—"

"Oh, don't thank me..." You keep on talking because he's so slow to respond that you feel you have to fill in the empty spaces. He just gives you a broad, easy smile as if to tell you to relax, you don't have to feel embarrassed for him. "And I see by my grade book that you haven't missed any classes either." He sits upright, absorbing what you say about him — his fist reaching into all that denim and fumbling around for that long white pointed dick you know he has and bringing it out through the zipper flaccid but slightly engorged, knees pointing in opposite directions; he pinches the cone of skin enclosing the tapered head and gently pulls, drawing it out like soft elastic, then stretching it like a web, eyes dilating, seeking your approval. "Kuh-come over h-here and and and thuh-thuck—"

He sits there smiling as if catching you in the act of hallucinating him that way, as if his imagination works in accordance with your own — but, nah, he's just pleased at what you've been saying about his class work. He's such a nice, reserved boy; he'd never say anything like that. "I'm-m-m thuh-thinking of ch-ch-changing m-my m-m—"

"Major?"

— or naked in his chair, leveling that black, smoldering gaze at you, he strokes his pale thing as if daring you to take a long look at it; about a yard of white, viscous fluid leaps straight up to his chin and gathers there momentarily like string, then drips off in a single blob —

"Y-yes. I'm-m-m t-taking all psych cuh-cuh-courses next them-them—"

"Semester. That's good to hear. You're a very bright student, and I'm sure you'll do well in psychology. Did my class help you to make up your mind?"

"Y-y-yes. Thuh-that and m-m-my own ditha-dithability. I'm-m-m fathinated by the buh-buh—"

"Brain? I know what you're saying, Ethan. I got involved in this for a similar reason."

He sits upright, knees together, the fat textbook in his lap, listening to what you have to say, trying to make a good impression.

"Remember the lecture about sleep and dreams, how most people cycle through the four stages of sleep, the deepest being when you experience rapid eye movement, erections, spontaneous ejaculations?" He nods slowly. "I have a sleeping disorder and don't cycle through the different stages normally."

"Whuh-whuh—"

"They're not sure what it is, but they think it's the result of a virus I had as a boy that left me with some kind of brain

damage. I remember being sick a long time and never really getting better. I was always sluggish, listless. I couldn't
concentrate on my schoolwork. It took me too long to complete simple tasks. I was a crabby boy; I cried a lot..."
Ethan nods, eyes wide, that absorbing thing. "I went in for
so many tests, finally sleep tests. They found I have a sleeping irregularity. This affects my waking life. I have my good
days and bad, depending on how my night has gone. During
bad days I fall into microsleeps and experience lucid dreams
and hypnagogic imagery. I can be sitting right here talking
to you normal as can be — when all of a sudden you stand
up naked and hairless in front of me and peel back that
smelly foreskin of yours to present me with the raw, aching,
pink head of your—"
"Huh-how did you know I have a fuh-fuh—"
— bending in half in his chair to suck and chew on it,
stretching it out in his teeth like taffy and growling like a
dog going at a bone and letting the skin snap back —
A knock, that Dean kid's buzz cut appearing in a crack in
the door, the powder-blue irises of his eyes squeezed down
to mere pinholes behind banks of lenses, face stony as ever.
"Did I leave a notebook in here?"
His demeanor is as unchanged as that of a graven image.
When he had been sitting where Ethan is during his
appointment first thing this morning, he had exhibited no
reaction to your critical comments about his paper.
"Television specials and religious circulars do not constitute
primary sources. On the level of research alone, this paper
fails, let alone the bad writing." As you were raking his
paper over the coals, you peered behind the devout poker
face and found a desperate lad sitting in a locked toilet stall
with his pants around his ankles, knees bolted together,
back ramrod straight, teeth clenched and sinews standing
out on his neck, sweaty glasses slipping down to the end of
his nose as — flick! flick! — come spurts onto the stall
door with a strangled cry of "Jesus! Fuck!"
The blond flattop in the crack in the door would be come-
ly but for the fact that the head comes to a bit of a point,

reducing the haircut to a sort of tuft growing out of the top of the boy's head. The two students exchange a glance — Dean's disturbingly pinched blue eyes averting from Ethan's level, absorbing, dilated gaze.

"I'm sorry, Dean, I don't see any notebook here."

— Ethan wrestling the elastic band of Dean's gym shorts down over his ass — "Huh-hold on to h-h-him for m-m-me!" — while you take him by the shoulders and pull forward, his blond stubble nuzzling into your lap as Ethan gets down on one knee behind him and slaps his dick repeatedly against the exposed hairless butt crack —

"Tuh-turnip head," Ethan says after Dean has gone, the image of the blond pointed head with the tuft of hair evoked so powerfully by the stuttering words that you laugh. As powerful as the vision you had while Dean was sitting across from you and you were trying to explain that his paper on homosexuality wasn't even written from a psychological point of view but a religious-polemical one: skein after milky skein shooting out of the boy's knobby cock and striking against his glasses, one spattering strand bunching up at his left nostril and then drooling down to his chin —

"Dean, you know what you're doing here? You're advocating murder. Don't you realize that?"

"You said we could take any position we wanted."

"But within reason. This doesn't even come close to being an academic essay. For example — let me see — ah, here we go: 'Take my psych teacher, for example, a fag, I bet he'd like me to plug his ass while all the boys in class beat their dicks against his face before sliding them up his ass tunnel, which I'm lubing up for them right now—'"

"Is 'turnip head' your own invention?"

"The kuh-kids in the duh-dorm call h-him thuh-that behind his buh-back. He came into m-m-my r-r-room once…"

— folded nearly in half on the floor, using the wall to brace his back, knees on either side of his face, aiming it toward his tongue, extended and flicking at the sparkling tip, when Dean knocks and enters and, seeing Ethan's ass presented before him upside down like that, enters it from behind: "Fuh-fuh-fuh-fuh-fuck!" —

"I seem not to be having a very good day, Ethan."

"Whuh-what's happening?"

— I'm getting up and locking the office door while your dark eyes follow my every move like you know what's happening. You sit back and smile up at me as I stand over your chair, heart racing, sympathetic nervous system in fight-or-flight mode, my twitching hand coming out to touch your warm, hairless cheek, the strong bone of your jaw, the blood vessel pulsing visibly at your throat; your hands reaching up to unbutton my trousers, I reach for the swirl of hair on the back of your neck and pull forward, my cock disappearing whole into your mouth as you look up submissive but in control, open mouth stopped up with my dick stump bulging out from the stubble of your upper lip — seven invisible throbs passing into your mouth, and in one gulp you polish them off and then stand to unzip your own pants while pressing your wet, friction-hot mouth against my own and coaxing my tongue out into the slippery sucking and bitter tang inside — then pushing me down by the shoulders with one hand, unsheathing your cock with the other, the blunt raw head of which I taste with my tongue, then the whole fat end of it in my mouth whole and round and slick as a still-warm peeled hard-boiled egg. Curious, I release it from my mouth and draw up the foreskin with my fingers and stretch it up away from the head and keep pulling until hair and balls creep halfway up the thickness of your shaft, which balls I then gather up into my mouth individually, separately in their soft hair sac while pulling harder on the foreskin until it seems I must pull even your asshole up into view for tonguing when you go *ulgh,* meaning enough. When I release, the hair slips back along the shaft, and balls drop back into place between your thighs, and the foreskin enfolds the thick head like the calyx of a ripe tomatillo, then begins its slow, fascinating creep back to form a pink frill gathering just behind the glans rim fully exposed, a mouthful — a few prods of your hips suggesting "Duh-duh-deeper, tuh-tuh-teach," then *ulgh* —

Door opens: "You're sure I didn't leave a notebook in here?"

Pulling out, your dick beginning to flop and drool, you get him by the front of the shirt, saying "Whuh-whuh-why are you always fuh-fuh-following me around and being a puh-pain in the uh-uh-uh" — then his pants down around his ankles — smack, smack — those gym shorts of his so easy to take hold of and in a single yank just rip off his bare blond ass, wrestling him to the floor until bent double in front of us — smack, smack — you leave pink palm prints on each of the exposed blond globular ass cheeks quivering, timid cock beginning to grow downward horse-like, taking on a club shape, bulbous at the end like a mushroom cap — then placing both hands firm against the now-red ass cheeks and smearing them apart to expose a dark hole tight as a coin slot and haired — "Luh-luh-luh-look at thuh-this, teach" — middle finger scooting to the center and scrubbing around and over the loosening soft flesh hole and then like poking a finger into a block of wet clay — a dollop of spit descending like a fat white spider on the end of its thread — the entry pliable and slippery now sinking a finger knuckle-deep and one more hard smack to the ass to stop his horse bucking — "Huh-hold the fuh-fucker for me!" — pinned chest-down to the floor and arms wrenched behind him, he shakes his head back and forth, glasses slipping off and those pinpoint powder-blue eyes finally regaining their normal enlarged shape, blossoming like a pair of cornflowers in the sun — "Oh-ho! Uh-uh — pretty boy, ain't he, now? Whuh-watch m-m-me pluh-plug him, teach."

Driving in like the compression stroke of a piston in its greased cylinder, that fat hot fucker peeled wide open, the kid lurching forward but reined in by the shirttail — "Whoa!" — I hold the kid's paper down under his nose and pulling the turnip head up by its tuft of hair so he can see it, say, "Read this paragraph for me here, Dean, would you?" Meanwhile engorged behind him you chug faster, faster at the fully unfurled hole adhering to you like a leech stuck fast.

"Uh! Uh! I have no problem with fuh! fags myself but their showing it right out in! in! public pisses! me off! — ah! — It's normal for us normal humans! to try to stop it! so if you're gonna do it — fuck! — in public you better get! to a hotel room or something because — fuck! — we'll stop at nothing — ow! — to reduce! the gay! pop! ulation... goddamn..."

"Okuh-kuh-kuh-kay, teach — now! " — unplugging, the hole popping shut, one jack and — bink! — the first shot goes wide, skipping hotly across cheek and ear; then shots two and three in rapid succession scalding lips, tongue retracting warm, odorous scum to swallow; not quick enough on the reopening — shot number four skims mouth and clings there like a cobweb, then stooping to catch five and six, which shoot high and splash murky against glasses, seven just a drizzle along the kneeling boy's back from stubbled neck to upraised tailbone now licked clean —

"Tuh-tuh-teach, y-you okuh-kuh-kay?"

Looking up — there bending over you is Ethan cradling your head, warmth squishing inside your underwear — the vision now reduced to a residue rapidly going cold and which, thank Christ, they can't see — they? Ah, your next appointment's here, number six, Gordon, a tall kid...

Next 14 Miles
by Sutter Powell

"Oh, no," Jared groaned when he saw the long string of vehicles stopped ahead. He eased off the accelerator, preparing to downshift. As the rig slowed he rolled past a sign flashing SLOW TO 35 MPH — ROAD CONSTRUCTION NEXT 14 MILES. Jared punched the heel of his hand against the steering wheel in frustration. "Ain't that just fuckin' wonderful?" He checked his watch: 4 p.m. He had exactly three hours to get to Petaluma, and he hadn't even made it over Donner yet.

Jared checked his mirrors. A red Wrangler was barreling up on the left, trying to get in front of Jared's rig. The speeding Jeep darted past another eighteen-wheeler just ahead of Jared and cut lanes quickly, narrowly avoiding a third truck in the left lane. Jared saw the trucks ahead hit their brakes, so he followed suit, lurching the rig slightly. *Not bad for a college boy*, he thought. He'd accepted the trucking job in order to earn money over the summer break. Jared checked his mirrors again. A silver Mercedes convertible was in the left lane, attempting to pass. "Sorry, buddy, not a chance," Jared said as he eased to a stop. The two rigs the Jeep had passed were now side by side in front of Jared's rig and the silver convertible. A fourth rig slid in behind the convertible, completely boxing the Mercedes in. The trucks ahead crept forward a few yards and then stopped, their brakes sighing.

The afternoon sun had warmed the interior of the cab, and Jared's white tank top was plastered to his lean torso. The seat of his faded 501s felt damp with sweat from the three hours he'd spent behind the wheel. Jared rolled his window down and leaned his head out, hoping to take a deep breath of fresh mountain air. He was met instead by the blasting beat of My Life With the Thrill Kill Kult. "Sex on Wheels" was blaring out of the silver convertible's expensive sound system. Considering the car and the driver, Jared was somewhat puzzled to hear the sex-rock anthem growling out of the Blaupunkt. The man behind the wheel looked like a typical conservative businessman, clad as he was in a white dress shirt and red power tie, his suit coat draped over the passenger seat. The driver wore mirrored aviator sunglasses, and his dark hair was cropped short. Jared spied just a touch of gray at the temples. *What's a sedate-looking businessman like him doing listening to Thrill Kill Kult?* Jared mused. The convertible driver turned and looked up. He smiled and said something to Jared, but it was lost in a sea of music.

"What?" Jared put a hand to his ear.

The businessman reached down, turned the music off, and cut the Mercedes's engine. He spoke again, but now Jared couldn't hear him over the truck's idle. The man cupped his hands around his mouth and shouted up to Jared, "I said, what's up ahead?"

"Oh, gotcha. I'll take a look." Jared opened his door and leaned out of the cab. By sighting through the space between the two trucks, he could just make out an enormous crane straddling the freeway about a quarter mile ahead. The crane wasn't moving, and there were several construction workers standing around pointing at it. "Looks like we'll be here for a while," Jared reported.

"What did you say?" the businessman shouted.

"I said, it looks like we'll be here for a while," Jared yelled back.

The businessman shook his head, indicating that he still couldn't hear. He reached for the console and retrieved a cellular phone. He held it up for Jared to see and called out, "You got a phone? What's your number?"

Jared nodded and climbed back into the cab, closing the door. He picked up the cellular that he'd checked out from Dispatch. He'd never used one, and it took him a moment to locate the number on the face of the unit. He leaned his head and shoulders out of the cab and pantomimed the number. Jared's phone rang several times before he discovered how to switch it on. "Sorry. I've never used one of these before," he apologized.

"I'd be lost without mine. I'm Antonio Franco, but you can call me Tony. Who am I speaking to?" The man's voice was so deep and masculine that the phone seemed to shiver against Jared's ear. Tony had just a trace of a Spanish accent.

"I'm Jared Walters."

"Pleased to meet you. What's going on up ahead?"

"A crane. It's blocking both lanes. Looks like it'll take a while to fix."

Tony laughed heartily, "Probably just out of gas, if I know anything about the highway department."

"Too right," Jared agreed.

"It's hot today," Tony remarked, loosening his tie and unbuttoning the neck of his white dress shirt. The sight of a few wisps of black chest hair caused Jared's ever-horny dick to stir in his damp jeans. "I'm headed to San Francisco, where I manage a restaurant," Tony said. "Where are you headed, son?"

"Petaluma — and who are you calling 'son'?" Jared demanded with a grin. "I'm almost twenty-two."

"No offense intended," Tony said, grinning back. "You just look kind of young to be driving a big rig like that. Most of the truckers I've seen are old fat guys like me, not sweet young things like you."

"You don't look like an old fat guy from up here," Jared replied. It was true; Jared could see that there wasn't an ounce of fat on Tony. The older man was in peak physical condition, with broad, muscular shoulders and a trim waist.

"Thanks, but don't flatter me. It's been many a moon since I was as young and firm as you are."

Jared blushed as he realized that Tony must have been checking him out when he leaned out of the cab. He knew that he was attractive, but he had a hard time accepting compliments about his looks. He'd always been shy as a teen, and he was just beginning to realize that he had matured into a handsome young man with blue eyes, blond hair, and a lanky six-foot frame. "Thanks. I worked out in the weight room all last semester."

"Well, you weren't wasting your time," Tony replied. "I'd give anything to be that lean. Enjoy it while you can, though. I have to work out five times a week just to keep from gaining weight." Tony unbuttoned his shirt the rest of the way, pulled his tie over his head, and spread his shirt-tails, baring his furry chest and well-muscled torso. Jared barely suppressed a gasp as he ogled the man. Tony's upper body was stunning: big, blocky pecs topped with silver-dollar–size nipples; bulging, imposing deltoids; corded, rippling arms with biceps like melons; and a washboard stomach layered with more slabs of muscle.

"Whew!" Jared whistled appreciatively. "I hope I look like that when I'm your age," he blurted. Instantly he realized what a gaffe he'd just made. He fumbled around for an apology, his face on fire. "Oh, shit. I didn't mean that you were old or anything. I meant that I—"

"Hey, kid, it's okay, it's okay. I know what you meant, and it doesn't hurt my feelings any. I'm flattered that a cute college boy like you thinks I still look good." Tony leaned back and tipped his sunglasses down his nose. Peering up over the silver frames, he spoke again: "Since we have some time to kill, would you like to see a little bit more?" Tony's free hand slid down and rested on his belt buckle.

Jared's cock pulsed at Tony's bold proposition. Surely he'd heard wrong. "Um...wh-what exactly do you mean?" he stammered.

"I mean, do you want to see more of my decrepit old body? Maybe you can give me some workout tips or something." Tony's resonant voice purred in Jared's ear, sending a shudder of lust down Jared's spine.

"Yeah...I guess that would be okay," Jared squeaked in reply.

Tony unbuckled his slim leather belt. He turned to face Jared and extended his long legs over the console and into the passenger side of the convertible's front seat, toeing off his black suede loafers. Jared held his breath as he watched Tony unzip his slacks. The older man lifted his hips and peeled his slacks down over his lean hips and powerful thighs. After his slacks were off, he lay back against the door of the convertible with one knee bent, his leg cocked up against the leather seat.

Jared's hands crept into his lap as his eyes feasted on Tony's body. He couldn't believe this was happening to him in broad daylight on Interstate 80! Tony was almost completely nude now, except for his black dress socks and a tiny little pair of knit briefs. The pouch of the black briefs could barely contain the man's hefty genitalia. The waistband was pulled down slightly in front by the weight of the stud's heavy cock and balls, revealing the beginning of his luxuriant black pubes. Tony ran his free hand over his broad chest and chiseled abs and then languidly down over his hip and onto his muscular quadriceps. "What do you think, Jared — do I need some more on my quads?"

"No," Jared replied, trying not to pant openly. "They look pretty good, actually." He looked around nervously. Could anyone else see what was going on in the front seat of the Mercedes? Probably not, he decided. To the right was a solid wall of rock, and in front, the back ends of two semis. Any motorist's view from behind would be cut off by Jared's rig and by the fourth truck that sat idling directly behind Tony's convertible. On the opposite side of Tony's

Mercedes was a hundred-foot drop down to the eastbound lanes below. Tony's convertible was almost completely isolated from view. Almost. The only potential witness to this alfresco peep show was the driver of the fourth truck. *What if he's some asshole who'll decide to call the highway patrol?* Jared worried. He peered over the tops of his sunglasses and tried to see who was driving the fourth rig. The truck's windshield was deeply tinted, and the sun glared off it, obscuring the driver from Jared's view.

"What about my calves? Do you think they need a little work?" Tony inquired, drawing Jared's attention back to the Mercedes. The man raised his right leg and massaged his bulging calf. This maneuver caused Tony's black briefs to creep deep into his ass crack, exposing the globes of his ass cheeks.

"No, no, I'd say your calves are just right." Jared surreptitiously popped the buttons on his jeans. He reached into his underwear and adjusted his sweaty, aching hardon to a more comfortable position, guiltily allowing his fingers to tarry on the sticky flesh of his rigid organ and cradling the phone in the crook of his neck.

"So, Jared, are you enjoying yourself up there?" Tony inquired seductively in his sonorous voice, arching one eyebrow. "You like looking at my body? And just where are your hands, young man? You aren't touching yourself, are you?" He slid his hand onto the packed pouch of his black briefs. "I've got one more muscle to show you. You want to see it?"

"You know I do," Jared groaned, groping his boner. "But what about the trucker behind you? What if he doesn't want to see it? You don't want to get us into trouble here."

"Hmm. You might be right. How inconsiderate of me. Well, let's just ask him."

Jared watched in amazement as Tony put his phone down, turned, and stood up. He waved one arm, grabbed his crotch, and shouted, "Hey, buddy! You, behind that black windshield — you want to see my dick?" The answer came in the form of a deafening blast from the truck's horn. "I'll take that as a yes," Tony said with a laugh as he resumed his reclining position. Retrieving his phone and cradling it between his square jaw and his shoulder, he began to caress the overstuffed pouch of his briefs with both big hands. "Sounds like we have quite a voyeur behind the wheel of the mystery truck," Tony purred, kneading his hardening dick through the flimsy black fabric of his briefs. "How about we give him something to write home about?"

"What do you mean?" Jared's eyes were glued to the older man's big paws as they squeezed and groped at the swelling cock flesh.

"I mean, let's really give him a show — show him something he won't ever forget." Tony's dick was now as stiff as a board and sticking straight up at Jared. The pouch of his briefs was pulled so far away from his crotch that his furry balls had spilled out of the leg openings. The swollen orbs lay in a fuzzy puddle against the seat of the Mercedes.

Jared tried to wet his lips but found that his tongue was even drier than his lips were. "What do you mean by 'we'?"

"I mean, let's give him two for the price of one. I bet he'd love to get a look at your hot young body. I know I would." Tony curled a fist around the base of his hard-on, molding the black fabric to his hard dick. He ran the fingers of the other hand teasingly up and down his engorged cotton-encased cock.

"Gosh, I...I don't think that's such a good idea," Jared stammered. "I mean, I'm...kinda shy."

"Bullshit! You've got a hot body, and you know it. Open the door of that rig and let me have a little look."

"What?" Jared whispered into the phone, shocked. "I just couldn't!"

"Oh, okay. Since you're obviously not interested, I guess I'll just tuck this away and put my pants back on." Tony released his hard-on and reached for his slacks.

"Wait!" Jared blurted. He just had to see Tony's cock, or else he would explode. "I guess I could show you a little something."

"I bet you've got more than a little something to show me," Tony chuckled as he leaned back once more. "But hurry up. That crane won't be stalled all afternoon."

Jared looked nervously at the black windows of the fourth truck and then opened the door of his rig with a sweaty, shaking hand. He placed his feet on the edge of the door frame, facing Tony below. Laying the phone on the dash, Jared untucked his tank top from his jeans and peeled the damp garment away from his glistening torso. Jared ducked his head and hooked the shirt behind his neck, baring his smooth, sinewy chest to the light summer breeze. He retrieved the phone and cradled it against one shoulder.

"Ooh. Nice chest, kid. Nice and smooth. Makes me want to run home and shave mine." Tony ran a hand over his furry pecs and pinched one of his brown nipples. "Why don't you pinch your little pink nipples for me?"

Jared's hands rose of their own accord. He groaned softly as his fingers tweaked his tingling nipples, stiffening them instantly.

"That's the way, son," Tony purred as he groped his bulging briefs. "But you're going to have to show me a heck of a lot more than that if you want to see this big cock." Tony slyly peeled the waistband of his briefs back and revealed just the broad head of his big dick. He stuck the tip of his index finger into his piss slit and collected some of his precome. He raised his shining fingertip to his lips and slurped his finger into his mouth, savoring his own juice and smacking his lips in Jared's ear. "Now kick those boots off and take down your jeans. I want to see some hard college-boy cock."

Jared leaned over and unlaced his steel-toed work boots. He pulled them off and placed them on the floor of the cab before peeling his socks off. He was about to tuck his socks in his boots when Tony piped up, "Wait a minute, kid! Toss me your socks."

Jared balled his tube socks up and tossed them down to Tony. When Tony caught them he separated them. He took one sock and pressed it to his handsome face, and Jared heard the older man take a deep sniff of the sweaty sock. Tony shoved the other sock into his briefs and rubbed it around his balls. Then he spoke again. "Hurry up and get those jeans off!"

Jared lay back across the seat of the truck, lifted his hips, and worked his jeans down to his knees. He sat back up, then slid them all the way off. The pouch of his white briefs was spotted with the lube that had been leaking from his hard cock ever since Tony had loosened his tie. Jared looked at Tony expectantly, his chest heaving.

"C'mon, Jared — you show me yours, and I'll show you mine. Your public awaits."

Jared was beyond caring what the mystery trucker thought at this point. He was so turned-on by Tony's horny words and salacious self-stimulation that he was ready to do just about anything. He hooked his thumbs under the elastic waistband of his briefs and very slowly began to slide the underpants off, giving Tony plenty of time to enjoy the show. When his stiff cock popped free, he was pleased to hear the hunky restaurateur's grunt of appreciation. Jared slipped his briefs off and spread his legs. He was now naked from the armpits down. He could feel the cool Sierra Nevada air stir his damp blond pubes.

"You've got a nice cock, boy. Toss me those shorts!" Jared immediately threw his briefs into the convertible. Tony pressed the white cotton to his nose and inhaled lustily. "Yum — hot, sweaty trucker undies. I know guys who would pay good money for a whiff of these." Tony laid the shorts aside and hooked his thumbs in his own briefs, "You ready, Jared? You ready to see what this old man's got to show you?" Tony lifted his brawny legs up and yanked his briefs down. "How about that?" he said proudly as he lay back and fisted his upstanding cock. Jared's hand flew to his own rod as he took in the sight of Tony's mammoth meat. His cock was enormous, the wide shaft entwined with thick, ropy veins. The plump purple head was as big as a small apple. "You like?"

"Yeah, I like!" Jared responded enthusiastically, his fingers slipping up and down his own quivering shaft.

"What about these balls?" Tony cupped his big brown testicles in his other hand and offered them for Jared's inspection. "You like hairy balls like these? Let me see yours. You got any hair on your hot trucker balls?"

Jared scooted his ass forward on the damp seat and dangled his balls over the edge so the other man could see them. "Yeah, those are some hot-lookin' nuts, kid. You wanna see my ass?" Tony hissed, rolling over onto his knees and elbows. Jared moaned at the sight of Tony's beefy ass cheeks. The older man's muscular butt was tight and toned, his hard glutes deeply indented. Tony pressed the phone to the driver's seat and held it there with the side of his face. Reaching back with two hands, he cupped his ass cheeks in both palms, spreading his hair-lined valley wide open. Jared could see Tony's tight anus puckering in the afternoon sunlight. "Look at that ass, kid. Not bad for an old geezer, huh?"

"Not bad at all," Jared murmured, his cock lips puckering in a reflexive imitation of Tony's asshole.

Tony rolled back over and hooked one leg over the back of the seat, pulling the other foot up close to his body, causing his ass crack to yawn open. He reached down into his fuzzy crevice and teased his ass lips with his fingertips. "Show me yours now," he said. "Show me what a college-boy trucker's butt hole looks like." Jared lifted his right leg and placed his foot on the armrest of the open door, leaning back into the cab. He could now feel the light breeze caressing his sweaty butt crack and tingling asshole. "Beautiful," Tony breathed. "Just beautiful. Now finger yourself for me. Reach down there and stick your fingers up your sweaty hole." Jared hurried to comply. Struggling not to drop the phone, he reached down to finger his pucker. Tony watched Jared finger himself, all the while tickling and touching his own clenching anus for Jared's voyeuristic enjoyment. Jared had inserted two fingers in his ass and was busily finger-fucking himself. Tony moaned as he

drove two of his own digits up his tight hole. "Careful,
Jared, don't make yourself come yet. I have something else
for you to stick up there."

"Huh?" Jared grunted, fingering away.

Tony pulled his fingers out of his ass and reached under
the front seat. He withdrew what looked like a shaving kit,
a bag of soft black leather. "Luckily for you, I have my
roadside emergency kit with me," Tony said as he unzipped
the shaving kit. He pulled out two enormous identical dildos and a bottle of lubricant. He held both dildos up for
Jared's inspection. "Choose your weapon, kid."

"Uh...I don't think I could handle one of those. They're
kind of big, aren't they?" Jared eyed the artificial phallus-
es warily, his butt hole twitching in anticipation as he withdrew his fingers.

"Nothing ventured, nothing gained," Tony said, laughing as he tossed a dildo to Jared. Jared nearly dropped the
phone and almost fell out of the cab of the truck, but he
managed to catch it in one hand. Jared's brow furrowed as
he inspected the latex cock. The dildo was remarkably life-
like, right down to the two lemon-size balls at its base. In
fact, there was something eerily familiar about it.

"I had these babies custom-made," Tony informed him
conversationally as he coated his dildo with lubricant.
"Had them molded directly from my own cock." Tony
closed the top on the lube bottle and tossed it to Jared.
"Grease that bad boy up, Jared. It's the next best thing to
me." He carefully positioned the glistening head of his
dildo against his puckered butt hole and pressed the wide
head in, grunting as his ass lips molded themselves around
the thick shaft.

Jared squirted some lube onto his Tony dildo and
smoothed the grease over the surrogate cock. He had never
tried to accommodate something this large, and his asshole was already twitching in expectation. Jared held the
dildo by its balls and lined it up with his pucker. By concentrating carefully on relaxing his anus, he was able to
get the fat head in without much strain, but there were

still eight inches of thick, veiny shaft to go. He looked down into the convertible and saw that Tony had already buried his dildo in his ass and was now easing it in and out with one hand while he jacked his purple cock with the other. "Now ask yourself: Is it live, or is it latex?" Tony panted into the phone. "Go ahead, Jared, slide a little more of me up your ass."

Jared braced his left shoulder against the seat and pushed the dildo farther into his clenching asshole. A shuddery moan escaped his lips as he pulled the big dildo out to the bulbous head and then slid it back up himself. Jared fisted his cock with his free hand and began to jack off forcefully, all the while watching Tony fuck himself with the other dildo. Jared could feel his balls tightening. With each thrust he shoved the dildo in a little more. He couldn't last long at this rate. His arousal was intensified by the knowledge that he was being watched by some unknown man in the mystery truck. "Man, I'm gonna shoot any minute," Jared groaned, his fist flying.

"Yeah, me too, kid," Tony gasped in Jared's ear. "I could lie here until next week and watch you fuck yourself with that dildo, but they're gonna move that damn crane any minute. We'd better hurry it up. C'mon, Jared, work that cock for me!" Tony's furry torso was covered in sweat, and his massive chest was heaving as he stroked and dildoed himself toward an explosive climax.

Jared felt his orgasm start in his toes, a rushing, tingling sensation that shot up his legs and into his inflamed crotch like an electrical current. Jared's asshole clamped down rhythmically on the Tony dildo, and his balls erupted. "A-a-ah!" he screamed into the phone as his pent-up sperm hosed out of his thumping dick. Jared's come arced out into the mountain air, one big milky glob landing on the windshield of the Mercedes. Tony growled in Jared's ear as his enormous penis detonated and spurted gobs of hot cream all over the leather interior of his car.

Jared eased the dildo out of his ass and laid it on the seat behind him, his head spinning as he thought about what had just transpired. His reverie was disturbed by a thundering blast from the air horn of the mystery truck. Jared looked up the road in time to see the crane lurch onto the shoulder of the freeway. Traffic began to move around it. "Oh, shit!" Jared fumbled for his jeans and quickly stuffed his legs into them. "Tony! Traffic's starting to move. We gotta get dressed!"

"Huh?" The hairy hunk raised his head and dropped the phone. "Oh!" He pulled the dildo out of his ass and reached for his slacks. Tony threw his shirt on, buttoning and tucking frantically. When he'd pulled himself together, he picked up the phone just as Jared pulled the door to his truck's cab shut. "Listen, Jared, here's my card and a little something to remind you of me," Tony said as he tucked a business card into his black briefs and tossed them up into the open window of Jared's rig. "You call me tomorrow, okay?" Tony turned the ignition key, and the Mercedes purred to life. "Can I keep your socks and shorts?" he asked.

"Sure. Hey, wait, don't forget your dildo!"

"No, you keep it — until next time," Tony said with a wink as he pulled away, leaving Jared shaking his head.

Just then the mystery truck pulled up alongside Jared and stopped. Jared blushed as he thought about the things the trucker had witnessed. The passenger-side window of the mystery truck was tinted like the windshield, but Jared could just make out a shadowy figure sliding across the seat. The window rolled down a few inches, and a slender, fine-boned hand with bright red nails emerged, proffering a folded white paper towel with something written on it. A flabbergasted Jared leaned out the window of his rig, reached over, and plucked the paper towel from the graceful female hand, then watched it retreat. The window rolled up, and the rig pulled away. Curious to read the message, Jared unfolded the towel. When he read it he threw his head back and roared with laughter. Written (in pink lipstick, no less) were these words: "Thanks for the show, boys. How the heck is a gal supposed to compete with that?!"

Tattoo
by R.J. March

Tommy "Digger" MacDougal was almost ready to get one.
Keith the Rock had one, and so did Hays and most of the
other guys. Those without were commonly known as tatless pussies. Digger once went so far as to pick one out: a
flaming heart with a knife stuck in it and the words LIVE
HARD, DIE HARD around it in a smoking wreath.

Where to put it, though, was a problem. The calf? The
arm? The shoulder blade? Hays had put his next to his left
tit — a small dragon whose tail encircled the nipple, seeming to flick at it. Hays was good at animating the dragon,
tensing and flexing his big, heavy hairless pec to shake it
up and down, but only when he was alone with Digger,
never in front of the other guys in the fraternity. Digger
and Hays were roommates, as close as real brothers.
Digger felt for Hays a love that was in some ways broth-
erly and in other ways not.

Most times, the way he felt about Hays was easy for
Digger to sublimate, to bury under the minutiae of every-
day life — history notes, Intro to Sociology lectures, what
the Tri-Delt girls were going to do for their Halloween
party. But there were other times, like when they were

both a little toasted — not too drunk — and alone, hanging out in their room, half dressed and talking about nothing in particular. Then Digger could not ignore what he felt for Hays, who lounged spread-legged in his boxers or paced in his sweatpants, the front of which showed every swing and sway of the boy's dick. And what he felt for Hays was something like an ache caught in his throat, a wanting that actually hurt. When he was alone with Hays, Digger tended to do too much — drink too much, talk too much, care too much, look too much.

He talked too much about his tattoo. They were lying around — Digger on his bed and Hays on the floor — not interested in studying tonight. Digger had bought a fifth of Jack Daniel's, and they'd started out with shot glasses. Soon they'd dispensed with them, opting instead to pass the bottle. Digger liked having his turn, the rim of the bottle still wet from Hays's mouth. He could press his tongue against it and feel something, a tightening, a tingle in his crotch. He eyed Hays, sprawled on the floor still in his soccer shorts and jersey, just in from practice. Hays lay on his back, one leg on the other knee, and shook his hanging foot, his soccer shoe dangling. Digger looked into the gape of his friend's shorts and saw plainly the jockstrap he wore and everything it did not cover. Digger threw himself onto his back and looked instead at the ceiling, willing away the erection that was steadily burrowing against the confines of his jeans.

"Christ," Hays said in a long breath. "I am hornier than hell." Digger got himself up on an elbow again and gave Hays a look. "Do you know what I mean, Dig? I am fucking horny." He took a swig on the bottle and planted the end of it on his groin. It glistened there and taunted Digger, who reached out for it, grabbing the neck, pressing it hard into his friend's crotch — a simple drunken mistake, but decidedly deliberate and bolder than Digger had ever imagined himself to be.

He took a drink and wiped his lips with the back of his hand, all the while watching Hays.

"You know what we should do, Dig?" Hays said. He sat up and took the bottle Digger was holding out to him. Digger felt a crazy sinking for a second, afraid of what Hays might have in mind but dying to hear him name it anyway — anything dirty, intimate, functional, necessary.

"What?" Digger said, his mouth sandy, cracker-dry.

"What we should do, buddy," he said, getting his face close to Digger's, "is go to Marco's and get you that tat you're wanting."

Marco's was where all the guys in their house had their tattoos done, with the exception of the Rock, who had done his own needlework, a crudely drawn yin-yang symbol on his meaty calf, halfway obscured now by the hair that lay thick all over the boy's hard body.

"Oh, I don't think—" Digger started, trying to come up with an excuse that would satisfy Hays, who was nothing but determined once his mind was made up. He looked down at his friend, blue-eyed, black-haired, with beard-blackened cheeks that dimpled when he grinned. He was grinning now.

"Don't tell me you're pussying out of this again," Hays said, laying his head on Digger's mattress, still very close to Digger's face. He could smell Hays's breath, the sweetness of the Jack.

"I don't have the money," he said weakly.

"I'll front you, asswipe," Hays said.

"I have an Italian exam tomorrow," Digger said, weaker still.

"Pussy," Hays whispered.

"Fuck you," Dig said.

"Pussy," Hays lisped, putting a finger on Digger's chin, pushing lightly. "It doesn't hurt much," he said, his finger moving up to Digger's lower lip.

Digger pulled back. His dick was beginning to twitch, to leak. He could feel the tip of it go wet. He rolled over onto his stomach and tried hard not to hump the mattress, not with Hays right there, his eyes softened with liquor, lingering, seeming to speak to Digger without really saying anything. *What would he say?* Digger wondered. *What is he going to say ever? Nothing I want to hear, probably. But those eyes — he has no idea what they do to me.*

Digger followed Hays to Marco's. He'd been there before and wasn't much impressed with the facilities, which reminded him of the barbershop his father used to take him to. The light was harsh, and it cast a sickening pall over everything in the room: the samples hanging on the walls, the chair — in fact, a barber's chair — the table loaded with needles, the gun.

Marco came out from a back room. He was tall and well-built, his arms bared in a sleeveless flannel shirt and strangely devoid of tattoos.

"I brought you one," Hays said, his face gone red. *From drink?* Digger wondered, feeling his own face redden. He looked again at Marco's huge tanned arms and wide hairy-knuckled hands and, lower, at the worn spot on the front of his jeans, under which lay — Digger could see this for himself — Marco's fat, soft cock. *No mystery there,* Digger thought.

"So what are you looking for?" Marco asked, and Digger's eyes nearly leaped in their sockets from the front of Marco's jeans.

"I'm not sure," Digger said, swallowing, wishing he had brought the bottle of Jack. Whatever courage Hays had pumped him full of was gone now. He suddenly felt stupid, eager to leave.

"Marco's got a cool one," Hays said, his eyes all soft on the tattoo artist. *The way he was eyeing me earlier,* Digger thought. "You should see it, Dig. It's crazy."

"Where is it?" Digger asked, looking the man over.

"Come on into the back room," Marco said, going over to the door and flipping the OPEN sign to CLOSED.

The back room was where the man lived, apparently. There was nowhere to sit, just a mattress on the floor. "Cleaning lady quit," Marco said, and Hays laughed. Digger stepped around a pile of clothes, on top of which was a balled-up pair of briefs. Marco offered some beer, bending over a small fridge, baring a patch of hair over his ass right where the crack smoothed. Digger noticed Hays staring and scooped up the wadded shorts, putting them into the pocket of his denim jacket. His fingers closed tight around the wad, and he felt himself going hard. He stepped over to the bed and sat down fast. Hays handed him a can.

"You okay, pal?" he said. "You look a little flushed."

Digger popped the top and took some hard swallows. "I'm fine," he said, burping. "Let's see this crazy tattoo."

Hays grinned as Marco handed him his beer. Marco touched the top of his jeans, undoing the button there.

"Hey," Digger said, but not in any voice to be heard.

Marco pulled on his zipper, and the jeans opened, revealing skin and hair and white cotton.

Digger sat with his sweating can of beer, his mouth open. He watched as Marco pushed his pants down to his knees, baring thighs that were pale, dark-haired, and channeled with muscles. Digger glanced at Hays, who looked solemn and rapt, his hands pressed flat on his crotch as though to still them or what lay under them. His fingers curled under in a caress, a grope.

Digger himself was hard, very hard, his prick snaking down and held fast in his pant leg. His cock felt superheated, burning against his thigh. He moved his hand to touch it, to lay his fingers along the length of it, as Marco thumbed down his underwear. The tattooist's cock jutted out from a dense bush of pubes, thick as a kielbasa and spiraled with blue, the whole shaft encircled with indigo ink from root to head — a crazy barber's pole.

"That is so cool," Hays said, dragging on his beer.

It seemed to Digger a strange choice, a strange decoration, since the man's prick looked as though it needed no embellishment. Especially now that it was twitching, coming to life, getting longer and longer, growing straight out from Marco's middle like a big ball-ended trunk.

"It says something," Hays was saying, just as Digger was beginning to notice words. The spiral of blue was a trail of letters that made words that made sentences.

"Why don't you come here and read it?" Marco asked Digger, who could not take his eyes off the tattooist's big, swinging club.

"Do it," he heard his frat brother say.

He found himself standing, handing his beer to Hays, who had to put down one of the two cans he was already holding.

He bent over to get a closer look.

"It reads better on your knees," Marco said.

"Yeah," said Hays.

Digger got on his knees.

Marco's cock seemed to float in the air, its fat head drifting closer and closer to Digger's face, until the boy's eyes crossed and his mouth opened. It hit his tongue, and Digger's lips closed around its hardness; he put his hands on Marco's hips to steady himself. He swirled his mouth over the thing, not really sure what else to do until Marco grabbed the back of his neck and showed the boy what he wanted. He slowly fed himself into Dig's mouth, a little at a time, telling Dig to take it easy when the boy took in too much at once.

"Now, why don't you get over here," Marco said in Hays's direction, and Digger heard Hays getting up off the bed and coming close. Out of the corner of his eye he saw his roommate walking funny, with his pants down around his ankles and his boner sticking up out of the piss slot of his boxers.

"Don't just stand there," he heard Marco say. "You know what I like."

Hays got to his knees behind Marco. Digger felt his hands being covered by his friend's hands, and their chins nearly touched as each went to work on opposite sides of Marco's crotch.

"You guys are doing great," Marco growled. "Get up that butt back there. And why don't you work on my balls, whatever your name is."

Digger pulled the great cock out of his mouth and said, "My name's Tom, but everyone calls me Dig—"

"I don't give a fuck what you're called," Marco snapped. "Shut the fuck up and eat those nuts."

Digger went red, heard Hays's muffled laughter, and nosed around the low-hanging nut sac before him. Like oversized marbles in a silky bag, Marco's balls rolled over Digger's tongue, tasting better than anything. He sucked hard on them, pulling them to the back of his throat, teething gently on the skin bag, pushing his lips up to the split of Marco's legs. The man's long, hard cock lay heavily across Digger's face, the head smearing goo across the boy's forehead. Marco let out a groan that sounded like approval.

Digger felt hands on his crotch, a tugging at the button fly of his jeans. He looked down and caught the huge head of Marco's dick in one eye; with the other he saw his buddy's fumbling hands trying to undo his pants. He leaned back to watch Hays's face working between Marco's butt cheeks, the tip of his chin wet with spit and bearded with the thick growth of ass hairs surrounding the tattooist's hole.

"He's real good at it," Marco said, and Digger looked up. The man's eyes were mere slits, his prick bobbing. "I bet you know that already, though."

"I don't," Digger said, a little hoarse.

"Man, you got to be kidding," Marco said. "Fucker makes me come this way." He reached around and grabbed Hays by the hair, pulling the boy's face out of his butt. "You telling me you never had this one?"

Hays looked at Digger.

"I wanted to," was all Hays said.

"All right," Marco said loudly. "Get the motherfucker's pants off, already."

In an instant Digger's jeans were off, and he was lying bare-assed on Marco's bed with his roommate's face buried between his ass cheeks. Marco got himself down on the mattress too and reached right in between Hays's legs, working his fingers in and out of the boy's butt hole, telling Hays how good he was going to get it, making Hays work all the harder on what Marco called "that boy's pussy."

Digger heard Marco blow a gob somewhere and say, "I'll bet you ain't seen your buddy here get fucked before either. I'm talking to you." And Digger felt a sharp cuff on his head.

"No," he replied lamely. He felt dizzy or something. Light-headed. Feverish, maybe. He was in some kind of heaven where everything happened too quickly. He felt every slip of Hays's fat tongue, every swipe and swallow. He wanted more of Hays inside him, his whole face, his whole body.

"You want to watch or what?" Marco said, and Digger slowly separated himself from Hays's wonderful mouth and got alongside Marco, looking down at the red gash the man was going to fill.

"See how bad the kid wants it?" Marco said, smiling at Hays's squirming butt. "He's just beggin' for it. Now, why don't you lube me up with some of that drool you got dripping off your chin there."

Digger went down on the man's tattooed prong, sucking up as much dick as he could. Marco fucked Digger's mouth with small strokes, massaging Hays's behind, pressing his thumb into the soft pucker. "Enough," he said, pushing at Digger's face.

Marco gripped the shaft of his pecker, touching Hays's hole with the end of it, pushing and poking until he had the head in and Hays's ass squirming for more. Marco fucked him with that, with just the head, and Hays started to whimper. "Give it to me," he said. "Just give it to me, man." And he tried to get more by pushing his ass onto the steely prong, but Marco gripped the boy's hips hard and continued to be stingy with his cock.

"Now I want you to see this," Marco said, "because this is a sight to fucking behold." Digger got close to Marco and watched as the man began to pump Hays for real, with powerful thrusts that shook the boy and made him cry out.

"Look at that cock, man," Marco said, grunting and sweating, "Looks like it's spinning, don't it?"

"Jesus," Hays panted. "Not so hard at first. Just ease into it, man."

"Ease, nothing," Marco said, wiping his face in the crook of his arm. "Suck my tits, why don't you, Pigger."

"Digger," Digger said.

"Suck them," Marco said sharply, and Digger bent over and took a salty nip into his mouth, swirling his tongue all around it, tangling up the hair there, and Marco said, "Put a little tooth in it." Dig bit down, and the tattooist moaned, banging into Hays, who moaned too.

Hays said something.

"What's that, baby?" Marco said, bringing his tattooed cock all the way out. It seemed to vibrate and stank of Hays's butt — a smell that made Digger's head spin and drop from Marco's tit to his fat red knob. He lapped at the underside of the head, just under the slit, and did not catch what Hays repeated. Marco cuffed him again.

"Appreciate the attention, Pigger, but your buddy wants you to fuck his face."

Digger crawled up to where Hays's head was.

"You do?" Digger asked his roommate.

"Oh, yeah," Hays said, his eyes soft and dreamy. Marco resumed fucking him, but softly now, with long and gentle strokes. He smoothed his hands over Hays's back, fingering the boy's knobby spine, pulling back and dropping a dollop of spit onto his fancied-up prick.

Hays opened his mouth, looking up at Digger. Dig pushed his upright cock down and in the general direction of Hays's parted lips. When he felt his friend's wet heat on his shaft, he leaned into it carefully but deeply. "Turn your head, Hays, and let me see," Marco said. "You like your buddy's dick, don't you?"

Hays grunted, Digger sighed, and Marco started picking up momentum. He got up off his knees and, squatting, began to fuck Hays's ass with short, fast thrusts. Hays sucked hard on Dig's dong, taking it all the way, snorting for air. Digger felt the hollow of his buddy's throat, how it tightened and went slack. He reached under Hays, searching for his nipples. The boy's pecs swayed heavily and then tensed up as hard as rocks, and Digger pulled hard on the fleshy points. Hays growled, and Marco panted, and Digger felt his nuts go tight. Marco slung an arm around Digger's neck and pulled him back, kissing him hard on the mouth, snaking his tongue into the boy's mouth. It was Digger's first kiss from another man, and not from the man he had wanted to kiss, but he kissed back and sucked on Marco's cocklike tongue, wishing it were Hays's instead.

Marco broke it.

"Fuck, man," he said, slapping Hays's ass. He laid himself flat on the boy's back and reached under for Hays's short, fat cock. "I'm there," he said, "I'm right there."

He pumped Hays's ass two, three times and pulled out with a yelp. Hays did a flip without losing a lick on Digger's prick, his own cock red-hot and dribbling. Marco beat his meat with a ruthless fist and sent a shot of white up across Hays and onto the wall behind the boy's head. The second shot hit Digger's cheek; the third and fourth fell in the center of Hays's chest. The rest flowed like hot honey over his fingers and down his balls, puddling in Hays's pubes.

Digger teetered on the edge. "That's it," he said and tried to pull out of Hays's mouth, but Hays wouldn't let him.

"He wants it, Pig," Marco said. "Give it to him."

Digger felt his prick rumble and his piss hole go wide, and he unloaded into Hays's hot mouth what he had been saving for a rainy day by himself. Hays choked and sputtered and drooled come, then went rigid, fisting himself with slow, short strokes, milking his cock, blasting a crazy spray of hot white jizz that amazed Digger and made Marco laugh.

"Jesus," Dig said.

"He always goes like that. Kid's a fucking show-off," Marco said, grinning.

They drove home in silence and went straight to their room, bypassing the poker game going on in the living room, unnoticed by the big, hulking drunks sitting around in their underwear. Digger sat on the edge of his bed, still in his coat, his hands jammed into his pockets. His fingers closed around the wadded-up pair of shorts he had stolen from Marco. He got hard just touching it.

Hays stood by the window. "I'm beat," he said.

"Me too," Digger replied.

Hays unbuttoned his shirt and shrugged it off. He touched his bare skin and looked over his shoulder at Dig. "I had a T-shirt, didn't I?" he asked.

"I think so," Dig said. He was staring outright at Hays, studying his roommate, the way his hair grew down to and stopped at the nape of his neck, the big curves of his deltoids, the jut of his ass. Hays unbuttoned his jeans and pushed them down with his boxers, baring his ass. The crack was spread, and Digger could see the dark hair the boy had there, how it curled over, covering his hole. A finger appeared between his legs, worming up around the hole, slipping inside. "I pretended he was you tonight," Digger heard, getting to his feet and moving over to his friend.

He stuck his face into the hairy crack, smashing his nose so hard, his eyes teared up. He lapped at the boy's fuzzy pucker, sniffing up the stink of it. He slipped out of his clothes and lay on the floor. Hays spit into his hand and jacked Digger, then squatted over the gripped dick, directing it up and into the little split between his legs. "Oh," they said together. Hays found the hard little knobs of Digger's nipples, pulling hard, twisting hard, causing Dig to buck and squirm and slam himself up into the heat of Hays's asshole.

"Oh, man," Hays was saying softly. "You are good, you are right there, right there." He bent over and put his mouth close to Digger's, and they kissed for the first time, a peck and then a smashing of lips and teeth, a fighting of tongues. The kissed for a long time, barely fucking, and the tightness of Hays's hole was driving Digger nuts. He felt around for the pair of stolen shorts. He rolled the boy over onto his back and hooked his legs over his shoulders. Hays's eyes went wide as Digger pushed all the way in, grinding his pubic bone against the boy's bottom, and he pressed the briefs under Hays's nose.

"Marco," Hays said, taking the underpants into his mouth. Digger sucked on his friend's toes, tonguing between them. As Hays grunted and gritted his teeth, tearing up the briefs and begging for more and more, his cock sputtered and gushed like an out-of-control fire hose, splashing Hays with his own creamy nut juice.

"Fuck," Digger said, pulling out and spraying jizz all over his buddy's stomach and chest.

They lay quietly side by side and listened to the noise their brothers made downstairs. "Leave my ass alone," one of them barked. *Probably Bishop*, Digger was thinking. Bish had a little red-devil tat on his butt cheek.

"Hey," he said, and Hays started out of a near sleep.

"What is it, man?"

"I never got to read Marco's dick. What does it say?" Digger asked.

Hays yawned, and Digger wished he could see his friend in the dark. He pressed himself closer, all along Hays's long body.

"It's the fucking Gettysburg Address or something," Hays said, curling up and spreading himself over Digger like a blanket, breathing into his mouth a good-night kiss. "To tell the truth, it never really made much difference to me what it said."

He bucked his hips, humping Digger's wet, tired crotch.

"And you're still a tatless pussy," Hays mumbled, drifting off to sleep while Digger imagined himself being worked on by Marco, who dispensed with needles and tattoos altogether and bore in with his artful tool instead. "I wish you could see this, man," Marco was saying in Digger's dream. "Dick's spinning like a barber pole."

"Feels like one," Digger said.

Downstairs, around the card table, the poker game degenerated into rowdiness, brothers sitting with cigars, legs thrown over the arms of chairs, dicks hanging out all over the place. Skipper emptied another beer can and threw it onto the pile with the others. "Looks like Marco's got another customer," he said, looking up at the ceiling where Digger and Hays slept. Everybody laughed except Keith the Rock. Bishop got a dreamy look on his face; his tat was just a week old, and he was already planning on returning for another.

"I don't see what the big deal is," the Rock said. He grabbed Bishop's shorts and pulled hard, tearing them off and baring the boy's bubble butt and his little red devil. "There's nothing special about this."

None of the brothers said anything. They all stared at Marco's handiwork, each admiring it for his own — private — reasons.

Hung Jury
by James Anselm

The foreman was running through his list of charges for
about the fifth time when I came, grunting just once as my
load spurted into David's handkerchief — at least I hope
that's where it went. I wasn't about to look.

From his end of the big oak table, the foreman fondled
his gavel and looked down to where I sat. "Did you have
something to say?" he asked self-importantly.

"No, I just yawned," I replied, trying not to show contempt. He shot me a dirty look and continued.

No one expects jury duty to be fun, so I had been pleasantly surprised to find David on the same panel. I hadn't
seen him since he had played an audition for me and we
had subsequently made some personal music together.

As a jury, we were an impossibly mixed bag and, oddly
enough, all men. But the attorneys hadn't questioned it,
and neither did I. David sat on my right, and a very young
fellow named Martin on my left. We were at the opposite
end of the table from the foreman. I was soon thinking of
most of them by nicknames. The boss, of course, was
Sarge. I took him for an ex-marine, an especially homo-
phobic one at that.

I hadn't yet thought of a name for the good-looking red-head on David's right, a man whom — under other circumstances — I would have liked to know better. In the next seat down, Barney resembled the neighbor in *The Flintstones,* cartoon-short and stocky with a permanent five-o'clock shadow. There was Al Bundy, the perennial salesman, and so on around the table.

Then there was Little Martin, as I called him in my mind. If he wasn't still in college, he couldn't have been out very long. His looks were only average, and the glasses didn't help, but I could see a very nice chest pushing at his spotless blue shirt, and I really had to restrain myself from reaching over to tweak one of his nipples just to see how high he'd jump.

At one point during the deliberations, David gave me a careful signal, then got up from the table and walked over to the bathroom. A couple of minutes later, I went to meet him. The room was a pathetically small affair for twelve people — two urinals and a single stall. I stood next to him and said, "I didn't even know you'd moved to the city."

"Just been here long enough to get jury duty," he sighed. "Still singing?"

"I was supposed to have a gig tomorrow night, but it doesn't look like we'll be finished here."

He shrugged, then looked down at his dick and asked, "You seeing anybody?"

"Nobody special. How about you?" My own rod started pulsing even before I saw him shake his head, and when I looked down, his was getting hard too.

We angled ourselves so we could watch each other get stiff but not be spotted from the doorway in case anybody came in. It was maddening to see those two cocks poking out big and proud but not have the privacy to do anything.

After a few frustrating minutes of eyeing each other, we returned to our seats. As I feared, we hadn't missed anything: Democracy was still in action, and the wrangling continued long beyond the limits of my interest, then past the limits of the normal court day.

We took a vote and agreed to stay overnight. I didn't really think we were all that close to reaching a decision, but if by some miracle we did, that would get us out a lot faster. The guard brought us dinner, then disappeared, though he said if we needed anything, we could use the in-house phone and someone would come around.

I had thought we were settling in for a boring night when I felt David's hand on my thigh under the heavy table. He had moved his chair closer to mine so gradually that I hadn't even noticed it, and now his hand was working its way to my zipper. I shifted in the seat to make it easier for him, and a minute later he had my joystick in his hand.

Recovering from my ejaculation, I excused myself to go to the john, not paying much attention when our foreman came in. Still, I can hardly ever resist glancing down to see what's next to me, so I checked him out as I was zipping up. It didn't look like an old man's dick, I was pleasantly surprised to note, but was full and pink.

To my horror I realized that Sarge had seen me looking, and I think I blushed. I locked my eyes on one tile directly in front of me, almost afraid to move. Then I heard him chuckle. "Go ahead and look, cocksucker," he snarled.

I pretended I hadn't heard him, but he said it again. "Look at it, cocksucker. I know you want to look at my dick. I know your type." Out of the corner of my eye, I saw him pull even more of it out of his fly, and it dangled in front of him.

"Would you like to see it hard? You don't have to answer me. I know you would." He began to stroke it slowly, and I gradually turned my head to watch as it started to elongate.

"Nice, isn't it? It's gonna get a lot bigger, just you watch." His hand moved up and down, seeming barely to touch the skin as it glided along, his pole growing with each gentle stroke. It was as though I were being hypnotized by the regular motion and his deep, soft voice, and I felt my own whang rising in my briefs in response.

I've seen an awful lot of cock in my day, both live and on video, but this ranked with the very biggest in my experience, and it kept getting harder as he taunted me. "Come on, boy," he sneered. "I'll bet you and your pussy boyfriend can't raise anything half as big as this."

Well, I am pretty big — though I couldn't match him — and since I was at full stretch myself by this time, I opened my zipper again and let the head poke out, pointing straight at the ceiling.

Then Sarge reached around behind me and grabbed my arm in a hammerlock. He was strong, and before I knew it he was marching me back into the main room, my rod leading the way. His poker nestling between my ass cheeks kept me from going soft despite my embarrassment.

I don't know what I expected — perhaps they would fall on me with cries of "Die, yuppie scum!" — but what never crossed my mind was the light that came into several pairs of eyes when they saw us come through the door.

"We've been at this an awful long time," Sarge said. "I move that we table further discussion until we've had a little recreation. All in favor?" There was a general buzz of agreement.

Releasing me, Sarge dropped his pants to the floor, and several of the others followed suit. David took my hand, but I was already making straight for Little Martin. As I moved away I could see Barney coming up beside David, so I didn't feel terribly guilty.

"Come on, Martin," I said. "We're all gonna have a good time." I held my hand out, but he shook his head. Then I pulled my shirt out of my pants and over my head, but the kid just wasn't buying.

"N-n-no, not me," he stammered. "You go ahead." I patted him on the shoulder and went back to the big table. David and Barney made room for me, and I got between them, putting one hand on each cock to complete the erections they had begun to generate.

Barney had not had the advantage of being jerked off ahead of time, so he was pretty quick to shoot his first wad. I felt him getting stiff and tried to slow him down, but he needed to pop so badly that he came before I could do anything to stop him.

I looked over at our college boy while Barney was squirting. Well, his lips may have said "no, no," but the "yes, yes" in his eyes was repeated in his crotch, which was sporting a sizable bulge as he watched us.

While Barney was catching his breath, I devoted my full attention to David, standing behind him to work his tits with one hand and his cock with the other and making encouraging faces over his shoulder at Martin all the while. David's hands were stretched around behind him, rubbing my sides and reaching for my ass.

The lump in Little Martin's pants was even bigger now, and it looked like it was still growing. He had pushed his chair back to the wall as far from us as he could get, but he couldn't tear his glance away. His expression of panic deepened, and I knew that he was getting harder by the second. Even his nipples were erect, jutting out from his tense pecs as though they would poke through the cotton that confined them.

I could tell that David was getting closer, and I wanted to feel him inside me. "Come on, David," I told him, "fuck me. I want you to fuck me."

Getting behind me and guiding his pole into my crack, David fed me inch after inch of it while I begged for more. Barney kept lapping at my length as though it were an ice-cream cone and my balls a double-scoop special.

Sarge had perched on the edge of the table; a blond fellow with glasses was trying to sit on his massive shaft, and he was not having an easy time of it. The redhead, hovering by them for a taste of the blond's cock, suddenly found himself thoroughly skewered by Al the salesman.

I looked over at Martin again; his eyes were screwed shut, and he had his hands over his ears. I had to laugh, but then I saw that his erection had poked right up over his belt. Bright red against his blue shirt, the head of his cock throbbed with excitement and glistened with precome. I wanted that whopper, but now I couldn't get free from my two fellow jurors.

David kept ramming into me, deeper than anybody had in a long time. In front, Barney was trying to deep-throat me — no easy job, thanks to my own size and the constant motion of David's thrusts from behind. I closed my eyes and let myself relax, giving myself up to their rhythms.

Then I heard cries in an unfamiliar voice — it was Martin. His hands clutched at the edge of the chair as his cock exploded; almost another inch of it surged out of his pants, and his load shot up the front of his shirt, hitting his chin and face.

The sight of him charged me up for my next orgasm, and I barely had time to warn Barney before I blew three big shots of jizz at him; still, he caught it like a pro. With my ass clutching David's cock, he too let out a yell and a blast of come.

I turned my head just in time to see Al Bundy come with a thrust that nearly knocked the redhead over. Then I could see the boss lean back from his partner, his heaving chest and tossing head making it clear that he was preparing for an intense orgasm. Sarge's blond blew a minute later, wetting the redhead down from the other side.

Once they disentangled themselves, Sarge went over to Martin and spoke to him so softly that no one else could hear. Then he put his arms around him and held him for several minutes. I could see that there were tears in the boy's eyes as the older man cuddled him and patted his back. Then he released him and began to undress him, gently loosening his tie and unbuttoning his soiled shirt.

Martin didn't protest this time; he stood quietly as piece after piece of clothing was removed until he stood stark naked, his smooth, muscled body shiny with sweat and his member growing again to full erection. I thought his chest had looked better when he was dressed, but that cock was just beautiful — slim and long.

Then Sarge bent over and offered his ass to the boy. I could see Martin didn't want to do it at first, but his lust

got the better of him, and he began to make a few tentative thrusts. Then, once he felt how good it was — you
could see it on his face — he started driving like the young
buck he was.

The rest of us stopped and watched, many stroking their
own hard-ons. Sarge encouraged him without words, urg-
ing him on to harder and deeper strokes through his
grunts and groans.

"Oh, God, I'm gonna do it again!" the boy gasped, and
we all cheered him on: "Go, Marty! Pull it out! Let's see!"

He stepped back a bit, and his cock slipped out of
Sarge's ass. He took it in one hand and had to give it only
a few twists before he shot clear over his partner's head on
the first two squirts, a few more drops landing on Sarge's
back as we applauded.

After that it was like the old days at the baths, with
every possible combination enjoyed — and a few impossible ones attempted. Making up for lost time, Martin shot
again and again, real gushers of come. "I don't know
where he's fucking getting it from," David said to me at
one point.

I didn't care where he got it from, as long as I got my
share. When I put my arms around the boy, his heart was
bouncing off his ribs, he was so excited. His dick went
from soft and limp to steel-hard in less than a minute.
"You're going to fuck me, aren't you?" he whispered.

"Only if you want it," I lied. He pushed his ass back
against my crotch, and I let him feel the size of my growing hard-on. "What do you say?" I didn't want to let him
think for too long; once I got fully erect again, he'd know
there was too much of me for his first time.

I leaned away, and his butt moved with me — that was
answer enough. Reaching for my pants, I managed to grab
a lubricated rubber, and I was ready. I squeezed the last
bit of liquid out of the foil, wiping it between his cheeks,
and started to invite myself in.

"O-o-oh, shit, it's so big...I can't, Jim!" He tried to get
away, but I held on tight.

"It's almost all in," I told him. "There's only a little bit more, and then you can relax." He kept saying no, but he stopped fighting me while I finished my penetration.

He never went soft all the time I was fucking him, which I guess is a compliment to my technique. Of course, knowing he was cherry inspired me to special efforts.

Leaning back against me, he gasped, "You're gonna make me come. I haven't even touched it yet, and it's ready to shoot." His hands wrapped around my ass, trying to push me into him bodily. "Oh, yeah, fuck me. Fill me up with that big cock. Make me come."

The more he talked dirty to me, the bigger and harder I got, pushing buttons inside his body that he didn't even know were there. How could he? They didn't teach this when I went to college either.

Finally he blew, hands-off, firing away like it was his first load of the evening instead of the fourth or the fifth. Meanwhile, his ass milked me for jizz I didn't know was still in me. I bucked deep inside him and shot again and again and again! If I hadn't been wearing a rubber, the come would have spilled out of his ears. We were both weak at the knees when that orgasm was over.

I held him close, and the son of a bitch started to get hard again. I moved my body against his, massaging his flesh with mine and gently squeezing his ass cheeks. His pulse had never really slowed down, and it was going faster now, as was his breathing. Between our stomachs his dick writhed like a living thing. "Oh, no, no!" he cried as though he couldn't believe it, "I'm gonna come again!"

You know, in the comic strips, when you see the word *sploosh*? I swear, that was the noise his come made when it shot out of his cock onto my chest.

While I was recuperating from that duet, the redhead came over and was willing to settle for a hand job while we exchanged numbers for another day. After watching him shoot a nice load, I was ready again. I wanted to try my luck with Sarge then, but he always seemed to be busy. The bastard had as much stamina as Martin.

Finally, eleven of us just slumped in our seats, exhausted, but Sarge was right back at he head of the table, the
damn gavel in his hand. "I think we should be able to
wrap this up in time for the morning session," he said.
"After all, we're clearly all of one mind."

The Afternooner
by Michael Cavanaugh

My desk chair was still spinning when I hit the hall. My boss had actually come over to my desk and asked me if I wanted to leave work early. I had looked up at him, waiting for the punch line. J.B. wasn't the kind of guy to let one of his minions leave the office early. Had he told me I'd be spending the evening or even the entire weekend tied to my desk, I wouldn't have batted an eye. Leaving early was another matter entirely.

"You did a hell of a job researching that Cantrell case for me, Mike," J.B. said, gazing down at me over the curve of his potbelly. "That extra effort kept me from making a fool of myself in front of those damned barracudas. They thought they had me when they mentioned the L.A. connection. Thanks to you, they ended up kissing my ass. Now go on and get out of here. See you on Monday."

Like I said, I was gone in a heartbeat. I skipped the elevator and shot down the stairs. I didn't want to be caught waiting for transportation if J.B. happened to change his mind. Stepping out of the building and onto the street was like walking into a convection oven, but I didn't care. I had a totally unexpected half day of freedom, and I was not going to be bothered by a little heat. I slipped out of my suit jacket, loosened my tie, rolled up my sleeves, and headed off down the street, whistling softly.

The Number 16 bus was jammed. To make matters worse, somebody had almost totally blocked the aisle at the rear of the bus with a huge packing crate. I was just about to curse the culprit for being a total shit-for-brains when I got a better look at the dude riding herd over it. One glance changed my opinion entirely — so much so that I began working my way to the back of the bus. I cozied up next to the crate and took a long, close look at its owner.

The guy was in his late twenties or early thirties and had the look of a man who was used to heavy-duty manual labor. His body was totally hot, and it didn't look like he'd built it at a gym. He was wearing a sweat-stained white undershirt, baggy and shapeless, that was doing a piss-poor job of hiding his buffed torso. He was holding on to the overhead handrail, a position that displayed one hell of an arm. The flexed biceps and triceps were awesome, and his furry forearm was thick and meaty. A big, solid-looking pec was also on display, coated with silky fur and capped with a big fat nipple that was perched on the swell of muscle like a candy kiss.

I sidled in next to him, positioning myself so I could cruise without being totally obvious about it. The bus was a hotbox, and within a couple of stops, I was starting to go into meltdown mode. So was the humpy guy beside me. I could see the dude's armpit, all pale and soft, matted with dark curls, the sweat beading up on them like little jewels. Sweat was glistening on his forehead as well, and before long, little trickles of water were running down his face and neck. I followed one salty rivulet with particular inter-est — it slid down his thick neck and onto his shoulder, then began to roll down over the full curve of his chest. It blazed a trail through the mat of hairs, cut across the dark areola of his nip, then stopped, quivering on the thick, meaty point of his tit.

You have no idea of the restraint — or maybe a healthy fear of getting my teeth rearranged — that was required to keep me from leaning over and licking that salty water right off the spot where it had come to rest. The drop grew larger, sparkling in the sunlight, until it finally let go and splashed down onto the toe of my shoe. I swear to you, I could feel that drop right through the leather! It shot a jolt up my leg right to my groin.

"Damn hot."

"Huh?" My head jerked up, and I found myself staring into the bluest eyes I'd ever seen. It suddenly dawned on me that this dude was as gorgeous from the neck up as he was from the neck to points south. The eyes were fringed with dark lashes, the nose long and straight, the cheekbones high, the chin and jaw firmly molded, the lips full and sensual. When he smiled at me, I could feel my heart slam against my rib cage like maybe it wanted to get out and be on its own for a while. Since that wasn't a possibility, a whole lot of the blood it was pumping found its way down to my cock, making it twitch and swell against my sweaty thigh.

"I just said it's damn hot." He smiled again, threatening me with cardiac overload. And that voice! It was deep and resonant with just a hint of a drawl.

"You got that right," I managed to say. My usual store of chatter had deserted me, leaving me floundering for something — anything! — to say. Fortunately, the hunk kept the conversational ball rolling.

"Off to a meeting?" he asked, rather pointedly eyeing my tie and the suit jacket I was carrying.

"Not this time," I replied. "I got lucky — my boss gave me the afternoon off."

"Good for you. I just got the rest of the month off. The OSHA inspector was snooping around the site I'm working on and shut us down for some piddling safety violation. Good thing I paid for this when I ordered it." He tapped the big box with his foot. "Otherwise, I would've been up shit creek."

"What is it?" I asked, unable to make any sense of the foreign words printed on the box.

"New stereo. State of the art. At least it damned well better be, considering what I paid for it." He looked out the window, then reached over and pulled the cord to signal the driver. "End of the line," he said. "Have a good day off, man."

"Thanks," I replied, my heart sinking at the thought of his getting away. Then fate intervened. The bus pulled up to the curb, and he began piling smaller boxes on top of the big one on the floor. It was too good an opportunity to let pass. "Let me help you with those," I offered eagerly.

"You don't have to do that," he replied, shaking his head. "Damn!" One of the smaller boxes started slipping. I caught it.

"No problem. No use breaking the damned thing — especially since it's paid for."

"Good point. Thanks."

"Lead the way." I followed him off the bus and along the street to a small brick apartment building. We climbed the stairs to the third floor and walked down the hall to 317. He unlocked the door, pushed it open, and stood aside for me to enter. I walked down a long hallway into a sunny living room.

"Just put it down right over here," he said, indicating a table under the front window. "Thanks a lot, guy. I really appreciate the help."

"No problem." That wasn't quite true. There was a slight problem — now that I was here, I didn't want to leave. I was searching for a reason to stay when he suggested one.

"Could I offer you a beer, uh...gee, I don't even know your name."

"Mike," I said. "And yes, I'd love a beer."

"Great, Mike. I'm Drew." We shook hands. "Make yourself comfortable." He gestured toward the couch and disappeared into the kitchen. I draped my coat over the back of a chair, removed my tie, and sat down. Drew returned with two cold beers, handed me one, then crouched on the floor and began ripping open boxes. When he had all the components spread out, inspiration struck. I offered to help put the stereo together, he accepted, and a couple of minutes later we were both kneeling in front of a bookcase, surrounded by connector cables and speaker wire.

"I don't want to set this thing down on its face. Looks like I need an extra pair of hands, Mike." I knelt behind him and reached around his shoulders, holding the component while he attached a series of color-coded wires to it. It took Drew a long time, but I was in no hurry. My arms were stretched out alongside his, and my crotch was pressing against the small of his back. The bittersweet aroma of sweat and musk tickled my nostrils. The effect on me was immediate — it stiffened my prick as if somebody had shoved a steel bar into it. I've got a pretty big dick, and my condition was too obvious to go unnoticed.

"Is it my imagination, or is something getting pretty lumpy back there?" he asked, his voice sounding different — pissed off or turned-on, I wasn't sure which.

"Lumpy?" I croaked.

"Yeah," he retorted, turning his head. "*Big* and lumpy." He grinned at me, and my apprehension evaporated, clearing the field for lust. "What are the chances that a tall, handsome businessman might be interested in tangling with a raunchy construction jock?"

"About a hundred percent," I said. I set the component on the shelf and slipped my hands inside the bagged-out armholes of his shirt, making contact with hot, slippery bare skin. I splayed my fingers out over his pecs and squeezed — they were every bit as solid as they looked. I rubbed his tits with the balls of my thumbs, and a soft moan of pleasure escaped him.

"You like to kiss?" he asked. Rather than answer, I demonstrated. I felt the pressure of his lips, then the hot, moist point of his tongue as it slipped into my mouth. My tongue poked back and parried his advances, twining around the sweet wriggling invader like a vine.

Without breaking the kiss, I rose to my feet, pulling Drew along with me. Still pressed tight against his back — my prick now snug against the lush curve of his ass — I pushed his undershirt up into his armpits so that I could explore his torso without anything to impede my progress. Drew's belly curved out slightly, hot and fuzzy against my palms. I tugged the curls around his navel, and his tongue shot deep into my throat.

My hands followed the curve of his belly downward, slipping inside the confines of his faded jeans, to his groin. Sweat-soaked pubes curled around my fingers, then I started touching tube. My fingers kept on moving, wrapping around the hot stalk of his prick. It flexed when I squeezed, and so did the globes of his ass, pressing back against my dick, offering irresistible temptation.

I unbuckled his belt and popped the buttons on his fly, then pushed down, shucking his pants onto his thick, furry thighs. I broke the kiss and followed the indentation of his spine from his neck to his tailbone. His butt was gorgeous — two muscular, pale, beautifully rounded globes of flesh, dusted with more dark fuzz. I licked him from his waist all the way down to where his cheeks cut back into his thighs. Then I centered myself and began sniffing around his hot crack. I wedged my tongue into the steamy crevice but couldn't quite get to where I wanted to be. Hell, I didn't see any DO NOT ENTER signs posted, so I planted my hands on his cakes and applied a little pressure. When I pried the mounds of sweaty flesh apart, Drew leaned forward and braced his hands on one of the shelves in the bookcase.

The move exposed a moist cleft with a tight brown pucker tucked at the base. A pair of furry pink balls dangled below, opening up enough possibilities to dazzle my horny brain. I nuzzled his nuts, licking the sweat off them, as I fumbled with the buttons and zippers that were standing between me and my nakedness. By the time I had achieved my goal, Drew's balls were rising up to hug the base of his cock.

"Nice," Drew purred, reaching back between his legs and fingering the bulging knob perched on the end of my hard-on. "That is one hell of a big prick."

"Thanks," I replied, tensing my groin muscles and making my pecker rise high in the air. Drew squeezed his fingers tight, and a big glob of goo oozed out the tip. He smeared it around the swollen cap, making it glisten.

"And this is one hell of a hot asshole." I demonstrated my sincerity by kissing the moist, quivering ring of muscle, then driving my tongue through it and up into the sweet heat of his chute. I wriggled my tongue, and Drew wriggled his ass. I had a feeling we were going to make a great team. I gripped his strong thighs and started eating him out, lubing him up with my spit.

While I was rimming him, Drew wasn't content to remain idle. He doubled over, grabbed his ankles, and managed to get his head back between his knees till he was able to make mouth contact with my cock. I moved in closer and thrust my hips forward, and he took my cock right down to the root — no mean feat, considering the size of my hang. The dude had a deep throat and knew exactly how to treat a man's meat. He slipped his hands under my ass and proceeded to fuck himself down the throat with my dick, all the while keeping his own ass pushed back so I and my tongue could have full and free access to his hot little slot.

"Want to fuck me, Mike?" he asked, his voice muffled by the throbbing obstruction of my cock.

"I could be convinced," I panted, licking his crack, the sensation of his ass pucker's pulsating against my tongue sending shivers up and down my spine. Drew straightened up, turned around, and hauled me to my feet, enveloping me in his brawny arms. He started kissing me again, and the feel of his soft lips — not to mention all those big, hard muscles shifting under his sweaty skin — was an incredible turn-on.

I zeroed in on his hot butt again. I smacked his cheeks, slipped two fingers into his crack, then crammed them into his slimy little bung, right up to the webbing. That accomplished, I began massaging the hard knot of his prostate. The muscle-bound stud practically melted, his springy ass ring squeezing my fingers tight.

I maneuvered him toward the couch and got him sprawled out over the cushions, facedown, left leg drawn up under him, his right knee braced against the floor. I stood there, staring down at him, eyeing his shaggy crack and the defenseless spit-slicked, slightly gaping hole I was poised to plunder. The sunlight was pouring through the windows, golden shafts of it slashing the couch, making the sweat on Drew glisten like crystal beads.

"In the drawer," Drew panted, pointing at a cabinet against the far wall. "I think you'll find some that fit."

"These?" I asked, holding up a foil packet, trying not to laugh. "Elephant brand?"

"I got them from a buddy as a joke. I told him I'd find a man to fill them someday. Looks like today might be the day." My big dick rose high, buoyed by the compliment. "Come on over here, stud," Drew continued. "Let me bag that dude for you." I stood at the edge of the couch, watching Drew as he opened the packet and rolled the lubed safe out along the shaft of my hard-on. "There we go, Mike. Nice and snug."

"I've got my eye on something else that's going to be nice and snug," I quipped, kneeling on the couch between his spread legs. I reached under him and gripped his cock and balls, pulling them back so I could see them. The move tipped his ass up, bringing his puckered lips within range. I tucked one of the sofa pillows under him, braced my hands on his back, and lowered my hips.

My knob touched the target, and Drew bucked. I watched the head of my piece disappear, then held steady as Drew shoved his ass up the long, thick shaft, not stopping until my bush was tickling his crack. He wiggled his butt, and I could feel the heat of his insides all along my meat. I yelped with pleasure, then fell on him, wrapping my arms around his thick chest as I started to fuck.

Fucking a man is a real turn-on, no matter how you put it. The thought of having about 210 pounds of sweating, flexing muscle pinned under my 167 pounds, totally at the mercy of my pistoning prong, was putting me right up there next to ecstasy. No doubt about it, Drew was loving my big, hard cock. He was moaning and whimpering, his body heaving and shuddering as I plowed his hole, driving in deep, then pulling out till I could feel his hole chewing on my knob.

"Come with me, man," I cooed, nibbling his earlobe. I pushed in deep, slipped my hands under him, coaxed him up off the couch. "Now," I said, standing behind him, my torso pressed tight against his broad back, "show off for me, Drew. Flex those hot muscles for me."

"Huh?"

"You heard me, man." I cock-walked him over to a mirror that hung on the wall beside the door to the hallway. I stood behind him, pumping his ass while he raised his arms and flexed, popping up a pair of cannonball-size biceps, complete with deep-cut striations and thick veins that snaked just below the surface of the skin. I felt him up, wrist to elbow, elbow to shoulder, squeezing the unyielding flesh, feeling his power pulsing beneath my fingertips. I tugged the damp curls in his armpits, then turned my attention to his pecs.

His whole body knotted when I latched onto his big tits. I pinched them a second time, savoring the spasms that shook him as I tugged on the little knobs that crowned the mounds of muscle on his chest. When my fingers trailed down the slightly convex wall of his gut, heading dickward, his hips kicked into overdrive, slamming his ass back against my pelvis, riding hard and fast on my throbbing cock.

"Nice," I growled, touching the tip of his piece, smearing the lube leaking out of him onto his trigger. He bucked harder, and his dick rose straight up against his gut. I cupped his balls in my palm, pulled them up against his flexing shaft, let him hump them till they were coated with his sticky juice. Drew was panting now, chest heaving, his asshole doing a virtuoso number on my meat.

"Down on your hands and knees," I barked, suddenly inspired to change positions. We hit the floor without missing a beat, Drew's ass high, his head resting on his crossed forearms.

"Fuck me, Mike," he gasped, looking up at me through lust-glazed eyes. "Fuck me hard." I obliged, slamming against him, spearing him with every throbbing inch of cock I had under my command. He grunted, the muscles in his shoulders knotting.

I fell on top of him, hips pumping frantically, my ass rising and falling as I threw all of my strength into the fuck. The harder I plowed, the noisier Drew got, egging me on to new levels of frenzy.

"Drive that big horse cock up my ass, man," he urged. "That's it! Harder! Deeper! Shit, yeah. Fuck me!" I thrust and bucked, found the knot of his prostate up in all that convulsing heat, and battered it mercilessly. "Oh, man, that's it. Fuck my ass hard. Hit that hot spot. Fuck it. Oh, yeah. Right there. Yes! Fuck, fuck, fuck!"

I reached under him, grabbed his dick, and began flogging it. I was about to lose it and was determined that he was going to go over the top with me. I wasn't disappointed. The shuddering in his channel increased as I pumped the come up out of him with my fist. I could feel the contractions as his orgasm began, his bowels grabbing my hard-on like a clenched fist. I pumped him that last, magic time, then collapsed on top of him, filling the rubber with my juices as he filled my palm with warm lube.

After it was all over, we humped a few more minutes, just for the hell of it — long, slow, lazy strokes, extending the pleasure for as long as possible. I didn't give up till my hard-on went limp and was finally ejected, his ass ring spitting me out into the cold.

We shared another beer, then Drew rummaged around, found a CD, and put it on the changer. We sat back to listen, only to hear an insistent buzz under the soft strains of the jazz. "Shit," Drew muttered, raising his head off my shoulder and glaring at the machine. "We must have a loose connection or a crossed wire."

"Oh, well," I sighed, rising from the couch and walking over to the components. "I guess we'll just have to check out those connections all over again."

"Yeah," Drew agreed, easing between me and the shelf unit and then crouching down, his ass against my belly. "Every damned one of them, Mike." He reached back and fisted my dick. "Every damned one."

First Story (Rough)
by Lew Dwight

I'm supposed to tell a story, but I'm not sure if I can, as I've never done it before. Especially writing it.

I have this true story I thought I might want to use but didn't know if I could, because I didn't think you'd believe me; but then I got to thinking how you said fiction's still fiction even if it's true, so maybe it will be good for the assignment.

The only thing is, I don't know what you'll think about me writing this story (it's about my first day at school). You might wonder what kind of a person I am, going through this. I don't want you to think that I think anything about you either by writing this. But anyway, I'm thinking of what you said about writing what you know, and this is about it.

The more I think about it, the more worried I am about embarrassing myself (or you), and the more likely I'll do some of what my grandmother called fudging the truth. She said you're fudging it when you tell a lie. When I begin to fudge here, I'll let you know, so maybe in our next conference we can talk about it. I'll say when I'm fudging, I just won't tell you what it is I'm fudging.

There was this kid who lived up north on a potato farm. His father made him know how to drive a tractor from the age of twelve to harvest potatoes. He knew a lot about potatoes and stuff, but he was bored because he was always alone. Not many kids his age in town, so he learned to play with himself. By this I mean he learned at a young age to lie on his back on the hay bales in the barn whenever he was feeling a little jittery and pull his pants down and massage himself, which was real relaxing. His dad had these big industrial-strength rubber bands he used for holding equipment together in the barn, and the boy discovered that they felt nice wrapped around his penis while he played with it. Never got caught either. This shows what a clever boy he was.

Dad was never too keen on him going away to college but wanted him to stay on the farm and learn about the business of raising potatoes and settle down there. The boy had other things on his mind. He figured going off to college would be a good way of finding himself. He decided this one day while lying on his back in the haymow stretching the rubber band over his penis.

He got accepted at Southern _____ Technical College (here I am fudging a little already), which is about a four-and-a-half-hour drive downstate. They have some interesting classes, even though he doesn't know what his major is going to be. When you're a kid who likes to lie on his back in the haymow and put a rubber band around your penis, it makes you think a lot about things you don't normally think about, but when it's all over and you're feeling kind of shitty afterward, you just push it all to the back of your mind. Well, being away at college allows those things you've pushed to the back of your mind to sort of creep forward and stay there, until maybe you'll get a chance to talk to somebody about them.

He was lucky enough to have his own car, a beater that he bought for fifty dollars from his uncle in Aroostook with no inspection sticker. He packed his stuff into it and drove down to the college a week before classes started, to familiarize himself with the place. Dad wasn't too happy with him driving down here because he thinks Portland is a little too racy, like Gomorrah or something, but what's he going to do, say I can't go when I'm already eighteen? It's a bitch having a father who looks at everything you do like it gives off some kind of bad smell. I used to think a lot about what would happen if he came up to the haymow while I was busying myself up there with the rubber band. Gives me chills just thinking about it.

Things didn't get off to the best start. I was there kind of early — in fact, I was the first one in the dorms — so I had no idea what to do, where to go, who my roommate was. I was feeling alone, just like I did up north in the country with nothing but potatoes all around. I was feeling real jittery, like, *Oh, shit, this is all a big mistake,* the dorm room so square and gross and dingy, with nicks in the dressers and desks, beds that squeaked. I went and lay down on the other kid's bed (whoever he was), a bare mattress stained with about a thousand other boys, and thought about him and what kind of friendship we might have, whether he would be some kind of jock or nerd or a nice kid. I was feeling hungry because the cafeteria wasn't open yet, and I was eating Hi-Ho crackers out of the box and getting drinks of water out of the drinking fountain. So my stomach's growling, and I'm lying in this pathetic room feeling shitty because no one's around, when I just push my pants down around my ankles and begin masturbating right on the kid's bed with all the lights on. I have my rubber band with me, which I double up and stretch around my dick at the base and up under my balls like a tourniquet. It hurts like hell at first, digging in and pulling the hair, but once I get it adjusted I like it because it squeezes everything up toward the head and makes my dick stand up big and hard and red as a Pontiac potato with blue veins wiggling out all over it. It's so big and sensitive that I almost can't stand touching it, but I do touch it, slowly and lightly, feeling every vein and bump and moving my soft fist over the bulbous head in polishing motions until all that jitteriness gathers up inside and explodes out all over my face. It strikes hot against my eye and chin three or four times (I'm careful to close my eyes at the last minute), then tapers off to little jets that make it only up to my chest.

Christ, do I feel like hell afterward. I need a couple of clean T-shirts to wipe up with, and I end up having to scrub stains off the mattress because a few of those shots went over my head. But you know how come stains are — you rub and rub, and they stay wet, so now I've already left my mark on my roommate's mattress. (I realize that I've changed the *he* to *I* here, but I guess I'll leave it that way for now and talk to you about it in our conference next week to see what you think is better, the *he* or the *I*.) Anyway, this doesn't make me feel any better. I'm hungry, I can't sleep, the room is bare and ugly, I'm feeling bad because I came on my roommate's bed already and can't get the stain out, it's late, and I'm still jittery as hell. So I decide to go out for a drive around town to maybe calm down and think what I want to do with my life.

Of course, after that drive from up north, I'm out of gas. I find this one gas station lit up like a spaceship — until I drive up, that is, and then the lights begin going out. I pull up to the pumps and ask the kid working there if he'll just take me as his last customer even though it's closed, because I'm almost on E and there's no place else open. He just looks at me a minute like, *You think you look like somebody I should stay open for?* He's this kind of tall kid with either a goatee starting or he forgot to shave, the whiskers outlining his mouth and chin giving him this mean-dog look. His hair's buzzed so close to his scalp, you can see this white squiggly scar on his head above his right ear. "I'd really appreciate it," I say, kind of dumblike.

He just comes around and flips open my gas flap, and I can hear him fumbling around for the cap. "How much?" he says, and when I ask him if he'll fill it, he just mumbles "Christ," the pump giving a loud dink as he turns it on. The nozzle clunks into the hole, and I listen to the hum of the pump and smell the gas vapors coming out. I scoot down in my seat a little so I can see him in my side mirror pumping the gas. His work shirt is rolled back tightly to the shoulders, and I can tell he's done this to show off the homemade tattoos that look like he drew them on himself with a Bic pen: a star in a circle, an upside-down cross, and at the shoulder, FUCK backwards. He's gripping the handle like a gun, like he means business.

I'm so busy looking at that thick hairless arm of graffiti holding the nozzle that I don't notice him right away glaring back at me in the mirror. What he must see in the mirror is my eyes wide with the jitters fixed on his arm, then looking up and seeing him looking back at me, then looking away too quickly. Oops.

"This thing don't hold much." Clank, rattle, clap. Done. He puts the hose away, then comes around and stands at my open window. I'm looking straight at this worn, peeling belt buckle that's a screaming death's head. "Where's your inspection sticker?" I hear this sort of gravel sound in his voice.

"I just bought this car off my uncle."

"If you get caught, you're fucked."

"Is there a fine?"

"Is there a fine? Fuck yes, there's a fine. Why do you think they want you to drive around with an inspection sticker?"

"What should I do?"

He's quiet; I can just hear him thinking to himself (in his gravelly voice), *What a stupid fucker, asking me what he should do.* "We can do inspections here. Come back tomorrow, and we'll have a look at it."

I get out my wallet and pull out a bill. His hand reaches down for my money, his fingers grubby, his nails chewed clean off to the pink meat. Gouged across the back of his hand, one letter on each knuckle, his favorite word again: F-U-C-K.

"Shit. I'm afraid to drive back to campus now."

He slides the bill out of my hand. "You going to that fucking hole too?" He leans over and looks in, his eyes giv-

ing the inside of the car a quick once-over like he's seeing
if there's anything to swipe. His teeth are kind of spaced
out like a pumpkin's, and with that goatee starting, he
looks like a bad dog that'll bite a chunk out of your ass if
you so much as look at him cross-eyed. "I'm in this program where I'm allowed to hold down a job and take a few
courses if I stay out of trouble."

He stands back up, with his waist up to my open window. He pulls out this big wallet on a chain and opens it
and puts my money inside. I wait for change, that death's
head screaming at me at eye level only about eight inches
away. I sit back in my seat and lock eyes with it. He seems
to be taking his time with that change, standing still at my
window like he's thinking something over. "Drive over to
the garage," he says finally. "We'll have a look at it now."

I don't know about this guy. He didn't give me my
change, and now he wants to inspect my car after closing
with no one around. He's in this program where he can
hold down a job and take a few classes if he stays out of
trouble. He's got a white scar above his ear and FUCK
carved into his shoulder and across the top of his left
hand. I'm so jittery now, I could puke, but I just put it into
gear and pull numbly up to the garage door while he goes
to the booth and turns out the rest of the lights in the lot.
I have a feeling this boy from the farm is about to learn
something about the city.

(I'm wondering what you're thinking about me right
now, like, *What a dummy, getting himself into such a situation*, but like I said, I'll be fudging some parts that
might be embarrassing, but I'll let you know when.)

After all the lights outside are out, he goes into the
garage and turns on the light in there, then raises up the
garage door from inside with one big upward yank. I drive
in, thinking I'm going to get my inspection sticker so I can
drive back to campus without worrying about the cops,
and he slams the door down behind me. I drive over the
lift and turn off the key, and he comes around and opens
my door for me and stands back with those big arms fold-

ed and those tattooed shoulders bulging out of the rolled sleeves. He says, "I saw you looking at me like you want to suck my dick."

"What?"

"What?" he says, sort of grinning. He takes an easy look out to the empty lot, like he's confident no one's going to show up, and his hand goes for the peeling death's head. He scoots down a little to unhook the buckle from behind, then pops open the top button — and it's like his dick just grows up out of his work pants, the zipper falling open by itself, and suddenly this big red arrow-shaped knob is sticking out. The pants and belt fall to the concrete floor with a clank, and he rolls his underpants down to his thighs. "You fucking college boys. You come out here all wide-eyed, not even knowing what you want, just to stare at my dick and my tattoos, looking like you want to fall on your knees and beg for it. I know what the fuck you're looking at."

"But I was looking at your belt buckle!" There's this spring-loaded ache in my groin so that I can't stand to be sitting there.

"Quit your fucking lying. Just take a look at this hog and tell me you don't wanna suck the piss out of it."

It's big and red and hairy, fat at the head and even fatter at the base, and he's got one big ball hanging lower than the other in his baggy-skinned sac, and when that underwear comes down, the meat just sort of falls forward like a plank and points at me, bobbing in place, the big purple tip like the split stem end of an overripe plum dripping something clear and syrupy in a single unbroken strand that touches the floor. It scares the shit out of me, it's so big, like he's just pulled some animal out of his trousers. That saying is so perfect — trouser trout — only this is more like an eel, mad as hell so the veins are popping out all down its wicked length and drooling at the mouth like it wants to come at you and take a nasty bite out of you.

By now I'm hurting, having never seen another guy's pecker so up close like this, only my own with the rubber band clamped around it looking like some kind of swollen boo-boo compared to this hairy monster staring at me now. I don't know, maybe it was just that the whole thing seemed bigger than it really was, being the first time I'd ever laid eyes on one, but it sure looked big to me.

"Get your little pussy ass down here and kiss this fucking pig on the mouth." Such a way he had with words.

"I don't know about this," I say, my boner feeling like it's about to break in half in my drawers.

"You little fucking liar," he says, reaching in and pulling me out of the car by my ear.

"Ouch!" I say, falling to my knees before him and losing my balance. I grab on to the only thing within reach, that telescope of meat, something going splat-splat against my forehead, then splat-splat against my face. I let go and fall back to wipe the come off my face with my arm while he finishes shooting off against the side of my car. He just laughs, his dick rising and falling with each shot, my car looking like someone's thrown eggs against it, those loads of his slumping down and sliding off in white lumps. "Jeez," I say.

"Guess I got fucking carried away," he says, giving his dick a few flopping shakes and grinning. "C'mere, punk. I'm not done yet." He lifts me by the shirt and plops me in front of him, that beast wavering drunkenly between us, slobbering. He sort of fist-levers the wet tip down my face, kind of roll-sliding the fat, greasy head down between my eyes and around my nose and back and forth over my mouth, smearing my face with more come. "C'mon," he says in that gravelly voice. "Open, I said. Stretch those little college lips of yours around my fuck stick."

So I'm kneeling here holding this double fist of dick up to my mouth like a beggar at a banquet, you know, stuffing my face, wondering how I ever got here and if it's really happening, when all the sudden he goes "Awfuck-umgunna—" but before I can pull away, he lets loose a couple of loads in my mouth, and I'm flooded with this kind of hot, acrid, nasty taste — but kind of nice too —

and it's still shooting away when I take my mouth off to gag — shooting in my face a few more times before I can maneuver it away, shooting over my left shoulder, shooting into my hair, shooting against the car again, gathering up on the glass and sliding off in lumps, and I'm thinking, *Jesus, this is like when I was a kid playing in the water sprinkler Dad set up on the lawn during a drought* — it would be going flit-flit-flit as I tried to put my face up to it for a drink, water spraying up my nose and making me cough until Dad came out and smacked me across the back of my fool head.

"Fuck. Guess I'm really trigger-happy tonight."

Wiping an arm down my face, I say, "I guess. Want me to try something?"

"What you got in mind, you little fuck?"

I fish that rubber band out of my pocket and show him. "It works good to hold it back," I say.

He just laughs and pushes his big dick at me, like, *Sure, I bet.* I know I won't be able to double the rubber band up like I do on myself, so I hold one end up under that low-riding sac of hairy balls of his, then loop the other end up over the top — and I really have to stretch it over the big, fat, wet head — then as I'm crossing it over and bringing it back down — snap! — it slips and snaps into place. "Awfuck! What the fuck are you trying to do, man?" His dick is so big — bigger than the biggest russet potato I've ever dug up — that the rubber band digs into the base like baling twine squeezing a bale of hay together, and he starts going like, "Take that fucking thing off, man!" the dick already ballooning out with blood and getting purple and shiny all over like it's filled up about as far as it can go. "That thing's too small, goddammit!"

He tries picking it off himself with his nail-bitten fingers but just ends up ripping some hair out. His eyes bulge, and beads of sweat begin to form in his blond eyebrows, but when I grab on to it and start tonguing the big puffy head, he changes his tune and goes like, "Aw-w-w s-s-sh-h-h..." and staggers back, eyes rolling back into his head, stum-

bling in his pants around his ankles and falling to the concrete floor, my mouth on him the whole time. Basically, he
wants to pop but can't. When I think he's had about
enough, I try to pick the rubber band out of the gutter it's
cut into the flesh at the base but can't get my finger under
it, so I try using my teeth, biting into the rubber and
pulling away, and as soon as it comes free, "Unnhh!" he
goes, letting off spurts of come that arc up over the hood
of the car my uncle sold me and splat up against the windshield like somebody's throwing boiled spaghetti against
the glass. I notice that if I let the rubber band snap to
again — "Son of a bitch!" — the load cuts off like when
you kink a hose — "What the fuck are you doing?" — the
flow trickling down to a thick dribble like glue over the
side and into his hair — "Get it off!" — and all over the
rubber band so I can't even pick it away from him with my
teeth, and he gets up on his knees — "Get it off!" — dick
dark and swollen like a zucchini now — "I said, get that
fucking thing off me!" — and starts boxing me.

"Wait a minute!" I say, and when I clamp my teeth
around the rubber band and pull — bip! — it goes sailing
off like a broken fan belt. I'm looking after my rubber
band. Meanwhile, he's dropping onto the floor, and when
I look down he's passed out on his back, shooting little
spurts of blood against his work shirt.

And now here's where I have to do a little fudging, like
I told you. I look around: I'm a mess, my car's a mess. His
come's dripping off everything and coming to rest in little
puddles on the concrete floor. He's crumpled over, that fat
pecker going flabby with a deep stripe cut into it where the
rubber band was, and also there's the fact that blood's
coming out of it. Shit! I have to get out of there, so I look
for my rubber band — it flew off to the other side of the
garage — and pull open the garage door and get in my car
and drive out of there, shaking like hell.

So that's the story of my little adventure on my first day
at college — though college hadn't really started yet and

that's not even all that happened that night. You notice I ended up leaving without an inspection sticker. On the way back to campus, this cop pulls me over for driving erratically, and he's like, "Where's your inspection sticker, son?" and I'm like, "I don't know, sir," and he's like, "So what are we going to do about that, son," looping his thumbs behind his big belt — but that's a whole other story. I've had to do some fudging, but I won't tell you what it is I've fudged. The story has a punch line too, and this is why I didn't think I'd be able to write about it, because it's so weird, but like you said, life is weirder than fiction.

A couple of days go by, and people start to show up on campus. One day there's this knock on my door, and I know my roommate's finally here (I already flipped his mattress over to the other side). The door opens — and guess who limps into my room. Guess who my roommate is. He's someone who's allowed to hold down a job and take a few classes if he stays out of trouble!

So you see, he's okay. The doctor told him it was just a rupture of some kind and will heal in a few weeks. I can only imagine what it was like for him to go to the hospital with a bleeding dick that looks like it's been nearly pinched off at the base. It's black-and-blue now, and he can hardly walk, and as you can imagine he can't do much with it right now. But he keeps telling me — he sits on his stained mattress across the room and points at me while he says in his gravelly voice — "You just wait, you little fucker. You wait till I'm better. You got something coming to you, punk." I'm a little concerned about what he plans on doing, but so far he's been a pretty good roommate.

So this is the draft of my story. I'm curious to see what you think about it and look forward to our conference next week to talk about all the fudging and the *he* changing to *I*. It ought to be interesting. I thought about rolling this up and giving it to you with a rubber band stretched around it to make some point. I'm not sure what the point is, but there ought to be one.

Road Test
by Kevin E. Barra

Missy grabbed my hard dick with both hands and licked her lips. "Shove it in my mouth, Kevin," she panted. "I want to suck your big meat till you scream." I couldn't believe it — she was gonna give me head! I lay down on the backseat of the Lexus and watched my throbbing cock disappear into Missy's soft, warm mouth. It was incredible...it was extreme...it was just a fucking dream!

I woke up with my alarm going off and my prick stretching my Jockey shorts into a painfully tight tent. Damn, that had been hot! I would have blown my wad in about thirty seconds if it hadn't been for that friggin' alarm clock. I slapped off the buzzer. Tonight was the night. Maybe. I rolled onto my stomach and pumped my stiffy against the mattress, pretending my pillow was Missy's hooters. Oh, yeah, I was gonna fuck that pussy hard tonight, man—

"Kevin, honey?" My bedroom door swung open. My mother. I froze, my cock quickly shriveling from eight to one-and-one-half inches. "The Department of Public Safety closes at noon on Saturdays. We'd better get going if you're going to get that license today."

"Okay," I mumbled around the pillow. I had to get my driver's license today. I just had to. Homecoming was tonight. I'd just turned eighteen, which put me two years behind everybody else in my class, even the geeks. Ever since I was sixteen, I'd been catching rides with my friends or taking my bike to cover up the fact that I couldn't drive a car. I'd failed the road test twice in the past six months. How fuckin' embarrassing. The second time I almost passed but screwed up parallel parking right at the end. Nobody made a big deal out of it, but I was the star half-back on the varsity soccer team, and I felt like I *should* be able to get a goddamned license before I graduated.

My dad promised to loan me his new Lexus to drive Missy to the dance tonight, which meant we'd be parking in style afterward. She'd been teasing and hinting around that I was going to get some action tonight, but if she had to drive her CRX, I could hang it up. Everything was riding on my passing this morning.

On the way to the test, I started worrying I'd get the gnarly old tub-of-guts state trooper who'd flunked me last time. It's hard enough to drive with a uniformed cop ordering you around in the passenger seat, but this old fart is about eighty and totally mean. When I bumped up against the flag in the parallel parking part of the test, he practically bit my head off, screaming about how I'd just smashed somebody's headlights and bullshit like that.

I'd already passed the written test, and they hold your score for a year, so there was nothing left for me to do but sign up and wait for the trooper to call my name. My mom was busy reading a Jackie Collins book and couldn't tell how nervous I was. In fact, the Pop-Tarts and orange juice I'd had for breakfast felt like they were about to come up. I took off for the rest room and locked myself in the first stall, ready to hurl.

The door to the men's room opened, and I heard boots clumping on the floor. One of the state troopers? I could just see myself puking in front of whoever was going to give me the test. I took a deep breath. The sick feeling was passing. I sat on the toilet and pulled my feet up so they wouldn't show.

I heard a belt buckle jingle, then a loud zip. Whoever it was seemed to be standing at the urinals. So how come I didn't hear pissing?

I leaned back and put my eye up to the crack between the side of the stall and the back wall. Holy fuck! It *was* a trooper. A big, strapping young dude I'd never seen before. He was standing in front of one of the urinals, but instead of taking a whiz, he was beating his huge cock, squeezing and stroking it with his hand.

I've seen guys fooling around in the locker room and at scout camp and never really given a shit one way or the other. But this was different. I don't know whether it was the uniform or 'cause he looked like Christopher Reeve and you'd never expect in a billion years that he'd be choking his fuckin' chicken in the men's room of the Texas Department of Public Safety or just that his dick was the biggest one I'd ever seen in the flesh, but my own cock was enlarging slowly but surely.

Was he going to come? I stopped breathing and slipped my hand into the pocket of my shorts just to check and see if I really, truly had a boner over another dude. Yup. The trooper spat in his hand and kept whacking away. With his other hand he pulled his underwear down, and a pair of hairless balls rolled into sight. Shit! I really felt like jacking off myself. I started to undo my pants. Then the rest room door banged open.

"Hey, Randy," a middle-aged guy I knew as a desk clerk said to the trooper, who hit flush right away and shoved his meat into his pants. He said hey and walked out. The other guy started to take a leak. I didn't feel sick anymore, but there was a new kind of feeling in my stomach, kind of like when Missy let me suck her tits for the first time, but stronger, weirder. I kept seeing the trooper's hard, fat dick and the way his jaw clenched while he beat off. I stood up and pointed my boner down my leg so it wouldn't show. I counted to ten after the clerk left and went out.

My mom looked up from her book. "Are you okay, dear?"

"Yeah, fine."

"Is Kevin here?" a crusty old voice asked. I looked up, and there was the old fart holding a clipboard. Damn! I got up and started shuffling forward.

"Good luck, Kev," my mother said, patting me on the ass. I followed Slim Pickens into the parking lot and showed him my permit, registration, and insurance. Then I had to prove that the blinkers and brake lights worked. I couldn't let this lard-ass coot stand in my way. I was gonna get this friggin' license if it killed me.

He got in the car. "Start the vehicle, son," he said. I hated being called "son." I turned the key.

Then all of a sudden someone shouted, "Bubba, phone call!" Randy, the well-hung dude from the rest room, came up to the car. "They say it's long-distance."

"Shit," Bubba drawled. "You're gonna have to hold on, son." He unbuckled his seat belt and pulled it off his fat stomach.

"I'll take care of the kid," Randy said. "Don't worry about it, Bubba."

"Fine with me," Bubba snorted. He got out, and Randy got in.

"I'm Officer Timmons," he said. We shook hands — the same hand he'd had his hard cock in a few minutes before. He put on a pair of mirrored sunglasses and adjusted the seat. "Let's roll, Kevin."

I started the car and pulled out of the parking lot like he told me to. Left turn, right turn, red light, green light. I tried to keep my mind on what he was telling me. But when I turned into a residential area, he stretched out his left arm and laid it on the back of my seat. For a second I felt his hand brush against my neck, and I started to get that weird dizzy feeling. I kept checking the speedometer to make sure I wasn't going over the limit, and sometimes I sort of looked over at Officer Timmons. His legs were spread wide apart, and his full lips were set in a line so that I couldn't tell if he was bored or annoyed or happy or what.

Who or what had he been thinking about while he was playing with his dick? Was he still thinking about it? Did he have a big old hard-on under those khakis? The air conditioner was on, but I was starting to sweat. We were coming out of the subdivision, but instead of having me turn around and drive back the way we came, he told me to keep going. In a minute we were on the outskirts of town. Something bogus was going on. This road test was already taking twice as long as my other two.

"Make a right up ahead," Officer Timmons said. I slowed down and turned onto this unpaved road that went into some trees for about fifty feet. There was some construction project somebody hadn't finished, the framework of a house or garage or something. I braked and shifted into reverse.

"Wait a minute, Kevin," he said.

I looked him in the face for the first time since we'd started driving. His skin was smooth and still tan from summer. I couldn't see a damn thing behind those sunglasses, though. I swallowed. My throat was dry, but my palms were so wet that they were almost slipping off the steering wheel.

"You've been doing a good job today, Kevin. There's been only one mistake so far that I can see."

"What?" I asked nervously.

"You've been staring at my crotch since I got in the car. I think I have to take off points for that."

"Wait a minute, man, you got it all wrong!" I protested. This was a nightmare! I was gonna end up in jail instead of between Missy's thighs. "I wasn't checking you out."

He nodded. "Then you won't mind if I check *you* out to make sure you're not hard." I didn't know what to say, but he wasn't waiting for an answer. He undid the seat belt, turned off the car, and planted his hand between my legs. It didn't take Perry Mason to find my cock: It was making a huge bulge in my baggy shorts, and it only got bigger when he started to massage it. I'd never been this turned-on ever, but I was also scared shitless.

"Officer Timmons, dude—" I started to say.

"You better call me Randy if we're going to suck each other's dicks." He took off the sunglasses. I looked into his light brown eyes and knew I wanted it as bad as he did. He put his hand on his chest. "Take off my shirt," he said.

My hands were shaking as I undid the buttons, mainly because *his* hand was working down the waistband on my pants. By the time I had the shirt open, he had two fingers in the fly of my underwear, tickling my rock-hard boner, pressing up against my dick slit, which was already wet and tingling. I grabbed Randy's white tank-top undershirt and pushed it up over his tan washboard stomach, then lowered my hands to his belt buckle. I felt him pull my dick out of my Jockeys and start to rub it up and down. Fuck, I was gonna shoot if he didn't—

Randy put his hand on the back of my neck and forced my head down onto his crotch. "Eat me," he growled. I buried my face between his long, sturdy legs and licked and slurped on his penis, which was burning a hole through his uniform pants. Randy moved my hand up to his massive pec. I squeezed the firm, slightly hairy flesh and pinched his big, stiff nipple.

He hooked his thumbs under my waistband and pulled my shorts and underwear down to my knees. How the hell had this happened — a state trooper feeling up my bare ass while I unzipped his fly and hauled out his flaming-hot cock? "Lick it, Kevin," he ordered. "Just pretend it's a big, tasty ice-cream cone."

I gave the shaft an experimental lick, and he moaned, loving it. I put my lips around the wide rosy-colored head and ran my tongue over it. It tasted great! I had to have more and slowly went down on the thick meat.

"Oh, yeah, Kevin," Randy whispered. "Eat it. You're doing great, man." He spread my cheeks, and I felt his saliva-covered fingers playing with my virgin butt hole and painfully hard prick. "Open up, Kevin," he breathed into my ear. My whole body tensed as one finger drilled into my asshole, then two. "You've never been fucked, have you?"

"No! This is the first time I've ever messed around with another guy."

"And it ain't gonna be the last," Randy said, smiling. "Get in the backseat, dude." We stripped off the rest of our clothes, and I sat in back while he slid between the front seats headfirst and swallowed every damn inch of my raging boner.

Not even in my wettest wet dreams did I imagine anything could feel this good. He was doing shit with his tongue I could not fucking believe. I opened my eyes and saw his naked butt and muscular back and shoulders. Randy had the most perfect body I'd ever seen.

"You've got a real big one, Kevin," he said. "I bet girls at school can't get enough of it."

For some reason I wanted to tell him I'd never had any pussy, so I did. He stroked my stomach with his big hands. "Then this'll be the first time you come in someone's mouth," he said. Then he started chowing down on my cock like he was possessed, fucking it with his wet mouth while he cupped my nuts in one hand and jacked my dick with the other one, using his soft lips and strong fist like a funnel. My balls were boiling over, and as much as I tried to make it last, I couldn't hold off another second.

"I'm gonna shoot, man!" I screamed, putting my hands on his shoulders. But he was staying right where he was, with his mouth around my spurting eight-inch cock. I fell back against the seat, thrusting into Randy's face until he'd sucked out every hot drop.

"You're still hard," he said, looking up at me. "How many times can you come?"

"Three or four," I stuttered, still reeling from that first orgasm.

"I bet my big fat dick in your little ass would help you pop off another load," Randy said. He climbed into the backseat and put his arms around me. Our naked bodies were pressed together, and I could feel his incredible muscles overpowering me. "You want me to fuck you," he said. "Admit it, Kevin."

Before I could say anything, he planted this amazing kiss on me. I tasted my own come and was just, like, totally floored to be mugging down with a guy! He made me want to surrender everything, and as he tongue-raped my hungry mouth, I knew I was going to let him use my butt hole however he damn well pleased.

Randy started kissing all down the front of my body, sucking my tits and teasing my cock and balls with the palm of his hand. He moved down to my crotch and pushed my legs apart so that my ass was right in his face. His monster meat was shoved back between his legs. I saw it, stiff against the seat, and wanted it inside me. But first he was rimming me, stretching my hole with his fingers and licking it with hot strokes of his nasty tongue.

"Suck my asshole," I groaned. I started to jack myself, but Randy grabbed my hands and pinned them over my head. His lips traveled up my hairless crack to my scrotum, then swallowed both nuts. It was awesome! I swiveled my hips around underneath him while my dick bobbed against his face.

Then he was ready. "Get up and bend over, Kevin." I did what he said. I was on all fours in the backseat, naked, with this buff state trooper's fingers working in and out of my butt. He took his pants from the front seat and got a condom out of his wallet. I watched over my shoulder as he rolled the lubed rubber over his gigantic bone-hard prick.

He squeezed some more stuff out of the package and smeared it on.

"Spread 'em and don't fight me," he told me. "It's going to be the most incredible thing you've ever felt." He pressed the head of his penis against my asshole and slowly prodded it open. "Relax. Yeah, Kevin, that's it. Man, you're tight. You're so fucking tight."

I can't say that it didn't hurt, but underneath the pain and soreness was an unbelievably hot sexual sensation that made me crave every inch of that cop cock. He eased all of it into my virgin hole, then started to screw me, slowly at first, then harder. He bent over and wrapped his arms around me. I felt his pointy nipples on my back as he pressed his massively developed pecs against me with every thrust.

I was going to come without laying a finger on my throbbing cock. Randy pulled out almost all the way, then slammed my aching hole at the same time I spewed hot semen everywhere. Five hot squirts, and still I was hard.

I felt Randy's teeth and breath on my ear. "I'm real close now, Kevin," he moaned. "I'm going to pump you full of my cream. I'm going to blow a load right up your hot little teenage ass. You're driving me *crazy!*" He grabbed my sensitive dick, and I groaned.

"Yeah, fucking shoot that come!" I shouted.

He did it, and if he hadn't been wearing that Magnum, my butt hole would have been overflowing with his boiling jizz. Randy finally took his big salami out and used his T-shirt to wipe up the backseat. I crumpled it up and shoved it out of sight. Next time I jacked off I wanted it close at hand. We went into the woods and got dressed.

"Congratulations, Kevin. You passed your driving test."

"What about parallel parking?" I asked. We were driving back to the Department of Public Safety station.

"Tonight you can park that juicy cock of yours right up my butt," he said, slipping on the mirrored sunglasses.

I nodded without saying anything. The dance wouldn't be over too late. And Missy wasn't that wild about parking anyway.

The Friday File
by Sutter Powell

Only ten minutes had passed since I'd last checked the time, and I had promised myself I wouldn't look for at least another hour. Friday afternoons at Aliandro, Dunhill, and Wade moved like molasses in January. Although the firm took up the entire nineteenth floor, there were usually fewer than ten people at their desks come Friday at 4 p.m. On Friday afternoons the partners and other big wheels migrated like ducks to the golf courses and country clubs of the Bay Area, leaving only the secretaries, paralegals, and bright young interns such as myself to answer their phones and pray for the week to grind to a close.

Even if I hadn't been watching the clock, I would have known it was nearing 4 p.m., because no sooner had my eyes returned to the brief that I wasn't writing than I heard the sound of efficient footsteps squishing toward me on the plush gray carpet. As befits a lowly intern, I was given a desk located in the law-office equivalent of Siberia — next to the typing pool at the entrance to the file room. My nameplate (MR. GOUGH — INTERN) identifies me as an insignificant serf, lest anyone mistake me for a real attorney. I lifted my eyes just in time to see Mr. Harrow pass my desk on his way into the file room. The older man's chiseled features were set in his trademark inscrutable expression, and he had what I had nicknamed his "Friday file" tucked under his arm. As the impeccably tailored attorney marched by in an exquisite Armani suit, he left just a whiff of Drakkar Noir in his wake. My dormant dick awakened from its boredom-induced coma and stirred restlessly. Every Friday for the past two months, I had watched handsome Mr. Harrow enter the file room with that damn folder under his arm. He would emerge about fifteen minutes later with a slight smirk on his face. This bizarre behavior aroused my naturally suspicious mind much the way the gorgeous older attorney aroused my naturally horny dick. Glen Harrow was the firm's star tax attorney and was rumored to be on the partnership track, so why would he be doing his own filing? On Friday afternoons? What was that all about?

I knew I should finish my brief, but I just had to know what he was up to. I glanced to my left. Mrs. Handerly, the busybody office manager who sat next to me, had her Dictaphone firmly inserted in her lacquered bouffant, and her pudgy little fingers were blazing away on her keyboard. I nonchalantly rose to my feet and meandered toward the file room entrance. I paused at the threshold and leaned my head in, scanning the photocopier area for Mr. Harrow. Not there. After another glance at the oblivious Mrs. Handerly, I slid into the file room. The floor was done in noisy ceramic tile, so I carefully toed off my shoes and continued on silently in my stocking feet.

The cavernous room had fifteen-foot-high ceilings, with gray metal shelves that ran from top to bottom. There were six rows of the double-sided shelves, each about twenty-five feet long. More shelves lined the perimeter of the room, and an aisle ran the circumference of the room between the ends of the rows and the wall units. From where I stood I could see that Mr. Harrow was not in the front aisle. That meant he was in the back aisle or one of the rows. I carefully made my way down the first row of shelving, moving away from the door and toward the back of the room. I peeked around the end of the row. The back aisle was deserted. He was in one of the interior aisles, between the rows of shelving. I crept from row to row, my pulse quickening. Second row, not there. Third row, empty. Fourth row, ditto. I crouched down and peered around the corner of the shelf into the fifth row. No Mr. Harrow. He must be in the very last aisle. I knew from my vast filing experience that the last row was reserved for "dead" files, a burial ground where inactive files went to decompose.

"Ugghhmm…" A low, throaty moan broke the silence, and I froze in place, my breath catching in my throat, my heart pounding. What the hell was that? I held perfectly still, straining to hear. "Ahhmmm…" There it was again. The moan was followed by a soft rustling of paper, perhaps cloth. I eased into the fifth row and slowly raised up to peek through the space above the tops of the files.

You could have knocked me over with a feather. About halfway down the last row of files, Mr. Glen Harrow, the hotshot tax attorney at Aliandro, Dunhill, and Wade, was busily beating his meat! With his slacks and underpants around his ankles, no less! I had to bite my lip to keep from laughing. I couldn't believe it! It was so out of character for Mr. Harrow. He was the most deadly serious of all the attorneys, and I had never seen him so much as smile. And here he was, spanking his monkey in the file room!

The half-naked attorney was staring intently at something he was holding in his free hand as he masturbated vigorously. His back was to me, so I edged closer to see what he was so engrossed in. It was the file I had seen him with earlier — his Friday file! It was a standard multisection contract folder, but what Mr. Harrow was so engrossed in was not contained in any of the firm's folders that I had reviewed. The wily attorney had removed the contract documents and replaced them with the latest issue of MEN magazine. Even from my poor vantage point, I instantly recognized Mr. July. (I'll confess that I myself had studied Mr. July's codicils and addendum in much the same manner as Mr. Harrow was now doing, only I had conducted my review in the privacy of my bedroom.)

I wanted a better look at the action, so I backed up carefully and tiptoed to the end of the row that separated us. I crouched down and peered around the corner. Mr. Harrow was really going at it now, his knees bending and straightening as he fucked his flailing fist. The tax attorney was now in profile to me, and I watched, mesmerized, as he stroked himself. Until this moment I had never noticed how incredibly built Mr. Harrow was. Hairy, deeply tanned legs rippled and bulged with muscle, the calves knotting up as he rocked up and down on the balls of his feet. Mr. Harrow's hair was a deep chestnut brown, and he wore it cropped close to his handsome head. I could see that he kept himself in great shape, because his stomach looked flatter than mine, and I was almost young enough to be his son. He was a complete and total stud. But as I could plainly see, Harrow's best feature wasn't his flat stomach, his chestnut hair, or his muscular thighs; no, top honors would have to go to his cock. The tax attorney's dick was absolutely exquisite — long, thick, and perfectly formed, the shaft a creamy tan color, the bulbous head a fiery purple-red. Two plump, hairy testicles the size of golf balls bobbed and weaved beneath the mammoth organ as he pumped away with his big hand, his Rolex flashing a masturbation Morse code under the fluorescent lights.

Watching the hunky older man pleasure himself made my dick as hard as a bone. My swollen shaft was bent painfully double in my slacks. I quietly unzipped my fly and reached in to adjust it, keeping my eyes glued to Mr. Harrow's enormous whang. I had been planning only to make my dick more comfortable, but the feel of my fingers on the sweaty cock flesh was so delicious that I drew my overheated hard-on out of my pants and began to stroke it.

"Arrghhh…o-o-oh!" Mr. Harrow moaned softly under his breath. He laid the Friday file open and leaned against the shelf, his eyes riveted on the centerfold. The attorney's firm, muscular ass was level with my face. Two delectable globes of ass flesh peeped out from under the tail of his crisply pressed dress shirt — a tight little bubble butt divided by a deep crevice. I ached to press my hard dick into that tempting crack.

Just then it hit me: Why couldn't I do exactly that? What was stopping me from stepping up behind him and pressing my cock into his luscious crack? Absolutely nothing, that's what. I had caught one of the firm's senior lawyers with his pants down. What was he going to do — have me fired for unprofessional behavior? I grinned wickedly as I contemplated my good fortune. Mr. Harrow was really working it now — his ass flexing and squeezing, his arm a blur. I decided I'd better make my move before he blew his load all over the dead files.

I rose silently to my feet and, with my hard-on leading the way, crept stealthily up behind the preoccupied tax attorney. Closer and closer I eased, holding my breath. When I was only inches behind him, I reached around his body, clamped one hand over his mouth, and caught his masturbating fist with the other.

"Let me give you a hand with that, counselor," I purred into his ear as I pressed my stiff cock into his sweaty ass crack.

"Mmmph!" Startled, Mr. Harrow grunted into my palm. He clawed wildly, trying to tear my hand from his face.

"Shhh!" I hissed in his ear. "Don't you dare make a sound. What if someone came in here and saw you like this?" I stroked my fist up and down along the shaft of his engorged dick.

"Ugghhhmmm," grunted Mr. Harrow, his ass cheeks tightening reflexively around my cock as I jacked him off. His rigid manhood was hot and moist, the skin velvety soft. I slid my fingers up to the head of his dick and toyed with the broad head, twiddling his spongy cock lips with my fingertips. Mr. Harrow inhaled noisily through his nose and tried to speak against my palm. "Oo arr oo?"

"Come again?" I whispered politely. "I didn't get that." Just to be ornery, I left my hand over his mouth.

"Ake urr ann off!" Mr. Harrow demanded.

"Okay, but only if you promise to be a good boy and keep your voice down. And no turning around!" I slowly dropped my hand from his mouth, all the while stroking his cock.

"Who is that? Is that you, Frank?" he hissed indignantly. Frank? Surely he didn't mean Frank Dunhill! Wow, Mr. Dunhill would do something like this? I filed this little tidbit of information away for future reference.

"No, it's not Frank," I replied. "Who I am isn't important at this point. What's important is that I caught you being a very naughty boy on company time. Which client were you going to bill your time to this afternoon?" I inquired teasingly, massaging his mammoth meat.

"Let go of me this instant! Whoever you are, I'll have your ass fired for this," Mr. Harrow threatened softly.

"Actually, I was thinking of having your ass, Glen." I worked my cock deeper between Mr. Harrow's ass cheeks, the moist curls of his furrow tickling my shaft.

"Stop that!"the older man hissed, reaching down to dislodge my hand from his organ. "If you let go of me right now, I might consider not having you fired."

I slapped his hands away and pulled him back against me, my palm against his chest. "Puhl-e-e-eze! You're bluffing, and you know it. On what grounds would you fire me? Masturbation interruptus? I doubt there are any legal precedents for that." I pressed my lips to Mr. Harrow's ear and kissed it, darting the tip of my tongue into his ear canal, then sucking his earlobe firmly between my lips. He sighed.

"No, I don't think anybody needs to get fired over this," I whispered. "The partners will never even hear about this incident if you play your cards right. I'd be willing to overlook your inappropriate behavior if you were to work with me on this. I think we can come to an equitable settlement here in the file room — say, your ass for my silence? We'll just have to keep our negotiations quiet." I made a trail of kisses down the side of Mr. Harrow's muscular neck as I began to undo the buttons of his crisp white shirt.

"Well, I, uh…"

"C'mon, Glen, you know you want to. Wouldn't it be hot to do it right here in the files? Isn't that why you came in here to beat off? The thrill of possibly getting caught?" I kissed my way around the nape of his neck to his other ear. I stuck my nose in his hair and inhaled the spicy scent of his shampoo. I had undone most of the buttons of his shirt, and I slid my hand inside to caress his furry pectorals.

Mr. Harrow tried to squirm away from me again. "No! I can't do this! It's too risky. Someone could come in at any second. I could lose my job. They'll have me disbarred."

"Shush, now, no one will ever know — unless you keep making so much noise. Or unless I'm forced to tell on you…" I let the threat hang in the air for a moment, and then I slid my hand down Mr. Harrow's shaft to his nuts. I cupped his testicles, squeezing the resilient orbs. With my other hand I located one of his gumdrop nipples and pinched it, teasing it to pebbled hardness. "Wouldn't it be easier to just relax and enjoy it? It could be our little secret."

"Damn you!" he muttered. "This is blackmail, and you know it." I found his other nipple and pinched it erect as I rolled and squeezed his gonads. Mr. Harrow groaned helplessly. "All right, all right. But hurry up, before we get caught."

"That's more like it, Harrow. Why don't you turn around and meet your blackmailer?" I released the attorney's balls and nipples, and he whirled around to face me.

"You're just an intern!" Mr. Harrow said indignantly.

"Shut up and kiss me," I whispered, pulling him to me by his necktie. Mr. Harrow's eyes widened, and he seemed ready to object, but he appeared to change his mind when our lips met. I pried his mouth open with my tongue and slid my hands down to his furry ass. I massaged the hard glutes and pulled his muscular body to mine, grinding his enormous dick against mine as we kissed. Mr. Harrow responded by wrapping me in his arms and thrusting his tongue out to duel with mine. "Take down my pants," I panted between kisses.

"Uh-huh," Mr. Harrow grunted enthusiastically, his tongue swirling around mine. His hands found my belt buckle and fumbled it open. He quickly shoved my suit pants and shorts down over my ass. When my dick popped free, he caught it in his sweaty palm and pumped it firmly.

Mr. Harrow pulled his mouth back and looked down at my erection. "Nice cock you got there — for an intern, I mean," he whispered sarcastically.

"Can you see it okay from clear up here?" I asked snidely. "Why don't you kneel down and take a closer look? At your age I bet your eyes aren't as good as they used to be."

"Yeah, I guess I can't see smaller things as well as I used to," he shot back with a grin.

"You got a smart mouth, Harrow. You need it washed out with dick." I placed a hand on his head and pressed down. Mr. Harrow dropped to one knee, eagerly running his fist up and down my eight throbbing inches. He locked his gaze on mine and pulled the head of my cock to his full lips, darting the tip of his tongue out to sweep around my leaking dick head. He coated my engorged glans with saliva, then drew my swollen organ between his lips, taking just the head and an inch or two of the shaft into his hot, moist mouth. He sucked his cheeks in, creating an intense vacuum effect, and began to pump his handsome head up and down as he twirled his rough, strong tongue around my tingling shaft. God, it was so good! The suction, the tongue work, it was all too much for me, and I was soon on the brink of orgasm. I reluctantly pressed my hand against his forehead and eased him off my dick. "Let's not get carried away with that," I said. "I believe the terms of our settlement included your ass."

"C'mon, kid, we don't have time for that. Just let me suck you off. We can't fuck in the file room anyway; we'd get caught for sure!"

"Sorry, Glen, no dice. Get up off your knees. I want that ass, and I want it now!" I commanded in my best butch top voice, although some of the effect was lost by my having to whisper.

"Oh, all right, but make it fast."Mr. Harrow peered nervously between the shelves as he turned around and presented his luscious lobes to me. "You have a rubber, right?"

"Of course I have a rubber. But why rush?" I knelt behind Mr. Harrow and grabbed his left ankle. I worked his foot, which was still clad in an argyle sock and an Italian wing tip, out of his slacks. "Put your leg up on this second shelf. Now move the other one out more — that's it. You don't mind if I kiss your ass before I fuck it, do you, Glen?"

"Just hurry up already!"

I cupped his furry globes and palmed him open. "Stick your butt out more." Mr. Harrow pushed his hips back, his ass crack yawning open to reveal his tightly clenched aperture. I dived in, pressed my lips to his hole, and kissed it. I stuck the tip of my tongue out and tickled the silky pucker of his ass lips. Mr. Harrow moaned, and I felt his anus blossom against my lips. I stiffened my tongue and inserted it into the satiny track of his ass. I reached under him and felt for his dick, then cupped my fingers around the rigid shaft and bent it back between his legs, forcing his balls up against my chin. I rubbed the pad of my thumb against the sensitive area of his dick right below the dripping head, and he squirmed, pressing my mouth deeper into his sweaty crevice. I fucked his asshole with my tongue and rubbed his pulsing cock with my thumb. I then popped my tongue out of his twitching pucker and let it dance down over his distended balls and along his turgid shaft. I washed the underside of his cock with my tongue and eagerly collected the salty drops of lube that dripped from the broad head of his dick. After savoring his precome, I resumed tongue-fucking. When his asshole was running with spit and clenching desperately at my tongue, I knew he was ready. I pulled my face from his humid valley and fumbled in my slacks for my wallet. I was shaking with lust, my fingers clumsy as they searched for a condom. I finally located one and tore the foil open. I rolled the rubber over my cock and stumbled to my feet, then grabbed Mr. Harrow by the hips and pressed my cock against his asshole.

"Here come da judge," I panted. "You ready for him, counselor? Any last-minute objections?"

In reply the lust-crazed attorney jammed his hips back and drove my cock all the way up his ass in one long thrust. I gasped in pleasure and bit my tongue to silence myself. "Just shut up and fuck me," Mr. Harrow grunted under his breath, clenching at my embedded member with his ass muscles.

I pulled out until just the head of my cock remained in his hot channel, and then I slowly slid all the way back in until my balls pressed tightly against his. I stroked in and out in this manner, mercilessly teasing both his tight asshole and my burning spear with long, deep thrusts. Mr. Harrow arched his spine, pressing his muscular ass back to meet each plunge. I slid my hands up under his shirttails and stroked the sweat-slick muscles of his broad back. He rose up, and my hands slid around his trim waist. I took his prick in my fist once more. Mr. Harrow moaned and ground his ass even harder against my groin.

Suddenly the sound of high heels on tile rang out as someone entered the file room. Click-click-click. We froze in place like some pornographic tableau. The high heels stopped just past the copiers. "Yoo-hoo, Mr. Gough!" Mrs. Handerly sang out in her annoying nasal voice. "Are you in here? You have a call."

I held my breath, and Mr. Harrow held his. Maybe she'd give up and go away. I felt Mr. Harrow's dick softening. I eased my hips from side to side, stirring my dick in his ass, and squeezed his organ in my hand. It hardened up again.

"Mr. Gough? Are you in here?" Click-click-click. Mrs. Handerly had moved farther into the room. Mr. Harrow tore at my hands in a panic, trying to get loose. I pulled him closer and buried my cock up his ass, holding him prisoner impaled on my cock.

I cleared my throat and called out, "Could you be a love and take a message? I'm deep into a legal matter, and I just can't pull myself away at the moment. I should be free soon, Mrs. Handerly."

"Whatever you say, Mr. Gough," she sniffed. Click-click-click went the heels out of the room.

Mr. Harrow heaved a sigh, and I could feel his heart pounding as he leaned back against me. "Jeez, that was close! What if she'd come around the corner? You're crazy, Gough. You are out of your fucking mind." He protested, but his ass was grinding against me, the close call obviously exciting him as much as it had me. He reached back and put a hand behind my neck, pulling my lips to his, kissing me deeply. "Now stop goofing around and fuck me before she comes back," he panted into my mouth. "Fuck me hard. Make me come." I grunted and shoved my dick up his ass. Holding it there, I worked in and out with rapid thrusts, grinding my hard-on against his swelling prostate. Mr. Harrow moaned his appreciation, thrusting his tongue into my mouth. I caught his swollen balls in my free hand and squeezed them firmly. With my other hand I roughly jacked him off, stretching and straining the moist skin. His asshole clamped down on my dick as I jerked forcefully on his cock.

In a matter of seconds we were both exploding. Glen's big body went rigid against me, and he tossed his head back onto my shoulder. His hands shot out to grab the shelves at our sides. His mouth opened, and I was afraid he was going to scream as he came, but the only sound he made was one long satisfied exhalation of air as his asshole convulsed around my dick and his engorged fuck pole detonated in my fist. Enormous blasts of thick, hot sperm arced out, spattering the tiles beneath us. That did it — with one last thrust I erupted. My shuddering boner was repeatedly stroked by Glen's milking ass muscles as I filled the condom with my seed. Glen turned his head, and I kissed him gratefully. I grasped the base of the condom with two fingers and eased my dick out of his ass, and we started to dress.

"That was the hottest fuck I ever had," he said, panting for breath. "Who'd have thought a pip-squeak intern like you could be such a love machine?" He grinned at me.

"Who'd have thought an old man like you would have such a hot ass?" I shot back good-naturedly, kissing him again.

"Now listen, kid, we have a deal, right? You won't say anything to anyone?" He reached for the Friday file.

I clamped my hand down on his and snatched the file away, tucking it under my arm. "Not so fast, counselor. I won't say a word to anyone, but I'll just hold on to this for you until, oh, let's say next Friday afternoon at 4, when we continue these negotiations?"

"Why, you horny little shit!"

I chuckled wickedly. "See you Friday, counselor."

NIGHT

Drop-kick My Heart
by James Anselm

I wasn't surprised to be enlisted in Coach Baxter's campaign to keep Bill Mitchell happy at Western University. He knew from experience that I was the best cocksucker the school had — and there was plenty of competition.

"He doesn't socialize with his teammates," Coach said as he paced his office. "He avoids talking to me. I'm afraid we're going to lose him, and he could be one of the best players I have. It pisses me off, after all the work I've put in on him."

Baxter explained how he made sure Bill always had plenty of spending money and how his rooms were about the nicest on campus. I had already heard the rumors that Bill would have flunked physics a third time without Coach's personal intervention.

"Nobody seems to know about a steady girlfriend, so maybe he's not getting any. If he just needs to blow his load to be happy, you might be able to help." Baxter put one hand over his own basket and said, "He's very nicely equipped, Jim, just the way you like."

I would be lying if I led you to believe that I was helping Coach Baxter for purely altruistic motives. In those days I was always on the lookout for something new, and little bait was needed to reel me in to this scheme.

It was easy for me to make arrangements to see Bill alone. We were only nodding acquaintances, but it would have been hard for him to turn me down. Even at a school as sports-crazed as Western, the editor of the university paper is a person everybody knows, and I made sure that the *Statesman*'s athletic coverage was excellent, since it gave me free access to all the locker rooms.

Having run track as a freshman, I had established my credentials as a "guy" in good standing before pursuing my literary bent. My craving for cock I pursued in a less obvious manner, but I don't have to tell you how many opportunities there are when a couple of thousand people in their physical and hormonal primes are assembled in one place.

Anyway, Bill seemed flattered to be interviewed about Western's chances this season and had no objection to having dinner while we talked — especially as it was on me. Nor did he have any objection to putting away a few beers while we ate. I found him easy to be with: not a great brain but far from stupid and a very funny guy.

When the restaurant shut down for the evening (I'd chosen it for its early closing time), it was only natural that he should invite me back to his place for another drink or two, on him this time.

I had the scenario pretty clear in my head, since I'd used it before. Butter up the big jock, get him out of his clothes, help him get his rocks off. He'd probably never speak to me in public again, but I could deal with that as long as he called my number when he needed a mouth to come in.

Only underclassmen had to share rooms at Western, so there wasn't much fear of our being interrupted, but I still locked the door while his head was buried in the fridge. I noted with envy that his room was quite a lot bigger than my own and his stereo was definitely state-of-the-art, though any boom box would probably have done for the music I imagined he listened to. "Not bad," I commented, pulling up a chair.

"Yeah, it's a nice room," he admitted, "but it's always so warm." I couldn't tell whether his complaint was justified, because I felt a flush come over me as he whipped the shirt over his head and tossed it on a chair. Of course, I'd known he was big, but I'd never seen him bare-chested before. Bill had the best body I'd ever looked at outside of a magazine, and it sent the blood rushing straight to my dick.

He had it all: size, symmetry, definition. His skin was completely smooth, and every muscle stood out in bold relief as he moved. Unlike most football players I've gotten to know, he didn't seem to have an ounce of fat on him. He had a stomach that made Brad Pitt's look flabby and out of shape — it was that small and tightly ripped. As my eyes moved up his body, his torso just kept getting wider and wider, from a perfect chest to shoulders that should have torn the seams out of every shirt he owned.

Bill stood there for a minute, shoving his blond hair back into place with his fingers, his bulging arms radiating a power that I could almost smell. If he did give up football, I thought, it would be for competitive bodybuilding. At that moment it became a point of honor for me to keep Bill Mitchell at Western. Happily, he seemed completely unaware of the effect his body was having on me.

When he brought his hands down, I saw him wince. "Anything wrong?" I asked.

"I must have pulled something in practice today. If I move my shoulder the wrong way, it hurts like hell." Then he looked at me as though seeing me for the first time. "I've got lotion for it, if you wouldn't mind rubbing some in."

"Why, sure, Bill, I'd be glad to do that," I told him. "I'm not in any great hurry to get back." As he went into the bathroom to get the bottle, I rolled up my sleeves, thinking there couldn't be a better lead-in.

"Coach got me this stuff," Bill said, handing it to me. "It works real good, but sometimes it's hard for me to reach where I want it." Taking the bottle, I squeezed a big glob onto one palm and rubbed my hands together. The fragrance was mild, vaguely minty, and I could feel the warmth of it immediately. Bill sat on one corner of the unmade bed, leaving room for me to perch next to him.

I worked the lotion into his powerful shoulders, trying to keep my body away from his so he wouldn't realize too soon that I had the woody of my life. Picturing this more or less as a job, I had never expected to get so turned-on by him; it was best for Bill to believe that nothing was happening that he didn't want.

"That feels really good," he sighed. "You have very warm hands."

Not as warm as my heart, I thought, but instead I asked, "Not so sore now?"

"Terrific. Could you put it on my back too? It relaxes my muscles when I'm tensed up." I reached away to squirt some more lotion on my hand. "Wait a minute; let me lie flat so you can do me better."

He peeled off his slacks to reveal not the boxers that most guys wore but Calvins! *I'm going to like doing you,* I thought. Fortunately, he threw himself on the bed immediately, so I didn't get even a glimpse of his basket. I started in working on that broad, sinewy back.

The muscle barely gave at all as I pushed at it, and I pushed hard — which he seemed to like, judging by his deep sighs. When I had coated his back thoroughly, he asked me to do his legs. My dick was throbbing away and leaking precome while I stroked his massive thighs, my fingers only inches from the crack between those two globes of flesh that formed his ass.

Then he turned faceup on the bed, and I could see that he had a hard-on of his own, as well-developed as everything else about him. The head had pushed its way past the elastic band of his briefs to glow red against the paler skin of his stomach, while the thick shaft remained shrouded in cotton.

"Would you keep going?" he asked, almost anxiously. "Is it okay?" I just patted his flat abdomen and squirted some lotion right onto his chest, kneading those tremendous pecs with my fingers. His nipples were rising bit by bit, and I could feel his heartbeat beginning to speed up. With my own cock trying to bust its way out of my jeans, I figured his was just about ready for the next step.

As I worked the rippled surface of his midsection, my hands kept sliding against his briefs, pushing them farther and farther down and exposing more and more of his hard dick. Finally I said, "What do you need these for? I'm just getting them all greasy." Bill lifted up his pelvis to help me as I slipped the briefs down his legs and dropped them on the floor.

Coming back to rub the tops of his thighs put my head just about where I wanted it. I opened wide and slipped the end of his cock between my lips before he realized what I was doing. I half heard him say "What the—" But he didn't finish the question, and he didn't do anything to stop me. In fact, I could feel him getting even bigger in my mouth.

At first I did most of the work — licking and sucking on that big, juicy man root — but before long he was moving his hips to meet me, trying to get his dick deeper and deeper down my throat. It was quite an effort to make room for him — Coach had been right about the size of his equipment. I think it must have been nearly on a par with Baxter's own legendary schlong.

His eyes were closed when I looked up, and his nipples were popped out about half an inch; capping those incredible pecs, they looked even bigger. I braced my hands against the mattress as I slurped his pole up and down, wanting to feel that chest (and all the rest of his wonderful physique) but still afraid of moving too fast. I was enjoying what I had for now, and I didn't want to lose it by rushing and possibly upsetting him.

But he was enjoying it too. Fucking my face like a son of a bitch, he kept saying "Feels good, real good" over and over, like a mantra. "Getting real close... I'm almost there. Mmm....so good...so good...oh, shit, yeah!" Then suddenly I could feel the head of his cock expanding again as he shouted, "Gonna shoot!"

If there had been college-level orgasm, he would have been an all-American. He thrashed and squirmed so, I almost lost my grip on his dick, which got even harder than it had been. He yelled incoherently, then started flooding my throat with bolts of hot come faster than I could swallow it, though I did my best. But there was more and more of it, and I had to let a lot go to waste.

When he was finally finished, he just lay there, gasping and half dazed. Watching his big chest heaving for air, I took one corner of the sheet and wiped his splooge from my chin. "Jeez, thanks," Bill said, catching his breath. "That was fuckin' great!"

"Well, I guess maybe I should go home now," I told him, ready for the usual excuses and rationalizations but nevertheless not wanting to hear them.

"Don't you want to come too?" he asked quietly.

"Well, yes," I started, "but—"

He interrupted me by placing one enormous hand over my crotch and sliding it up and down. As his fingers made contact with the wet spot there, his eyes widened, and he smiled a little. "Come on," he ordered. "Get those clothes off!" I didn't have to be told twice.

My rod popped right up when I opened my jeans — there was no way it was going down by itself now, not after all my work on Bill's fabulous body. He took it in one hand and started stroking it, using the lotion as grease. The tingle it gave me turned me on almost as much as seeing this football star playing with my cock.

His biceps swelled and relaxed as he frigged me, his hand moving back and forth on my eager member. I tried to make it last longer, but it wasn't any use — I'd been wanting to release this load ever since Bill took his shirt off. I threw back my head with a grunt and let go. One incredibly long blast of come hit him in the center of his chest, dribbling down along that washboard belly.

Bill smeared it around with his fingers and brought them close to his face to smell. He breathed deeply, expanding that chest again, and I heard him sigh with satisfaction. Then he sat up and put his arms around me, crushing me close against him for a long moment. He whispered "Thank you" into my ear again but didn't say anything else.

After we separated at last, he went over to the stereo and pushed a few buttons there. I guess my face must have showed my surprise when the slow movement of Mozart's C Major Piano Concerto — one of my favorite pieces of music — issued from the speakers. Bill chuckled at my expression.

"I know, football players aren't supposed to like Mozart better than Madonna," he said. "And they're sure as shit not supposed to like other football players. Do you know — win or lose — I always get out of that locker room as fast as I can? I get a boner every time I watch some of them shower — and they'd all be sick if they knew!"

"Not all, Bill," I replied.

He snorted, but his jaw dropped when I told him, "Jack Cotter wouldn't."

"Jack? No, no way...Jack?"

"Well, you didn't hear it from me, okay? But if you tried the same business with him you did with me tonight, he'd probably let you suck his cock."

"No shit. Would he let me fuck him?"

"I doubt it, but you could ask." In fact, I knew Jack saw himself as God's gift to bottoms, but Bill needed to find that out for himself.

"Jim, can I..." My heart lurched as I waited for him to finish the question. "Would you let me fuck you?"

"Bill, if you've got a rubber here, you can do anything you want with me!"

He went over to his dresser and rummaged in a drawer while I stood behind him, running my fingers up and down along his lats. Leaning against the dresser, he spread his legs to let me play with his rump for a few minutes.

His ass cheeks were glorious — smooth skin over hard muscle — and I kissed and licked them, tasting the salt of his sweat as it trickled down from the base of his spine. I slipped one hand between his legs to play with his mighty balls while I nuzzled against the hole I knew wouldn't open for me that night.

Bill turned around then and expanded his chest very slowly so I was able to put both my hands on it and enjoy the sensations. I could feel his rib cage shifting and his pectorals growing in size as he tensed them. I nibbled at his tits and licked his armpits clean of sweat while he flexed and pumped for me. Soon we were both rock-hard again, though we had come only a few minutes before.

"You've got such a great body," I said, and he actually blushed. "Don't act like nobody's ever told you so!"

"It isn't that," he replied quietly. "It's one thing to hear it from a coach who just sees you as a big piece of meat he can use to get the ball to the other end of the field, but it's kinda different hearing it from someone who's just come all over it."

As I put the rubber on him, I wondered how I was going to get this much meat inside of me. Sitting on it seemed to be the best way to go, and Bill held his cannon steady as I inched my way into his lap. Somewhere along the way, I came to the conclusion that he wasn't as big as I'd first thought, because it felt awfully good having him inside me.

Bill fucked me like a lover, so gently that I wondered if it was his first time in another man's ass. That was fine with me — I hate getting roughed up, and he could easily have really hurt me with his big dick.

After a while I straddled the bed so he could stand and fuck me doggy-style, which enabled him to increase his speed. Then we both settled onto the mattress face-to-face, my legs over his shoulders.

He hit my buttons every time the full length of his huge cock pushed into me, and I squeezed it with every muscle I had as he pulled back. Occasionally he reached around to give my rod a few strokes with his hand — as if there were any way on earth I could go soft at this point. After a while I lost control and started jerking myself off furiously.

I came first, watching in amazement as my cock gushed out twice its normal load. Bill was getting more turned-on as he watched my sperm flying through the air, and he started driving into me even faster, breathing hard.

"Gonna come again. Almost there, Jim. Gonna come big, I can feel it—"

"Oh, yeah, Bill, let me see it this time...come on me!" He quickly pulled his cock out of me and ripped the condom off, his hand flashing along his meat. Then he sprayed me with a load at least as big as the first one, that deep voice yowling like an animal as his balls pumped out his hot jizz.

After that second orgasm we lay there for several minutes, just listening to Mozart. As we sat side by side on the edge of his bed, Bill heaved another of those deep sighs. I asked, "What's wrong? Shoulder still bothering you?"

Bill gave a bark of a laugh and said, "It never was!" Then he got serious: "I don't think Coach has been that happy with my performance lately, and I'm worried about getting dropped from the team. You know everybody; do you think you could put in a good word for me?"

"Bill, leave it to me," I told him. Putting my arms around his waist, I could feel his dick stirring again. "I'll fix it with Coach Baxter somehow."

Electricity
by R.J. March

Ben turned over in bed, trying to avoid the hard shaft of early-morning light that stabbed through the window. He heard the soft sound of footfalls and the low hum of music from the apartment above. He waited for the sound of water, the boy up there taking his shower. He could see the boy clearly in his mind's eye: dark short hair, eyes the color of slate, a heavy brow, a nose not quite refined. He could almost see the boy standing naked outside the shower stall, pushing back the plastic curtain, stepping into the streaming water. Ben had not actually ever seen the boy without his clothes but had seen him enough times in just shorts, the boy's smooth torso muscled but not overly built-up, the tiny dots of nipples that looked like small coral-color pearls. He had stared once, while the boy had pointed out a leaking pipe under the kitchen sink, at those pinkish dots, which had also reminded Ben of peas — early peas, new peas you buy at a farmer's market, the ones you have to shell.

The boy often reminded Ben of food.

Ben was twenty-three that year, the Year of Short Hair as he called it, because all the guys seemed to have their hair cut to the scalp. Ben would walk into the college barber-shop and sit in his favorite chair and tell his barber, "Show me some skin and leave a little on the top." The house Ben was living in was his grandmother's, and she was in Florida year-round. Ben rented the upstairs apartment to students at the state university in town, where Ben was taking the long road to a B.A., which for Ben stood for bachelor of anything.

The boy upstairs wasn't much younger than Ben — probably just this side of twenty-one, Ben was thinking — but he had a boyish face, a boyish figure. Maybe five foot eight, slim-hipped and smooth, the boy had a long, muscled torso, a killer stomach, and legs that Ben dreamed about wrapped tighter than a belt around his waist. The boy's name was Chris, but Ben, in the privacy of his own bedroom, called him Boy.

Chris was the perfect neighbor: He made hardly any noise, lived like a monk, and was all wrapped up in his studies. Sometimes Ben would be sitting at his desk with his big, fat *Norton's Anthology of English Literature, Vol. Two*, in his hands, and he'd catch himself staring at his ceiling for minutes at a time, just staring, as though he had Superman eyes and could see his little Jimmy Olson padding around upstairs in ragged boxers, eating crackers out of a box, reading about marketing strategies, criminal law, corporate holdings. What he wanted was to be up there with him, stretched out on the couch, staring between the vee of his two feet at the boy, the boy's pale legs shocked with black hair, cute little butt hidden in the bag of his shorts, sweet cock knocking at his fly as he walked around the room with a heavy tome of Russian poetry. Just hearing the boy's feet on the floor overhead could give Ben an aching boner.

What he liked best was the sight of the boy's laundry up on the second-floor back porch, a line hung with hand-washed boxers, limp jockstraps, pairs of sweat socks — all the intimates of a boy's life. He watched out the window for Chris to come back from his evening runs, red and sweating, as if from athletic sex, and he wanted the boy's hot, wet skin against his own.

But he barely acknowledged his neighbor when they passed each other coming and going. Chris seemed so self-contained, and Ben was more than a little unsure of himself. He had had quite a few girlfriends until Chris moved in as well as a couple of really strange sexual encounters with a couple of really strange guys, so he wasn't quite sure what he wanted. Whatever Ben was feeling about his neighbor, however, was intense and seemed to center at his crotch. Thus the sight of the boy's laundry made him twitch in his own shorts, and seeing the boy at school, however distant, could prompt Ben to make a trip to the nearest men's room stall to pump a load into the white porcelain toilet bowl, not caring much if there was anyone on the next crapper to hear him.

Ben was trying to write a paper for his art and cultures class — "Art as Spiritual Participation" was the title of his essay, and that was all he had so far. He stared at his word processor, his face lit by the screen, the only light he had on in the house. He had just worked out and showered and slipped on a pair of sweats and a T-shirt. Upstairs the boy was playing some new music, the latest from Erasure, and Ben tapped his foot to the beat that wafted down through the ceiling.

Suddenly the screen died and the music too, and Ben stood up in the unexpected darkness, cursing the ancient electrical system that frequently went on the fritz like this. He went looking for a flashlight, unable to remember where he'd put it last. For all he knew, it could be down in the cellar next to the fuse box — the result of his tending to the last mishap. He lit a candle and listened to the boy, who walked across his living room, opened his door, and ran down the stairs, skipping steps. Ben heard him at his own door, knocking softly.

Ben opened the door. Chris was barely recognizable in the dark. The boy said hey and Ben said hey back.

"It's like the whole city or something. It's all black," Chris was saying, standing in the foyer.

"I was just going down to the basement," Ben said. "I thought we blew a mess of fuses." Chris went to the front door of the foyer and opened it as if to prove what he was saying. Indeed, the sky was pitch-black, and every house he could see was dark.

"There wasn't a storm, was there?" Ben asked. "I didn't hear any thunder or anything."

"I don't have any candles or anything. Do you?" Chris asked as he closed the foyer door, moving closer to Ben's threshold.

"I've just got this one," Ben said, motioning to the one that was burning on the table in the living room. "You want a beer or something?"

Chris followed him to the kitchen. Ben opened the refrigerator door and was stupidly surprised that the light inside didn't come on. He squatted, feeling his dick swing freely in the dark cave of his sweatpants, and grabbed a couple of bottles, handing one to Chris.

"I'm not afraid of the dark — usually," the boy said. Ben heard the twist of the cap and the little gasp the bottle made as it was opened. He palmed his own cap off and chugged some beer. They stood together in the kitchen, and Ben wished like anything that the lights would come back on right then so he could look at the boy, look at him all over.

"We could go into the living room," Ben said. The kitchen was so narrow that with Ben leaning against the fridge and Chris up against the sink, there was only enough room to pass a fist between them. They both turned to exit and knocked shoulders and hips, and Ben realized the boy was shirtless, wearing just a pair of boxers.

"Excuse me," they said together and tried again, and Chris got out first and stood by the sofa. Ben followed.

"Sit down," he said, and the boy sat, and Ben stood looking down at him. The candlelight made his skin seem even more pale. Ben saw that the fly of Chris's shorts was open, showing nothing. He eyed the nipples that hung at the outer curve of the boy's pecs. Chris put his bare feet up on the coffee table, his giant boxers hanging wide at his angled thighs, offering another glimpse into nothing.

"I was writing a paper," Ben said.

"I wasn't doing anything," Chris said. He was looking around the room at what he could see by the candle's flame. Ben had the walls painted the color of Dijon mustard, hung with prints he found at flea markets. Near the ceiling was a narrow shelf that circled the room, filled with the junk he'd collected so far — books, old toy trucks from when he was a little boy, pieces of pottery — a bunch of nothing but for some reason compelling to Ben.

"I was rolling a joint," Chris added. "That's what I was really doing. I could get it, if you wanted."

Ben wrinkled up his face in the direction of the paper he was supposed to be writing, and Chris said, "But if you're not into that—"

"It's not that," Ben said. "It's just that I was planning on getting a jump on my paper tonight." He was doing his best to keep his eyes out of the valley the boy's two raised legs made. "But what the fuck," he said, and he saw Chris break into a smile.

When Chris returned, they had a couple more beers and shared the joint Chris had rolled. It was fat and potent, a wicked stogie that made Ben feel buzzed and just a little anxious. "This isn't very mellow, is it?" he said, handing the roach to Chris.

"No, this shit's goofy," Chris said. "I can do some good work on a little bit, you know — papers and reports and shit like that — but..." He trailed off, and his face broke into a big stoned grin.

"What?" Ben laughed.

Chris sat up and put his elbows on his knees. "Man, I swear, this weed just goes straight to my dick. Like it's laced with Spanish fleas or something."

Ben laughed again, harder this time, the kid was so cute and funny.

"I feel like you're my older brother," Chris said suddenly and seriously, and Ben stopped laughing, but his mouth was still laugh-shaped.

"Do you have one?" he asked.

Chris nodded.

"Yeah, well, sometimes I feel like I'm looking out for you, you know?" Ben said, wishing he hadn't. The boy fell back against the sofa again, and his legs fell open. He looked about ready to sack out.

"Am I losing you?" Ben said, regretting that too.

"Huh?"

"I was wondering if you were tired," Ben said.

"No," Chris said. "I was just thinking about how cool it was that this weird shit with the lights happened, and I've been upstairs for a couple of months, and we've never hung out. I didn't think you were into it, and now I find out you're totally cool. I figured you were some hyper-brain. I don't even know what you're studying."

"Me either," Ben smirked.

"No girlfriend?"

Ben shook his head.

"Me either," Chris said.

They sat quietly for a long time, listening to each other breathing. They kept looking at one another, asking the same silent questions: *Do you? Will you?*

"I've got a fucking boner," Chris said, breaking the long silence. They both began to giggle like kids. "You want to see it?" he asked Ben.

"Sure I do," he said, his mouth feeling cakey. He sipped the rest of his beer and wanted another but couldn't leave his seat, awaiting the unveiling.

Chris worked his dick out through the slit of his shorts. It poked up tall and white with a big, fat head that kept it from standing on its own. Ben became aware of some action going on in his own pants. Chris held his cock at its base and waved it around like a little bat.

"I can take these off," he suggested, pinching the front of his shorts.

Ben nodded, and the boy pushed at the waistband that curled and rolled down his hips. His pubes were pitch-black and thick as a head of hair. He put his fingers into it, scratching himself, his cock lying heavy against his hipbone. "This is kind of cool," Chris said lazily, taking up his rod again. "I like you watching me."

Ben shifted in his chair. He spread his legs wide, and his dick, half hard, pointed at the boy, kept from full ascent by the drum-tight stretch of sweats. Chris gripped his shaft and chucked his fist up and down. With his free hand he fingered his hard and tiny nipples, those pink sweet peas, and Ben wanted nothing more than to put his mouth on one and then the other. He groaned with the thought, and Chris smiled. Chris's eyes were red and half closed with pleasure. He licked his fingers and touched them to his tits again.

"Let me see yours," he said softly, and Ben stood up fast. Stars swirled in his eyes, and he felt a little dizzy, but that passed, and he undid the string that, along with his suddenly jutting cock, held up his pants. He felt fourteen years old, reminded of times he and his buddies had showed off the wages of puberty: spurts of growth in the dick department, a patch of pubes finally coming in, the quickest shooters. He bared his bone, and Chris said, "Cool." Ben's dick stood out fat and long, nestled in a patch of gold-colored hair. The air swirled around his pecker and made it sizzle. He touched it to make its end weep with stickiness. Chris sat up and brought his head close to Ben's cock head.

"Take off your shirt," he said, and Ben complied, lifting the T-shirt over his head. His chest was smooth, twin sheets of muscle with a deep slit at the center. His stomach laddered down to his pubes, and his lateral obliques, those funny wing-shaped side muscles, curved, marking the tops of his hips. He put his hands there, and his cock ached to be touched.

"You look good," Chris said. "I like the way your muscles stand out."

Ben watched the boy jack his cock, his own cock wanting hands, mouth, the tight suck of butt muscle, the boy's ass ring.

"Come here," Ben said, moving his hips and making his pecker swing.

Chris looked up at him, his mouth just opening. A bit of tongue slipped out and moistened his lips. The candle was beginning to gutter; it sparked and spit, threatening to go out at any moment. Ben wanted to see the boy, see him bent over and sucking, bent over and taking the tip of Ben's cock, then the shaft, all the way down to the pubes. He wanted to see the boy's eyes when his own dick got sucked down Ben's throat. The candle sputtered out. The boy sat glowing.

A hand closed around his swinging meat, and then Ben felt the boy's tongue on the underside of his shaft. He put his hands on the boy's head, curling his fingers against the dark bristles of hair. "Good," he said when he felt the heat of Chris's mouth on his dangling sac, sucking the baggy skin, tenderly chewing, nudging with his tongue Ben's pendulous balls. The boy licked up, kissing the veined kielbasa-size cock, slipping his mouth over the head swiftly, going down on Ben slowly, surely. Ben came up against the back of Chris's throat, and he pulled back again, the boy's teeth lightly along the top, catching the head and drawing Ben's thick rod in again, lips taut, tongue teasing. He felt Chris's hands now, slipping up Ben's thighs, fingering the curling hairs that grew lightly at the base of his dick. They circled his balls, making a tight ring, and tugged, and Ben felt his dick dribble. He heard the boy moan, sucking up the ooze. He backed off.

"What do we do now?" Ben heard Chris ask.

"Well," Ben said. He wasn't sure what to do next. His experience was limited, but he didn't care to divulge this information to Chris. This was as far as he had ever gone, getting his joint sucked, shooting his load on the floor with some stranger who milked his own cock as he squatted at Ben's feet.

"Do you want to go to bed?" Ben asked.
"I guess," Chris said.

They walked back to Ben's room, and Ben flipped the light switch, forgetting again that there was no power. He turned quick to say something, and Chris knocked into him, his hard cock bumping against Ben's thigh. The boy's lips smashed into Ben's shoulder. They grunted together, and Ben slipped his arms around the boy, crushing him into a bear hug. His hands followed the trail of Chris's backbone to his tailbone, and they grabbed hold of the boy's full ass cheeks, fingers at the rim of the boy's butt pucker.

Chris made some crazy noises and humped himself against Ben's leg. "Man," he said when Ben moved his hands up again to the boy's shoulders, "that's the other thing about this pot — it makes my hole all wacky. The other night I was so horny for it, I used a long-neck beer bottle. I'd just squat on the bottle and jack, then I'd take a break and take a swig from the bottle. I was out-of-my-mind horny."

"You feeling that way now?" Ben asked.

"Oh, fuck, man, you know it," he said, turning around and rubbing his ass up against Ben's crotch. Ben dropped to his haunches and started biting the tops of Chris's ass cheeks. He put his hands between the boy's legs and gripped his balls, pulling them back and wetting them with his tongue. He sniffed around the hypersensitive hole, which smelled hot and musky and ready for reaming. He touched it with the tip of his tongue, and the boy whimpered. He pushed the boy over, and Chris sprawled surprised across the dark bed. Ben found the boy's pulsing hole again and started eating it, gnawing with his teeth, probing with his tongue. He fucked into it with spit-slicked fingertips, and the hole seemed to gape. He went deeper with his fingers as Chris fucked against the bedspread, and with his free hand Ben got himself ready with a gob of saliva and a few short strokes on his own fiery rod.

"You want my cock?" he asked, and the boy started begging for it, his hips bucking. He flipped over onto his back and lifted his legs, and Ben took him by the heels and leaned into him, feeling the plush hole sigh around his cock head, inviting him in.

He never imagined fucking would be so easy. Chris's hole was more than easy; it was a coach, coaxing him in smoothly, then a drill sergeant, tightening up when Ben withdrew. Finding a comfortable rhythm, Ben handled his cock the way he handled an oar on the rowing team: stroke, stroke, stroke — nice and easy at first, but slowly and almost imperceptibly picking up speed.

He hooked the boy's feet around the back of his neck, and he fingered those tiny nips. His hips were now slapping against Chris's fanny, and they both grunted. Chris reached up for Ben's head, pulling him down and wrecking his tempo, and he fell into the boy's mouth for an unbelievably hot kiss that very nearly cost him his load. He crawled up on the bed, still fully engaged with Chris's mouth and asshole. He smeared his lips across the boy's mouth and whispered wetly into the boy's ear without really thinking, "Little brother."

Chris flipped out, turning into a fuck monster. He wrestled and twisted and got himself astride Ben's hips, supported like a tripod by his own two legs and Ben's concrete cock. He rode on Ben like a broncobuster, coming down hard on Ben's hipbones, and Ben wondered what sort of internal damage the boy could be causing himself. Then he forgot about the boy's innards save for the heat and the gritty slide, and he felt himself being sucked up — he felt as though he just might fall up the red inside of the boy. He pumped his hips and met the boy's ass with sharp slaps, and Chris twisted on Ben's pecs. Ben felt the heavy whack of Chris's cock against his belly, the hot juicy spray of it as the boy shot and shot, his teeth clenched.

"Stay on it," he whispered. "Stay on it, buddy," and Chris continued the ride until Ben's dick burst, great gobs of milky seed scattering up inside the boy's buttery asshole.

They were asleep when the lights came on in the room. It was close to dawn, and they were wrapped around each other. The overhead light shocked their eyes. From upstairs they heard the music Chris had been playing. They got themselves up and sleepily stumbled around. Ben shut down his computer, his essay title lost in the storm. He went upstairs with Chris to shut off the tape player and the lights. With everything black again they fell into Chris's bed, hard and ready and recharged, both of them eager to generate their own electricity.

Into the Night
by Ira Tea

It wasn't all that late, but Nelson felt worn-out when he got home from work. He went into the kitchen and poured himself a drink. Listening to the heavy rain pounding the ground outside his windows, he figured the city would be quiet tonight, even though it was Friday.

Thinking a short nap might revive him, Nelson went into the bedroom, took off his shirt, and gazed down at his neatly made empty bed. As tired as he was, he still felt decidedly horny and restless. Unfortunately, his energy level was too low to go to a bar, and phone sex never turned out to be enough to satisfy his desires.

Thinking masturbation might quench his lust, he pulled the blankets back from the bed to expose his newly purchased sheets. He took his pants off but left his underwear pulled down around his knees. If he yanked them up at just the right moment, he would shoot his load into them and leave the whiteness of his new sheets unstained.

He ran one hand down his chest to his stomach. His body was completely shaved, and he took some pleasure in feeling the smooth skin. He had been swimming since he was a little boy — he had even won some ribbons in high school — and still swam a few times a week to maintain his fine-tuned physique. He thought about some of his favorite locker-room scenes and touched himself again, near his inner thighs. Anticipation made him hard, and he knelt down on the bed, supporting himself with one hand while he adjusted the pillow with the other. Then he lay down on his stomach and rubbed himself against the cool, crisp bed linens. He didn't use his hands to stimulate himself, only the effortless back-and-forth motion of his hips against the mattress. His breathing grew heavy.

Chills washed over his body, and he shivered in the breeze coming through the slightly open window. He ground his pelvis against the mattress and bit into his pillow. He considered putting a video on but instead thought about an affair he'd had with a college swim coach. The memory of the coach's hard, eager cock made him moan.

Nelson raised himself up onto his hands and knees, moving his body with animal rhythm and force. His fingers teased the sensitive head of his dick until he began to feel a tingling deep in his groin. He knew he couldn't hold off much longer; he was reaching the point of no return. His load was boiling inside his balls, ready to flow the length of his dick and explode.

At last his come burst from his piss hole in hot, milky bullets. His wad shot across the bed, landing on the now-wrinkled white sheet. Too late to trap it in his underwear, Nelson felt more jizz erupting from his cock and wetting the soiled sheet. He bent over and lapped up the creamy mess with his tongue. It was a taste he enjoyed.

Feeling relaxed and no longer frustrated, Nelson remade his bed, got dressed, and decided to fix himself some dinner. He stared at the snapshots on the refrigerator, held in place by the force of magnets. His friends' faces seemed awfully gentle for guys who were involved in S/M photography and temperature torture. But the wilderness shots got him thinking as he quietly chewed his dinner.

Nelson would sometimes venture out late into the night, crossing the highway to make his way through the dark park by the river. Wearing a skimpy T-shirt to show off his toned body, he always felt like a wild man, his sexual desire building along with his testosterone level. Nelson was fascinated by the joys of brief sexual encounters; there were always surprises in store with people who, in the dark, had no faces.

Returning home before dawn, Nelson usually discovered that he'd left something behind in the park. He never knew what it would be, but if he returned the next day, the belt, the sock, the leather strap — whatever — would be gone.

Staring at his empty plate, Nelson wondered who might be out tonight. He always felt excitement in the air just after a storm, and tonight was no different. He had to know what might be happening just out of sight, under cover of darkness. The mere thought of what might lie ahead of him made his cock swell pleasurably in anticipation. He put on a fresh T-shirt and went out to explore.

Nelson had no desire to stop in at a bar. He headed straight for the cruisy park, preferring the bold directness the men displayed there. Nelson was always drawn to adventure, and he admired the spontaneity and lack of inhibition he found under the trees.

The park lay just on the far side of the road. Following the well-worn footpath into the park, Nelson was glad the way was so familiar; it was dark inside, and his eyes took a long time to adjust. With a surefootedness born of long practice, Nelson made his way along the pavement, searching the shadows for a lurking figure. He heard the sound of piss splashing against a tree and soon after spied the man, his body turned so the dim light from the nearby path illuminated the back of his leather jacket and a pair of worn jeans covering his ass. As the spray slowed, Nelson watched the man's hand work its way down the length of his cock and then shake off the last few drops. Nelson moved closer to the tree. As he walked he was highly conscious of the crunching noise his boots made on the many broken twigs scattered on the rain-dampened ground.

The man turned deliberately, leaving his jeans unbuttoned. Nelson licked his lips, aroused by the sight of someone fully clothed with his dick hanging out. The man showed off his prize, holding his oversize cock in one tight fist. Careful to keep his lure in the light, he slapped his dark cock a few times in the open palm of his other hand. The noise was quick and sharp. Nelson watched as the dick got harder, signaling this man's clear availability.

Nelson approached and reached out his hand to squeeze the ready cock in front of him. He liked to measure it with his hands, judging the thickness by wrapping his fingers around it, calculating its size by adding a second hand to its length. As Nelson's fingers touched the hot smooth flesh, the man pulled his prick away.

"If you want it, use your mouth," he said in a whisper.

Emboldened, Nelson took a step forward.

"Get on your knees." The stranger pushed Nelson down onto the ground. He took his cock and hit Nelson across the face. Nelson experienced pure pleasure, feeling the full force of the slap. Then he felt the hard, fleshy mass against his cheeks. Back and forth the dick went, tracing a pattern on his face. The man pushed the head of his cock against Nelson's face, trying to find a place to enter. He jabbed his boner at Nelson's eye, his ear, and finally his lips.

"Lick my dirty prick clean," the man growled.

Nelson opened his mouth, wanting to suck this monster to climax. The man's hard-on filled his jaws and pushed against the back of his throat, making him gag slightly.

"Watch those teeth. I want to fuck that throat of yours."

Stimulated even further by the stranger's dirty talk, Nelson opened his mouth wider.

"Take it all in. Come on, cocksucker — swallow my big piece of meat. Work for that hot load. Isn't that what you want, cocksucker? Huh? Isn't it?"

Nelson nodded greedily, heedless of the fact that he was gagging on the man's pulsating joint.

"Take it all in. You love that fucking cock, don't you, pig? Isn't that what you are, a come-hungry pig?"

Nelson moaned with passion, loving the impossibly hard swell of the man's cock in his slobbering mouth. He became dimly aware of someone new standing nearby. He cast his eyes from the wiry black pubic hair in front of him toward the side. A new dick, this one smaller but uncut, jutted stiffly from another anonymous crotch.

Nelson worked his way out to the head of the cock he was so feverishly blowing, digging his tongue into the satiny piss slit in search of those first precious drops of precome. The slit was wide, and he worked at it with the pointed tip of his tongue.

He glanced to the side and saw two fingers pull at the foreskin of the second cock until the piss hole was covered. One finger poked into the opening of the hood, stretching the loose skin wide.

The man Nelson was servicing grabbed the back of his head and rammed his prick back down his throat. Nelson could almost taste the hot come surging up the iron bar of the man's cock shaft.

Seconds later the man yanked his cock out of Nelson's mouth and began to spray the air with his steaming juice. Nelson's tongue sought vainly to catch some of the hot spunk until he felt a load of sperm oozing down his neck. He looked up as the man pumped the last dribbles of jism out of his softening cock. Nelson rubbed the load all over the skin of his throat.

He stood up unsteadily and wandered along the edge of the water, looking up through the trees toward the rocks. Sometimes he saw the shadow of bodies against the hard surface of stone. When he got closer he saw men covered in sweat. They glistened like bodybuilders at a competition.

Many nights the men would strip down to their underwear, the soft cotton barely containing their hidden treasures. As the night wore on, the men would end up naked; they'd display their cocks like trophies, polishing them proudly in anticipation.

Nelson's practiced gaze zeroed in on a pumped-up dick bouncing inside a pair of sweatpants. As he passed, Nelson looked up to see a latex shirt, the sleeves hacked off to reveal a pair of muscular arms.

Circling back around, Nelson saw the man stop by a massive boulder and drop a small bag at his feet. In seconds he'd removed both his shirt and his pants; Nelson knew he had found what he was looking for this night.

The man leaned back against the rock and began to cover his body with oil. When he oiled his balls and pulled them up from between his thighs, Nelson approached him.

"Could you help me out here?" the man asked. "I'm having some trouble with my reach."

Nelson climbed onto the rock. With the bottle in one hand, he spread a thick line of oil along the man's thigh with his finger. Then he placed the finger between the man's legs and started to massage his ass. Instead of shrinking back, the stranger pulled his legs up and wrapped his elbows around his knees. His crotch was hairless and smooth, and Nelson had no trouble slipping a finger inside the guy's puckered hole. Soon Nelson had a second finger inside the man's hot, steamy butt.

When the man pulled Nelson's arm closer toward him, Nelson started finger-fucking him in earnest. Slick with precome, the guy's prick was bouncing with each thrust of Nelson's hand.

"Mmm...you've got magic fingers," the guy moaned, reaching down to jerk his cock.

Nelson leaned over to inspect the contents of the man's bag, hoping to find a fat dildo there.

"I love men who work with their hands," the guy whispered hoarsely.

Nelson let go of the satchel and felt along the surface of the guy's stomach. His muscles were tight.

"Oh, man," the guy gasped, "this is too fucking hot."

Nelson took the words as an invitation and pushed his hand in deeper. The guy spread his legs wide and jerked himself with increasing urgency. "Oh, shit!" he cried out. "I'm gonna blow!" He must not have come for weeks because his cock seemed to explode, spewing buckets of hot jizz. A huge load of come landed on his chest, and he smiled with blissed-out relief.

Nelson continued to probe the inside of the man's ass, but he knew the scene was over. With no particular destination in mind, he sauntered off among the trees. Although his line of vision was blocked, he heard soft voices nearby making noises he recognized as the sounds of sex. He had always thought of outdoor sex as relatively silent, but tonight the air was filled with the siren song of animal lust. He came upon a group of men ranged in a circle, which appeared to be empty at the center. After a moment he made out the figure of a man bent over at the waist being fucked. He was wearing nothing but a pair of gloves.

"Fuck me with that hard cock, you bastard," he was saying. "Yeah, pound my hot hole, you motherfucking piece of shit!"

The man doing the fucking responded by viciously shoving his cock so far into the bottom man's ass that all the helpless guy could do was shout with a mixture of shock and pleasure.

Nelson rubbed his swelling crotch. The guy being plowed looked up at him and reached out his arm. Then another strong fuck thrust came, and he winced.

Nelson walked over to the bottom man's side and started pinching his nipples, which were hard and round like pellets. He pulled at them harder and harder, torturing them with his fingertips.

"Make him groan," the fucker panted.

Nelson clutched the bulge in his own pants. He watched a river of sweat roll down the bottom guy's back and disappear in the mat of pubic hair that was being wedged between his ass cheeks with each hard thrust of the top's ramrod cock.

"Let's have that meat," the bottom guy urged him.

Nelson opened the fly of his pants and yanked out his dick. The head was swollen, and the slit was pouting, open and ready to shoot.

The guy being fucked struggled to maintain his balance long enough to take Nelson's boner into his hungry mouth, while the top man jammed his cock deeper and deeper into him. His legs shook as he wrapped his arms around the bottom's waist, and his face began to tighten; Nelson could tell he was close. Then he saw him buck and heard him grunt. The intense action slowed rather abruptly.

The top slid his shiny meat out of the bottom's ass and pulled the come-filled rubber off with his hand. Nelson noticed a leather cock ring keeping the man's dick hard and red. But there was no lingering; the top buttoned up his jeans and walked away.

The bottom proved to be insatiable, especially with more cock around. He dropped to his knees and turned back to Nelson, taking his cock back into his mouth and sucking on it hungrily. He reached up between Nelson's legs and pushed against his ass, wanting every inch of Nelson's cock in his mouth.

Nelson spread his legs farther apart and undid his pants. They fell to his ankles. The cocksucker took Nelson's shaved balls into his mouth, saliva dripping down his chin. Then he returned to Nelson's cock, swallowing it greedily.

Nelson backed up. His cock was wet and hard, and he wanted it drained. He fit a condom over its head and unrolled the tight latex down the shaft. There was a hot ass available, and Nelson wanted to pack it.

The guy got up off his knees and bent over. He spread his butt wide, waiting to be entered. "Fill me up. Fill my sloppy hole with your big fucking prick."

"If you want this meat, let me hear you beg for it," Nelson said.

The bottom grabbed Nelson by the legs and pulled him up against his ass. Nelson teased him by pushing just the head of his cock in and then pulling out again. The guy squirmed.

"Put your dick in there. I need to get fucked, man."

"Then take it, bitch," Nelson growled.

The bottom centered his hole over the head of Nelson's cock and pushed back. In one slick move he had Nelson's cock buried to the hilt inside him.

A muscular man moved in closer and bit Nelson's nipple. Somebody else's hand probed his ass, but, unable to maneuver, it disappeared. Then Nelson felt the same hand tugging on his balls. He pumped his hips furiously, willing himself to come. The bottom stretched his legs, jerking frantically at his own prick.

Someone nearby was being spanked. The sound spurred Nelson on, and he fucked the guy even harder. His balls slammed against the bottom's ass, which sucked his cock in like a ravenous mouth. After a few more thrusts, Nelson knew he couldn't hold back. His cock grew even harder, and he spewed his juice into the bottom's gaping hole until he was spent, empty. But he kept pounding away at the guy's butt until he came too, in long, shuddering waves.

They held on to each other until Nelson's cock grew limp. He pulled out and threw the jizzy rubber to the ground. He wondered if it would still be there when he came back tomorrow night.

Queer Punk
by Bob Vickery

I'm still half asleep, staring up at the ceiling and wondering whether I should get up. Part of me just wants to roll over and catch a few more z's, but I don't think my body can take the lumps in the couch anymore. (Darlene told me she'd found the couch on trash day in front of some apartment building a couple of blocks away.) I can hear Darlene and her dickhead boyfriend, Buck, in the bedroom; it sounds like they're having a fight. I guess that's better than the times when I have to listen to them fuck, hearing Buck groan like he's got a bad case of the trots. I can't make out most of what they're saying, but every now and then I hear my name. Ol' Buck is probably ragging on Darlene again about how much longer her deadbeat little brother is going to be hangin' around. If it weren't for me, I don't think they'd have anything to talk about.

The bedroom door opens, and Buck walks in wearing nothing but his underwear. He gives me the evil eye as he makes his way to the kitchen. I give him my best "Fuck you too" look. A few seconds later he's back with a carton of orange juice in his hand. He takes a swig from it. "So, Jamie," he says, "how's the job hunt going?"

I shrug. "No luck yet, Buck," I say. I catch myself checking out his body again. It really pisses me off when I do that. Buck works out regularly with his weight set, and his body is tight and cut, but he's such an asshole. I'd cut off my dick before I had anything to do with him. Still, I can't help copping a look at him every now and then.

Buck takes another gulp of orange juice. "You know, they're looking for a busboy over at that Italian restaurant on Haight."

I turn my head and stare at the ceiling again. "Thanks. I'll check it out." *When monkeys fly out of my ass,* I think.

I can feel Buck's eyes on me. "Another thing, Jamie," he says. "I don't want you using my weight set anymore. You never put the weights back right."

I ignore him, and he goes back into the bedroom. A little later he comes back out again, dressed for work (he runs a forklift at some Kmart in Daly City). We don't look at each other, and when he leaves he slams the front door. What a douche bag.

A few minutes later Darlene walks in wearing a bathrobe. "Good morning, Jamie," she says.

"Hi," I grunt.

Darlene scratches her head and yawns. "You want some breakfast?"

I shake my head. "Naw. Maybe a cup of coffee."

As I sit at the kitchen table with her, I can see that Darlene is trying to work herself up to say something. I decide to make it easy for her. "I *am* going to look for work today, Darlene," I say.

She looks apologetic. "I'm sorry about Buck."

I laugh. "So am I." I shake a cigarette out of the pack and light it. "What do you see in him, Darlene? He's such a fucking loser."

"Yeah," Darlene snorts, "unlike the parade of winners you've called boyfriends." She bums a cigarette from me and lights it, though I know she's trying to quit. She breathes out a cloud of smoke. "Listen, Jamie," she says. "I have to go to work soon. How about you doing the laun-

dry? Buck's been grousing about running out of clean
shirts, and I just don't have time to do it myself today." I
make a face, and Darlene's eyes shoot daggers at me.
"Don't give me a hard time about this, Jamie," she says,
sounding pissed. "I've already had to deal with Buck's bullshit this morning, and I don't want any attitude from you."

I don't say anything. "Okay, fine," Darlene snaps. "I'll
do the damn laundry myself when I get home from work."

I push my chair out and get up. "Oh, chill out, Darlene.
I'll do the fuckin' laundry."

Darlene still looks pissed; I guess I didn't agree nicely
enough. She gets up and piles the dishes in the sink. When
she leaves, the good-bye she throws over her shoulder at
me is like a fuckin' icicle.

As soon as she's gone, I go to the bedroom and work out
with Buck's weight set. I check myself out in the mirror as
I do my curls. I look fuckin' good, my biceps pumped up
nicely, my pecs hard and defined. I put the dumbbells
down and pose, flexing my arms, checking out my definition. Hot stuff. I drop my shorts and stare at my reflection.
My dick flops against my thigh, half hard. Under my gaze
it stirs and stiffens, the head flaring out. I fuckin' love my
cock: the meatiness of it, its redness and thickness, how
the veins snake up the shaft. I wrap my hand around it
and begin stroking, slowly and easily at first, then picking
up the tempo till my balls are a bouncing blur. I pull my
dick down and let it slap against my belly, then shake it at
my reflection. "You want to suck on it?" I croon at the hot
naked stud looking back at me. "You want me to fuck
your face, ram this dick down your throat?" A sexy punk
with too much attitude stares back, sneering and shaking
his dick at me as well. I walk up to the mirror and start
humping my reflection, my body pressed tightly against
the glass, my hands grabbing the corners of the closet
door. The mirror feels smooth and cool on my skin as I
thrust my cock up and down against it. It doesn't take
long before I'm ready to shoot. Groaning, I squirt my load
on the mirror and watch as it drips down over my reflec-

tion. I wipe my hand across the spattered jizz and lick my fingers clean. Then I clean off the rest of the load with my Jockeys and get dressed.

I gather all the dirty laundry and take it to the Laundromat just down the block. The place is empty, and as the clothes are washing, I sit out on the front step, soaking up rays and smoking my last cigarette. I think about my living situation. I gotta line up some kind of gig, get some money so I can get my own place. I've been in San Francisco about three weeks now, and it's pretty clear that I've just about milked dry the setup I have going with Darlene.

When the laundry's done I toss it into one of the dryers and walk down to Haight Street for more cigarettes. I pass the winos lined up by the supermarket and the panhandlers, runaways, and dopers on the street corners and buy some Marlboros at the mom-and-pop store over by the park. On my way back I check out the neighborhood piercing studio. It would be bitchin' to get my nose or my eyebrow pierced, but that shit costs more money than I can afford. I push the idea out of my head.

The first thing I see back at the Laundromat is the open dryer door. *Oh, shit!* I think. A quick check shows that everything's been cleaned out — not just Darlene's and Buck's stuff but most of the clothes I own as well. The fucker didn't even leave any of my old ratty underwear behind. "Fuck!" I shout, kicking the dryer door as hard as I can. It slams against the dryer and bounces open again, and I kick it again, hard enough to put a crack in the window. I storm outside and cross the street without looking. A car screeches to a stop, and the driver gives me a twenty-second blast on his horn. I spin around and kick one of his headlights out. The dude gets out of his car, and I just wait with clenched fists. He has second thoughts, calls me an asshole, and drives off. I laugh, but I still feel like ripping someone's head off.

Darlene is the first one home. Even before I open my mouth, I can see she's had a bad day and isn't in the mood for any shit. When I tell her what happened, she freaks.

"What a stupid thing to do, Jamie!" she shouts at me. "I can't believe you just left that stuff by itself for anybody to rip off!"

She goes on like this for a few more minutes. I smoke a cigarette, slouched in a chair, and pretend like I don't hear her. After a while she storms off to the bedroom, but when she reaches the doorway, she turns around again and glares at me. "When Buck gets home, you can go ahead and tell him what happened," she snarls. "You tell him you lost his favorite shirt, the one he always goes bowling in." She slams the door. *Jesus fuckin' Christ,* I think.

I'm not about to hang around to hear Buck piss and moan at me. I change into my one last T-shirt, the one that says QUEER PUNK, and head out to Haight Street. A few guys are jamming on one of the street corners, playing guitars and congas, and I hang out there for a while, toking whenever the joint they're circulating comes back to me again. Later I grab a burrito somewhere and wash it down with a couple of beers, then wander up to Club DV8 to see what's happening. Some group called Hog Maw is playing tonight; even out here on the street, their music is loud enough to pop an eardrum. The doorman sits on his stool by the entrance, cracking his knuckles and staring at the world with his fat biker's face. I wait till a large group of people show up and push through the door, and I crowd in with them, slipping by without paying. By the time the doorman sees me, I'm already in. "Hey, you!" he yells, but I dive into the bodies crammed on the dance floor and lose the fucker.

The band sucks, but I like the way the noise just sweeps over me, pushing everything else out of my head. I grab a beer at the bar and watch the dance floor, checking out the guys. There's some hot meat out there tonight, bodies pumping to the music — slick with sweat, ripe, smelly, pierced, tattooed. My eye suddenly snags on one of them — not because of his tight, muscular body (which is hot) but because of the T-shirt he's wearing, with THE BOOGERS written across it in black and red. I bought that shirt in a

Chicago punk club last year. Any doubt I might have had that this is the same shirt goes out the window when I see the grease stain on the back that I got from changing the oil in my car. That's the fucker who ripped me off!

It looks like he's dancing by himself. I push through the crowd toward him, sometimes losing him in the crush of squirming bodies but then catching sight of him again, closer each time. I finally squeeze through right behind him. His shaved head, muscles, and the ring in his left ear make him look like a punk Mr. Clean. Just then the band stops playing. I put my hand on his shoulder, and he turns to face me, his eyes narrowed. Along with his ear, he's got his nose and left eyebrow pierced. I smile at him. "Hey, man," I say. "I like your shirt." Then I slug him in the face as hard as I can.

The dude falls against the stage but then comes back at me like a hound from hell. We start slugging it out on the dance floor. He gets a good one to my right eye, but I connect flat on his nose; blood streams down over his nose ring and spatters my stolen shirt. He tries a head butt on me, but I jerk away in time and hit him with a body tackle. We're down on the floor now, sometimes me on top, sometimes him. The crowd around us is cheering us on. When I'm on top again, I pull my fist back to give him a pounding so hard, his parents will feel it. But before I get a chance, somebody grabs my arm and yanks me to my feet. It's the doorman. "Okay, you little bastard," he growls, "you've caused enough trouble for the night." He pins my arm behind my back and shoves me forward through the crowd. People are hooting and jeering on both sides of us. My upper lip is cut, and I can taste my blood as it flows into my mouth.

When we reach the door, the bouncer gives me a final hard shove, and I go crashing into a parked car. A couple of seconds later, the other guy comes flying through the door as well. The doorman stands at the entrance, glowering at us with a face like raw ground chuck. "If I see you guys here again," he snarls, "I'll rip your fuckin' heads off." He points a fat finger at me. "That goes especially for you, asshole." He goes back inside the club.

I climb to my feet and spit the blood out of my mouth. The other guy has pulled off his (or rather my) T-shirt and is dabbing his bloody nose with it. His body is lean and muscular, his abs cut like a six-pack, his pecs hard and ripped. Both his nipples are pierced too. His arms are covered with tattoos; I can't make them out in this light, just a few scattered images: tits, skulls, knives with blood, that kind of shit.

"You want to give me my shirt back?" I growl.

He looks at me and then at the shirt in his hand. "Oh, is this yours?" he asks, his eyes wide. He blows his nose into it. "Here," he says, tossing it to me. I let it fall to my feet. We glare at each other.

His eyes flick down to my QUEER PUNK T-shirt and then back to my face again. "You queer?" he asks.

Okay, I think, *here comes the bullshit.* It looks like we really are going to have to take up where we left off in the club. "Yeah," I say, squinting my eyes. "What of it?"

"Nothing," he says, shrugging. "Except I'm queer too."

I didn't see that one coming. "So?" I finally say after a couple of beats.

He grins, and for once it's not a "Fuck you" grin. "So d'you want to fuck?"

"Are you for real?" I reply, laughing. But I start wondering what he would look like naked.

The dude shrugs. "Hey, it was just a thought." A few seconds go by. "We could keep on fighting if you want to do that instead," he adds. It's like we're on a date, trying to figure what movie to see.

I take in the muscles, the tattoos, the piercings. In the glow of the streetlight, his body shines with sweat, and I can see the meaty bulge in the crotch of his torn jeans. His lip is puffed up where I hit it, pushing his mouth into a permanent sneer. His dark eyes sneer too, looking hard at me, challenging me. I feel my dick growing hard. I haven't been laid since I moved to this city, and I'm getting real tired of fucking my fist. "Okay," I say slowly. "If I get to choose, then I choose fucking."

The dude laughs. "All right!" he says. He sticks out his hand. "I'm Crow."

I take his hand and shake it. "Jamie," I say.

Crow lives in a dingy apartment on Fell Street, one long hallway with a whole bunch of rooms branching off it. He tells me he shares it with four other guys, but it feels as if half of fuckin' Haight Street is crammed into this place. A tape deck blasts from one of the rooms in the back, playing something from Smashing Pumpkins, and I hear laughter and loud voices. People wander in and out of the kitchen, mostly guys but a few chicks too. The place smells of grass, incense, and ripe garbage. It makes Darlene and Buck's apartment look like Graceland.

Crow's room is nothing more than a storage closet with a mattress on the floor. There's no other furniture in it — no other furniture could fit in it — but there are piles of clothes stacked along the walls. I recognize some of my stuff, and damned if I don't see Buck's bowling shirt, a neon-blue polyester piece of shit that should be burned.

Crow sees me staring at the clothes. "You can have them back if you want," he says, grinning.

I don't say anything, I just pull him to me and pry open his mouth with my tongue. Crow wraps his powerful arms around me and starts grinding his crotch against mine. I can feel the bulge of his dick rubbing against mine, a slow, circular massage of cocks separated by blue denim. With a sudden jerk he topples us both onto his mattress. He grabs my wrists and pins my arms down as he continues to dry-hump me nice and slow. His tongue pushes into my mouth and down my throat, almost deep enough to taste the burrito I had for dinner.

I bury my face in his armpit and lick the sweat from it, breathing in the smell deeply. Crow's body squirms on top of mine, and he bends his neck so he can stick his tongue in my ear. I trace my own tongue across his firm pecs to his left nipple. It's huge, sticking out sharp and erect like a little toy soldier, the ring in it gleaming in the light from the bulb overhead. I place the metal hoop between my teeth and tug at it. Crow reaches up to yank the string that turns out the light, but I pull his arm away. "I want to see your body," I tell him.

Crow's mouth curves up into a slow smile. "Okay, man," he says, "if you want a show, I'll give you one." He stands up at the foot of the mattress and kicks his boots off. I lie back with my hands behind my head and watch. He unzips his jeans and drops them, revealing a pair of bright red bikini briefs. He looks fuckin' hotter than hell in them.

"Nice briefs," I say. "You've been hitting some high-class Laundromats."

Crow just laughs. Slowly, teasingly, he pulls them down, first showing his pubes, then the base of his dick shaft, thick and promising. He stops there. "You want to see more?" he asks, eyebrows arched.

I don't answer but just reach over and yank his briefs down. His half-hard dick swings heavily between his legs. It's a beautiful dick, fat and meaty with a dark red head that flares out from the shaft. His foreskin is pierced with a thin steel ring. I almost shoot a load just looking at it.

"Christ," I whisper. I never saw anything like it before.

Crow looks proud. "I had it done a couple of months ago." Under my eyes his dick begins to lengthen and get harder. "Check it out," Crow urges. "It won't bite."

I get up on my knees, but Crow holds me back at arm's length for a second. "Get naked first," he orders me. Only after I strip does Crow let me take his dick in my hand. I work the foreskin back and forth over the head, watching as the ring winks in and out of sight. Crow's fat dick is fully stiff now, and the feel of his warm, hard meat against my hand gets my own cock all stiff and juiced up. I squeeze his dick, and a drop of precome oozes out of the piss slit. I lick it up, whirling my tongue around the head, tasting the saltiness of the spermy pearl. I look up at Crow and grin. "My favorite flavor," I say.

I work my lips in small nibbles down the length of Crow's shaft until my nose is buried deep in his pubes. I inhale deeply, breathing in the musky, pungent scent of Crow's cock and balls. Crow begins pumping his hips, and his dick slides easily in and out of my mouth. I feel the ring scrape the inside of my cheek, and I run my tongue over it. I wrap my hand around Crow's balls; they have a solid heft to them that feels like they were made for my palm. I squeeze them as I twist my head from side to side, giving his dick the full treatment with my tongue. Crow groans loudly. He seizes my head with both hands and thrusts his dick deep down my throat, mashing his pubes into my face. Then he pulls back and continues fucking my face with long, steady strokes. My other hand plays over his body, kneading the muscles of his torso, feeling his hard ass, and tugging his tit rings. With his dick still in my mouth, I look up past the cut abs, the muscle-packed torso, and the bull shoulders to his face. Crow grins. "You're a real pig for dick, aren't you?" he croons. "You just can't fuckin' get enough of it." And he's right. I'm a dick pig for sure, and I've got my face buried in the trough tonight.

I take his cock out of my mouth and start flicking his balls with my tongue. They hang loose and heavy above my face, furred lightly, the left nut lower than the right. I suck them both into my mouth and slobber my tongue over them, drool running down my chin. Crow starts beating my face with his dick, gently slapping my cheeks, nose, and eyes with it.

My tongue blazes a wet trail down the hairy path to Crow's asshole. His ass cheeks are fleshy and muscular. I bury my face between them and then burrow in deep, probing his bung hole with my tongue. Crow goes crazy, writhing around and grinding his ass into my face. I replace my tongue with my finger, working it slowly up his chute to the third knuckle and then screwing it around.

Crow groans loudly. "How do you feel about fucking my ass?" he rasps.

"I feel just fine about it," I tell him.

He rummages under a pile of clothes and comes up with a jar of lube and a rubber. "Lie down on your back," he growls. He straddles my hips and wraps his greased hand around our dicks, squeezing them together. I look down at the sight of it: our two cocks being stroked together, slipping and sliding against each other inside Crow's big, rough hand. Crow bends over, and we kiss again.

I take the lube from him and grease up my hand as well. Reaching behind, I pry apart Crow's ass crack and slide my grease-slimed finger inside his bung hole again. Crow squeezes his asshole tight, and I feel the muscles clamp down around my finger. I slowly pull it out, wiggling it all the way, then shove it back in hard. Crow's body squirms against mine, and I push a second finger in. Crow groans loudly. "Lie down on your back," he gasps.

I do so, holding my wrapped dick straight up as Crow lowers himself onto it. It slides smoothly into his ass, and Crow eases onto it like he's sinking into a hot bath. He closes his eyes and sighs loudly, and the look of pleasure on his face is so intense, I almost laugh. He begins riding my dick, pushing off my body and then sliding down again, and I pump my hips to meet him stroke for stroke. It's such a fuckin' hot sight: his pierced, tattooed, muscle-packed body sliding up and down my cock. I wrap my still-greasy hand around his dick and stroke it slowly. With my other hand I tug on his nipple rings, first the right one, then the left, then back to the right again. Crow's eyes glaze with pleasure, and something close to a whimper comes out of his open mouth.

I pull his head down and kiss him hard, pushing my tongue deep down his throat as I pound his ass. Crow turns into a fuckin' maniac. He wraps his arms around me, and we roll around on the mattress, Crow snarling and howling like some wild animal. I feel like I'm in a segment from *Mutual of Omaha's Wild Kingdom*. I hear footsteps down the hallway outside and then a laugh. "Go, Crow!" someone yells.

Crow's on his back now, and I shift into overdrive, roaring down his ass like he's just so many miles of bad road. Each pounding I give him seems to shove Crow deeper into the mattress. One hard thrust gets my dick in full to the balls, and I grind my hips and tear up his ass. Our eyes lock; Crow's are bright and sharp, not missing a thing. I see the challenge in them. He wraps his legs around me and clamps his ass muscles tight. My dick feels like it's gripped in soft velvet, and as I pull out and then thrust back in, I feel like my whole fuckin' body is about to implode. Crow's lips are pulled back, and his eyes are laughing. The message in them is clear enough: *Don't even think you're running this show.* I pump my hips a few more times, and Crow matches me thrust for thrust, drawing me to the edge with a skill that blows my mind. The things I could learn from this guy! I groan loudly, and Crow reaches down and pushes hard against my nuts. Sweet Jesus, I just explode in that boy's ass, my dick squirting what feels like a couple of quarts of jizz into the condom.

Before the last spasm is over, Crow flips me on my back and sits on my chest. As he fucks his hand, I reach up and pull down hard on his tit rings. He gives a whimper that trails into a long groan. His balls are pulled up tight now, and his dick is as stiff as dicks get. He's going to blow any second now. He begins to shudder, and then the first load of jizz squirts out of his dick and onto my face. Crow cries out as his wad rains down on me, sliming my face and dribbling down my chin and into my open mouth.

Crow collapses on top of me. Through the closed door I can hear Pearl Jam on the tape deck down the hall. After a few seconds Crow raises his head and starts licking his own pearl jam off my face. When he gets to my mouth, we kiss again — not like before, just nice and tender. I close my eyes and drift off to sleep with Crow's naked body sprawled on top of mine.

The next morning Crow gives me back all the clothes he swiped. I catch him looking at Buck's butt-ugly bowling shirt. I hand it to him. "Here," I say. "Do you want it?"

Crow's happy to take it. He tells me one of the guys is moving out in a couple of days, and if I'm looking for a place, the room is mine. I accept without seeing it.

The sun is just rising when I finally step out onto Haight Street. The homeless are just beginning to stir in the shop doorways. As I walk by, one of them sleepily asks if I have any spare change. I give him another one of Buck's shirts and then just head on toward home, grinning.

Careless Love
by Derek Adams

I sat on the front porch, drinking a beer after work and contemplating for about the millionth time the shitty state of my life. Things had gone to hell early and stayed that way ever since. The first time I was called a queer, I had no idea what the word meant. I was five years old at the time, prancing up and down along the creek that ran beside the old house where I grew up. I was wrapped in an old quilt that my mother had banished to the attic, waving a stick — or was it a scepter? — at passing cars, then curtsying if they honked or waved. I have the vague memory that I believed I was the queen of some mythical realm where people like me fit in.

"You're a queer, aren't you, Eddie Wickham?" Tommy Marks and Bobby Joe Purdy had been standing on the opposite bank of the creek, pointing at me, when they first broke the news. I dropped my stick and fled into the shrubbery, where I stayed till Tommy and Bobby Joe were well out of sight.

Even though I didn't know what the word *queer* meant, I knew enough not to ask my father about it. He was already distant and disapproving, and I didn't want to add any ammunition to his arsenal. I found out what a queer was soon enough — other kids in the neighborhood took up the cry, and I was branded before I entered first grade.

I endured the name-calling, bullying, and social ostracism by retreating even further into my fantasy realm. I surfaced only on those frequent occasions when the bullying escalated to beating and I got my skinny ass smeared all over the playground. I finally got fed up with that when I turned sixteen and sent off for a bodybuilding course that was advertised in a *Superman* comic book. I admired Superman more for his physique than for his commitment to fighting crime and figured that if Clark Kent could do it, then so could I.

Much to my surprise, the program worked, and I developed muscles where there had been nothing but skin and bones a few months earlier. When the inevitable encounter with the local Neanderthals took place at the beginning of the next school year, nobody was more surprised than I when I creamed Jimmy Loggins in the hallway outside junior English class. I didn't gain any friends from this display of physical prowess, but I never had another black eye either.

I thought I had a ticket out of Harmonville when I graduated from high school, but disaster struck again. My grades were good — hell, I had nothing to distract me from my studies — and I was favored to win a scholarship to the state university. I was elated at the prospect of beginning life anew in a place where nobody knew me — someplace where I'd no longer be called a queer.

As it turned out, Tommy and Bobby Joe had been absolutely correct in their assessment of my sexual profile. Up until the end of my senior year, I had never even so much as considered the idea of having sex with anyone other than my own right hand. I knew the rumors about who was sleeping with whom in my peer group — I was unpopular, but I wasn't deaf — but I had never been foolhardy enough to entertain a grand passion for anyone at school, male or female. Then, in a weak moment the week before graduation, I accepted an invitation to go to a party. Actually, I was so shocked at having been asked that I failed to heed the many warning signals that anyone in my situation should have noticed.

The party was a boys-only bash thrown by one of the most popular guys in the senior class. I arrived, got real nervous, drank too much beer way too fast, and got talked into smoking some pot. It all got a little fuzzy after that, but I have vague recollections of rolling around naked with an unknown number of drunken, horny seniors on an old mattress down in the furnace room. The next morning my mouth tasted terrible and my asshole ached something fierce. I gathered up what clothing I could find, climbed over the snoring bodies littering the house, and made my way home.

Naturally, word got out about the party, and every day brought new horrors to light. Evidently, I had taken on damn near the whole senior class that night, sucking any cock that got shoved my way and wiggling my ass around like a two-bit whore in a lumber camp on payday. My scholarship was canceled, my father died of a heart attack soon thereafter, and my dreams of starting a new life withered on the vine.

Now here I sat, my twenty-fourth birthday looming on the horizon, still stuck in Harmonville, still an outcast, with no one to talk to and no place to go. My world pretty much consisted of television, beer, and my low-wage job in a local factory that produced ball bearings for precision machinery. My mother never missed a chance to tell me that supporting her was the least I could do, since I had killed my father and made her a candidate for welfare. She grumbled that the money I brought home wasn't enough, but anytime I offered to quit and look for work in another city, she threatened to have a stroke. Life was a bitch.

I drained my beer and was going in to fix some supper when I saw Charlie Ferrin walking along the street that runs in front of the house. Charlie was my age, but we'd never been in class together because Charlie had always lagged a couple of grades behind. He'd quit school as soon as he turned sixteen, but if he'd ever wanted to leave Harmonville, he hadn't made much more progress than I had.

Charlie had never been a friend, but he had saved me from serious injury on more than one occasion when I was the school punching bag. I suspect that he intervened more for the joy of a fistfight than from any feelings toward me, but he had enabled me to escape from my tormentors a number of times, so I had a soft spot for him in my memory.

I'd always thought Charlie Ferrin was the sexiest man I'd ever laid eyes on. Charlie actually had biceps when he was ten and hair on his chest at an age when the rest of us were fruitlessly searching for pubic hairs. Time had only made his body bigger and harder. Nature had given him chiseled good looks and thick raven hair, which he wore in a long ponytail that almost brushed his broad shoulders. I swear, he turned my crank every time I saw him.

Poor Charlie had also had his share of tough luck. After countless juvenile scrapes, he'd beaten the living shit out of some guy in a nearby town during an argument. Nobody ever found out what the argument was about, but it didn't matter for Charlie — he'd been sent up for assault and battery. After he'd gotten out of prison and started doing odd jobs to keep his parole officer happy, the old lady who lived next door to us, Mrs. Staley, had been one of the few people in town who'd actually hired him — I guess everyone else was afraid of him.

I prayed for Mrs. Staley to have him come around on weekends so I could be there to enjoy the show. Charlie always wore baggy old overalls when he came to cut the brush out back or to paint her front porch, and anybody who cared to look could catch glimpses of Charlie's splendid physical assets. There were buttons on the sides of the overalls, but Charlie never bothered with them, an oversight that bared his silken flanks and exposed a fair portion of his tight, furry ass. His impressive chest and incredible arms were also much in evidence, making Charlie a sight to behold.

This afternoon it was humid, so Charlie had his shirt stuffed into the back pocket of a pair of tight faded Levi's. I swear, just seeing the sunlight glinting off the silky hairs that dusted his massive chest made my heart beat faster. While I was focusing in on the little tattoo emblazoned above one of the big, dusky brown nipples that crowned those spectacular pecs of his, Charlie looked my way. I smiled and waved jauntily. He saw me, and he may — or may not — have nodded. I wasn't able to decipher the tattoo, but I did have the satisfaction of seeing the ridges in his washboard belly tighten when he briefly turned my way, and I went inside the house, feeling uplifted.

I fried up some chicken and steamed some vegetables, then sat in the dining room and ate while my mother complained about the reception on the television in her bedroom. I wasn't listening too closely, but I got the general idea that she wanted me to work enough overtime to be able to afford a new set for her. I said something noncommittal and hustled her back to her room so I could clean up the kitchen.

It was Wednesday night, and that meant Cal Purdy. Now Cal wasn't the most exciting man who ever walked the streets of Harmonville, but he did have his good points. He was a few years older than me, and his gut was starting to grow a little, but he was still pretty easy on the eye, and he had a nice pair of arms. He also had the biggest dick I'd ever seen or heard tell about.

Cal's cock was a subject of considerable interest to the women of Harmonville. Cal had never married, and the women he'd dated over the years all seemed to have a couple of things in common — admiration of Cal's equipment and a great deal of difficulty in getting it geared up to go where they most wanted to put it. I'd heard that some gals had spent the better part of the evening trying to wake his old one-eyed buddy up, only to have Cal himself pass out on them. People were beginning to whisper that Cal was

impotent — and wasn't that a hell of a shame for a man
endowed like he was.

Well, I knew for a fact that there was nothing wrong
with Cal's prick. Given the proper encouragement, it
would get hard and stay hard for hours at a time. The
truth was, those gals were at a distinct disadvantage. Cal
played the ladies' man, but the dude was as queer as I
was. The only difference between us was that Cal was in
the closet — way deep in, like where you keep the suit you
wear only to funerals.

I heard his truck pull up just a few minutes after 10. I
turned out the lights in the living room, tiptoed down the
back steps, and slipped into the tumbledown garage at the
back of the property. I saw the burning ember of Cal's cigarette before my eyes adjusted to the gloom, and I used it
to guide myself over to where he was standing.

"Eddie," he muttered gruffly, dropping his smoke and
grinding it out under his heel.

"Cal," I replied, dropping to my knees and getting down
to business. Cal had already popped the buttons on his fly
and shucked his pants down around his hairy thighs. I
stroked the thick pendulum between his legs, amazed, as
always, by the sheer size of it. Cal had a dick that mea-
sured thirteen and a half inches long — yes, I checked it
out myself — and the sucker was as thick as my wrist. The
knob on the end was as big as a medium-size apple.

Cal got stiff quicker than you could say "hard-on." He
stood there whimpering softly as I began licking his stick,
savoring every fat, veiny inch of him. I hung off the end of
it and sucked for a while till he started getting juicy, then
leaned back and jacked him, letting his hot lube drizzle
down on my bare chest. When I finally let go of the big
fleshy stalk, it swung up majestically, pointing high in the
air. Impotence was definitely not a problem I ever had
with Cal.

Cal pulled me to my feet, and his huge log of a prick
throbbed against my belly, getting harder and leakier by
the second. I kept my hands planted on his bulging biceps,

feeling the big muscles twitch and flex as he worked his thick fingers up into my hungry hole.

When the critical moment came, Cal spun me around, forced my legs apart, and drove his mighty spike deep into me. I bit my tongue to keep from crying out, jarred as usual by the sheer immensity of what he was forcing up my fuck chute. He packed me full, and I started doing a slow dance on his rigid dick, bumping and grinding and squeezing my ring down tight as he braced his hands on my shoulders and started to fuck.

Regardless of what Cal told himself or anybody else, he definitely got off on fucking guys. I knew for a fact that he had nothing against grabbing another man's stiff cock and pumping it. He had a firm grip on mine right now, his fist flying up and down the shaft, making me twitch and squirm. He was also rubbing my belly and playing with my tits and balls till I was damn near banging my head against the top of the old workbench.

Cal loved getting me to shoot while he was porking me. When I blow, I contract long and hard, and when he played it right, old Cal could make me have spasms for a good five minutes, with my ass ring battened down nice and tight on his pistoning love muscle.

I leaned back against Cal's shaggy torso and let fly, my first thick blast of jizz hitting the wall. Cal really got off on the volume of spunk I shot — something else those gals couldn't give him. He drove deep and squeezed my nuts hard, making me shoot off another gusher. Once I'd stopped pumping, Cal pushed me back onto the bench and kept on driving. After a couple of minutes, his cock jerked, his knob blew up big, and he blasted me full of juice.

The thing with Charlie Ferrin would probably never even have come to a head if I hadn't decided to go out to Josie's Place, a honky-tonk about halfway between Harmonville and Vidalia. The place was straight and redneck, but the music was good, and a man can watch only so much television before he starts to believe the commercials.

Anyhow, I was sitting at the bar, minding my own business, when some drunk asshole swaggered over to where I
was sitting at the bar. "Faggot!" he slurred, trying unsuc-
cessfully to knock me off my stool. I was ready to ignore
that, but then he went and spit in my beer. "Drink that,
cocksucker," he bellowed, shoving me again.

"Knock it off!" I barked, hoping to bluster my way out
of the situation. My tormentor, however, was too drunk to
be intimidated. He made a fist and planted it in the middle of my chest before I could move out of the way, sending me sprawling. The place got real quiet, then three
more drunks came over and started egging the guy on.

Well, needless to say, nobody was coming to my rescue,
and I was beginning to think I was going to experience a
repeat of one of my childhood playground experiences
when a man suddenly came between me and the drunks.
One look at the man's long black ponytail and the full,
rounded ass packed into the faded Levi's, and I knew it
was Charlie. I couldn't quite figure why he was willing to
intervene, but I didn't lose any time worrying about it. I
scrambled to my feet and stood beside him, proud to claim
him for an ally, at least temporarily.

"Well, well, looks like we got us two faggots to whip,"
the man who'd pushed me said, taking a step forward. I
glanced over at Charlie. The veins in his neck were standing out like cords, and his face was scarlet. When his
hands balled into fists and his shoulders hunched forward,
I leaned over and put a restraining hand on his arm. His
biceps were hard as a rock — a big warm rock.

"Don't get in a brawl over me," I whispered. "You'll
break your parole and get your ass thrown back in jail."

"Don't care," Charlie growled, his voice all menacing
and raspy.

"Well, I care, damn it!" I snapped. It was true — the
idea of Charlie going back to jail where I couldn't see him
for three to five years suddenly struck me as unbearable.

"Don't care," he repeated sullenly. I knew that I had to
take action immediately. There was no way in hell that I

could physically stop Charlie Ferrin, but maybe, just maybe, I could stop the situation. With that in mind, I doubled up my fist and, putting my entire weight behind it, smashed my tormentor in the jaw. The man's eyes rolled back, and he hit the barroom floor like a ton of shit. His buddies muttered curses and glared at me balefully but melted back into the crowd that had gathered around, unwilling to risk getting decked by a pervert.

I turned around, ready to buy Charlie a beer, but he had already disappeared. It occurred to me that that wasn't such a bad idea, so I stalked out of the place, staring down any man who dared to look my way.

The friends of the guy I'd decked hadn't wasted any time: All four tires on my old Chevy were flat, and the windshield had been bashed in. There was no way in hell that I was going to go back into the bar, especially now that Charlie was gone. I stomped out of the gravel parking lot and headed back to Harmonville, cursing a blue streak all the way.

When the pickup pulled over alongside me about a half mile down the highway, I figured I was a dead man. I started breathing again only when I recognized the sound of Charlie's voice. "Get in," he said, scooting over on the seat and throwing open the passenger door. I climbed in gratefully and leaned back, watching the familiar scenery glide by in the glare of Charlie's headlights.

The truck was permeated with his acrid, musky scent, a smell that was distinctly masculine and very comforting. Neither of us spoke during the ride, and when he pulled up in front of my house, shut off the engine, opened the driver's door, and got out, I felt too nervous to say anything. Charlie followed me up the walk and into the house. My heart was pounding so hard that my rib cage hurt, and my damned tongue was stuck to the roof of my mouth. Charlie wasn't being much help either. His hands were shoved in his pockets, and he was staring sullenly at the floor. Whatever it was he wanted, he obviously wasn't going to ask for it verbally.

"Come on," I finally croaked, motioning for him to follow me. My bedroom was at the back of the house, as far from my mother's room as possible. It had once served as a storeroom, but I had converted it after I tumbled to the fact that I wasn't leaving Harmonville anytime soon. You had to go out the kitchen door and across the side porch to get to it, and my mother never came near it. I wasn't sure what was going to happen with Charlie, but I didn't want it to take place in the garage. That was fine for Cal, but it didn't seem right for Charlie Ferrin.

Charlie stood by the door as I lowered the shades and turned on the light. I closed the gap between us and locked eyes with him. One look into his large, dark brown eyes, and I realized that Charlie Ferrin was scared shitless. The poor fucker looked like a deer caught in the headlights of an oncoming truck.

As I stared at his handsome face, his full reddish lips suddenly seemed irresistible. Hell, I'd never kissed a man before in my life. None of the men I'd ever been with saw me as anything more than a couple of holes with a dick attached, so kissing had been out of the question. Now, though, it seemed right. I leaned forward slowly, and since Charlie didn't jerk his head away, our lips met.

An incredible surge of feelings jolted me at that first kiss. The sex heat was there, sure, but there was also this feeling of tenderness and protectiveness that damn near made me feel like crying. Charlie didn't resist when my tongue slipped into his mouth. He tasted like beer and cigarettes, and the inside of his mouth was all wet and warm. I traced the tip of my tongue around the roof of his mouth, and Charlie moaned softly.

We stood there for the longest time, no point of contact between us except for lips and writhing tongues. Oh, yes, Charlie's tongue started squirming around after a bit, rubbing against mine and flickering delicately against my teeth. But it was mostly me, probing and thrusting, penetrating his body, desiring to be inside his warmth, his strength.

When I finally broke the kiss, my knees were weak. Charlie's eyes were shut tight, his cheeks flushed. He looked like a little boy in that instant — well, like a big boy anyway. He just stood there, not moving, lips parted slightly, a bead of sweat trailing slowly down his neck.

"Can I touch you, Charlie?" I asked finally, my voice shaky. The kiss had been electric, erotic beyond anything I'd ever felt, complete in and of itself. To go further without his permission seemed like a violation of his privacy. Besides, the asking carried its own special magic.

"Don't care," Charlie murmured breathlessly, not moving when I pressed my hand against the bare skin in the V of his faded shirt. I twined the long hairs on his chest around my fingers, and I could feel his heart slamming against his sternum. The heat of his body shot up my arm and right down to my groin.

I slowly unbuttoned his shirt and slipped it down over his shoulders. His skin was like warm silk, stretched over the unyielding muscles beneath. I traced the veins that curved over his swollen biceps down his thick forearms to his wrists. His pulse was racing, and his breath sounded harsh in his throat.

Charlie stood passively as I knelt to unlace his dirt-caked boots. I pulled them off and tucked his white socks inside, delighted by the little patch of dark hairs growing on the tops of his feet. I unbuckled his belt and popped the buttons on his fly, then peeled him out of his faded jeans. His muscular legs were pale in the lamplight, more hair feathering over the bulge of his calves and down the insides of his thighs.

Charlie may have been scared, but his body was definitely interested. His prick was pointed right between my eyes like a loaded gun, the crown flared, the piss hole gaping. I leaned forward and nuzzled his crotch, sniffing his spicy musk. As I started licking his furry balls, my hands wandered up the backs of his legs to his ass. It was covered with a soft down that tickled my palms and sent the blood surging to my cock.

He remained motionless, uttering only a soft moan when I swallowed his engorged piece to the root. He groaned a second time when my fingers wedged into the cleft between his ass cheeks, seeking out the tight little pucker that was hidden there.

I reached my goal and rubbed my finger across the moist, tender flesh. Much to my surprise, Charlie shifted his feet, spreading his legs enough to give me access. I continued sucking him, running my tongue up and down along the tender underside of his prong.

I tensed my arm and pushed my hand up until my middle finger sank into Charlie, right up to the webbing. For just a moment I thought that maybe I'd gone too far, exploring Charlie's body in a way he wouldn't appreciate. His thighs tensed, he sucked his belly back toward his spine, and his hole clamped down on my digit like a vise. I felt one of those big hands flutter against my shoulder before coming to rest there. When I looked up, his eyes were shut tight, but there was a faint smile playing around the corners of his mouth.

Honey was bubbling out of Charlie by the time I stopped giving him head and stood up to get naked myself. In the few seconds it took me to tear my clothes off, Charlie stepped over to the bed and sprawled across it facedown. I asked no questions, just knelt between his outspread legs and buried my face in his crack.

He tasted of salt as I licked the short hairs away from his asshole, then crammed my tongue deep up inside him. The walls of his funky little butt hole were soft and smooth, making my prick thump against my belly in anticipation. I slipped my hands under Charlie's torso, and he raised up on his elbows. I tweaked his tits, popping them up into points, then rubbed the balls of my thumbs against them till he was vibrating like a harp string.

After kissing Charlie's asshole one last time, I braced myself above his passive form and dragged my cock up and down along his crack. He quivered and bucked, his ass flexing, grabbing at my tingling shaft. I held my breath as my knob finally made contact with the pulsing mouth of his rear entry. There was a moment of resistance, then I breached his defenses and sank slowly into his clutching man channel.

"Oh, Eddie!" Charlie groaned, the muscles along his spine knotting as I probed his steamy depths.

"Am I hurting you?" I whispered, stroking his muscled sides and kissing the throbbing veins in his strong neck.

"Don't care," he gasped, shaking his head from side to side. His ass bumped back against my pelvis, a sign I took to mean he wanted me to continue. So I fell on top of him, wrapped my arms around his thick chest, and started to fuck. Charlie twisted his head around, lips parted, his mouth blindly seeking mine. Our tongues touched, and I realized with a pleasurable jolt that that portion of my anatomy was every bit as sensitive as my pistoning dick.

Topping a man like Charlie damn near shorted all my circuits. He was so hot and tender and defenseless inside, sort of like finding a soft spot in a rock wall. I hunched my hips, driving in deep, then drew out slowly, not stopping till his sphincter caught the flaring rim of my crown. Charlie was cooing now, his big body twisting under me as he writhed around the spike of flesh crammed up his asshole. When I started pounding his prostate with my cock knob, Charlie squealed and bucked up under me. I reached between his legs and groped him. His prick was like a steel bar, and his balls were drawn up so tight on either side of the shaft, I couldn't even get a grip on them.

My urgency increased with every pile-driving stroke I made. I was on the verge of losing control anyway, and when Charlie's asshole started to have spasms around my aching cock, I lost it. I reared back, braced my hands on his shoulders, and rode him as hard and as fast as I could. Our moans rose to two cries of ecstatic pleasure as we both started coming together. I could feel the strong contractions racking his frame as he started pumping jizz out onto the bed just as I began pumping it up his chute. Spunk gushed out of me as if it would never stop, blasting deep into Charlie's asshole. He obviously felt my spouting heat, whimpering as each shot seared his bowels. When I had finished, I collapsed on top of him, totally wrung out.

"Eddie," Charlie whispered, his hands closing over mine. It soon became clear that he had no plans of letting my hands go, so I pressed my face against his neck and fell asleep on top of him, my dick still poked up his hole.

When I woke up the next morning, I was on my back, and Charlie was squatting over me, pumping my prick to get it hard enough to sit on. Needless to say, it didn't take him long, and we greeted the day with an exuberant fuck. He was smiling as my cock drove up into him — a big, goofy grin that made him look like an overgrown kid. I reached up and pressed my hand against his chest, feeling his heartbeat, strong and steady. Then I remembered the tattoo. I brushed away the wisps of chest hair until I could read the crude block lettering: HEART'S DESIRE.

I looked up at Charlie inquisitively. "Heart's desire?"

Charlie shrugged his shoulders, then squeezed his asshole down nice and tight around my throbbing dick. "Got it in the joint. Never knew why. Till now, I guess."

"Heart's desire, Charlie." I tugged the hair on his chest. He leaned down, his hair brushing against my lips.

After we finally managed to get up out of bed and into our clothes, I walked Charlie out to his truck. He put his arms around my waist and pulled me tight. Our crotches ground together, and I could feel his prick stiffening against me.

"You're a horny bastard, Charlie Ferrin." I laughed and planted my hands on his hard ass, not giving a damn about any of the scandalized faces appearing in the surrounding windows. Hell, the neighbors needed some new gossip to keep things interesting.

"I'll come back tonight, Eddie," he said softly, his face suddenly serious. "If you'll let me."

"Sure," I replied, noticing for the first time that his eyes had little gold flecks in the irises. Just before I let him go,

I ducked my head and kissed the little marked spot on his pec one last time.

Maybe it was sudden, but it felt right. Being with Charlie, I didn't feel like such an outcast for the first time in my life. You're only an outcast if you have no friends, and now I had a buddy.

"Who was that?"

I started and turned around. My mother was standing at the kitchen door, her hair done up in big, unattractive pink rollers.

"Charlie Ferrin, Mother," I said, wishing that she'd just go away.

"That criminal?" Mother wrapped her old robe tighter around her lumpy body. "What's he doing here?"

"He's a friend, Mother," I said patiently.

"I don't want him hanging around here," she snapped, her face turning scarlet. "What will the neighbors say?"

"Don't know, Mother," I said, shrugging my shoulders and turning away from her. "Don't care."

Bobby Baby
by Leo Cardini

Contrary to popular rumor, the first time I met Bobby Champion was not at the Mineshaft but here at the Julius. That was back in 1979, when the Village was a much different place.

He was standing at the bar, more or less where you're standing right now, staring straight ahead into his thoughts, one foot on the bar stoop and one hand loosely wrapped around the drink in front of him. He was dressed in tight new Levi's 501s that strained against his beautiful butt, inching up into his ass crack, and a plain white T-shirt that hugged every glorious plane and contour of his thickly muscled shoulders, well-defined chest, and trim, taut waist.

I took a fortifying sip of my vodka and tonic and turned to him with a familiar "Hi," knowing perfectly well he wouldn't know me from Adam.

He turned and looked at me, a tentative smile slowly making its way to the surface. Close up, his face was even more stunning than on the stage. His beautiful mane of thick blond hair, parted in the middle, fell across his forehead like a half-drawn stage curtain just above those distinctive arched eyebrows, which give him such a mischievous look. Animated hazel eyes, a square jaw, full lips, and perfect teeth completed the drop-dead–handsome effect.

"Hello," he replied cautiously, clearly trying to recall who the hell I was.

"Don't you remember me?" I asked.

"Uh…well, frankly, no."

"I guess I didn't make much of an impression on you then. Or do you always forget the men you kiss?"

"Hmm. The Mineshaft, maybe?"

Just imagine — Bobby Champion at the Mineshaft, prowling around through all those dimly lit, shadowy rooms full of hot and horny men!

"No, not the Mineshaft," I said. "Actually, the Summerlawn Theatre."

His face broke into a more relaxed smile. He was so fucking handsome, it was almost unbearable.

"Oh! Orchestra left, row K, seat 126. Right?"

"Right."

Let me explain, in case you never saw it. At that time Bobby was playing Tomcat Tugger in *Pets,* a new musical. Early in the first act, during his solo, he'd leap off the stage into the left aisle and kiss whoever happened to be seated in row K, seat 126.

How I thrilled to his touch as he grabbed me by the jaw, turned my face upward, and planted an exaggerated kiss right on my lips, his raw animal magnetism hitting me like a whiff of fresh poppers. Not that his snug-fitting feline costume didn't help, considering the way it emphasized a sizable tomcat-on-the-prowl bulge in his crotch that looked like it was in desperate need of attention.

"Well, then," he said, "you must know I kiss an awful lot of guys."

"Eight times a week, in the theater alone. And that's not including places like — since you were the one who mentioned it — the Mineshaft."

"You're pretty fresh, aren't you?"

"And pretty horny."

His interest in me was as obvious as mine in him. By now we were leaning against the bar facing each other. His knee brushed against my shin, and I caught him eye-balling my crotch. I too was wearing 501s — though worn and faded, with two of the metal buttons refusing to stay put in their buttonholes.

And then it hit me. But of course!

"But there's also something else I want from you besides…"

I let a quick glance down at his crotch finish my sentence for me.

"Oh?"

"That is, if you don't think you'd mind mixing business with pleasure."

He stared at me with a puzzled look.

"I've written a musical. Well, music and lyrics, anyhow. I'd like to play it for you because I think you'd be perfect for the lead."

"And I suppose you just happen to live around the corner, where you could play the score for me?"

"Why, as a matter of fact, yes. Over on Waverly. By the way, my name's Steve. Steve Hammerheim. Composer, lyricist, and — alas — piano tuner."

As we shook hands, he asked, "Did anyone ever tell you you look like—"

"Like Tom Aria, the dancer-slash-choreographer?" I interrupted.

"Yeah."

"All the time. Except that at six foot four, I'm about an inch shorter than he is."

Another glance at my crotch, this time with the intention of my noticing it.

"I can't speak to being an inch shorter there too, but if that's the case, then frankly, he's one lucky guy."

"Hmm," was all he replied, the drawn-out syllable resonant of his unmistakable interest in the size of my cock.

He polished off his drink and motioned to Billy the bartender to pour us another round.

"So tell me a little about your show."

"It's called *Bobby Baby*. It's about this gay man — same first name as yours — living in the Village today. His closest friends are these five pairs of lovers, and the show concerns his observations of their relationships as he examines his own inability to establish any lasting relationships himself."

"Pretty heavy stuff for a musical."

"I know, but I really believe in this show, and I think the time's right for it."

Well, we talked about the show, and we talked about our careers, our sexual interest in each other coming through loud and clear, and half an hour later we were walking through the front door of my apartment.

I invited him to sit next to me at the piano, pulled out the score, and went through my standard forty-five–minute backers audition, starting with the opening number — "So Glad to See You" — and moving from song to song with a brief description of each scene.

And he absolutely loved it! He sighed after the melancholy "Grateful to Be Sorry," laughed at the tongue-twisting "I'd Love to Move In With You, But...," declared himself drained after the devastating "The Boys at Brunch," and jumped up from the piano bench to applaud me when I'd completed the final song — "Roomfuls of Ricky."

"So?" I asked. "You interested?"

"*Interested*'s not the word!"

"I mean, I'm really serious about this."

"I know you are. So am I."

We talked shop for a few minutes, then I gave him a copy of the script and arranged for him to meet Hal, my collaborator.

With the business part of our meeting taken care of, I quickly tried to figure out a way to segue into pleasure. "You know," I said, "there's one other thing we should consider about your playing this part."

"Oh?"

"The San Francisco scene." Which is actually the name of a song. The scene itself is Bobby's bedroom. It's 5 in the morning, and the airline steward he brought home the night before gets up to leave for a flight assignment to San Francisco.

"What about it?" Bobby said.

"If you remember, the two of them are in bed naked, which means when Bobby gets out of bed to take down the steward's phone number...well, there are a number of references in the show to Bobby's being...generously endowed." (I was actually making this up on the spot.)

His face immediately brightened with that familiar devilish smile of his.

"So you want to see if I'm hung."

"For purely professional reasons, of course."

"Of course. Well, since it's for the sake of my career..."

He was clearly relishing the scene we were about to improvise as much as I was.

Taking much longer than necessary, he slowly removed his T-shirt, luxuriating in the feel of his animal physicality as he stretched and flexed his body. He showed off a tight "innie" of a navel set in remarkably flat, well-defined abs, clearly the result of a rigorous exercise routine. A narrow line of blond hair bisected his torso as it ascended his chest until it finally fanned out between his gracefully contoured, gym-sculpted pecs. Farther up, as his head momentarily disappeared inside his shirt, I spied the damp hair nestled in his armpits, so tempting that I could've lapped the sweat out of them right then and there with very little coaxing.

Shirt off, he looked at me as if to say, *Well, what do you think?* He was posturing madly, chest pushed out, his hard-nubbed nipples daring me to take them between my thumbs and forefingers and massage them.

Tossing his shirt onto my sofa and looking me straight in the eyes, he slowly unbuckled the wide black leather belt he was wearing, pulling it through his belt loops with one efficient, biceps-bulging yank. Then he slowly undid his Levi's button by button, the ever-widening opening revealing more and more firm, tantalizing flesh below his navel, at least until his low-cut white bikini briefs came into view. Lowering his jeans to mid thigh, he shook his legs, and his pants dropped to his ankles.

He paused, standing there to let me fully savor the way his underwear strained to contain their clearly substantial contents.

But before I could really gorge myself on the sight, he fell backward, gracefully landing on the edge of the sofa, pulling off his sneakers, socks, and Levi's.

Then he stood up again, clad in nothing but those ever-so-brief bulging shorts. Oh, he was a cockteaser, all right, as adept as any experienced stripper at holding an audience's interest.

He flashed me another smile that seemed to say, *And now for what you've been waiting for,* then slipped his thumbs under the waistband at the hips and slowly lowered his shorts. The lush forest of his blond pubic bush gradually came into view, spilling out of his briefs, driving me crazy with the promise of what was to come.

And then the pale brown base of his cock presented itself to my appreciative gaze. Was it really as thick as this partial view suggested?

He continued lowering his briefs. Inch after inch of fat, spongy dick came into view, far exceeding my wildest expectations.

With one final effort he leaned forward and quickly pulled his briefs down to his knees. Then he stood up again, beaming with obvious pride.

My God! He was so well-hung that I actually gasped. And not only was his cock huge, but it was also perfectly formed, a monumental thing of beauty. His soft cut cock hung down heavily between his legs, covered with a network of blue veins that emphasized its thickness, capped with a large purple-pink head. Behind, his two oversize balls hung low in their loose ball sac, lightly sprinkled with bristly blond hair.

"So what do you think?" he asked.

"You'll do...I guess."

Truth to tell, it was all I could do to restrain myself from sucking him off right then and there.

"What do you mean, 'I guess'?"

"I can't say for sure, 'cause the fact of the matter is, I figure when Bobby gets out of bed, he'd have a hard-on, wouldn't he?"

"So you want to see me with an erection? Is that it?"

He was clearly eager to show me.

"Professionally speaking, yes."

"Shit. The things I do for my career."

He gripped his cock, knuckles topside, fingers encircling it below, and gave it a slow, downward yank, pulling it over to one side.

All that soft, pliable meat he was manipulating — it was too much to bear. I slid off the piano bench onto my knees and planted myself in front of him.

He leisurely tugged on his swelling dick, clearly appreciating the rapt, openmouthed audience he had found in me. Soon he had it hard enough so that it stood up on its own, enabling me to examine the tender-looking, mouth-watering underside of his stiffening shaft.

"Would you like some help?" I asked, surprised at the urgent tone in my voice.

"That's okay. I can manage."

The fucker! He knew damn well he had me in the palm of his hand — so to speak — and he was milking it for all it was worth — so to speak yet again.

"The important thing is for you to judge if it looks right for the part," he said, pretending to be serious.

"Oh, it does!"

And as he continued stroking himself, a bead of pre-come appeared in his piss slit, increasing in size until I knew that at any moment it would begin to trickle down his dick.

"I wouldn't want you to get your fingers sticky with all that dick juice," I offered.

"Why, that's damn considerate of you, Steve. You can lick it off if you like."

I stuck out my tongue and scooped up the bead of clear, precious liquid. His cock head twitched in grateful response.

"Thanks," he said as he continued stroking his tool.

"Ah. Look at that. There's more already."

This time I didn't wait for permission to tend to his oozing piss slit but instead quickly trapped his cock head between my lips before he had the chance to refuse me. It felt as firm and fleshy as a ripe plum. Wasting no time, I slithered my tongue along his piss slit, cleaning it off, and then began licking the sensitive underside of his glans.

"Oh!" he shuddered from above as his free hand fell lightly on my shoulder.

I reached for his balls, encircling the sac with my thumb and forefinger and pulling down until his balls were snugly enclosed. My remaining fingers were wrapped around his huge nuts as I tried to go down on his dick. I was unsuccessful, though, except for the first few inches, because he continued to hold it on display with his fist.

I pried his hand away. He offered only token resistance and then rested it on my other shoulder.

By now his rugged upturned cock was rock-hard — so stiff and unyielding that it could have been carved out of granite. Inch by inch I went down on him, feeling his ever-widening shaft slide past my lips and into my mouth.

His cock head reached my throat, and it took me several attempts to maneuver it inside. But even at that, once I got it down my throat, I had to stop short of the final few inches. There was simply too much of him for me. And though I don't mean to brag, I've had a lot of experience sucking on big dicks.

I closed my eyes and worked my way up and down his cock, giving it my full concentration, greedily noting its every detail: its length, its texture, its circumference, the way it filled my mouth, and the relentless way it taxed my throat.

Like an audience reaction from the upper balcony, variously modulated groans indicated his appreciation of my cocksucking efforts.

Finally, with one loud staccato "Ah!" he pushed me off his dick. I fell back onto my heels. His huge, spit-shiny dick — a good nine inches — rose up magnificently in front of me, throbbing with excitement.

"So what do you think, Steve?"

I took my time surveying it from several angles as he stood there, resting his hands on his hips, putting on a lively cock-twitching show for me.

When I'd had my fill of inspecting it, I said, "Yeah. Like I said before, you'll do."

He let out with a surprised laugh, then said, "Is that all you can say?"

And then, clutching his dick again and shaking it at me like a scolding finger, he added, "I've been around long enough to know that you don't see one like this every day of the week."

Rising to my feet and placing my hand over my own trapped and aching hard-on, I replied, "Well, as a matter of fact, I do."

"Oh?" he said, looking down at my crotch with unmistakable interest.

"Yeah. See for yourself."

I took his right hand and placed it on my crotch. As he fondled me through my tight Levi's, I pulled off my T-shirt, tossing it onto the sofa next to his.

I looked at him again. Still investigating the dimensions of my denim-bound dick, he stared at my bulging crotch, mesmerized by its contents. The proud, playful manner he had assumed up to that point was upstaged now by lust — passionate, deadly serious lust. In places like the Mineshaft, I'd seen many a man enter that realm of raunchy desire in which nothing else matters but raw, unmitigated man-to-man sex, and I realized that Bobby was one of those men who would stop at nothing once the craving came over him.

"Aw, shit!" he exclaimed in an awed half whisper as he dropped to his knees.

I began to unbutton my Levi's, but he shoved my hands away and impatiently undertook the job himself as if he were a man possessed. In no time he had my 501s down around my ankles. My underwear bulged with the huge boner it could hardly contain.

He pulled my briefs down, and my cock flopped out in front of him. Fat, smooth, and cut, it hangs down, even when it's hard — all ten inches of it.

"Jeez!" he said. "I figured you had to be hung just because of your height — and your hands. But this!"

With one hand he fondled my large, low-hanging balls, jostling them around in my loose ball sac. As big as they are, they're really sensitive, so the feel of his fingers manipulating them practically made me go weak in the knees. With his free hand he gripped my dick and held it up, examining it as thoroughly as I had just examined his.

"Oh, man!" was all he could say as he fell into rapt contemplation.

Then he suddenly encircled my cock head with his warm, wet lips and quickly sucked it down into his throat until he gagged.

But he refused to retreat. The gagging diminished, and soon he was sucking up and down with a steady rhythm, fondling my balls with one hand while stroking his own dick with the other.

Finally dismounting me, he looked up at me glassy-eyed and said, "I'd sure like to have you up my ass."

"Is that the kind of scene you get into at the Mineshaft?" I teased.

His mention of the Mineshaft earlier had piqued my curiosity because, as you might already have guessed, I often went there myself to indulge in the marathon sexual workouts for which it's known.

"I get into a lot of scenes at the Mineshaft," he said.

"So do I."

"I can give it, and I can take it."

"Me too. You want to discuss this scene in advance?"

"Let's improvise."

Ah — a man after my own heart. "You're on," I said.

As soon as I could pull off my boots and Levi's, I led the way into my bedroom. Once there, Bobby suddenly grabbed me from behind, wrapping his powerful arms around me and pulling me tight against his chest. I had to struggle to free myself so I could turn and face him. Once I did so, he pulled me hard against him again and plunged his tongue into my mouth, brutally taking possession of me, his hard cock trapped between our stomachs and his balls brushing against the base of my pendulous dick as he overwhelmed me with his testosterone-fueled passion.

It was clear he liked to play rough, and I played back just as ferociously. Flesh against flesh, muscle against muscle, we struggled with each other as if attempting to force our way into each other's skin.

Somehow we managed to fall onto my bed, thrashing around, repeatedly forcing the headboard to bang against the wall. At one moment he was on top of me. At the next I was on top of him. I thought maybe we'd break the bed, but I really didn't care.

Now, I might be strong, but I was no match for him. Soon he had me on my back, pinning my arms above my head. He straddled me, knees pressing into my sweaty armpits, and shoved his cock down my throat. There was so much of it, and he plunged it into me so insistently and repeatedly, I wouldn't have been able to plead for mercy if I'd wanted to.

Savoring the pummeling action of his muscular glutes as he force-fed me his dick, I kept pushing up with my legs, rebelling against his restrictive straddle, with no more effect than to raise my butt off the bed.

My cock was so hard and I was so fucking horny, I finally sought to free myself from him in earnest. With one passionate surge of energy, I struggled toward liberation, quickly wrestling Bobby into a reversal of positions and shoving the first four or five inches of my cock into his mouth. Then I paused to capture the image of him at that moment: sweaty and wide-eyed, his mouth full of dick.

I slowly eased the rest of my rod down his throat. I'd learned a long time ago that there are very few men who can manage to swallow my entire dick. Bobby was one of them, squirming below me with obvious satisfaction as he took it in. Soon I could barely make out the base of my shaft beyond the obstruction of my pubic hairs as they spilled over his upper lip and bristled against his nose.

I pulled out of him several inches and then eased back in again. The sensations were overwhelming. Repeating this four or five times, I realized I'd soon reach orgasm if I didn't watch out.

I quickly pulled all the way out of him and shoved my balls into his face.

"Lick 'em!" I demanded. Which he did enthusiastically, sucking one large ball into his mouth and then the other, tugging at my ball sac while giving my nuts a thorough tonguing.

I freed his hands and slowly rubbed my cock back and forth across his face. Lubricated with his own spit, it slid easily across his handsome features.

After a while, however, I became aware that he was trying to say something. I raised myself up and pulled my balls out of his mouth.

"Fuck me!" he pleaded, breathing heavily. "Please!"

I slapped him across each cheek with my cock and then, dismounting to sit on the side of the bed, ordered him to get up.

He rose compliantly and stood in front of me, his stiff, throbbing cock inches from my face. Acting the slave, he lowered his head respectfully and clasped his hands behind his back.

Spreading my legs and slowly stroking my dick, I asked, "So you want this cock up your ass?"

He nodded yes.

"Do you think you can take all of it?"

He nodded again, this time a little more eagerly.

"There's some Vaseline and a towel under the bed. Get them for me now."

Which he did.

"Now, turn around and bend over."

Which he also did, rewarding me with the sight of his firm, muscular butt, pale with tan line and adorned with a triangular patch of blond hair just above his ass crack.

"Spread your cheeks."

He pulled his buns apart, exposing his puckered, sparsely haired butt hole, then clenching it repeatedly as further inducement for me to examine it.

I brushed my fingers lightly across his rear entrance, then opened the jar of Vaseline, applied some of its greasy contents to his hole, and eased one finger in.

"Oh!" he exclaimed.

I managed two fingers in.

"Oh! O-o-oh!"

Finally three fingers, which I proceeded to slide in and out of his asshole, getting him all loose and lubed. I realized that I could've fisted him (imagine him in a sling at the Mineshaft, putting on the performance of his life!), but this was not the time for it.

"Turn around," I ordered, pulling my fingers out and wiping my hand on the towel, "and grease my dick."

"Yes, sir. Anything you say."

He got down on his knees between my legs. He lifted my cock, studying it for a few seconds, then kissed it on the tip and proceeded to apply the Vaseline. I could tell he was getting into it, the way he lavished it with such loving attention. Soon it shone with lubricant, constantly twitching in response to his conscientious manipulation.

"Now, wipe your hands off and get back in bed — on your back," I said.

He obediently followed my directions and got into position, legs spread apart and cock throbbing. As I positioned myself between his thighs, he lifted his legs, raising his ass off the bed and exposing his shiny, receptive butt hole.

I pushed his legs back until his knees met his shoulders, and I pressed my cock against his hole, holding it there. As our eyes met, I thrilled at the sight of him. Just imagine — Bobby Champion, Broadway heartthrob, here in my own bed, staring up at me in desperate anticipation of my over-size dick making its way up his ass.

"Oh! Fuck me! Fuck me hard!"

I slid my cock in — one, two, three inches — as he moaned, tossing his head from side to side.

Four inches, five inches, six inches —

"Oh, shit!" he cried out.

"You okay?"

"Yeah. Keep going."

Once I had all ten inches inside him, I began working my way in and out, quickly finding the right rhythm for us. He grabbed his cock and stroked it, imitating my thrusts, which caused his balls to rise and fall at the same fevered pace.

The headboard began tapping against the wall in time with my lunges up Bobby's ass. As I increased the speed and force of my jabs, the taps became bangs, and soon the pictures on the wall had joined in accompaniment.

We fell into a blissful state — sweating and straining with the industry of our exertion but nonetheless blissful. It might have lasted a minute. It might have lasted an hour. It didn't matter.

Soon I felt myself galloping toward an enormous erup-tion. As my breathing grew labored, Bobby began stroking his flushed, swollen dick with increased enthusiasm.

I accelerated my thrusting, the heady feeling of pending orgasm surging up from deep within my balls.

Bobby suddenly stopped stroking his cock, his hand gripping it mid-shaft. He was himself clearly on the verge of coming.

"Shoot it, you fucker!" he yelled at me. "Shoot that load up my ass!"

I plunged into him one more time, letting fly with a pow-erful gusher of come. The intense, overwhelming ecstasy of release quickly spread throughout my entire body. I plunged my cock deep into his hole again and again, each time shooting what felt like quarts of jism.

Once I was spent and had savored the sweet sensation of orgasm still lingering in my balls, I quickly pulled out of Bobby and relinquished my hold on his legs, letting them fall to either side of me. I wrapped one hand around his balls, pushed his hand from his cock, and pulled on his ball sac until I had his hard, throbbing dick pointing straight up.

Wasting no time, I went down on him as if my life depended on it, taking the entire length of his rigid shaft in one fell swoop.

He was indeed on the verge of coming. After only a few strokes of my mouth, I felt his unbelievably hot load shooting down my throat. His head thrashed violently from side to side, and his entire body shuddered as he shouted "Oh, shit!" so loudly, I knew Bill and Leo next door would be pressing me for details the next morning.

When he'd shot his wad and returned to a more relaxed state, I simply closed my eyes, savoring the feel of his cock in my mouth. I didn't want to give it up. Instead I just let it soften inside me, experiencing every detail of its metamorphosis into a gentle monster at rest. When he was finally soft, I opened my eyes again and looked up at him.

He'd raised himself up on his elbows and was staring down at me with that wonderfully wicked smile of his.

"So," he asked, "do I get the part?"

Letting his soft dick slip out of my mouth, I moved up alongside him and replied, "Only if you promise to stay the night."

"Well, since it's for the sake of my career—"

I pressed my lips against his, preventing him from finishing his sentence.

And the rest — as they say — is history. Bobby and I became lovers, and *Bobby Baby* ran off-Broadway for four years, establishing my reputation and boosting Bobby to star status. Then came *Can That Boy Fox-trot!* which you probably know is about a reunion of aging gay men who were once chorus boys together in the same '50s Broadway musical and which, of course, also starred Bobby.

But what got me on the subject of how Bobby and I met? Oh, yeah, that persistent rumor you mentioned about Bobby and me meeting at the Mineshaft — not that we didn't stir up many a scene there after we became lovers.

You're too young ever to have gone there, but it's clear to me you'd have fit right in.

Oh, yes. Definitely.

Anyhow, since *Fox-trot*'s closing soon, we're casting for my new show, *A Weekend on the Island.* It's about three mismatched gay couples who spend a weekend on Fire Island. Which is why I wanted to meet you, since I...well, we...think you'd be perfect for the role of the superstud nephew home from college who secretly lusts after both his uncle and his uncle's boyfriend.

Bobby? Oh, he's playing the uncle.

So if you like, I'd love to play the score for you. And our apartment's just around the corner.

Yes, Bobby'll be there.

Sure, you can try out a scene or two with him.

With both of us?

Actually, that's what we had in mind.

Australian Crawl
by Parker Vreeland

You could almost see the mist rise from the frost in the air.
My friend Ben Anderson, who was hosting his annual
Academy Awards party, had just introduced me to Mike
Hargar. I had been introduced to Mike at least ten times
over the past few months. And, for the tenth time, he was
giving me a haughty, oddly vague look that betrayed not
even a hint of recognition.

He had no legitimate excuse. It was just that, as an
architect who had spent the past few years working for a
prestigious firm in Sydney, Australia, he held those of us
acorns who didn't fall very far from the tree in ridiculous-
ly undisguised contempt.

Well, he wasn't the only one who could serve attitude. I
have in my veins the blood of Southern women who
endured the Yankee occupation, and they wrote the book
on attitude.

"No, Ben, I don't believe I have met Mark."

"Mike."

I shot him a cool glance that clearly said, *Like it matters.* I turned to Ben. "Well, I'd better go before the show
starts and pick up that ice you said you wanted."

He all but pushed me out the door. "Why bother, dear? We can just let you hold the drinks for a minute — and pray they don't freeze."

I glared back over his shoulder at Mike. "I wouldn't put any money on it if I were you. Be back in a little while."

My party mood had evaporated, and I was in no hurry to get back. Instead of driving the five blocks to the 7-Eleven, I decided to walk.

I didn't get very far.

The lights were on in a tiny house on the corner. In the unfurnished front room, I could see a shirtless man bent over, running a roller in a tray of paint. Then he stood up. I couldn't help letting out an audible "Yum!"

Even from the street I could make out an incredibly defined set of abs and awesomely developed pecs. He was wearing nothing but a pair of sweatpants that had obviously been dried on the HIGH setting too many times and fit accordingly.

I stood at the end of the driveway awhile, drinking in the movement of his body and the rippling of his muscles. Then the porch light of the house next door came on. It dawned on me that I probably looked a mite suspicious lurking about in the shadows, so I reluctantly moved on.

But it was impossible to get him out of my mind. My imagination, seizing the moment, ran away on an erotic little holiday. I pictured myself leaning against the doorway of his bathroom, watching as he showered off the flecks of paint that had spattered his body. Large globs of soapsuds coursed over his tanned muscles, and his hand lazily scrubbed at the paint on his skin.

I stepped in, and now they were my hands scrubbing away. I kneaded his thickly muscled back and shoulders, the soap making his skin erotically slippery. Losing himself in the feel of my hands on his body, he stretched, and a whole new series of shadowed muscles erupted.

Pressing myself tightly against him, I reached around and played with his chest, tweaking his nipples in the spray of the water. He leaned his head back, his cool, wet hair falling against my cheek. It smelled clean and fresh from the herbal shampoo, smelled good enough to eat. I bit his ear lightly and licked at the drops of water that clung to the side of his face.

Then my hands traveled down, sliding over his flat stomach till I felt the bush of his pubic hair. I circled the thick shaft of his dick, which was sticking straight out in front of him. It swelled in my grip, growing bigger and bigger like a bicycle tire being pumped full of air. I pressed my own erection tightly between the cheeks of his ass.

Over and over I impaled my fist on his shaft, the water and soap lubing the thick, veined meat. As I gripped it tighter and pumped it faster, his breathing grew ragged and heavy. His ass flexed around my turgid cock. I picked up the pace. He started grunting softly and pressed closer against me. Faster, driven, my hand flew up and down the length of his cock till a series of sharp shouts announced that he was about to come.

His hands clutched at the shower curtain and the tile wall as great milky geysers shot through the stream of the shower. His dick felt like a beating heart, and the power of that pulsing flesh brought me to the brink as well. Jamming hard against his tight butt, I ground myself against him, the tight, burning feeling in the head of my cock finally finding release...

Yes, well, I had hardly found release. What I had found was that it was uncomfortable as hell to walk around with a big old hard-on down your jeans. Instead of walking back with the ice, I decided to go back to Ben's and get my car.

I would, of course, have to pass the hunk's house on the way there.

I was all prepared for a surreptitious sneak peek through the windows again but was surprised to find him out in the middle of the front yard, hosing off the rollers and paint tray. My heart nearly stopped, and so did my feet — those tight little gray sweatpants had gotten completely soaked.

"Nice night," he said, startling me further.

"Yeah," I replied, not really knowing what to do. Should I keep walking or stop for a neighborly chat? "A bit cool, though."

"Not too cool for a beer to hit the spot, though, eh?" The accent was unmistakable. Dear Lord, he's Australian! I've always had a weakness for the accent, and the unpleasant Mr. Hargar's recent residence in that country was not enough to make the magic pall for me. He shut the hose off. "Care to join me for one inside? I hate drinking alone. Something seedy about it."

"Uh, sure," I said, glancing down the street toward Ben's house.

"Your mates won't miss ya," he said, winking. Funny, even in the darkness I could see the bright blue of his eyes and his white, toothy grin.

"My mates?" I followed him up the walk.

"You're a friend of the fella who drives the old Mustang convertible, aren't ya? I've seen you over there from time to time."

This big old hunky stud had noticed me before? How the hell had I missed him?

The house had the sickeningly sweet smell of wet paint. Both the front room and the kitchen were shiny with the stuff, and I was already getting light-headed by the time he got the beers out of the refrigerator.

"Just moving in?" I asked, staring at the sweat glistening on his back.

"About six months ago, actually. My wife and I decided to separate, and when all the shouting was over with, I felt that the more separation, the better." He winked at me again. "A few thousand miles ought to do the trick, don't you think?"

"Gee, I'm sorry. Well, I mean, I'm glad you're here. Welcome to Austin...a bit late." I was stumbling over my words like an idiot schoolboy.

"Let's go in there," he said, motioning to a dark room beyond the kitchen. "It's the only place fit to breathe, I'm afraid."

I went in and immediately found myself sprawled across the floor. Well, not the floor, actually. Across a mattress on the floor. He flicked on a low-wattage light.

"Sorry about that. You okay?"

"Oh, sure. I've landed face-first on more mattresses than—" Oh, shit, I thought. Campy remarks to straight men when you're in their beds under innocent circumstances are not cool, Parker.

He laughed and tossed me a can of Miller Lite. "That's all right then, eh? My name's Dirk, by the way." He flopped down beside me and leaned against the wall, popping open his beer.

"I'm Parker." I was staring like a fool — Dirk, in a manly gesture, had spread his legs wide open as he sat down, and that poor, abused cotton fabric that strained across his crotch just wasn't going to stand much more. I could make out both balls and the thick vein that ran up the underside of his dick to the helmetlike head. I started sweating like a whore in church.

"Well, Parker, glad to meet ya. I haven't met many people since I've been here. Not the right kind of people, anyway." His hand slid down from his knee to his crotch. He gave it a squeeze.

"The right kind?" The phrase had me thinking of Mrs. Astor wrinkling her nose at nouveaux riches trying to crash high society in old New York. It really didn't seem to apply to Austin, Texas, in the 1990s. Or maybe I was being obtuse.

Dirk leaned back, causing his straight blond bangs to fall seductively over his narrowing eyes. "You're the right kind, aren't you, Parker?" As he moved his hand away, it was quite obvious that the bulge had grown bigger. The dome-shaped head of his dick, previously outlined by the wet fabric, was now starting to poke out of the waistband.

Obtuse to a point. You don't have to hit me over the head with an anvil. I smiled. "You betcha!"

I crawled over between the fleshy arches of his legs. I slowly slid my hands down his thighs, and they came to rest on the soggy cotton bunched up around his dick, which leaped at my touch. Gently kneading it like bread dough, I got the thick, veined shaft to slip farther and farther out of the waistband until the oozing, sticky head slapped up against his navel.

"And they say things grow big in Texas," I murmured, leaning in to kiss his ear, then his cheek and jaw, moving along to his soft, parted lips. He received my tongue hungrily, and I felt the full import of being the first man Dirk had "met" in six months.

He pulled me down against his chest, and I lost my balance. My full weight fell on top of him, and he growled happily as his arms tightened around me.

"Sorry about that," I mumbled into the crook of his neck, but Dirk took no notice. He was busy shoving my jeans down my legs and squeezing the cheeks of my ass. An electric shock shot through me as our bare flesh touched. His skin was hot, almost feverish, and slick with a light film of sweat.

Rolling me onto my back, Dirk soon had the rest of my clothes off, and he discarded his own soggy shorts and shoes. He flopped down on top of me, and we began to wrestle passionately, kissing and biting and licking each other almost as if in combat.

I loved the feel of his body, the rounded firmness of his muscles, the light dusting of blond hair on his arms and legs. A full-length mirror on the closet door reflected the strong contractions of his ass cheeks as he pumped his rock-hard cock along the length of mine. Watching the live-action porn show from over his shoulder, I clamped my legs to his flanks like a human vise and met each thrust with one of my own.

Dirk rolled over onto his back, pulling me with him. I sat up, straddling his torso, and ran my hands over his chest as it rose and fell with his heavy breathing. I leaned down and lapped at his nipples, gently at first, then building to a frenzy of sucking and pinching with my teeth. Dirk dug his fingers into my hair, pressing me closer.

When I felt I had gotten his nipples to their peak of sensitivity, I brushed up against them with the light beard stubble on my cheek. Sitting up again, I ran my dick up the length of his body, grinding it between the mounds of his pecs and then sliding it over to tease his nipples with the slippery precome that was oozing out of me like water from a leaky faucet. Dirk growled and nearly bruised my thighs as he tightened his grip in a spasm of pleasure.

"Jesus, Parker," he gasped, his thighs bucking up uncontrollably. "I want to get fucked."

This sounded great to me. "Do you have all the right supplies?"

I was afraid that after six months of inactivity, Dirk wouldn't be prepared for an impromptu encounter. Fortunately, I was wrong, and he dug condoms and a tube of lube from a box next to the mattress.

I maneuvered Dirk onto his stomach. Spreading his muscular thighs slightly apart, I slid my dick between his ass cheeks and reached underneath him to grab hold of his eight-inch cock. Slippery with sweat, his ass cleft was firm and smooth, and Dirk flexed the mounds against my shaft as I slid back and forth. He began to emit sharp, animalistic grunts and cries as he picked up my rhythm, and the massive flesh pole in my hand swelled even more as it raced toward climax.

I backed off and rolled the condom onto my dick. Smearing a dollop of lube around the puckered entrance to his ass, I warmed it up with my finger before gently shoving it into his chute. He gave a little gasp as I worked it past the tight sphincter muscle.

I got into position, mounting Dirk's body. I drummed the small of his back with my cock, working myself up to full hardness again. Then I traced the path down between his cheeks to his fuck hole and punched my rod into Dirk's velvet-soft ass.

I was too wound up at this point for a gentle fuck, and I was pounding into him with a frenzy in no time. His body jerked with each impact, and the sight of this fantastic man sprawled out beneath me on the crumpled sheets, twitching with pleasure, drove me even harder. The sharp clapping sound of our skin slapping together echoed in the nearly bare room, but this was soon drowned out as Dirk and I groaned louder and louder, bellowing obscenities.

A tight, burning sensation welled up in the head of my dick. Roughly grabbing hold of his hips, I let an explosion erupt into the rubber up Dirk's ass. I ground myself around inside him, losing myself in the sensation of his clamping down on me, holding me tight. Then, coming back to my senses a bit, I could tell from Dirk's moans that he too was coming close to orgasm.

Slipping out of him, my right hand still slick with lube, I reached around his body and grasped his thick, throbbing shaft. He let out a throaty gasp. Pumping up and down, building the speed to a flying pace, I soon felt the pulses of his orgasm jerk within my hand, and he muffled his frantic cries with pillows. I rolled the palm of my hand around the slippery dome of his cock till he was bucking violently with unendurable pleasure underneath the pressure of my body.

Finally we both lay still. I eased off his back and onto the mattress. Dirk threw his arm over me and pulled me up against him.

"I knew it," he murmured breathlessly, gently playing with my softening dick and kissing the back of my neck. "You're the right kind of people."

Dirk's definition certainly gave me a whole new perspective on Mrs. Astor's exclusivism. I suddenly thought of Mike's haughty attitude.

"Say, Dirk, you wouldn't want to go crash a party, would you?"

Dirk smiled. "Sure. I'd love to meet your friends."

"It's not my friends I want you to meet," I mumbled, pulling on my jeans.

I should have seen it coming, I suppose, but the fact that I didn't made it all the more delightful. Among those whom Dirk counted as "not the right kind" was the newly repatriated Mike Hargar. Dirk was, in fact, his boss. And Mike was not out to him.

Mike all but had a breakdown and dashed off to lock himself in the bathroom, reeling with embarrassed confusion. Ben shook his head at me as I loaded a plate with chips and salsa for Dirk.

I grinned at him. "Don't fuck with us Southern girls. We don't just serve attitude — we make sure you choke on it."

Mike managed to remember who I was the next time we ran into each other.

I still called him Mark.

Border Crossings
by Phil Cole

Yes. Yes. Yes! I'd know that ass anywhere. No other ass over there like that ass over there. Turn around, Dmitri, turn slowly around and look in my direction. Fucker winked. Fucker smiled. Fucker's back. Thank the Lord for Bausch & Lomb. Thank the Lord for the signal corps. Nine hundred bucks a pop for these binocs, they tell me. Worth every penny. Just a little fine-tuning here...Dmitri! You've got a pimple on your nose! What have you been up to? The fleshpots of Leningrad is what you've been up to. Left me back here to wank myself to death while you laid waste to Leningrad and got a pimple on your nose for your trouble is what you've been up to. Zoosh! I don't want to hear about it; I'll come in my pants.

That's it, comrade, pick up the binoculars, rest them on those high Tatar cheekbones, look at me with those big black Slavic eyes. Oh, yes, the signal: thumb and index finger in a circle, just the way you do it when you slide down my cock, just before you lean into me and suck me till I go into orbit. "I am not Rooshian, I am Azerbaijani. There is much difference." Really? Could have fooled me. I am not American, I am New Yorker. There is much difference.

Dmitri, you are too much. But you are knock-down-drag-out to die for. Welcome back, tovarich, we have much catching up to do. But don't tell me about Leningrad.

This was all going on one summer just before those idiots who thought they were in charge said that the Cold War was over now and we could all go home, that due to their unswerving efforts and magnificent diplomacy, the evil empire was no more. Bullshit! Dmitri and I had worked out a separate peace long before George Bush ever got his silver foot out of his mouth.

Dmitri and I were tank commanders. I commanded an M48A1 with twin Chrysler 400-horsepower engines that got about three miles to the gallon. Fully loaded, it weighed in at fifty tons and had enough firepower to take on the planet Mars. I had so much high-tech communications gear, I could call up Mars to let them know I was coming. Dmitri, in his Soviet equivalent, didn't lag even a hair behind in total awesomeness. Until our owners launched us on missions of intergalactic mayhem, however, our orders were to keep an eye on each other, me from an encampment east of Tirschenreuth in West Germany, him from an encampment west of Planá in Czechoslovakia. From day one did we ever keep an eye on each other!

We kept an eye on each other across 500 yards of no-man's-land. In the middle, equidistant from us, was a clear-cut strip with an ugly fence running in both directions as far as the eye could see. Dmitri's top guns had put up the fence; the U.S. of A. had had nothing to do with it. But, truth be told, the U.S. of A. was quite happy with the arrangement. It kept things simple: You're there, we're here, and never the twain shall meet. They failed to take into account our ingenuity, Dmitri's and mine.

The first day my battalion took up its position, I'd come up out of my hatch, binoculars at the ready, and begun to scan the landscape for filthy commies. Lo and behold, there was a filthy commie scanning the landscape for filthy jackals of capitalism. He lowered his binoculars, and there was Dmitri. It was unconditional surrender — not a shot fired. If I'd known how, I'd have defected that very instant. Dmitri was standing on the ground next to his tank. That summer in Central Europe, it was hot, hot, hot. Our uniform regulations had been relaxed — as, apparently, had his. The only things he had on were shorts and boots — camouflage shorts. What a hoot! The Russkies camouflaged their soldiers' private parts. He was leaning over the side of the tank, one hip hiked up a little, and he was the most beautiful thing I'd laid eyes on in my twenty-one years of laying eyes on my fellow man. Dmitri was big — not fat big, no fat on Dmitri, just huge all over. Even in that slouch against the sponson, he towered over his tank. Dmitri had to be seven feet tall. Swirly black hair spread out across his pecs, defining his abs. A thick black line of hair disappeared into his shorts. His black hair was cut fairly short but not so short that a little lock of it didn't fall over his forehead. He turned to say something to someone not within view of my binoculars, smiled, and then brought his binoculars back up to his eyes. I lowered mine so that he could see what a filthy capitalist jackal's face looks like when he's shooting his wad all over the turret controls of an M48A1. Luckily, none of my crew was aboard at the time. Luckily, my hand and my cock were down there below the hatch. Luckily, I was able to clean my mess off of the turret controls before my crew came back from their mess. Luckily, I hadn't gone to the mess tent with them. "Shit on a shingle" they said it was. To the uninitiated, that's creamed beef on toast. It is bottomlessly horrible.

Dmitri must have seen and correctly interpreted the look on my face or had seen my arm jerking away — maybe both. I mean, I found out later that he instantly realized that a furtive wank was taking place in the enemy camp. Even more fascinating, I found out that having observed this, Dmitri retired to the privacy of his own tank and wanked, my silly face in his mind's eye. Wanked twice, if he's to be believed. Anyway, that's what got everything going.

The next morning there he was. I'd raise my binoculars to find him looking at me through his. He'd lower his, grin and wink, and then raise them again. That was my signal to lower mine and grin and wink. This went on, back and forth, until even I began to think it was getting pretty fucking absurd. Then we tried fierce, menacing looks. I had to try to match the way he splayed his fingers and pulled down his lower eyelids, crossed his eyes, and let his tongue loll. I was no match for him in this, as I found when I looked at him and discovered him looking disgusted and waving his hand dismissively at the rank amateur in the terrifying-looks department. Well, even when he was doing those awful things with his eyes and his tongue, he was still the most gorgeous thing I'd ever seen.

We couldn't have kept this up all day without getting caught. My crew wasn't blind. I had the only pair of binoculars, so they couldn't see Dmitri, but just looking at me, they'd know that I was either communicating with someone across the border or going stark raving bonkers. I did not go to the mess tent for lunch, instead asking my driver to bring me a plate of whatever was on offer as long as it wasn't shit on a shingle. Then I got out some three-by-five cards and a black marker and wrote 1200–1300 TODAY—EVERY DAY, cursing myself that my entire Russian vocabulary consisted of *da* and *nyet*. I needn't have worried. Dmitri was looking at me when I raised the binoculars and held the card in front of me. I saw him bend forward as he stared at the card. Then he disappeared down his hatch, shot back up, showed me paper and pen, then began writing:

OKAY. 12 HOURS–13 HOURS. ALL DAYS. I AM DMITRI.

Son of a bitch! He could write English. My hand began to shake so much, I almost couldn't.

I AM PHIL, DMITRI. HOW ARE YOU?

I AM OKAY, PHIL. HOW DO YOU DO YOURSELF?

Well, I won't bore you with a sign-by-sign replay. Suffice it to say that over the next few days, Dmitri and I got acquainted — very acquainted. So very acquainted that it would have been crystal-clear to anyone else reading our signs (God forbid) that the next step had to be a fuck, and the sooner the better. But how? I found out the next day at 1210 hours.

PUT GLASSES ON FENCE WHERE I POINT. SMALL SIGN. KM14.

It took me a while, but I finally found the little sign nailed to a post on the border fence. It had to be a kilometer marker to indicate how far along it was from where the fence started. I signaled that I could see it.

THERE I WILL BE AT 24 HOURS. THERE IS HOLE UNDER KM14. I MADE IT IN NIGHT. YOU WILL BE THERE. WE WILL BE THERE. THERE WE MUST BE. DO NOT FAIL.

The cards flashed by so fast, I barely had time to read one before he was holding up another. Dmitri looked to be getting hysterically horny. How nice. I shot him a ROGER AND OUT and slid down into my tank for a wank. I was so excited about getting my hands on Dmitri that the danger of some horrendous international incident that might result from our rendezvous never crossed my mind.

Until 2355. At 2345 I was working my way down a hill and through some woods. It was pitch-dark, but the Germans are so meticulous about gathering debris from the forest floor that as long as I worked my way from tree to tree, I didn't worry about tripping over something and breaking a leg before I had a chance to throw it over Dmitri. I stopped at the edge of the clear-cut and raised my infrared binoculars. The Army thinks of everything except the extracurricular uses the troops might come up with for all the fancy gear. The fence was clearly visible, if a little reddish. I hadn't a hope in hell of picking up on something as small as the KM14 marker, but with a little triangularization help from my range finder that afternoon, I'd worked out exactly how far it was from the tank and the angle of approach I'd have to use, give or take a meter. When you're using the range finder to show you where to lob a high-explosive round, even if you're off a meter, your target is still going to get blown to smithereens, so don't fret about the meter. I was virtually certain that I was directly in front of KM14, ten meters distant. But where was Dmitri? It was 2355. For the next five minutes I thought about international incidents. I have to admit, I thought more about international incidents than I did about Dmitri.

A shadow — or was it? It stopped moving. Then it started to move again, became a form, a man, a big man, moving fast, coming straight toward the fence. For a second I thought he planned to pole-vault. Impossible — it was fifteen feet high, and he'd surely go splat right against it. Just as I was getting a good fix on him in the glasses, he disappeared, vanished. Of course! He was in the hole or trench or whatever he'd dug the night before. I started forward just as he came out of it, running. Christ! Thundering hoofbeats. Dmitri picked me up under one of his arms without breaking stride, had us back out of the clear-cut, and was on top of me on the forest floor, holding me with huge arms in a bear hug, kissing my eyes and my ears, grinding his huge body into mine. I could feel his chest heaving from his sprint, feel the hair, a thick, soft mat tickling my nipples. His cock, flat against his gut in his shorts, pressed against mine. His arms were under me, holding me hard, huge biceps against my rib cage squeezing the breath out of me.

"You did come. I knew you would not fail. Now for a moment we must be very still to hear if there are pursuers. I do not think so. I am very careful; they are very stupid. If we kiss, that will make us very still. You will kiss me?"

I'm not sure how still that kiss made us. It more than likely made us sound like wild boars rutting, but that would have served the purpose just as well. Humans, in pursuit or otherwise, give rutting wild boars a wide berth, and there were a lot of wild boars in that forest. I'm quite sure that that kiss made us impervious to the sound of pursuit. A tank could have roared up and started firing, and I wouldn't have noticed. It went on and on, and the one other thing I did notice was Dmitri's cock getting harder and harder.

When we did come up for air occasionally, it was to murmur sweet nothings of a very apolitical kind. Dmitri finally let go his death grip, and I was able to get my arms around his huge, muscled back and down to clutch his tight, hard ass. I'd memorized every square inch of him from 500 yards except what was camouflaged by those shorts. He seemed to know what a nudge of my shoulder meant. He rolled off me and lay on his back, his arms flung up behind his head, waiting. I sat up slowly, very much aware of the weight that had been on me, then swiveled around until I was astride him on my knees. As I started to pull his shorts down, he raised his ass to help, and then I felt his hands on my shoulders. As I went down, the smell of sex and fresh sweat became stronger and stronger, like some delicious drug. My hand squeezing his enormous cock, I opened my mouth wide and took his balls into it, closing my mouth and swallowing.

And swallowing and swallowing. His cock stiffened, and an ass cheek in my other hand went very hard as he poised to thrust up. Dmitri gasped, then succeeded in suppressing a bellow. His hands were clutching my shoulders to the point of pain. When I took my hand off his cock, it slapped hard against his gut. As I eased his balls out of my mouth, his whole body jerked. My tongue still working frantically, I started up the cock shaft. I moved my arms and hands up his body. He was rigid, all of his muscles taut, but his hair under my forearms was soft and yielding. When my hands cupped his pecs, I had licked my way up his cock to the head, running my tongue around it. As my mouth closed around it and I started down the shaft, I found his nipples and pinched hard. Dmitri's pelvis shot up, and I almost gagged. I was all the way down on that enormous cock, my nose buried in hair. The smell was almost too much. I felt my cock jerk, felt the dampness of precome on my gut. I pinched his nipples harder.

"Stop! I want you also. I want us to do this first time so we will remember that we did this first time together, not me alone. Turn around over me. Let me have you."

Without taking his cock out of my mouth, I managed to swing around until I was over him, my knees against his

massive shoulders. His hand came up my leg. He made a
circle with his thumb and forefinger and ran it down my
cock, getting a firm grip at the base. He gripped my ass. I
felt his mouth on the head and let him push me all the way
in. His arms came up around me, and I held tight to the
backs of his thighs. The forest was very still; we were very
quiet as we sucked each other, savoring the smell of each
other's damp balls. We came together — Dmitri was right,
it had to be together. Even the tall, silent trees seemed to
look down on us with approval.

We lay together under the tall, silent, approving trees,
exploring each other's bodies and tongues, holding on
tight to each other.

"You will be long here, I hope," Dmitri whispered.
"When will they move you to some other place?"

"My tour is for six months, so I'll still be here when the
snow is too deep for us to do this here. Unless our owners
find some excuse for us to shoot at each other. Then it
won't matter anymore; we'll have to find somewhere else."

"We will not shoot even if they tell us to, and we will
find someplace warm to love. I have been here one year. I
know this place like my hand. We will disguise you to be
Rooshian and smuggle you."

That prospect was more than a little scary. My cock
whomped up a notch or two, but that was probably
because Dmitri was squeezing it. Maybe he decided he
should squeeze it because I was squeezing his, maybe he
thought of it all on his own. Whatever, things were getting
very heavy again. I put his ear in my mouth and whispered, "I want you to fuck me. I want to sit on your cock
and feel it shooting in me. That's the shooting I want."

Next to my cheek I could feel a grin broadening. Frank
and open discussions were under way; entente was the
fuck at the end of the tunnel. I got astride, spit in my
hand, and reached under me for his cock to lube it. Then
I lowered myself. His hands came to my waist to push me
down. When he was all the way in me and I could feel his
pelvis against my ass cheeks, I began to ride it slowly,

leaning into him, rubbing him all over, feeling huge, hard shoulders and biceps and soft, swirly hair on pecs and abs. I ran my finger down the thick line of hair from his navel. Dmitri made soft, contented noises. His huge hands came off my waist and caressed my thighs. I ran my hands up his arms, reached into his armpits, and twisted the thick hair in my fingers. His hands found my cock and balls and began to stroke in rhythm with my riding. A finger on the hand on my balls stole up under me to join his cock in my ass. When he did that it was only a matter of seconds, and we both knew it. I rode faster, and he jerked harder. He started to meet my ass with hard thrusts of his pelvis. I pinched his nipples as hard as I could. We couldn't see each other in the darkness, but I, for one, was making my filthy capitalist jackal's grimace as I shot my load up that thick black line of hair. Dmitri gasped, and his body shuddered under me.

Soaked in each other's sweat, we lay there for a long time, little kisses, little intentional muscle twitches exciting each other's skin.

"We have this week to love. The next week I go to Leningrad on leave. It has been arranged for long time. Then I would want it, now I would not, but it must be. When something is on paper with stamp on it, it must be. It will be week only. Then we will love again. I will give Leningrad my love for one week only."

Dmitri heard it before I did even though he'd been the one whispering. He stiffened and raised his head slightly, moved it from side to side like an antenna.

"Old German women, faggoting," he said.

I slid off him and sat, my hand on his shoulder as a needless signal for silence, and listened. Our listening was palpable. Then I heard it too: old women's voices — two? three? — slightly echoing in the forest, no possibility of telling how many, how far away. Midsummer nights are very short in Central Europe. My watch told me it was only 0330, but already the trees were more than vaguely discernible. In half an hour a bird here and there would try out a tentative chirp. The old German peasant women, bent from the fields, wrapped in black shawls, would be on the prowl for sticks and twigs, kindling — faggots. That's what kept the forest floor so pristine: old German women clearing out the faggots, wrapping them with vines into bundles to take them home to start the morning fires. I snorted. It was too fucking funny: Dmitri and me, tied up with vines, being dragged back to kindle peasant fires.

Dmitri said, "What?" but I didn't think I'd be able to explain. I doubted very much that his grasp of American slang went that far. Besides, he might be offended, and I certainly didn't want to risk that.

"We'd better get out of here, comrade," I said. "Tomorrow, 2400. And keep your guard up. This may be a piece of cake, or it may have been beginner's luck."

Getting out of there took another ten minutes of body lock. Then I watched through the infrareds as he took off across the clear-cut, disappeared for a moment under the fence, came up running, and vanished into Czechoslovakia.

Working the Road Gang
by Bob Vickery

It was one of those August days when the heat just bears down on you like slow death. Nothing but burned-out cornfields to my right. Over on my left a couple of fishing boats chugged down the brown, sluggish waters of Hull Creek, heading out to the Chesapeake. No air conditioner in my old clunker; the only way to survive was to keep all the windows rolled down and pray for a breeze. As I cruised down the dirt road, my car kicked up clouds of fine red dust that billowed inside and coated everything: the dashboard, the seats, the inside of the windshield. I could taste the grit in my mouth when I swallowed: good ol' red Virginia clay. Up ahead I could see the dark ribbon of Highway 17 cut perpendicular to the road I was on; asphalt never looked so good.

There was a road gang working on the highway. A beat-up old truck was parked on the shoulder, two men standing on its bed and pouring hot asphalt down on the road. Three other men were on the ground, raking the asphalt level. They all stood under the blazing sun, shirtless and sweating buckets, pushing that steaming tar around like they were the damned from hell and this was what they had to do to set things straight. Off to the side a few good ol' boys — foremen, I guessed — stood quietly by, watching them. Their faces had all the expressiveness of two slabs of tenderloin.

I stopped at the intersection and watched the crew for a couple of seconds. It made me squirm just to think about what it must feel like out there on that hot tarmac. Fried beef. One of the men on the road straightened up and wiped his head with his forearm. Instinctively I checked him out. He looked like the youngest guy there, mid twenties, about my age. Sandy hair streaked with dust, the high cheekbones and wide mouth of Appalachian white trash, and a tight, compact body packed with muscles and ready for trouble. Guided by some mountain hunter's instinct, he must have felt my eyes on him. He raised his head and looked directly at me; though his eyes were squinting in the sun, I could still see that they were as blue and hard as cold steel. Sweat trickled down his face in a steady stream.

I turned onto the highway and pulled alongside him.

Impulsively I reached into my back pocket and pulled out my old bandanna. I handed it to him. "Here," I said. "You need this more than I do."

Instead of reaching for it, he backed away. The two foremen stiffened and stepped forward. *What's this all about?* I wondered. "Hey, you!" one of the foremen yelled at me. I decided it would be a good idea to move on, and I pulled away fast.

Old man Edwards was holding his usual position behind the counter of the Kilmarnock Grocery Store. He grinned at me as he rang up my six-packs and groceries. "This heat done you in yet, Pete?" he asked.

I shrugged. "I'm taking it all in stride. In the evening the breeze comes in from over the creek and cools things down a bit." I gave a small laugh. "I hope the state is paying that road crew back there a hefty salary. That's sure shit work to do in this kind of heat."

Edwards snorted. "Hell, the state ain't paying those guys nothing but three squares a day. That's a prison gang, son. They're just serving time."

I stared at him. "You're kidding me!"

Edwards shook his head. "Hell, no. If it wasn't for the prison labor, most of the roads back here in these parts wouldn't never have been built."

I considered this. "I thought prison gangs were kept in chains and the guards all carried shotguns."

Edwards laughed. "You been watching too many movies. It ain't like they're letting murderers out on the crew. These guys are all just two-bit criminals."

I thought of young Sandy Hair. If he wasn't mean enough already going into prison, working out there on the hot asphalt all day would sure finish the job. I thanked Edwards and went on with my errands.

By the time I was ready to head back, the sun was low in the western sky. If the heat had slacked off any, I sure as hell couldn't tell.

The road crew was still at it, a couple of miles closer to town now. One of the lanes had a new layer of asphalt and was shut down to traffic. Sandy Hair waved me down, and I braked to a halt. He came up to my car and leaned down.

"We're lettin' the cars from the other direction come through first," he said. "You're goin' to have to wait a couple of minutes." My initial hunch was right; his drawl was pure Appalachian. If he recognized me, he gave no indication. I looked over his shoulder. A Greyhound bus was inching down the one lane between the traffic cones. Both guards were off with the other men, directing it through.

I turned back to Sandy Hair, but he wasn't looking at me. He was staring at the six-pack of Buds sticking out of the top of the grocery bag. He was looking at them the way a Baptist would look at a piece of the True Cross.

"You want one?" I asked.

His gaze shifted back to me, and he gave me a hard look, his blue eyes narrowing dangerously. *This is not a guy to fuck around with,* I thought. After a couple of beats, his mouth curled up into a slow grin. "Mister," he drawled, "I'd slit my grandma's throat for one right about now." He glanced behind him. One of the guards was looking over at us. Sandy Hair straightened up.

"But I better not. I could get into deep shit if I tried to sneak one." He stepped back as if to walk away, but before he did his eyes slid down my body in unmistakable appraisal. His glance met mine again, and he winked. "Thanks for the offer, though. Both the beer and the bandanna." He turned and walked away. After a couple of minutes, he waved me and the cars behind me through.

That night I lay in bed with not even a sheet over me. The heat pressed down on me like a flatiron on wrinkled cotton. The fan on the bedside table did nothing but push the hot air around a little, and my pillow was damp with my sweat. *Fuck it,* I thought. *There's no way I'm going to be able to sleep in this weather.* I got up, pulled my jeans on, and grabbed my flashlight. Sometimes when it got like this, I just lay down on the dock by the creek. It was cooler down there, and if there was a breeze anywhere around, it would come from over the water.

The rough wood of the dock felt good under my back, and I just lay there quietly, looking up at the night sky. There was no moon out that night, and the stars blazed. The only sounds I could hear were the creek frogs croaking and the waves lapping against the pilings. I was just drifting off when I heard a loud thunk come from inside the boathouse. Nothing in there but my beat-up old motorboat and my fishing gear. But sometimes raccoons squeezed in through one of the loose boards and got into the bait bucket; the little bastards made an unholy mess. I decided it was worth getting up to scare them off.

I sneaked up to the door, flung it open, and shone my flashlight inside. There weren't any raccoons, but Sandy Hair was there, stretched out in my boat, his long legs dangling over the edge. He bolted up, squinting in the light's beam. I just about dropped my light in surprise.

"What the hell are you doing here?" I demanded.

Sandy Hair said nothing. He just kept on squinting in my direction. After a while he finally spoke. "Mister, would you mind not shining that goddamn light in my eyes?" I shifted the light so that he was caught just in the edge of the beam. Neither of us said anything for a few moments. It was pretty easy to figure out what had happened.

"You're on the run, aren't you?" I asked. Sandy Hair didn't answer. He didn't have to. I thought about how I should play this. "Come on up to the house," I finally said.

"You got a gun?" Sandy Hair asked. It was clear that with the beam shining in his eyes, he couldn't see who was talking to him.

I shook my head, a gesture wasted in the darkness. "No," I added quickly.

"Then why the hell should I do anything you tell me to?" he asked. His tone was more practical than belligerent.

"Because it's a hell of a lot more comfortable in my house than in my damn boat," I replied. I swung the light around so that my face was lit up. "Remember me? The guy who offered you the beer?"

Sandy Hair's face remained expressionless. There was another long pause. "Yeah," he drawled. "I remember you. You alone?"

I wondered how smart it would be to admit that. "Yeah," I finally said. "I'm alone. You coming?" Sandy Hair just sat there, looking at me with narrowed eyes.

He finally stood up, swaying to keep his balance in the rocking boat. He stepped out onto the planking that ran along the boathouse wall. "Just lead the way."

"So what are you gonna do?" Sandy Hair asked. He was sitting at the kitchen table, a chicken leg in one hand, a beer in the other.

I shrugged. "Nothing. You can spend the night here, but I want you out by tomorrow morning."

Sandy Hair looked at me speculatively. "How do I know you ain't gonna call the sheriff as soon as I drop off?" He took a long swig from the can in his hand. "Maybe I'd be better off just tying you up."

I met his gaze. "You could try." Sandy Hair had bigger muscles than I did, but I was taller and broader in the shoulders. I didn't know if I could take him on, but I figured I had at least a fighting chance. "Listen," I said. "I got no stake in turning you in. What you did is none of my business."

Sandy Hair stretched. "Then I guess I'll just have to trust you." The way he smiled made what he said seem like a joke. He finished off his beer, crushed the can, and tossed it in the garbage. He looked at me. "You know what I want more than anything else right now? A bath. I stink like a damn pig after working on that goddamn road gang all day."

"The bathroom's down the hall," I said.

His mouth curved up into a slow smile. "Don't mean to offend you, buddy, but I'd just as soon not leave you alone in the kitchen with the telephone." His grin widened. "I didn't say I had to trust you completely. Would you mind stayin' in the bathroom with me while I wash up?"

I looked at him stretched out on the chair, taking in the muscular body, the powerful arms, the distinct bulge in the prison-issue trousers. I felt my dick begin to stiffen.

"Not at all," I said, keeping my voice calm and easy.

Steam rose up from the tub as it slowly filled. I sat on the closed toilet seat as Sandy Hair pulled off his shirt. Once more I got a chance to check out his fine, lean body, the torso packed tight with muscles, the skin gleaming with a light sheen of sweat. The nipples were nut-brown and wide, the size of quarters, and they begged to be chewed. A light crop of brown hair dusted his pecs and trailed across his tight belly into the waistband of his pants. He was right about needing a bath. Even from where I sat, the smell of old sweat was pungent, almost rank. I closed my eyes and inhaled deeply.

Sandy Hair pulled down his trousers and kicked them off. All he had on now were his frayed prison-gray undershorts. His legs were long and muscular, good legs for out-running prison guards.

Something about the slow, deliberate way he was strip-ping made me wonder if he might be testing me for my reaction.

"You've really kept yourself in shape," I said.

Sandy Hair looked pleased. "When those assholes don't have me out pushin' tar, I spend a lot of time in the prison yard pumping iron." He pulled down his shorts and kicked them away.

His dick was fat and meaty, uncut, the head peeking out from the dark foreskin. It flopped against his thigh in a way that made my throat tighten up. His balls hung low and heavy in the summer heat. Sandy Hair turned around and stuck his big toe in the water to test it. His ass flesh was pale and creamy, a sharp contrast to his deeply tanned torso. It was an ass you could write poems about. My dick was as hard as a pile driver, and I just hoped my old jeans were baggy enough to hide that fact.

"What were you in for?" I asked. I was trying like hell to keep my tone of voice conversational.

Sandy Hair stepped into the tub and eased himself down. He closed his eyes and sighed. After a few seconds he looked at me. "I knocked off a 7-Eleven over by Roa-noke. It was my second offense, so they gave me five years. I have another eighteen months before I'm up for parole."

I rolled this over in my mind. "What's your name, any-way?" I asked.

Sandy Hair lathered up. "Virgil." He grinned. "Pretty fuckin' stupid name, isn't it? What's yours?"

"Pete," I said.

Virgil reached over, and we shook hands. "Glad to know ya, Pete. You're a real friend in need." He waved his hand in a way that seemed to take in the whole house. "Must get pretty lonely out here, all by yourself."

"I get by," I said.

Neither of us spoke for a while. I watched Virgil soap up his pits, feeling a twinge of disappointment. I would have loved to bury my face in them and sniff them for days. He scrubbed his torso and arms and lifted up his legs to scrub them too. I was getting so damn horny, I felt I could shoot a load right there. Finally Virgil stood up, the water running down the length of his naked body.

"You got a towel I can use?" he asked.

I reached over to the towel rack and tossed him one. Virgil began to dry his body vigorously. He put the towel behind his back and rubbed. I watched as his dick and balls swung heavily back and forth. When I looked back up, my eyes met his, and he smiled.

"You can suck it if you want to," he said amiably.

"Wh-what?" I stammered.

Virgil's expression was friendly. "I said you can suck my dick if you want. God knows, you been looking at it like you was a starving dog and it was a T-bone steak." He tossed the towel on the floor. "In fact, you'd be doin' me a favor if you did. It's been a helluva long time since I last got a blow job."

I didn't say anything for a while. There wasn't a single sound in the room except the gurgle of bathwater going down the drain.

"It's been a long time for me too," I finally said. "It's slim pickings around here for a guy like me."

Virgil's grin broadened. "Well, then, hot damn, Pete! Let's get down to it!"

That was all the invitation I needed. I dropped down on my knees in front of Virgil and took his dick in my mouth. I rolled my tongue over it, savoring the feel of another man's meat down my throat. I couldn't remember how long it'd been since I'd last tasted cock. It didn't take much work on my part to get Virgil's meat to start stiffening. I felt it swell in my mouth, getting longer and thicker, the cock head pushing against the back of my throat. Sort of like inflating a life raft inside your house; you didn't know if the room would be big enough for it to fit.

I made room. I began to slide my lips up and down the shaft, twisting my head from side to side. Virgil groaned.

"Yeah, buddy," he crooned. "Work that dick." He began pumping his hips in time to my sucking. I reached back and cupped his ass, feeling the muscles tighten and relax with each thrust.

I pulled away and buried my face in his balls, inhaling deeply. Even after Virgil's bath, I could still smell their musky odor. I took his ball sac in my hand and hefted it.

His nuts hung low and heavy in my palm. I looked up at him and grinned. "Hell, these things are a meal and a half all by themselves!"

Virgil laughed. "Well, then, chow down, Pete!"

I kissed his balls gently, pressing my lips against the loose flesh; the light scrotum hairs tickled the skin around my mouth. I opened my lips and sucked his balls in, teasing them with my tongue the way I had done his cock seconds before. I raised my eyes, my mouth full of scrotum meat. High above the expanse of tight, muscular flesh, Virgil's face loomed over me.

"You having a good time?" he asked, his eyes mocking.

Before I could answer, Virgil hooked his hands under my armpits and tugged me to my feet. He pulled my face to his and kissed me, slipping his tongue deep into my mouth. I folded my arms around his naked body and pressed him tightly against me.

His torso squirmed against mine, and I felt his dick dry-hump the front of my jeans. Virgil pulled back. "You know what your problem is, Pete?" he said. "You got too damn many clothes on."

I grinned. "Well, let me see if I can do something about that." I unzipped my fly.

Virgil stepped out of the tub. "You got a bedroom around here somewhere? Or do you just go hang yourself up in a closet at night?"

"Down the hall," I said, laughing. "Let me show you."

As I pulled off my pants, I watched Virgil lie stretched out on my bed, stroking his dick. "I been wanting to see you naked since I first spotted you on the road," he said.

I stood at the foot of the bed, my hands on my hips. "Well, you got your wish, Virgil." I grinned. "Now what?"

"Come over here and fuck my face," Virgil growled. "Nice and slow. Make it last."

I jumped onto the bed and straddled him. Holding his head with both hands, I slid my dick deep into his mouth.

Virgil's tongue played over it like something with a life of its own. I began pumping my hips in rhythm with his sucking, closing my eyes as the sensations swept over me. I opened them again. I didn't want to miss the sight of my dick crammed into the mouth of this hot mountain man.

I took my cock out and dropped my balls into Virgil's mouth. He sucked on them eagerly as I slapped his face with my dick meat.

I spat on my hand and reached behind me, wrapping my palm around his cock. He thrust his hips up, and his thick meat slid up and down inside my spit-slicked fist. He groaned, his voice muffled by a mouthful of scrotum.

Virgil wriggled farther under me until I was sitting directly on his face. His tongue squirmed between my ass cheeks and probed my bung hole. His tongue licks were like electric jolts up my body, and I gasped from the sheer pleasure they gave me. I rolled off him.

"I want you to fuck my ass," I growled.

Virgil looked up at me with a sly smile. "Anything to keep you from calling the sheriff, Pete."

I reached into my nightstand and pulled out a condom and a jar of lube. Virgil laughed. "I thought you told me you never get laid!"

I shook my head. "Not never. Just not often enough."

I slid the condom down Virgil's cock as he lubed up my ass. He threw me on my back and slung my legs over his shoulders. I felt his cock head press against my bung hole, and then, with excruciating slowness, his dick slid up my ass. He skewered me good, thrusting deep inside me, his balls pressed hard against my ass cheeks. When he ground his hips in a circular motion, it felt as if there were at least two feet of dick up my ass. I groaned.

"You gettin' your money's worth, Pete?" Virgil grunted. He started pumping his hips, driving his dick in and out in long, rapid strokes. I moved my body in rhythm with his, matching him thrust for thrust. I reached up and pinched his nipples, not gently. His eyes narrowed, and a mean blue light came into them, but his mouth curled up into a lazy smile. "Yeah, that's good, buddy," he growled. "Play rough." He bent down and planted his mouth over mine, never missing a stroke.

I squeezed my legs around his torso and flipped him over. I rode his dick like he was a runaway train, working it with my ass, squirming on his torso. Virgil scooped a dollop of lube out of the jar and started jacking me off. Perspiration dripped down from my forehead, into my eyes, and onto Virgil's chest. I could see that Virgil was drenched too; our bodies were slippery with sweat. The heat made our fucking take on a slow-motion, dreamy quality, like fucking underwater, like fucking in thick, hot mud. The only sounds in the room were our grunts and sighs and the steady slap of wet skin on wet skin. I squeezed my ass muscles tight and then loosened them as I slid up and down Virgil's fuck pole. It wasn't long before that cool, hard light in his eyes was gone, replaced by a feverish gleam. His mouth was half open, and he gasped in the humid air with a ragged breath just shy of a groan.

I bent down and licked his nipples, and this time he did groan, a long, trailing one that seemed to come from his gut. "Ah, baby, that feels so good!" he whispered.

I reached behind and cupped his balls in my hand. They had pulled up and were tight against his body, and I knew he was ready to squirt. I gently squeezed his nuts, and Virgil shuddered. "Jeez, I'm about to shoot," he moaned. I pressed between his balls hard, and that pushed him over the edge. He cried out, arching his back, thrashing around in my bed like a bronco, and I just hung on for the ride. I felt his dick pulse inside me, squirting load after load of sweet jizz into the condom up my ass. His lube-smeared hand was still working my dick, and I could feel my own load rising out of my balls. I fucked his fist with a couple of long, hard thrusts, and that was enough to do the trick. I threw back my head and hollered. The first spurt of jizz hit Virgil just below his right eye. A second load came, then a third, until his face was dripping with my come. A drop of it hung from his lower lip. I bent down and licked it off, and we kissed long and hard, our tongues pushing toward each other's throats.

I collapsed beside him. I meant to get up and get Virgil a towel to clean up with, but my body felt too heavy to move. We lay motionless in the sweat-soaked sheets, too exhausted to do anything but drift off to sleep. I woke up once, briefly, a couple of hours later. Virgil was snoring gently. By the light coming from the hall, I could still see smears of my come on his face, mingled now with his sweat. I drifted back to sleep.

Virgil left the next morning, wearing some old clothes of mine and carrying with him thirty-seven dollars, all the money I had in my wallet. His escape was big news in the local papers for a couple of days, but after a while, when nobody found him, the story moved to the back pages and eventually disappeared.

Two months later I got a postcard from him, postmarked Memphis, with a picture of a riverboat on it.

"Hey, Pete," his scrawled note read. "So far, so good. Wish me luck. Stay away from those road crews. Those bastards are a mean bunch. You were lucky with me. V."

I keep it in the top drawer of my night table. Every now and then, when the weather's thick and humid and I can't sleep, I pull the card out and jerk off, holding it in my hand. It's not as good as the real thing — not by a long shot. But it helps me remember that hot summer night when an escaped con plowed my ass but good and fell asleep with my come all over his face.

alyson
books

B-BOY BLUES, by James Earl Hardy. A seriously sexy, fiercely funny, black-on-black love story. A walk on the wild side turns into more than Mitchell Crawford ever expected. "A lusty, freewheeling first novel.... Hardy has the makings of a formidable talent." *–Kirkus Reviews*

2ND TIME AROUND, by James Earl Hardy. The sequel to the best-seller *B-Boy Blues.* "An upbeat tale that—while confronting issues of violence, racism, and homophobia—is romantic, absolutely sensual, and downright funny." *–Publishers Weekly*

MY BIGGEST O, edited by Jack Hart. What was the best sex you ever had? Jack Hart asked that question of hundreds of gay men, and got some fascinating answers. Here are summaries of the most intriguing of them. Together, they provide an engaging picture of the sexual tastes of gay men.

MY FIRST TIME, edited by Jack Hart. Hart has compiled a fascinating collection of true, first-person stories by men from around the country, describing their first same-sex sexual encounter.

THE DAY WE MET, edited by Jack Hart. Hart presents true stories by gay men who provide intriguing looks at the different origins of their long-term relationships. However love first arose, these stories will be sure to delight, inform, and touch you.

THE PRESIDENT'S SON, by Krandall Kraus. President Marshall's son is gay. The president, who is beginning a tough battle for reelection, knows it but can't handle it. *"The President's Son* ...is a delicious, oh-so-thinly veiled tale of a political empire gone insane." *–The Washington Blade*

THE LORD WON'T MIND, by Gordon Merrick. In this first volume of the classic trilogy, Charlie and Peter forge a love that will survive World War II and Charlie's marriage to a conniving heiress. Their story is continued in *One for the Gods* and *Forth Into Light.*

HORMONE PIRATES OF XENOBIA AND **DREAM STUDS OF KAMA LOKA,** by Ernest Posey. These two science-fiction novellas have it all: pages of alien sex, erotic intrigue, the adventures of lunarian superstuds, and the lusty explorations of a graduate student who takes part in his professor's kinky dream project.